June Tate was born in Southampton and spent the early years of her childhood in the Cotswolds before returning to Southampton after the start of the Second World War. After leaving school she became a hairdresser and spent several years working on cruise ships, first on the *Queen Mary* and then on the *Mauritania*, meeting many Hollywood film stars and V.I.P.s on her travels. After her marriage to an airline pilot, she lived in Sussex and Hampshire before moving to Estoril in Portugal.

June Tate, who has two adult daughters, now lives in Sussex.

Nothing is Forever

June Tate

headline

First published in 2002
by HEADLINE BOOK PUBLISHING

First published in paperback in 2003
by HEADLINE BOOK PUBLISHING

4

ISBN 978-0-7472-6549-8

Typeset in Times New Roman by
Letterpart Limited, Reigate, Surrey

Printed and bound in Great Britain by
Clays Ltd, St Ives plc

HEADLINE BOOK PUBLISHING
A division of Hodder Headline
338 Euston Road
LONDON NW1 3BH

www.headline.co.uk
www.hodderheadline.com

To my friends, Molly, Marjorie, Netta, Jilly and Heather. We meet most mornings in Harvey's restaurant, and over several cups of coffee, we support and care for each other. Often we laugh until we cry and very occasionally, we cry until we laugh. It's called, friendship.

ACKNOWLEDGEMENTS

To my lovely and talented editor, Shona Walley. My thanks for pulling everything together – separating the wheat from the chaff, and therefore making a much better book.

And with love to my two wonderful daughters, Beverley and Maxine, who watch over me like two guardian angels. I am blessed with my girls, and my cup runneth over.

Chapter One

Flora Ferguson raced down the steps of the Royal Herbert Hospital in Woolwich, thankful to have come to the end of the day's training. It was late spring and she carried her coat over her arm, as she made her way to her digs, desperate to change out of her nurse's uniform, wash her hair and bathe away the smell of disinfectant and carbolic. Yet not for a moment did she regret joining the Voluntary Aid Detachment, known as the VADs.

Prior to this, she had been at home in Glasgow, listening to the news of the war, the one everyone said would be over by Christmas 1914, getting more and more frustrated as her brothers-in-law had answered Kitchener's call and joined the army to do their bit for King and country. But what on earth could she, a mere woman, do? Then one day, whilst shopping, she saw a poster advertising for VADs and instantly joined. Her mother was incandescent with rage.

'Of all your hare-brained schemes, Flora, this is the worst by far! What on earth possessed you to do such a thing?'

'I felt I could be useful!' she said defiantly.

'You know absolutely *nothing* about nursing. You are entirely unsuitable for such a task.'

'At the moment, maybe, but they train you for three months.'

'And after that, all you'll be good for is emptying bedpans. Ugh!' Janet Ferguson shuddered at the thought. 'At twenty-three, you should be settled down with a suitable husband and raising a family, like your two sisters.'

Flora glared at her. 'That's your idea of what my life should be, Mother. It certainly isn't mine.'

At a loss for words to win her argument, Janet fell back on her usual retort. 'What your father will have to say when he comes home, I don't know!'

Alistair Ferguson was used to being the peacemaker between his daughter and his wife but, unlike Janet, he was forward-looking, admiring the spirit in Flora and encouraging it whenever he could.

Later they sat together in his study and discussed the situation. 'Is this what you really want to do, my dear? Have you thought of all the possible consequences? What if they send you to France? It could be very dangerous. Remember poor Edith Cavell. The Germans shot her!'

'Yes, Dad, I know all that, they explained to me everything that being a VAD entails. What's the point of joining them and then saying, "But I want to stay at home, safe and sound"? I might as well not bother!'

'No, I suppose not.'

'There is one thing, though: we are volunteers so we don't get paid.'

Alistair looked at the worried expression on his daughter's face and said, 'Well, I had better increase your allowance then.'

She rose from her chair, flung her arms around his neck and kissed him. 'Oh, Dad, I do love you.'

★ ★ ★

And here she was in early 1916, away from home and the restrictions her mother tried to force upon her, learning to give injections, change dressings and clean the ubiquitous bedpans as Janet had prophesied!

As Flora turned a corner rather sharply she collided with another pedestrian. Her study books and papers flew into the air, and a strong pair of arms caught her as she almost fell. She looked up into the face of a man who had the deepest blue eyes she had ever seen.

'Goodness, I'm so sorry. Are you all right?'

Over his shoulder she could see several of her papers blowing across the road. 'My notes!' she cried, and made to run after them, but he stopped her.

'You pick the stuff up on the pavement, I'll get the other.' And with that he dashed out into the road, deftly sidestepping a horse and cart, and a new Model T Ford car whose driver angrily pumped his horn. This frightened the horse, which reared, causing the man on the cart to curse them both loudly.

The man on foot returned to the safety of the pavement and handed Flora a rather untidy mess of papers. She saw now that he was wearing the uniform of the Royal Flying Corps, and she thought how the collarless jacket, Jodhpur-style trousers and long boots suited him.

In a deep voice, with the softest Irish burr, he asked, 'Did I hurt you?'

'No, honestly, I'm fine.' She looked at the papers and frowned.

'Important, are they?'

'They are the notes I have to study tonight. But it's all right. I can soon straighten them.'

'Look,' he said, pointing across the street at a small tearoom, 'why don't we go there and sort them out?' As

Flora made to protest he added, 'It's the least I can do. After all, tea is good for shock – you must know that being in your profession – and I don't know about you, but I am deeply in shock. I might even need medical assistance!'

She had to laugh at his audacity. 'All right,' she conceded. There was something solid and reassuring about him.

He took her arm and led her to the tearoom, where they settled at a table near the window. 'Are you hungry?' the airman asked.

Flora realised she was starving, and nodded. The stranger ordered a pot of tea, poached eggs on toast and some scones. As the waitress walked away he said, 'That will do to start with.' He held out his hand. 'Flynn O'Connor.' His grip was firm and sure.

'Flora Ferguson,' she replied. 'What are you doing in London?'

He stared deeply into her eyes. 'Do you believe in fate, lovely Flora?'

'I don't know that I do. I've never thought about it.'

'Well, I certainly do. Here I am at the beginning of a month's leave and within hours I meet up with an angel of mercy. Now *that* is fate!'

She chuckled softly. 'I've heard about the Irish and their silver tongues,' she joked. 'Are you a pilot?'

'Yes, that's right. At the end of my leave they are sending me back to France.'

Flora became serious. 'What's it really like over there?'

'You don't want to know,' he said.

'Oh, but I do! As a VAD, they will be sending me there when I finish my training.'

Flynn's smile had disappeared and Flora suddenly saw the face of a man who was under strain. She recognised it immediately, having witnessed the same expression among some of her patients.

'War is hell, Flora, and I wish with all my heart a lovely young woman like yourself could be spared the experience of seeing the devastation that it causes to man and beast.' He paused as if lost in thought, then quietly asked, 'Would you do me a great favour?'

'It depends what it is.'

'Would you have dinner with me tonight? I am in desperate need of female company. I have been surrounded by men and war for months. I would like to dine some-where splendid and then dance – hold a woman in my arms. Would you do that for me, Flora?'

There was such a note of yearning in his voice she said without hesitation, 'Yes, I will.'

His smile was so warm she could almost feel the glow from it.

He walked her back to her digs and said, 'I'll pick you up at eight o'clock. Wear your glad rags, Flora, because I have the feeling this will be a night we'll both remember for the rest of our lives.'

Once inside the house, she quickly bathed and washed her hair before seating herself at a small table in her room to study her notes. Although her mind was on the young man who had almost bowled her over, she forced herself to work until it was time to get changed. Her mother had insisted that she pack two evening dresses in case she needed them. Flora had only done so to stop Janet from nagging; now she was pleased that she had.

She slipped the russet-coloured gown over her shoulders, and smoothed the silken material over her hips, patted in place the coffee-coloured lace inset of the bodice, then brushed her long nut-brown hair thoroughly, before twisting it up on the top of her head and anchoring it with long pins and combs. She applied a light coat of mascara and a touch of lipstick before standing back and looking at her reflection, tweaking her cheeks to add colour. A cream tulle scarf around her shoulders finished the outfit and she wondered with girlish delight what her escort would think when he saw her.

Flynn was on time. As Flora opened the front door to him, he said, 'My, but what a vision of beauty you do look, Miss Ferguson. I'll be the envy of every man this night.' He took her by the arm, leading her towards the waiting taxi.

'The Ritz Hotel,' he said to the driver as he entered the vehicle.

He held her hand as he sat beside her, but didn't say a word as they drove through the streets of London, and Flora was content to gaze out of the window and wonder about this handsome stranger sitting beside her, but once they were settled at a table in the hotel's sumptuous dining room, with its wonderful chandeliers and tall pillars, the conversation flowed effortlessly.

Flynn asked her about her home life and laughed when she told him of the running battles she had with her mother. 'I am a big disappointment to her,' she remarked, 'because I'm not settled with a nice husband, like my sisters.' Her green eyes shone as she said, 'She says I'd rather muck out the stables than look after a man!'

'Do you ride?' asked Flynn.

'I do. I have two horses. Jasper, a gelding, is my favourite. He's black with a white forelock, and Sheba is of Arab stock. She has such a high opinion of herself, we called her after the Queen of Sheba.'

'Then you would be happy at my place just outside Dublin,' said Flynn. 'I have a stud farm.'

6

'How wonderful!'

'After the war, I intend to buy more stock and breed a long line of winners.'

They tucked in to their Châteaubriand, supped their red wine and learned of each other's hopes and dreams, many of which they shared. Then Flynn took her to a nightclub in the West End. They settled at a table and he ordered a bottle of champagne.

'Good heavens!' Flora exclaimed. 'I won't be fit to work in the morning.'

As Flynn took her hand and led her on to the dance floor, he said, 'Believe me, you must live life as if today is your last, always.' He took her into his arms and held her close as the band began to play a waltz.

Her body melted against his as they moved around the floor. Flynn rested his head against hers and she felt the warmth of his skin, was aware of his strong physique, the breadth of his shoulders. The scent of him gently invaded her nostrils – and she felt wonderful.

When the dance came to an end, he didn't release his hold, just looked into her eyes, waiting until the band began to play again, ignoring everything else. 'I am such a lucky man, Flora Ferguson, to be here with you tonight and to be able to feel you in my arms. You know you belong here, don't you?' he said softly.

Returning his gaze, she whispered, 'Yes.'

Later they took a taxi, and then, dismissing it at the Victoria Embankment, they strolled, pausing by Cleopatra's Needle, to look out over the Thames. The sky was clear, and, arms entwined, they stopped to look at the reflection of the moon against the water, and listen to the movement of the boats on the river.

'We have only four weeks together before I leave for France,' Flynn said. 'Let's not waste a minute of it.'

He gathered her to him and kissed her. As his lips moved over hers with a growing intensity, she returned his kisses willingly, clinging to him, wanting this moment to last, and gasped for breath when he eventually released her.

He cupped her face in his hands and said, 'Why the hell did we have to meet in the middle of a war?'

'Fate isn't always kind, is it?'

He gave a half-smile, 'Ah, so now you believe in it, do you?'

'I still don't know, but whatever it was that brought us together, I'm glad that it did.'

They clung to each other in an embrace that was filled with desperation.

Flora was aware of the perils of war. She read the papers avidly every day and knew how heavy the casualties were; how the 'Old Contemptibles', the regular army, at the beginning of the war had withstood the German might, only to lose the bulk of their trained men; how the British troops had been forced to withdraw at Loos, with many thousands killed. She also listened to the stories of her patients with growing horror. Flynn was already part of it . . . and soon she would be too.

It was late when he took her home. He kissed her good night and asked, 'What time do you finish tomorrow?'

'Four o'clock.'

'I'll be waiting outside the hospital for you.'

'Good,' she said.

During the following ten days they were inseparable. They walked around London together, and if Flora was off during the daytime they went to various museums and art galleries, where they argued with good humour about the works of the masters. They went to the races and studied the mounts as they paraded around the paddock, Flynn sharing his knowledge of horses and bloodlines . . . and they fell in love.

One evening after they had dined on board a riverboat, Flora stood by the rail with Flynn behind her, enclosing her in his arms. 'You know, don't you, that we are meant to spend our lives together? You are going to marry me, darling Flora, aren't you?'

She turned round within his hold and looked up at him, this man whom she had met only recently, but whom she felt was to be a part of her life and whom she already loved, and said, 'Of course I am. Did you ever doubt it for a minute?'

He chuckled as he shook his head and, taking her by the shoulders and drawing her even closer, he said, 'You know, you are an extraordinary woman.'

'I know,' she said. And then she kissed him.

'Tomorrow, I'll buy you an engagement ring, before someone else comes along and takes you from me,' Flynn said.

'I don't want anyone else,' she murmured as she snuggled against him.

As this was such a special day, Flora dressed with care, wearing a dark blue linen suit, and a navy toque hat trimmed with a small white plume. Then she set off to meet Flynn in Bond Street.

They entered a jeweller's shop and looked at various rings before Flora eventually chose a square sapphire, flanked by diamonds. As she tried it on and held out her hand to see it glitter beneath the lights, she asked, 'Can you afford such a ring? Have I found myself a wealthy husband after all?'

The male assistant behind the counter frowned and coughed at her indiscretion.

Flynn just laughed and said, 'Darling, I have enough to keep a wife in style, unless I find a really expensive horse to buy, and then you might have to put it in hock for a while!'

They went to a nearby hotel and ate oysters and champagne to celebrate.

Flora smiled across the table at her fiancé and said, 'Oh, Flynn, darling, I am so happy.'

He took her hand and kissed her palm. 'And so am I, but you realise we can't possibly marry until this war is over?'

'But why?' she protested.

'Listen, darling, I don't want to make you a bride *and* a widow in a short space of time, do I?'

Her heart seemed to miss a beat, and she caught her breath. The very idea that Flynn might be killed was more than she could bear. 'Please don't talk like that,' she pleaded.

'Flora, darling, I have been there, I've seen and experienced war, and you will do the same, far too soon. Nothing is certain in such times. You are an intelligent woman, you know what I mean.' He paused for a moment before saying, 'I don't suppose it would do any good asking you not to go?'

She shook her head and with quiet determination said, 'No, Flynn. I really feel I have to do this. Please try and understand.'

He squeezed her hand. 'Then you should. I would never stand in your way of doing anything, I want you to know that. You are like me, darling, a free spirit. We can't bear to live in any kind of cage.'

Flora realised then how fortunate she was in this man. The only other person who understood this feeling was her father. 'I'll wait,' she said, 'until after the war, when we are both safe. It must end sometime. After all, nothing is for ever.'

Flynn stared into her eyes and traced the shape of her mouth with his finger. 'There is one thing I can't wait for and that is to make love to you. You don't have to be back at the hospital until the morning. If the hotel has a room free, will you stay the night with me, and all the other nights, until I go back to France?'

She didn't care about anything else, all she wanted was to be in the arms of the man she loved, for however long she had. 'Yes,' she said. 'I can't bear to let you out of my sight.'

'I'll take care of you, darling,' he said. 'I will make sure I don't leave you pregnant. Not until we're married, anyway.'

'And that had better not be too soon after we're married, because I want a chance to work the horses with you. You don't know it but I'm as good on the back of a horse as any stable lad or groom!'

He started to laugh at her indignation. 'For the love of God, will you calm down! Of course you can do all these things. We will need time together after the war to really get to know one another, before we surround ourselves with kids.' He stopped laughing. 'You do like them, I hope? Children, I mean.'

'Yes I do, and we'll have a fine family.'

'Ah, we'll make wonderful babies together,' he said quietly.

She felt the rush of colour to her cheeks.

He paid the bill, then taking her by the hand, he led her over to the reception desk, and booked a room.

Chapter Two

Flora wondered why she didn't feel embarrassed, once they entered the bedroom. After all, she had never had sex, or slept with a man before. She felt shy, certainly, but as Flynn took her into his arms, everything felt so right, even when he undid the buttons of her dress and let it slip to the floor. She stepped out of it, picked it up as she would do at home and placed it over a chair, before turning back to him. She saw the look of amusement on his face.

'What's so funny?' she asked.

Gently catching hold of her arm he pulled her towards him. 'You are! Here am I, bursting with passion, and you – you stop to pick up your dress!'

'Well, I do have to wear it tomorrow when we leave here,' she explained, 'and I don't want to look dishevelled now, do I?'

He removed the pins and combs from her hair and as it tumbled around her shoulders, he ran his fingers through the luxurious tresses. 'You don't mind being mussed up in the bedroom, I hope?'

'Not at all,' she said as he kissed her. 'In fact I think I might like it.'

He picked her up in his strong arms and carried her over to the large double bed and carefully laid her down. He removed his uniform jacket, then his boots, took off his socks, undid his trousers, switched off the overhead light, leaving just the small table lamp on, and then he lay beside her and stroked her face. 'Mrs O'Connor. I like the sound of that.'

'So do I,' murmured Flora as she wound her arms around his neck.

Flynn kissed her gently on her forehead, her nose, and then her mouth. Her lips opened to respond as he moved his expertly over hers, and fondled her breasts, caressed the roundness of her hips and whispered, 'You are so beautiful. I love you, my darling girl, and one day we'll spend the rest of our lives together.'

'I hope we don't have to wait too long,' she said.

Mindful of her virginity, Flynn was a thoughtful lover. He didn't rush her but slowly caressed her, coaxing her gently so that she relaxed as they became more intimate, and he made sure she was ready for him before he moved over her and finally consummated their love.

Afterwards they lay together, arms entwined. 'Oh, Flynn, I do love you so,' said Flora as she snuggled into him beneath the bedclothes. 'I wish we could just stay here until you have to leave.'

He chuckled softly. 'If we did that, I wouldn't be fit to fly my plane.' He smoothed her hair away from her face. 'Tomorrow I'll find a hotel nearer the hospital, and then you can collect your things and we'll register as man and wife.' He pinched her nose teasingly. It will be good practice,' he said, his eyes twinkling with devilment. 'You can tell your landlady you're going away for two weeks' honeymoon!'

'You are a wicked man, Flynn O'Connor! Incidentally, I have to be on duty at eight o'clock in the morning and I'll need time to go home and get changed first,' she said.

He reached out and picked up the telephone. 'I had better ask for an early morning call,' he said, 'otherwise we might sleep in.'

When eventually Flora entered the hospital the following morning, ready for duty, she was floating on air. The nurses were not allowed to wear jewellery and her engagement ring was on a chain around her neck, beneath her uniform. It was her secret, not to be shared with others.

Flora liked most of the other nurses with whom she trained, but deliberately hadn't made a special friend during her time there, having seen how so many of her patients fretted for friends who had died on the battlefield. She figured she would have enough to cope with when she was eventually sent to France, without any added burdens. It wasn't difficult for her; even as a child she had been a solitary person, the youngest of the three sisters, different from the others, content to be with her horses. She didn't need anyone else then either, except perhaps her father. But now, of course, she had Flynn and she did need him.

She tried not to grin when she thought of her mother. Janet would have a fit if she knew what her daughter was up to. As she changed the beds in the ward, she thought how ironic the situation was. There was her mother, who had strived to get her to settle with one of the various young men she invited to the house, who had been furious when Flora showed no interest in any of them, and now, not only was she engaged, but she was also sharing a bed with her fiancé.

She smiled at the patient in the bed before her as she placed a thermometer in his mouth and took his pulse. 'How long have you been married, Sergeant?' she asked, as she eventually removed the thermometer and read it.

'Four years, Nurse.'

'Would you recommend it? she enquired.

Although he had lost a leg during the fighting, the man still retained a sense of humour. 'Certainly. It's great to have someone to clean and cook for you and keep you warm on a cold winter's night!'

'Sergeant! That's an awful thing to say.'

He grinned at her. 'But every word is true!' As she made him more comfortable and adjusted his pillows, he added softly, so no one could overhear, 'But it's also great to have someone to share the good times and the bad. My wife can't wait to have me home, chopped up as I am. That's true love, Nurse, and you can't bloody well beat it.'

During the final days of Flynn's leave, Flora continued to spend every available minute with him. Sometimes they took a bus and walked on Plumstead Common; at other times they stayed in their room and talked.

Flynn told her about his family: his father, an accountant; his mother, who was a great homemaker, who loved to garden and who grew enough vegetables to feed an army – and of his love of horses. He described his stud farm.

'At the moment I have ten horses being trained by a friend and my head boy. That's enough to keep them busy whilst I'm away. You'll love the house. It's big – you could live in the kitchen.' He looked at her and asked, 'Can you cook, Flora?'

She looked at him archly and said, 'What if I say I can't. Will you take back your ring?'

He gave her a sideways look and said, 'Well, I would honestly have to think about it most seriously.'

She climbed on his knee and ruffled his soft brown hair.

'As a matter of fact I can. Cook used to teach me. It was her way of keeping me out of trouble if I went into the kitchen.'

'Thank the Lord for that!' exclaimed Flynn. 'I'm getting used to you; I wouldn't like to have to start all over again with another woman.'

She playfully put her hands around his throat. 'You just try,' she warned.

The days passed far too quickly and it was soon time for Flynn to leave. On their last evening, to her surprise, he took Flora inside a local church and walked her up to the altar steps. They stood together and he took her hand in his. He stared into her eyes and said, 'Wilt thou, Flora Ferguson, have this man to thy wedded husband?'

She felt the tears well up in her eyes. 'I will,' she answered.

'I, Flynn Thomas O'Connor, take thee, Flora Ferguson, to my wedded wife. That will have to do, darling, until this war is over.' He drew her slowly towards him and kissed her.

She threw her arms around his neck and in a choked voice said, 'I couldn't feel more married to you than I do now. I will always love you, my darling Flynn.'

They dined in a small intimate restaurant, but neither could find the words to say very much and both were relieved when it was time to return to their room. Once there, they climbed into bed and clung together.

Flora tried hard to bite back the tears, but failed miserably. 'What will I do without you?' she sobbed. 'These past weeks have been the happiest in my entire life.'

He kissed the tears from her cheeks, tasting the salt of

them, and held her close. 'I'm going to an airfield in Fienvillers. When you get to France, try and contact me. If there is any way possible for me to get to you, I'll be there, I promise. As soon as I have an address, I'll write.'

They made love that night with a feeling of desperation, holding each other in a tight embrace as if to make the most of their final night together, and when eventually they lay back against the pillows they were breathless and exhausted.

The following morning, neither could face breakfast. They placed their clothes in their separate cases and went downstairs. Flora was near enough to the hospital to walk, but Flynn had ordered a taxi as he had a journey to make to meet up with other pilots, as they were all to fly new aircraft over to France.

He put his case inside the vehicle and told the driver his destination. Then, turning to Flora, he clasped her in his arms and said, 'You take care. I'll see you sooner than you think.'

She kissed him. 'Be careful. Remember how much I love you, how much I need you.'

As he was driven away, she turned and walked to the hospital with tears streaming down her face, and that night, back in her digs, alone in her bed, she gazed at the ring she had taken off the chain and placed on her finger. She lifted it to her lips and kissed it as she silently said her prayers, asking for her love to be kept safe.

It was in the middle of June when Flora finished her training, and she joined a detachment of nurses travelling to Southampton, to cross The Channel on a hospital ship. Once in France, for several days they passed through war-torn towns in military vehicles, and Flora began to understand the devastation and destruction that Flynn had spoken of. When they arrived at the field hospital near the Somme, they were shown their cramped quarters in a tent, then immediately put on duty.

In the makeshift ward where Flora was to work, there was a stench of foot rot and death in the air. As she and her colleagues tended to the sick and dying, she could hear the sound of gunfire and the whine of shells, followed by explosions, muffled only by the distance. But nothing could muffle the cries of men in pain.

Flora had thought she was used to the sight of injured men from the time she'd spent in Woolwich, but nothing had prepared her for this. But as she looked around at the beds, packed side by side, as tightly together as was possible, the men in blood-soaked bandages with horrific injuries, she knew that this was the reason she had joined the VADs. Here at least she was needed. Here she could be useful.

Before she had left England, she had received a letter from Flynn telling her that he had arrived safely, giving her an address to write to and telling her how he missed and loved her. He sounded bright and cheerful, which had helped her as she herself had to prepare for her journey into the unknown. At least, she told herself, she was nearer to him now.

The Somme offensive started on the first of July, two weeks after Flora arrived. As the men climbed out of the trenches, they were cut down by German machine guns. The brave soldiers continued to obey the orders of their obstinate generals and the only thing that was achieved was the loss of thousands and the mutilation of others. The field hospital could not cope with the number of wounded, the doctors and nurses were working almost round the clock, yet somehow they found the strength and the will to continue, and to show their patients that they cared.

One morning Flora was changing the dressing on the shattered leg of a soldier who, despite his injury, suddenly grinned at her. 'Can I take you back to Blighty with me when I go?' he asked.

'And what would the other poor devils do if I deserted my post?' she retorted, pretending to be horrified by his suggestion.

'It's only that I've been looking for a woman with a touch like yours all me life!' he said, winking at her.

'All your life!' The lad was no more than nineteen.

'We grow up quickly in the country.'

As she gazed at the pinched features of her patient, she thought how much he needed the time spent in good clean country air. Air that was not polluted by cordite and rotting flesh. She had seen the effects that life in the trenches had upon her patients. In the eyes of each of them was an expression of fear and desperation, and in those who were wounded sufficiently to ensure their passage home, there was a look of glee, but above all, relief. She recalled one patient whom she'd discovered putting penny pieces inside his bandages, over his open wound, trying to infect it even more. When she had asked why, he'd told her in anguished tones, 'I can't go back there, Nurse. I just can't take any more.'

She turned her attention back to her young patient.

'I live in Newmarket,' the boy confided. 'I was going to be a jockey, but I grew too tall. Maybe it was just as well,' he said, looking at the bandages on his leg. 'Bloody lot of good I'd be now.'

'I ride myself,' said Flora.

The boy looked surprised. 'Go on. Is that right?'

'Yes, I have two horses: a gelding, fourteen hands high, and a part-Arab. And my fiancé has a stud farm in Ireland.' They spent the next ten minutes talking about horses, which seemed to cheer her patient considerably, but they were interrupted by the call of one of the doctors.

She followed him outside with a sister and another nurse to where there were rows upon rows of wounded, lying on stretchers, waiting for attention. It broke Flora's heart to see them lying thus, but there was no more room inside and the wounded kept arriving by ambulance.

The doctor began at one end of the line, examining each man, giving orders as to their treatment. For a few it was too late and the doctor covered their faces with their blankets. He made no comment. By now this was too common an occurrence and he kept his observations for the men whom he *could* help.

Hours later an exhausted Flora went off duty. In her quarters she removed her headdress, undid her white-bibbed apron, now bespattered with blood, and lay upon her narrow cot, too tired to take off her dress. She immediately fell asleep.

Her dreams took her away from the fields of battle and the results of the war. She was riding Jasper across the Scottish heathlands, breathing in the scent of the heather, along the banks of Loch Lomond, letting her horse drink from the water. Flynn was with her on a chestnut roan. They both dismounted and he held the reins of his horse with one hand and pulled her to him with the other. His mouth was hungry on hers and she returned his kisses with ardour.

Her dream world was shattered as an orderly awakened her. 'Time to get up, Flora,' he said. 'I hardly like to disturb you; you were smiling . . . at what, I'd like to know?'

She blushed as she sat up. It may have been but a dream, but she could still feel the imprint of Flynn's lips on hers.

Seeing the flush in her cheeks, the orderly laughed. 'If you were a fellow, I'd say you were having a wet dream, my dear.'

She swung her legs off the bed and said, 'There's no need to be crude, Jim.' But she smiled at him nevertheless. Alone she quickly washed and cleaned her teeth in the bowl of cold water, changed into a clean uniform, then brushed her hair, twisting it up off her neck, holding it with tortoise-shell combs kept in place beneath her headdress, which she anchored with a small hatpin.

As she made her way to the hospital she wondered just how much longer this dreadful war would continue. How many more lives would be lost before an armistice could be agreed? In all honesty, she didn't think it was imminent.

The Battle of the Somme continued for months, and by mid-September Field Marshal Haig's hope of capturing ground quickly had failed, and even the tanks ordered were of little use. They had never been used before, and most broke down before reaching their destination, or sank in the mud, caused by the neverending rain.

Flora sat beside the bed of a soldier from the 7th Shropshire Light Infantry. The young lad had caught a burst of gunfire in his chest, which was now riddled with shrapnel, and he wasn't expected to last the day. Flora held his wrist to take his pulse, but he caught hold of her hand.

'Is that you, Mum?' he asked in all but a whisper. 'I never thought I'd see you again.' He coughed and a small trickle of blood ran from the corner of his mouth.

Flora gently wiped it away.

'I'm sorry I didn't write more often,' he said.

She placed a damp pad on his forehead in an effort to cool his fever. 'Whist now, my son. Try and get some sleep.' She gently stroked his cheek and he closed his eyes. Moments later, she felt for a pulse, but there was none. She called over a doctor to confirm her opinion, and then an orderly to remove the body and bring in another patient.

This was the pattern of Flora's day, every day, but being strong-willed, she coped. There were occasional letters from home, but it was news of her beloved that she was always desperate to receive.

Chapter Three

Flynn O'Connor sat at the controls of his biplane and pointed downwards. The observer, sitting behind him, gave him the thumbs up and proceeded to take pictures. Flynn traced his course from the map in front of him. They were passing over the Somme and somewhere not too far away from Flora. God, how he missed her! He remembered with longing the time they had spent together in London. How soft had been the feel of her skin as he'd held her. He remembered the scent of her, how the corners of her mouth twitched when she was amused, and the sound of her laughter. And he wished he could turn back the clock.

A sudden nudge to his shoulder brought him back to reality. The observer was pointing. Flynn looked up and saw two German Albatross biplanes bearing down on them. Grabbing his control stick he quickly manoeuvred his aircraft into a turn and headed for his base. He could hear the rattle of the mounted machine gun being fired by his observer at the approaching enemy aircraft, but fortunately the returning gunfire only nicked the tip of one wing of his machine.

Eventually they landed safely at their own airfield, taxied across the grass and Flynn turned off the engine. As the two of them climbed out of the cockpit, the observer said,

'That was a bit bloody close!'

Flynn laughed. 'Don't worry, we have the luck of the Irish on our side.' But as they walked towards the ops room to report, he gave a sigh of relief and thanked his lucky stars he hadn't been surprised by Baron von Richthofen in his scarlet biplane, the leader of the notorious 'Richthofen's Flying Circus', the flower of the German air force. The Red Baron, as he was known, had accounted for several British planes. The air ace had a reputation they all respected and every one of the pilots yearned to be the one who brought him down.

A week later, Flynn had two days' leave, and in a borrowed staff car he made his way along battle-torn roads to the hospital to surprise Flora. He drove past tanks, now utterly useless, stuck in the mud, lines of men marching along with an air of despondency. He passed deep craters filled with water, where the dead bodies of gallant soldiers were half submerged and thought: Christ! What a terrible waste of life.

On his arrival at the hospital, he watched unobserved as Flora bent over a patient and spoke softly to him, then helped the soldier to take a drink. Flynn looked around the crowded ward. The smell of blood and ether filled his nostrils and the sight of the many wounded made his heart heavy – so many young lives changed through this bloody war. But at least these boys were alive. Not only today on the road had he witnessed the carnage, but from the air he had also observed the dead bodies of both sides, lying in the mud, draped over barbed wire. Every decaying corpse belonged to somebody. Many a family would mourn in the days to come.

'Flynn!'

He looked up to see a delighted Flora rushing towards him. He swept her up in his arms and kissed her warmly, to the loud cheers of those patients well enough to watch.

Flora blushed but kissed him back. She wasn't going to let an audience stop her from being in the arms of the man she loved. 'Come with me,' she said, and led him away to a small anteroom. Now alone and away from prying eyes, the two of them clung to each other.

Flynn rained kisses on her, muttering, 'God, it's good to see you, to feel you. It seems so long since I last held you.' He drew back slightly and with a look of concern he said, 'You've lost weight. Are you all right?'

Flora cupped his face in her hands and gazed adoringly at him. 'I'm fine. Oh, darling, it's wonderful to see you. How long can you stay?'

'I have to leave again in the morning. Are you working tonight?'

'I come off duty in an hour's time, and I'm free then until the morning.'

'Then we mustn't waste a moment. I have found somewhere for us to eat and they have a room for the night. I've booked it in the hope that we can make use of it.'

'Good Lord! How in this godforsaken place did you find it?'

'Darling, wherever there is life and a few people, you can always find something if you know where to look. You go and finish your duty and I'll meet you here in an hour.'

As Flora walked back to her ward, Flynn made his way over to a line of stretchers and handed out cigarettes to those who were able to talk and smoke.

'Thanks, mate,' said one man. Then, looking at Flynn's distinctive uniform with a winged insignia of the RFC on the khaki jacket, he asked, 'Royal Flying Corps?'

27

Flynn nodded.

'A flyboy. I wouldn't 'ave your fucking job for anything, mate. The infantry 'ave more chance of surviving than you lot!'

'It's all in the lap of the gods, my friend,' stated Flynn with a broad grin.

'Well, I've caught a Blighty,' said the soldier, nodding to his heavily bandaged arm. 'They say it might 'ave to come off, but I don't give a shit. All I want is to get 'ome to me wife and kids. I don't want to end up 'anging over some barbed wire, shot to pieces. Without this arm I can use the other to take a piss, and as it's the left one I can still keep the wife 'appy.' He winked at Flynn.

Laughing, Flynn moved away. This was not the first brave man he'd spoken to during the fighting. There was the usual black humour that prevailed under such circumstances – humour that only those involved in the fighting would understand. Those at home would never be able to appreciate it, but then they hadn't seen action on a battlefield, never stood in trenches filled with water, worn clothes covered in lice, had to kick out at the rats that were frequent visitors, or seen a wounded man drown in the muddy water because he had slipped off the duckboards where there was no one to save him. Neither would they have witnessed the hundreds of men who climbed up the ladders to get out of the trenches and go over the top, ready to fight the enemy; who met with sudden and immediate death.

Later, Flora, now changed into a jumper and skirt beneath her overcoat and ankle-length boots to allow her to cope with the mud, climbed into the vehicle Flynn had purloined. They drove for about fifteen minutes before Flynn turned the car through the arched gateway of an old house. Many windows were boarded up, and around the battle-scarred garden were roof tiles that had been removed by blasts of gunfire. The Boche, who had occupied the building, had been moved on by the troops who had liberated the owners, and now they had also left.

'What is this place?' asked Flora as she alighted from the vehicle.

'It's an old manor house, but the owners, suffering financially from the war, have opened it as a hotel. When the Germans captured the surrounding area, it was closed and it's not really open now.'

'So how did you discover it?'

'I had to make a forced landing here recently. The owners came running out to see if I was all right, and that's how we met. I brought them a few stores afterwards and a couple of chickens, and I said I was looking for somewhere to bring my girl.'

Flora smiled at him mischievously. 'If you hadn't joined the service,' she said, 'you could have become a master con man. It's that Irish charm. It works every time.'

He ushered her towards the front door and said with a soft chuckle, 'I certainly intend it to tonight.'

Inside the large entrance hall was a highly polished table with a huge vase of wild flowers in the middle. A servant stepped forward and led the visitors to a nearby room. Before a log fire was set a table for two, with a bottle of red wine uncorked and, in an ice bucket, a bottle of champagne.

'Dinner will be served in ten minutes, monsieur,' the manservant announced. 'Later, when you wish me to, I'll show you to your room.' After opening the champagne and filling the two glasses, he moved away quietly and left them alone.

The two lovers sat closely together on the cosy settee before the fire. Flora sank back into the arms of her fiancé. 'I could stay here for ever,' she murmured.

Flynn kissed her forehead. 'I know what you mean. Just for a while we can forget the war and be two ordinary people who are in love.'

When the roast chicken was served it was succulent, and the crispy roast potatoes were perfect. There were only a few vegetables but they were delicious, and to follow there was fruit and cheese.

Flora gave an exclamation of delight. 'How did you manage all this?'

Flynn chuckled. 'It's best you don't know.' He took her hand and kissed it. 'Let's take what's left of the bubbly to our room. We have only tonight and I want you so much.'

Rising from her chair, Flora said, 'Then what are we waiting for?'

Their bedroom, in an earlier time, must have been quite sumptuous, but even now the somewhat shabby drapes at the windows and the covers on the chairs had an air of elegance.

There was a small fire burning in the grate to take away the chill, and the light from the flames cast dancing shadows on the walls as Flynn turned out the lights.

'Open the curtains so we can see the moon,' Flora requested.

The couple stood together before the window, their arms wrapped around each other. 'Looking out from here at this peaceful scene,' said Flora softly, 'you wouldn't believe the carnage that is just over there, out of sight, would you?'

Flynn had been thinking that on such a clear night the soldiers in the trenches had little chance of survival as they went over the top to meet the enemy, but he kept his thoughts to himself. He caught hold of Flora's chin and gently turned her face towards him. 'Those are things we are here to forget, darling. Come on. Let's go to bed.'

They lay together and Flynn ran his fingers through her hair. He gazed into her eyes and in his soft Irish burr said, 'I have dreamed of this moment for so long and now we are together it seems unreal. I'm worried that I'll wake up and find it was all a figment of my imagination.'

She pulled his face down and kissed him. 'Believe me, it's real,' she whispered. She placed his hand on her left breast. 'This is me, Flynn, darling.'

Locked in each other's arms, the two of them soon forgot the stark reality that was war as their love and need for each other took control. Flynn kissed Flora's eyes, her neck, then his mouth moved to her full breasts. As his teeth gently raked the pert nipple, she moaned softly as her body cried out for him.

'Oh, Flynn, darling. Love me, please love me.'

There was a deep hunger in their kisses when eventually he lay on top of her. She clasped him to her with her legs, as he slipped inside her.

Much later, they lay side by side, their naked bodies close and warm beneath the covers. As she snuggled even closer to Flynn and caressed his broad chest Flora said, 'I wonder how long it will be before we are together again?'

He didn't answer. Knowing the dangers that were still ahead for both of them, he couldn't bring himself to speculate about the immediate future. 'I love you, you know that, don't you?' he asked.

'Of course I do and you'll see, one day we'll be able to put all this behind us.'

They lay together talking softly, planning their future.

'We'll buy good stock,' said Flynn. 'And one day we'll train a racehorse that will win the Irish Derby, and if we are really lucky, maybe an English Derby winner too. After all, Irish horses are the best in the world.'

Early the following morning they made love again, then washed and dressed, eating their breakfast downstairs. The slightly stale bread and hot bitter coffee seemed to them like a feast. They barely spoke but gazed longingly at each other, trying to drink in every detail, committing it to memory, knowing that soon they would have to part.

Flynn drove Flora back to the hospital. They had only time for a brief kiss. They clung together for just a moment.

'You take care,' urged Flora, her voice choked with emotion.

He smoothed her face. 'And you watch out for those patients of yours,' he said, summoning a smile. 'You tell anyone who gets fresh that you belong to an Irishman with a big fist!'

With a lump in her throat Flora watched him drive away. 'God, keep him safe,' she prayed as his vehicle was driven out of sight.

Chapter Four

It was now October. The battle of Thiepval Ridge in late September had brought forth the usual rush of wounded, and the damp and the mist in the air didn't help. There were soldiers in the hospital from the 8th Suffolks and the 8th Norfolks, and the medical staff heard that one company had been reduced to ten men during the attack on High Wood. The carnage continued whilst the generals discussed tactics over their fine wines, away from the mud and mayhem.

Everyone at the field hospitals was working flat out and one day just fused into another with the same problems. Medical supplies were often meagre and the surgeons worked under impossible conditions, sometimes operating day and night for long periods. When things were at their worst, all Flora had with which to change the stinking wads of dressings was a pair of forceps sterilised in a jam jar of methylated spirit.

In addition to those who had physical injuries, there were the other poor devils whose minds were the victims of war and who suffered from shell shock. Some would sit for hours, staring into space, others trembled all the time from head to foot, unable to keep still, and the sound of gunfire sent others scuttling into corners or under beds, shaking with fright. Flora knew that for many there would be no cure, and it tore at her heartstrings, but when she heard of ignorant people calling the men cowards, her anger was awesome.

She would sit holding their hands, talking softly to them, trying to get through that vacant expression behind the eyes. Just occasionally there would be a sign of recognition, but almost immediately the patient would escape the world of reality and return to his own dark place where he felt safe. It was heartbreaking.

She had not heard from Flynn since their last meeting, but she told herself that no news was good news. Deep inside, however, was the constant fear for his safety. Grim news from the battle zones came in with the patients. As the weeks passed, the weather became colder. Beneath her nurse's uniform, Flora wore two of everything. If she left her vest over the back of a chair at night, it would be frozen stiff in the morning, so she only removed the garment when it needed changing. And sometimes she would do her rounds wearing a topcoat.

In November, the bad weather finally brought the Battle of the Somme to a close, but the wounded were still arriving at the field hospital, staying there until such times as arrangements could be made to move them either to other hospitals or shipped home. Eventually the field hospital prepared to close and Flora was told she was going on leave. This should have pleased her because, like everyone else, she was exhausted and mentally drained, but she didn't want to be too far away from Flynn. She sent word to him and hoped fervently that he would receive her message.

The day before she was due to leave the hospital with the

last of the staff, she heard the sound of an aircraft approaching. Looking up at the sky she saw a plane circle a nearby field and descend to land. With her heart racing, she watched and waited until a figure appeared in the distance. The pilot, dressed in his flying gear, walked with a gait that she immediately recognised, and she started to run towards him. The man removed his flying helmet and waved it vigorously at her.

Soon she was enveloped in his arms. 'Oh, Flynn!'

When he let her go at last she felt the tears trickling down her cheeks. Burying her head in the depths of his jacket she was racked by sobs.

Flynn just held her until she stopped, then he tilted her chin and looked at her tear-stained face intently. 'It seems to me, my darling, that it is you who needs to be taken care of.'

She wiped her eyes and took a deep breath, trying to collect herself. 'I'm fine, I was just so relieved to see you all in one piece. I have been out of my mind with worry, wondering if you were alive and safe. How long can you stay?'

'Only an hour.' At the look of disappointment on her face he added softly, 'I couldn't let you leave without saying goodbye, could I? Now tell me, are you still my girl?'

She punched him playfully on the shoulder. 'Don't be ridiculous! You know how much I love you.'

'Then show me.'

She put her arms around his neck and kissed him with such longing, she thought she would die. 'I wish you could come on leave with me. I need you so much,' she whispered.

He caressed her cheek. 'I know, darling. If only I could. There is nothing I would like better, but sadly this damned war is still going on. I just can't get away right now.'

She placed an arm in his and they walked back to what was left of the hospital. 'Well, at least I can rustle you up a cup of tea on the Primus stove,' she said.

As they sat together on upturned crates, Flora gazed at her love and was saddened to see just how strained he looked. But don't we all? she thought. Everyone has experienced such dreadful times. One day, far into the future, we will be able to forget, but not yet. Certainly not yet.

'Are you all right, darling?' Flynn asked. 'You look even thinner than when I saw you last.'

She gave a wry smile. 'It's army rations! I'm fine, and I'll be better still, now that I have seen you.' She didn't want to tell him about the acute shortage of food. He would only worry more.

'Where are they sending you?' he asked.

'To a hospital in Rouen, but I have a week's rest before I go on duty again.'

'It's not nearly long enough,' he said. 'You look exhausted, but at least there you will have better conditions, a proper hospital and, most important of all, not be so near the battle lines.' He took her hand in his. 'You are far too close to the fighting here. I'll feel better knowing that you are safe.'

And how much longer will *you* be safe? Flora wondered. The more sorties he flew, the more chance Flynn had of being shot down. So far he'd been luckier than most, but . . . She pushed such thoughts aside. After all, here was the man she loved, near enough for her to reach out and touch him. Which is exactly what she did. She ran her fingers through his hair, pushing back a wayward lock that fell over his brow. His flesh was warm beneath her fingers. He caught hold of her hand and kissed her palm.

'One day, darling, we'll ride over the hills of Ireland

together. We just have to be patient, that's all.' He rose from the wooden crate and pulled her into his arms, kissing her tenderly until his lips became demanding and passionate, bruising her mouth, but she didn't care.

'That will give you something to remember me by until we meet again,' he said, staring at her intently.

'As if I could ever forget you, my darling Flynn,' she said softly.

They walked together to the boundary of the field where he had landed. He gave Flora a quick hug and said, 'You keep well, and I'll see you as soon as I can get away.'

She watched until he reached his plane, then waited until she heard the engine start, and when she looked up as he flew over her and circled, dipping his wings in salute, she waved frantically until he disappeared over the horizon.

The station hospital at Rouen was completely different from the one Flora had recently vacated. This was a proper building instead of a collection of tents, although the staff still slept on canvas beds as the iron beds were desperately needed for the sick and injured.

During her week's rest, Flora slept a great deal. When she realised she didn't have to get up to go on duty, it was as if she suddenly let go. Exhaustion overcame her and her body at last received the rest it needed.

One day a couple of weeks later, two of the medical officers borrowed a car and gave Flora a lift into the town. Despite the devastation caused by the war, some shops were open and a couple of restaurants, where they were able to get a meal of sorts, but Flora's delight knew no bounds when she found a shop where she could buy shampoo and a new lipstick. She doubted that another trip would be possible in the near future, especially as petrol was in such short supply.

There was not the severe shortage of food at her new posting. Not that anything was in great supply, but there was sufficient to keep body and soul together. The casualties kept arriving and Flora began to wonder if there was a man left at the front who was fit and well.

She did receive a letter from Flynn three weeks after she arrived at Rouen, telling her that he was well, how much he missed her and how much he loved her, but there was not the same exuberance in his writing as there used to be. She thought that was only to be expected under the circumstances. He must be exhausted. She read the letter again and again, clutching it to her breast, knowing that he had held these few pages. But at least she was able to sleep easy for a while, especially as he wrote that he would do his best to come and see her soon.

Christmas came without another word, but Flora, although disappointed, busied herself decorating the wards with whatever they could find or make. She was up a ladder trying to drape some foliage she'd picked, whilst below her stood one of her patients, a crutch under one arm, one leg in plaster and his free hand holding on to the ladder trying to keep it steady as Flora reached out to place a large bough safely.

The man looked up anxiously and said, 'Now then, Nurse, you be careful. I don't want you tumbling off this thing. There isn't much I can do to save you in my condition.'

She glanced down and, with a grin, said, 'Just think how awful it would be if I fell on you and broke your other leg!' And she started to laugh.

'I don't think that's very funny! he protested.

Hanging on to the ladder for dear life as she was laughing uncontrollably, Flora said, 'I thought it was hilarious.'

'You would! You medical types have a very strange sense of humour if you ask me!'

Those patients who were able went to a church service in the hospital, and a choir, who went to every ward and sang carols, visited those still confined to their beds, which had been decorated with strips of coloured crepe paper that had appeared from an unknown source.

As she listened to the words of 'Silent Night', Flora felt a lump in her throat. At home in Scotland, despite the war and the shortages, her family would no doubt be sitting around a huge log fire, drinking mulled wine, handing out mince pies and eating their fill, surrounded by friends and relations. A sudden overwhelming sense of loneliness encompassed her and she felt the tears well in her eyes. As a volunteer, she could hand in her notice at any time, but it never entered her head to do so. Here she was needed and here she would stay. Besides, she couldn't go home and leave Flynn. How could she?

It was New Year's Eve and Flora was making her final round of the ward before lights out. She tucked in a loose corner of a bed, checked that each man was as comfortable as he could be, and was about to move on to the last bed when she looked up. Standing in the shadows at the end of the ward was a man. She couldn't see his features as the lights were low, but she recognised the uniform. With mounting excitement she settled her final patient for the night and hurried towards the doorway.

'Flynn!'

But before her stood a stranger. 'You are Flora Ferguson?' he asked.

She felt the blood drain from her face as she saw the anxious look in his eyes.

'It's Flynn. He's dead, isn't he?'

The stranger took her by the arm and led her to a chair in the hallway. He stooped down beside her. 'Yes, Miss Ferguson, I'm afraid he is. His plane was shot down last night. It all happened very quickly.'

She could visualise the aeroplane plummeting down to earth. It would take minutes. Minutes of knowing you were going to die. She could scarcely bear to think about it.

'Was he burned?' she asked fearfully.

'No, he wasn't. When the plane crashed some locals pulled him from the wreckage. An enemy bullet had killed him. He wouldn't have known anything about the accident,' the stranger said, trying to give her some kind of comfort.

'Thank God for that,' she murmured.

'Flynn named you as his next of kin, that's why I'm here. Outside I have a suitcase with his belongings.'

It seemed as if this person was talking to her through a haze and she was on the outside looking in. There was a great rushing sound in her ears. It was totally unreal; it couldn't really be happening. Her wonderful Flynn couldn't be dead. This was some terrible nightmare . . . Then the haze lifted. She could hear clearly – and she knew it was fact.

Gazing up at the stranger, she saw he was wearing a dog collar and realised for the first time that he was a padre. How many times, she wondered, had this man and many like him had to break such news?

'Thank you for coming,' she said quite calmly. 'If you'd

like to bring the case here . . . only I can't leave the ward, you understand.'

He laid a hand on her arm. 'You can't stay on duty, my dear,' he said. 'I'll go and fetch one of the orderlies. I'll be back in a moment.'

Dazed, she watched him walk away.

She remained seated, unable to move or think. It was as if someone had switched off all her feelings. She was frozen to the spot, her mind blank, her eyes unseeing as she gazed into space. And here she remained until one of the male orderlies came along with Sister James.

'Flora!'

She looked up, confused.

Sister James helped her to her feet. 'Come along,' she said, and led Flora to her room. From her pocket she took out a small flask of brandy and poured a tot into a glass. She handed it to Flora. 'Drink this,' she ordered.

Feeling the liquor warm in her throat Flora looked up. 'Flynn is dead,' she said flatly.

'I know. I am so sorry,' said her superior. The sister sat beside her on the bed. 'Would you like me to stay with you, Flora?'

'I should be on duty.'

'Not tonight. I have arranged for someone to cover for you.'

'Thank you,' said Flora, not really listening.

There was a knock on the door and Sister James went to answer it. She came back with a small suitcase. 'Here are Flynn's things,' she said. 'Is there anything I can do?'

Shaking her head, Flora said, 'No, I'll be fine. I just need to be alone.'

'I'll look in on you later,' said the sister as she quietly left.

It was with a dispassionate look that Flora eyed the

battered suitcase. Is that all that's left of him? she wondered. She closed her eyes and remembered the last time that her darling Flynn had held her in his arms, the kiss that all but bruised her lips. The one he said would give her something to remember him by. But there was so much more to remember. His light brown hair, his deep blue eyes, the way he walked, laughed, teased her – made love to her. How could such a bright light be extinguished? She felt the tears well up in her eyes and trickle down her cheeks, unchecked.

She undid the case and took out his uniform jacket. She buried her face in it, breathing in the scent of him – and she wept.

Early the next morning, as the dawn was breaking, Flora put her cloak over her nightdress and walked outside, clutching Flynn's jacket to her chest. She wandered aimlessly around the grounds of the hospital, unaware of the cold, tears streaming down her face, wondering how she could possibly face the future without the man she adored. They had such plans – the stud farm, raising a thoroughbred to win the Irish Derby, his children she would no longer bear. Her body and her heart cried out in torment. She sank to her knees on the damp grass.

'Flynn! Where are you? Flynn, come back to me I need you!' she cried. She beat her fists on the ground in anger and pain, then lay sobbing into his jacket until there were no tears left. Then she returned slowly to her room, feeling exhausted and empty, as if everything inside her had been torn out by some cruel avenging spirit.

Later that morning, the matron sent for her. 'I heard about the death of your fiancé,' she said. 'I am sorry. Do you want to go home? It can be arranged. I will understand.'

'Go home! Whatever for?' How could she explain that was the last place she needed to be? Much as she loved her family, she couldn't bear them fussing round her. How could they begin to understand what it was like to be so near the front line, the fear of being killed by an enemy shell, or what she had seen – the mutilated bodies brought in on stretchers, the way things were here . . . the war? The fact she had lost the man she loved whom they had never met? Her pain . . .? The comfort of her home was the last thing she needed. She had to stay; it was her only salvation. Without the hospital and the patients, she would be lost. 'Thank you, Matron, but I need to work,' she said quietly.

And that is precisely what she did. Flora Ferguson shut her grief away in a small black compartment at the back of her mind and worked until she blotted out the pain of her loss, until she was too tired to think, but would fall into her bed every night completely exhausted, until weeks passed into months and months into another year. Until she began to learn how to face up to a future without Flynn O'Connor.

Chapter Five

The war was over! On the eleventh hour of the eleventh day of the eleventh month in 1918, an armistice was finally signed. When the news was heard at the hospital in Rouen, loud cheers echoed along the corridors, grown men wept, the women too. Those men who were dreading their return to the fighting shed tears of relief; others, for the many friends who would not be going home. Flora, though filled with relief that the carnage would now end, unlocked her grief at last and let her tears fall, sobbing uncontrollably, knowing that her hopes and dreams were in tatters, now that Flynn was dead and they would never ride together in the Scottish Highlands, that their plans of a life in Ireland would never come to fruition. And the loss she felt was deep, painful and devastating.

It took time to arrange the evacuation of the hospital, and although her work as a VAD was now at an end, she insisted that she stay on to see the men sent home. They were to be transported by train to a French port, then across The Channel to Southampton. There, she would take her leave of them. As she told the matron, 'You'll need all the help you can get to look after the patients on the trains and on the sea crossing.'

Flora was proved right in her estimation, and the nursing

staff were run off their feet. Not only did they have to cope with seasickness, as the sea was so choppy, and the disabling effect of injuries, but many of the men who had lost limbs were anxious now the time had come to face their families, as to how they would be accepted, and for many the future would indeed be bleak, their chances of employment negligible.

'I've got a wife and two kids, Nurse,' confided one. 'How am I going to keep them without army pay? Can you see anyone employing a bloke with one leg and a bad back?'

Flora was hard-pressed to find words of encouragement. 'I'm sure the Government will help,' she said. 'After all, didn't they promise a land fit for heroes, after the war?'

'That's just talk,' the man said. 'I don't trust any of them bloody politicians. They'll say anything to get elected.'

As the last patient was taken ashore in Southampton, Flora took her engagement ring off the chain around her neck and placed it on the finger of her left hand. Then, picking up her case, she walked down the gangway of the ship and put behind her the past two traumatic years of her life.

She hailed a taxi and asked the driver to take her to a decent hotel.

As she signed the register she said to the receptionist, 'I don't know just how long I'll be staying at the moment.'

'That's perfectly all right, madam,' she was told.

Once in her room, she took off her coat and lay upon the bed. She shut her eyes and thought how comfortable the mattress was after the canvas beds she had been used to. She walked into the bathroom, put the plug in the bath and turned on the tap. What a luxury this was going to be! She put the complimentary bath crystals into the water and slipped out of her clothes, stepped into the bath and sank into the steaming water, breathing in the scent of the crystals. At last, a touch of civilisation.

After a meal in the dining room, she undressed and sat on her bed and suddenly felt lost and alone. There was hardly a sound. For two years, movement had surrounded her: nursing staff, tending to their duties; the cries of her patients. In the beginning, when she was near the battle front, there had been the sound of the German howitzers being fired, the explosions of the shells. Now . . . there was nothing. It was like being in an alien world, away from all that was familiar. What on earth was she to do with herself? And she wondered just how she was going to be able to settle down to a normal life, without Flynn.

The following morning, Flora went to the reception desk, picked up the receiver of the public telephone then gave the operator the telephone number of her father's office in Glasgow. When she heard the familiar voice on the other end of the line, she was choked with emotion.

'Hello, Dad. It's Flora.'

'Flora! How lovely to hear from you! Where the devil are you?'

'I'm at the Dolphin Hotel in Southampton. I came over from France with the hospital ship yesterday.'

'Thank God you're safe. Are you all right? When are you coming home?'

Taking a deep breath she said, 'I'm fine, Dad, but I need a few days to be alone, to get myself together before I see the family. You do understand, don't you?'

'Of course. You come when you're ready. Let me know when and which train, and I'll be there to meet you. I'll tell your mother I've heard from you, but I'll not give her the name of the hotel.'

'Thanks, Dad. I have missed you so much.' She replaced the receiver. How well her father understood her, and how well he knew his wife. Flora guessed that her mother would be making plans for her return the moment she knew she was home. Had she the means of reaching Flora, there would be immediate pressure, and that was the last thing she needed. That, she couldn't have coped with. She wanted no homecoming party; the house filled more with her mother's friends from the various committees – which seemed to take up every spare moment of Janet's life – than friends of Flora's.

Flora decided to explore her surroundings, and put on her coat and hat, winding a scarf around her neck to keep out the chill November air. She stepped out of the hotel and turned to her left, heading for the waterfront. From there she wandered off towards the dock area, past the dock gates and into the Chapel district. She was appalled by the shabby houses alongside each other like small boxes, mostly in need of repair.

Children played in the narrow street, none of them dressed sufficiently well, in her opinion, to keep out the cold, but the little ones didn't seem to mind as they bowled wooden hoops around or jumped over skipping ropes made out of worn hemp. She felt something tugging at the back of her coat and turned to see a small child dressed in a torn jumper, and a shabby skirt to her ankles, both of which were in need of a wash.

'Got any change to give me so I can get some food?' asked the waif. 'I'm hungry,' she said plaintively.

'Where is your mother?' asked Flora. The child shrugged her shoulders. 'Do you live in one of these houses?'

'No I don't. You gonna give me something or not?' she demanded.

Flora hid a smile at the spirit of the little mite. She opened her purse and took out a half-crown, removed the warm scarf from her own neck and wound it around the small neck. As she handed over the money, the child's eyes were bright with excitement.

'Cor, miss. Thanks.' And she took off around the corner like lightning.

Flora watched the children playing for a while, thinking how the simplest of things gave them the most pleasure. She took in every detail of the place as she continued to look around: the shabbiness of the area, how at some windows the curtains were freshly washed, at others, they hung in torn ribbons. She carried on walking until she came upon Kingsland Market, with its fruit and veg stalls and barrows selling second-hand clothes, all the sellers vying with each other for business.

'Loverly spuds,' called one. 'Only a penny a pound!'

'Git yer apples 'ere,' called another. Flora was enchanted by the place, but as she watched the busy scene before her, she saw that there were several children wandering about, pilfering the rotten fruit thrown in boxes behind the stalls, and others pinching good stock when the vendor wasn't looking, which wasn't often. The market traders were used to such tricks and kept their eyes open.

'Come back 'ere, you little bleeder!' called one man to a small boy, who was running off. 'I'll have your bloody 'ide if I catches you round my stall again.' He fussed over the display on his barrow, muttering angrily under his breath.

Flora frowned. The children who were pilfering weren't doing it for fun, she'd observed. Those who had been successful were away tucking in hungrily to their pickings. She stopped a passing policeman.

'Excuse me, officer,' she said, 'but these children that are running around the market, where do they come from?'

He smiled benignly at her. 'Not from these parts, are you, miss?'

'No, I'm just passing through.'

'These kids, well, some of them, that is, don't belong nowhere in particular.'

'What on earth do you mean?'

'Many of them have no proper homes to speak of and those that have, poor little devils, have to make do. The parents are usually to be found in the pub. The old man anyway, spending money on beer instead of food for the family.'

Flora was shocked. 'But that's appalling. Can't the council or someone do something?'

'They do, miss. Many are sent to the workhouse, but the others make out as best they can. There is a soup kitchen, but unemployment is rife here and lots of blokes back from the war can't find work. There's not a lot anyone can do.'

'But what happens if the children get sick?'

'Who knows? Some of them die, I expect. They can't afford a doctor, that's for sure.'

She looked at him angrily. 'How can you stand there and tell me that so coldly? Doesn't it make you sick that children are left to fend for themselves and that maybe they will die and no one cares tuppence about them?'

The policeman looked somewhat ruffled. 'Of course I care! I've got a couple of kids myself, but there isn't anything I can do about these here, is there?'

'And I suppose everyone thinks the same and so no one does anything!'

He became quite huffy. 'If you feel so strongly, miss, why don't *you* do something?'

She looked at him and said, 'What a good idea, officer. I might just do that!' She turned on her heel and walked away, leaving the policeman muttering beneath his breath about do-gooders, always interfering in things they know nothing about.

The following day Flora ventured along Canal Walk, or the Ditches, as it was commonly known. It was a narrow street closed to traffic, with one-storey shops on either side. She looked in the window of a costumier's, but walked on when the owner came out selling his wares.

'Want a nice frock, maybe, madam? We have a good selection. Come inside.'

Flora shook her head and looked in the pawnbroker's shop a little further up. There were a couple of pubs too, she noticed. She turned up her nose at the stale smell of beer that wafted beneath her nostrils as she passed. Prostitutes stood around, plying for trade among the seamen who walked past. She looked at them with interest, thinking there would be no business from the men who had fought in the war and were seeking employment. It had saddened her to see some of these men on street corners, selling matches for a pittance, after fighting for their country. They certainly wouldn't be seeking comfort from prostitutes. But, being a seaport, Southampton would always be full of seafarers with money. She watched one woman with fiery red hair approach a man, who obviously knew her.

'Hello, love,' she said. 'You back already? Where the hell does the time go, eh?' He pinched her bottom. 'Hello, Jessie. Ready for a tumble then?'

'You got the money, dearie?'

'Of course I have. Been saving it up to spend on you.'

'Then what are we waiting for?' And they walked away arm in arm.

Flora spent the following three days wandering around other poor areas of the docklands. Each day she returned to the hotel deeply depressed at what she'd seen. On the fourth day she came upon a building that was vacant, with a For Sale sign outside. The main gate wasn't secure and she pushed it open and walked in. She peered through dirty windows, trying to see the interior. She walked round the back of the building and did the same, with a feeling of mounting excitement. She took down the telephone number on the sign and rang the estate agent, making an appointment to view the premises the following morning.

When the estate agent met her and opened the front door to the premises, she saw that the building looked in a good state of repair, although it needed a thorough clean and a lick of paint. Downstairs there was a fair-sized kitchen with an old dirty oven and cupboards on the walls. There were several smaller rooms that appeared to have been used as offices, and upstairs there were six decent-sized rooms and a bathroom.

'This place used to be a builders' merchant's,' explained the agent. 'The family lived upstairs, and rooms on the ground level were used as offices. The plumbing's in good order,' he added.

'What about damp?' enquired Flora.

'None of that, miss. It would have affected the merchandise. No, this building is pretty sound.'

'If that's the case,' said Flora, 'why is it empty?'

The agent cleared his throat and in a conspiratorial tone said, 'Well, you see, miss, the owner went bankrupt. He liked too much of the hard stuff, I'm afraid, and the debts piled up.'

'I see,' said Flora. 'I'll go away and think about it. I'll be in touch.'

'What was you thinking of doing with it, if I may ask?'

But she didn't answer. At the gate she shook the man's hand and said, 'You'll hear from me within a couple of weeks. Good morning.'

The estate agent scratched his head as he watched her walk away. 'That one plays her cards close to her chest,' he muttered.

That evening, Flora checked on the trains to Scotland, rang her father and arranged for him to meet her in the late afternoon the following day. She sat in front of the mirror of the dressing table in her room and brushed her hair. Now she was ready to face her family, because she knew exactly what she was going to do with her future.

Chapter Six

A gentleman in the same train carriage as Flora helped to lift down her luggage from the rack as the train pulled in to Glasgow's main station. She thanked him; then, as she stepped down on to the platform, she summoned a porter to carry her case. She could see her father waiting by the exit, and waved. He greeted her warmly as she emerged from the crowd of passengers.

'Flora, my dear! What a sight for these old eyes you are.' He embraced her and kissed her cheek, then, holding her shoulders, stepped back to look at her.

'I can see you are in need of a rest, my dear.' He took the case from the porter, tipped him and said, 'Come along. We'll go to the nearest hotel and have a wee dram before we face your mother.' His eyes twinkled. 'It will give us both a bit of Dutch courage!'

As they settled in the comfortable lounge of the Caledonian Hotel, her father quietly asked, 'Was it really bad where you were?'

'Yes,' Flora answered simply. 'It was awful, but I was glad to be there.'

'I am so very proud of you, dear Flora. I'm sure you don't want to talk about things at the moment, but if ever you do . . . well, you know, don't you?'

She gazed fondly at him. Alistair Ferguson was an imposing-looking man: tall, with a military bearing, his dark hair turning white at the temples, his jawline and features strong. His grey eyes, as he looked at his daughter, were filled with sympathy and understanding.

'Yes, Dad, and one day soon we'll talk, but not yet. How's Mother?'

'She doesn't change, dear. Still involved with her committees, but it keeps her busy and fulfilled. She immediately wanted to start arranging a homecoming party for you, but I put a stop to it. I said she was to ask you first.'

Flora chuckled softly. 'I bet she didn't like that.'

'Your mother doesn't stop to think, Flora, but she means well.'

'As long as she doesn't want to marry me off. That's the last thing I need!'

He laughed loudly. 'You don't change either – fundamentally that is. But I *can* see a change in you. When you left us you were but a girl; now I see before me a woman.' He squeezed her hand. 'You have grown up, Flora, my dear.'

'Yes, Dad, I certainly have.' She downed the last of her Scotch. 'How is the distillery business?'

'Fine. The Scots will always have a taste for good malt, and fortunately so do others. Despite everything, we are doing all right.'

'Good. I'm glad to hear it. Well, I suppose we had better go and face the music.'

Once outside the confines of the city, Flora feasted her eyes on the old familiar scenery. Now, in late November, the tops of the mountains were already snow-covered. There was a bite in the air and she thought the only thing she needed to hear, to complete her homecoming, was the sound of bagpipes.

Mr Ferguson turned the car off the road, drove through the tall wrought-iron gates, up the driveway and stopped in front of the large house. 'Are you ready for this?' he enquired.

She nodded, grinning at him mischievously. 'It can't be worse than a barrage from enemy guns, can it, Dad?'

He frowned at her. 'Now that is unkind!'

'I know,' she said.

A housemaid who had been with the family for years opened the door. 'Welcome home, Miss Flora,' she said, and stood back to let them enter. 'Your mother is waiting in the drawing room.'

Janet Ferguson rose from her seat by the fire. 'Flora, my dear. Welcome home.' She walked towards her daughter with open arms, and kissed her on both cheeks. 'Come and sit by the fire. You must be frozen!' Turning to the maid she said, 'Mary, make a fresh pot of tea and ask Cook for some sandwiches. Miss Flora has had a very long journey.'

'I'm not hungry, Mother,' protested Flora.

'Nonsense! Of course you are. Now let me look at you. Mm, well, you do look a bit peaky, but some good Scottish air and food will soon put that right and then we'll have a party and invite all your friends. It will be a real homecoming.'

Flora glanced across at her father, who raised his eyebrows, then, looking at Janet, she said firmly, 'No, thank you, Mother. I don't want any party. I just want to spend a week or two here, ride my horses, visit a few of my favourite places, get some clothes together, and then I'm returning to Southampton.'

Her father looked surprised, but her mother was positively shocked. 'But, Flora, you have only just returned home. We haven't seen you in two years. I need to get you back into the social scene.'

Flora tried to be patient with her mother. 'I know and I'm sorry, but I have things to do. Important things.'

'What could be more important than being with your family after so long?' asked Janet indignantly.

The tenseness of the moment was lifted as Mary brought in a tray laden with sandwiches, a sponge cake and a silver pot of tea. 'Leave it on the table,' ordered Janet. 'I'll pour myself,' she snapped as the maid started to do so.

Oh dear, thought Flora, I've only been in the house five minutes and already I'm at odds with my mother. Some things never change.

Her father intervened. 'Now, Janet, my dear, we must leave Flora to do what she wants.'

Her mother looked very annoyed. 'I only wanted to give her a good homecoming. People are interested to know what she's being doing these past two years.'

Flora sighed and sipped her tea. 'Mother, please try and understand. I have been in the middle of a bloody war.'

'Flora, please!'

'I'm sorry if that shocks you, but had you seen the carnage that I have, the last thing you would want is for it to be the conversation at a party.' As her mother made to interrupt, she continued, 'I have seen men mutilated by gunfire, torn to ribbons by barbed wire, limbs blown to smithereens. People don't want to hear this.'

Janet, horrified at these revelations, took a handkerchief from her pocket and wiped her brow. 'No, of course not,' she conceded.

'I just need time to try and taste a little of normal life for a couple of weeks. That is the best homecoming you can give me. Is that too much to ask?'

Janet was completely taken aback by the firm tone of her daughter's voice and the steely look in her eye.

'No, of course not. If that is what you want, then so be it.' She suddenly saw the ring on Flora's finger. 'You are engaged! I had no idea. Who is the man?' she demanded.

Flora fingered the ring, twisting it round. 'Flynn O'Connor, a pilot in the Royal Flying Corps.'

'An Irishman? Does he come from a good family?'

'I really don't know. I never ever asked him. It wasn't important.'

'But of course it's important. When are we to meet this man?'

Her mother's condescending snobbery was just about the last straw. 'I'm afraid you won't. You see, he was killed in action a year ago.'

Janet was speechless, but her father said, 'I am so very sorry. I'm sure he was a fine chap.'

'Yes, Dad, he was and I loved him dearly. Now if you don't mind I want to go to my room. I am feeling very tired and I'm mentally drained.'

'Of course,' said Alistair. 'If you don't want to join us for dinner, I'll have Cook make you up a tray and send it to your room. It will give you time to sort your things, then I'll see you in the morning.'

'Thanks, Dad. That would be lovely.' She turned to her mother. 'I'll see you at breakfast.'

'Good night,' Janet said. 'I am so pleased that you are home safely.'

Flora went and kissed her and her father, then made her way to her old bedroom. She sat on her bed and thought: poor mother. She does her best . . . But she knew that, with the best will in the world, Janet would never understand her. Thank heavens for her father!

* * *

Downstairs, Janet Ferguson was trying to come to terms with her daughter's homecoming. She turned to her husband and said, 'I'll never understand that girl.'

Alistair looked at her and said, 'But you never have.'

Janet glared at him. 'Well, it certainly isn't for the want of trying. I just don't know what to do about her.'

'She has been through a great deal. She's been in the middle of a war, for God's sake! Leave her alone.' He took a cigar from the box on a side table and lit it. 'Your trouble, my dear,' he said, 'is that you tried to bring up Flora in your own image, and she is a very different kettle of fish. If only you could accept that she has a mind of her own then all would be fine.'

'Stubborn is what she is! I tried time and time again to find her a suitable husband and she couldn't have been more difficult. Now she swans in wearing an engagement ring and we knew nothing about it, or the man!'

Alistair sighed. 'Does it matter? The poor fellow is dead!' He wasn't sure which of the two women was the more stubborn. But he did wonder just who the man had been whom Flora had chosen as her husband. One thing he was sure of: he must have been a strong character. And how sad that he had died. That must have been devastating for Flora. Poor girl, she had been through some terrible times – how would she cope with being home? He was puzzled as to her reason for returning to Southampton. Why there, where the family had no connections? But knowing his daughter, he guessed they would be told when she was ready.

Flora, in fact, wasted no time at all in informing her parents of her plans. At breakfast the next morning, she told them about the poor living conditions she'd seen in Southampton's docklands and the stray children, begging for money to buy food.

'That's appalling!' exclaimed her mother. 'But I don't see that you can do anything about it.'

Flora tutted angrily. 'That's exactly the attitude of everyone, and therefore nothing gets done at all. Well, I'm going to do something about it!'

'And what might that be?' asked her father.

'I shall offer these children a bed and a home and see that they are fed and looked after.'

Janet looked askance. 'But how on earth are you going to undertake such a task?'

'I have the money that Aunt Lena left me, which is mine now I'm twenty-five, and I've seen a building for sale. It needs decorating and furnishing, but I've worked out that I could run it for a year.'

'And what happens to those poor children then?' asked her father quietly. 'After giving them food and shelter, it would be cruel to have to turn them out on to the streets again.'

Flora was undaunted. 'Ah well, I am to stir the conscience of the Council and the people of Southampton. I have to find some funding from somewhere.'

'How on earth are you going to do that?' demanded Janet.

Flora gazed across the table at her. 'Frankly, Mother, I have no idea, but I'll get the money somehow. I have to. No one else gives a tinker's curse about these children, it seems. Well, I do!'

Janet looked at her husband for some support, but he ignored her and said, 'That sounds an admirable thing. Just what you need to get your teeth into. I wish you luck.

If there is anything I can do, you let me know.'

'Thanks, Dad. I knew you would understand.'

'Well, I confess I don't,' said her mother. 'It sounds like another of your hare-brained schemes to me. You will probably need permission from the authorities to open such a place – have you thought of that? – and if you don't get it, what then?'

Her mother had brought up a very valid point, one that Flora hadn't thought about. 'Surely they'll agree when they see the place and understand that with my nursing experience I can take care of any sick children, and if they are seriously ill call a doctor.' She looked pleadingly at Janet. 'Some of these children are dying, Mother, for want of medical care. Don't you think that's obscene?'

Janet's tone softened. 'Yes, Flora, I do. I think it's unforgivable. And I do realise after what you have been through it makes it even worse to see lives wasted in those so young.' At the look of surprise on Flora's face her mother added, 'I confess that I don't always understand your motivation in life, but I do see that this would be a very worthy and important step to take. I just don't think you have gone into things deeply enough, that's all.'

Flora sighed. 'You are probably right, but I feel so strongly about it. It is something I absolutely have to do.'

'Then nothing will stop you. I wish you luck. I only hope in time I don't have to say I told you so.' Janet left the table. 'Now I must be on my way as I have a meeting in an hour. I'll see you both later.'

Her father rose from his seat and said, 'I must be off too. Why don't you take Jasper out for a ride? It will help clear the mind, give you some thinking time. I told the groom to prepare him.' He smiled. 'I knew the stables would be first on your list this morning.' He glanced at the breeches she was wearing. 'It appears I was right.'

Flora beamed at him. 'How well you know me, Dad. That's a good idea. See you at dinner.'

Jasper was her favourite horse, and as Flora called his name as she approached his stable, he whinnied in recognition. She entered the stall and saw that he was already saddled. She stroked the horse's head, fed him a carrot she'd taken from the kitchen and nuzzled her head against his neck. 'Hello, old friend,' she said. 'Come along, let's get out of here.'

As Flora rode over the heathland her mind was filled with thoughts of Flynn. How much she wished he was here with her, but she felt he was, in spirit, as she rode amongst the heather, her face wet with tears. Later, as she stopped to give the horse a rest, she thought how peaceful it was. How quiet, how beautiful. How perfect. But life wasn't perfect, not by a long chalk . . . and for those poor children struggling to survive in the docklands of Southampton, life was very hard. As she climbed back into the saddle, kicked her mount into a gallop and felt the wind in her hair, she knew that nothing was going to stop her from trying to help them. She couldn't fail . . . wouldn't fail! She would fight tooth and nail to try to help at least some of them. Now, she had a purpose in life.

That evening at dinner, the atmosphere was back to normal. The tenseness of the morning forgotten. Flora caught up on the news of her sisters and was surprised to hear they both had new offspring: Thelma a son and Margaret a daughter. Both their husbands had enlisted in the war, but had fortunately returned physically sound. It seemed that both of the girls were happily settled.

'As I had hoped to be with Flynn,' she said sadly. She looked at her parents. 'We met in London when I was doing my training. He was on leave, due to be sent to France.'

'What did he do for a living?' asked her mother.

'He had a stud farm in Ireland,' explained Flora. 'We planned to raise thoroughbreds, maybe a Derby winner.' She took a sip from her glass of wine. 'But there, the best plans can fall apart, especially during wartime. He was shot down over France, but not before a German bullet had killed him as he sat in the cockpit. At least I'm grateful that he didn't know anything about the crash.'

'I wish we had been able to meet him,' said her father quietly.

'So do I. You would have liked him, Dad. And you, Mother. He could charm the birds from the trees.' She smiled. 'Being Irish, you see. The Irish have a certain something about them. I certainly found him irresistible.'

'Life often seems unfair,' said Alistair.

'True, Dad, but at least he wasn't left maimed like many of my patients, coming home to an uncertain future after fighting for their country. But let's not think on these things now. Tomorrow I'm going into Glasgow to do some shopping.' She grinned at her father. 'That is always a sure-fire way to cheer up any woman.'

Alistair put his hand in his pocket and took out his wallet. 'Here,' he said, handing her four crisp five-pound notes. 'Treat yourself. I think you deserve it.'

With a cry of delight, Flora took the notes. 'Thanks, Dad. It's ages since I went shopping. The last time was in Rouen, when I found some shampoo and a new lipstick, and believe me, that was exciting!'

Laughing he said, 'Well, let's hope you do better tomorrow.'

★ ★ ★

The following morning Flora caught the local train into the city, and wandered around the familiar streets, looking in the shop windows. She walked along Sauchiehall Street, and entered a smart store where she bought the things she would need for her return to Southampton. She went to a different shop and purchased three nurse's uniforms. She thought it ironic that she would once again have to wear this uniform when she had been so happy to discard it and the memories it evoked. But this time it was to be worn for an entirely different purpose.

During her final days, her two sisters and their families visited, and the girls spent hours chatting about old times. Her brothers-in-law didn't mention their time spent in the war, which Flora could understand, and she didn't enlighten them about the horrors she had seen. What was the point? The war was over and they were all trying desperately to forget such painful memories. It wasn't easy, and sometimes her dreams turned into nightmares, bringing the past back far too vividly.

When it was time for her to take her leave, she kissed her mother goodbye.

'I hope everything works out as you want it to,' said Janet a little abruptly. She wasn't very good at showing her emotions.

Alistair drove Flora to the station and on their arrival, he found a porter to take her luggage, gave her a big hug and said, 'Don't forget where I am if you need me.'

'Thanks, Dad. I'll be in touch. You take care.' She settled in a carriage and as the steam from the train hissed out around the wheels as it started to move, she wondered just what was ahead of her now.

Chapter Seven

Flora was somewhat weary when eventually she arrived at Southampton. She asked the taxi driver to recommend a good bed-and-breakfast place, and he suggested one in Wilton Avenue.

'Is that anywhere near the docks?' she enquired.

He looked horrified. 'Good Lord no, miss. I wouldn't take you to a place near there, not a lady like you. You can get a tram to the docks from here if you want,' and proceeded to tell her how.

The boarding house was clean and comfortable and the rates reasonable, the landlady was pleasant and Flora decided to book in for a week at first. After a good night's sleep and a cooked breakfast, she made her way to the office of the estate agent who had shown her around the premises she now desired.

The agent recognised her and again they walked round what used to be the builders' merchant's. Flora was even more excited as she saw the building for the second time, but she was a canny Scot and didn't show her enthusiasm.

'Well,' she said slowly, 'it would do for what I want at a push, but I don't know . . .' She walked round the downstairs rooms. 'It would need a lot of money spent on the decoration to make it habitable.'

The estate agent, anxious to make a deal, jumped in. 'No doubt we could come to some arrangement about the price.'

Flora hid a smile and knew that he was hooked. After much haggling, she brought him down to the price she wanted to pay. The man looked somewhat fraught as they shook hands on the deal. He smiled ruefully. 'If ever you need a job, Miss Ferguson,' he said, 'you could always come and work for me. I feel as if I have been run over by a tram!'

She laughed with delight at the compliment. 'It's my Scottish blood,' she explained.

'You don't come from a long line of vampires, I suppose, only I'm sure I've had the blood sucked from me.'

'Nonsense! You will still make a profit, but I know I have a reasonable property, one at the market value rather than the inflated one you originally wanted. I'll be in tomorrow to sign the contract.'

'And what do you intend to do with this when it's yours?' he asked.

'Live in it, of course.'

'What, on your own? It's too big for one person, I'd have thought,' he said, fishing for details.

She wasn't to be drawn. 'I like a lot of space.'

She bought the local paper and looked for a painter and decorator in the advertisements, writing down several numbers to call the following day, and wandered around the High Street and Above Bar, looking at the furniture shops. She frowned. There must be somewhere that sold beds in bulk, like the iron beds they had in hospitals. Buying them singly from a furniture shop would be hideously expensive – far beyond her tight budget. She would have to look into this during the following weeks.

★ ★ ★

The next morning she visited the bank where she had money from her account in Glasgow transferred, and spoke with the bank manager, who was very helpful when she told him she had bought some premises that needed decorating. He gave her the address of a man he knew. But Flora again kept to herself the reason for buying such a place. She didn't want anyone to know of her intentions until she had looked into all the possible difficulties that might face her. When the building was ready, she would approach the proper authorities, but until then, it was her secret.

She then made her way to the estate agent's office, handed over a bank draft for the required amount and came to an agreement whereby she had the keys whilst the papers were being drawn up. As she walked towards the docks, she could feel her heart beating wildly, she was so excited. Flora stopped in front of the building that was now hers and, unlocking the gates that kept out the passing public, she undid the front door and slowly, walking from room to room, she started to plan her children's home.

The month of December passed in a flurry of activity. Builders came and knocked down an inner wall between two rooms upstairs to turn it into a room big enough for a dormitory, Flora reasoning that it was easier to keep an eye on children in one big room rather than two small ones, and if eventually the big one was full, there were others that could be put to use. Old dirty lino was removed, to be replaced with new, and everywhere was to be painted after Christmas. Downstairs the walls were white, but the rooms upstairs were to be in bright colours: yellow in one and apricot in another, the remaining rooms yet to be decided.

She had paid for the builder to hire extra hands to do the decorating, anxious to get as much finished as she could before the festive season.

Flora bought a second-hand sewing machine and made curtains, buying the material in the market to save money. She set herself up in a room downstairs out of the way of the builders and began to work. The kitchen she had scrubbed clean and a new bigger cooker had just been installed. She knew the workmen were puzzled by this as she overheard them talking among themselves.

'That's a bloody big cooker for just one person,' said one.

'Maybe she's going to open a boarding house . . . or a brothel,' laughed another.

'No, not a lady like her. She's from good stock, you can tell.'

Flora grinned to herself and was about to walk away when she heard the first man say, 'Well, it's just as well it ain't a brothel. Jack la Salles wouldn't like that. This is his patch; he wouldn't like no competition.'

Flora was intrigued.

'He's a twisted bugger if ever there was. His liking for young girls makes me sick to my stomach. You'd think the police would have put him away by now.'

'I heard they never could find the proof. He's a smart bastard,' another voice chipped in. And the conversation changed, leaving Flora wondering about this man with his perverted ways.

Christmas was drawing near and Flora knew that her mother would be expecting her to make the trip home, but there was too much to do. From a public call box, she rang her father at his office and explained, leaving him to pass the news on. 'I know it's not fair to ask you to do this, Dad, but it would be the easiest way in the end.'

'It's all right, my dear. I don't mind. How are things going?'

'Fine. I've been staying at a guest house ever since I arrived, but tomorrow I'm moving into my own place and that will make life a lot easier.'

'And what will you do over Christmas?' he asked.

'I haven't given it much thought,' she said, 'but I'll be fine, don't you worry.' As she replaced the receiver, she thought it ironic that the last two years she had been so homesick at Christmas, and now she had the opportunity to be with her family, she declined to do so.

In fact the problem of Christmas was solved in an unexpected way.

The day after Flora took leave of her bed-and-breakfast accommodation and moved into her new abode, she had a visitor. She was in the kitchen, resplendent with its new cooker and pots and pans, making tea for the workmen, complete with cakes she'd baked that morning, anxious to try out the oven, when there was a tap on the kitchen door. Looking up she was surprised to see a young priest standing there.

'Good morning,' he said. 'Forgive the intrusion, but I am Father Duggan, from St Joseph's, the local Catholic church. I thought it was time we met. I have been watching the activity here with great interest.'

Flora looked at the tall good-looking young man with fair hair that seemed somewhat unruly, as he kept running his fingers through it to keep it off his forehead. She smiled at him. 'Please come in,' she said. 'I'm making tea for the workmen, perhaps you would care for some too?'

He looked longingly at the tray of cakes cooling. 'I must confess it was the smell of the baking that drew me in this morning.'

'Then you must taste them.' Flora poured a cup of tea and placed two cakes on a plate for him, then excused herself for a moment to take the big brown teapot, mugs and the cakes on a tray out to the men. When she returned Father Duggan had made himself comfortable on one of the chairs in the kitchen and was tucking in.

'My, but these are good.'

Flora sat in another chair and joined him. 'Flora Ferguson,' she volunteered, and shook him by the hand. 'If you are looking to add another member to your flock, Father, I'm afraid you'll be disappointed. I am not a Catholic.'

He laughed heartily. 'That was not my intention,' he said. 'Mind you, it would have been a bonus! But the cakes more than make up for it.'

Over their tea, they chatted congenially. He was from Cork and had been in Southampton for more than a year. Flora pressed him for anything he could tell her about the children she had seen begging on the streets. It was a similar story to what the policeman had told her.

'Many of them are from poor homes run by bad parents. Others know no other way but to live by their wits. We do have a home for some of them,' he said. 'Nazareth House is a Catholic home for Catholic children, run by nuns.'

'But what about the others?' Flora asked. 'The non-Catholics?'

'There is the workhouse and one or two children's homes, but they usually don't want to go there,' Father Duggan said. A frown creased his forehead. 'And I can't say I blame them, to be honest.' He looked perturbed. 'The staff who run them are not the most Christian of people, and can be quite cruel, I've heard, but if a case is looked into, nothing seems to come of it and they are allowed to carry on.' He gazed sadly at her. 'It is a problem, Miss

Ferguson. One that gives me many a sleepless night.'

'What if someone wanted to open such a home – would they require permission from the council?' she enquired tentatively.

'Yes, they would. Why do you ask?'

Flora liked the young priest and felt she could confide in him. 'Because that is my intention,' she declared. 'I intend to open this place to house these poor little creatures, to take care of them and keep them off the streets. Let me show you round,' she said.

She took Patrick Duggan upstairs and showed him the one large dormitory, the other rooms and the bathroom, then downstairs to what was to be a playroom, she explained. On then to what was to be the dining room. 'I shall have a long table down the middle,' she said, 'probably with bench seating and comfortable chairs around the side where after the meals they can sit and read books.'

'I doubt if any of the children can read,' the priest said.

'But they can look at pictures and I'll teach them to read.'

He looked at her with raised eyebrows. 'I'm wondering if you are real or have you been sent from above?' he asked with a broad grin.

Flora chuckled. 'I'm no angel, Father, make no mistake about that. But fortunately I'm in a position to do something about these street children, if I can get round the bureaucracy. Do you think I have a chance?'

'Well now, Miss Ferguson, it seems that fate may have brought us together after all. The chairman of the council is a parishioner of mine.' His eyes twinkled. 'I take his confession. I might just be able to help you in this matter. Put a little pressure on, if I have to.'

'Father Duggan! That sounds almost like blackmail.'

'How could you say such a thing?' he exclaimed. 'I am a man of the cloth, after all.' But his mouth turned up at the corners as he tried not to smile. 'I will, however, introduce you to Richard Goodwin, our local GP. He's a good man, as concerned about these children as I am. With him in our camp, we should be able to pull it off between us.'

It was the 'our camp' that did it. Flora knew that she had the priest on her side and if the doctor was of a like mind, then she stood a good chance of being successful.

She thanked Father Duggan profusely, and they began to talk of other things, the impending festive occasion just a week away.

'Your busy time,' Flora said.

He agreed.

'No doubt you have a housekeeper to look after you at the presbytery,' she said.

'Usually there is a very good woman who comes in every day to take care of me, but she's in hospital at the moment. Appendix,' he explained.

'So how are you managing? No doubt with your good looks your women parishioners are flocking around like flies, anxious to look after your welfare!' she teased.

He gazed at her knowingly. 'They are very kind, and one of them comes in to clean, but as for meals, I am quite resourceful. I'll have you know, Miss Ferguson, I'm a pretty good cook. My mother taught me well. You should taste my Irish stew!'

'And at Christmas? Will you be having stew then?'

'To be honest, I've been too busy to even think about it.'

'No doubt you will have a host of invitations, but I'll be here on my own – why don't you come here for your Christmas dinner?' she suggested. 'I'll have company and you won't have to worry, which is a fair exchange. At least it will give you a chance to see how well the children will be fed – if I ever get any, that is.'

He studied her with mild amusement. 'I would say, even on such a short acquaintance, that you are a very determined lady who won't take no for an answer about anything. That being the case, thank you. I'll be delighted to share your Christmas meal with you.'

Flora beamed at him. 'Excellent. What are you like with a paint brush?'

At his look of consternation, she burst out laughing. 'I'm only joking, Father.'

His look of relief made her laugh even more. 'I am anxious to get things finished, and there is so much yet to do, but you can relax. I won't ask you to help.'

When the room that was to be her bedroom was ready, Flora furnished it quite simply with just a single bed, dressing table and wardrobe. The curtains were pale green to match the walls, but she had purchased a vibrant bedcover from one of the second-hand shops, to give a spark of life to the otherwise peaceful room. The burgundy and gold pattern looked unusual, but fabulous.

In the kitchen was a large farmhouse table, and two comfortable chairs, pulled up near the fire, and along the corridor, she had turned a small room into a sitting room when the decorators had finished, with comfortable second-hand furniture, cheering it up with her handmade curtains and cushion covers. She decorated the mantelpiece with greenery bought at the market, placing coloured baubles among it. As she did so, she thought of the hospital at Rouen and how she had decorated that. How times had changed for her, but she wondered then, as she often did in her quieter moments, how the men she'd escorted home had settled in. In her heart she knew that many of them would be having a hard time.

She would have loved to have gone out on to the streets and gathered up some of the children and brought them back to the house now, but she didn't want to fall foul of the law. She told herself she would have to be patient.

On Christmas Eve, she decided to go to Midnight Mass and made her way to St Joseph's. After all, it didn't matter which church you attended, she thought. They were all houses of the Lord, but she had to hide a smile when Father Duggan gave her the sacrament. The look of surprise on his face was something to behold. She wondered what he would have to say about it when they shared their Christmas meal the following day.

At the appointed time, Patrick Duggan arrived at the kitchen door, clutching a bottle of white wine and was ushered in by Flora, who said, 'come and sit by the fire. You must be frozen. It's like the North Pole out there.' And, indeed, earlier that morning there had been a light flurry of snow.

As he sat down beside the fire, the priest said, 'When I saw you at Mass, I wondered if you were going to join my flock after all.'

Flora said, 'No, Father, but I was sure the Good Lord wouldn't mind where I took communion.' She studied his face. 'For a young man, you are looking somewhat weary today, Father.'

'I was up half the night,' he explained. 'One of my parishioners passed away in the early hours of the morning. I had been there to give him his last rites.' He looked saddened. 'Not an easy time of the year to lose someone, when people are celebrating the birth of our Lord.'

'I have never found it acceptable at any time,' she said softly.

'It sounds as if you have experienced such a loss.'

As she lifted the turkey from the oven she said, 'My fiancé was killed in France two years ago. I was out there as a VAD, from nineteen sixteen until the end of the war.'

'I see. Then you are probably more experienced at dealing with death than I am.'

As she rested the bird and turned the potatoes, Flora told him of her years in France, and the things she had seen. It was the first time she had spoken of it to anyone since her return, and although it was still too painful to talk about Flynn in any great detail, it was like a cleansing of her soul when she had finished, and she told the priest this.

'I am privileged that you felt that you could tell all this to me.' He took from the pocket of his cassock a corkscrew and opened the bottle of wine.

Flora grinned at him as she reached for two wine glasses, thankful that she had purchased some the day before. 'You came well prepared!' she teased.

'I'm used to opening the communion wine,' he explained. 'Some of my flock have a rare thirst and I'm not averse to a glass of wine myself with a meal.'

When at last they sat at the table and were eating their turkey with all the trimmings with the roast potatoes, sprouts, carrots, and cauliflower covered in a delicate cheese sauce, Patrick looked up and said, 'You wouldn't like a live-in priest when you open your home, would you? This is the best meal I've had since I left Ireland.'

'You get me permission to open and you can name your own price!' she quipped.

'What are you going to call this establishment when it's finished?'

'I don't really know. To be honest I hadn't given it a thought.' She was silent for a moment, thinking over the prospect. Then she smiled. 'Of course. I will call it Harwood House.'

'I like the sound of that,' he said. 'But why? You must have a reason for your choice.'

She explained, 'My Aunt Lena, Mother's sister, was also my godmother, and when she died she left me a legacy in her will. As it is her money which enables me to do all this, I think it fitting that the house be named after her, don't you?'

'An excellent idea. I think we should toast the good lady.' He raised his glass, as did Flora. 'To Aunt Lena and Harwood House!'

Later, after the plum pudding, they sat in the small sitting room by the fire, drinking coffee. Flora, filled with curiosity, turned to her guest and asked, 'How did you become a priest, Father?'

'It was decided when I was born that I would go into the Church.'

She looked surprised. 'Decided by whom?'

'My mother. I was the first son born after four sisters. She was so delighted at having a boy after praying for one, that she decided in return for having had her prayers answered I should dedicate my life to God.'

'Didn't you have any say in the matter?'

'To be honest I never ever questioned it. I grew up knowing what my future was to be and I'm happy being a priest.' At the expression of disbelief on Flora's face he smiled at her and said, 'The Lord calls us all in different ways, you know.' He looked at the clock ticking away over the mantelpiece and said, 'I really have to go, Flora, but thank you so much for your hospitality.'

As he rose from the settee, she got to her feet and said, 'Let me cut you some cold turkey for your supper later, just in case you get hungry.'

He began to protest but she would have none of it. 'I know men and their stomachs: you may be full up now but later tonight you'll need a snack.'

And so Father Duggan left, thanking her again, clutching his food parcel.

'After Christmas,' he said, 'I'll bring round the doctor, Richard Goodwin, to meet you and look the place over. Then when you are ready to open, we'll approach the local council. Thanks again, Flora. I'll be seeing you soon.'

As she cleared away and washed the dishes, Flora wondered just what Patrick Duggan might have been had his mother not decided his future. The good-looking priest might well have ended up in the Church, but maybe he wouldn't. It was an interesting thought.

Chapter Eight

It was New Year's Eve and Jessie Maxwell was not looking forward to it. She threw back the blanket and swung her legs out of her bed in the shabby room that was her home, situated in the docklands of Southampton. She stretched wearily and then held her forehead. It had been a boozy lunch hour at the King's Head, but at closing time she had taken home a punter. He hadn't been any trouble; in fact he had consumed so much beer that he had fallen asleep. When he did wake up and Jessie had told him he owed her for the sex they had, he was so confused that he paid up and went home.

If only she could always earn her money so easily, she thought. 'Stupid bugger! It served him right,' she muttered as she began to brush her hair. Her mouth had a foul taste, so taking her toothbrush, flannel and thin towel she locked the door to her room and went to the bathroom along the corridor, which was shared by the six inhabitants of the house.

Jessie looked at her reflection in the broken mirror hanging from a nail with a bit of string above the basin. At twenty-four, she knew she looked older. The years of being on the game and spending so much time in the local pubs had wreaked havoc with her skin. Through bleary eyes she looked with disgust into the mirror. She washed her face, cleaned her teeth, then made her way back to her room.

'Better get ready for the night shift,' she said aloud. After Christmas Eve, business had been slow. Most of her punters had been at home with their families and no ship had docked for several days – not one with crew that had any money, anyway. So the pickings had been very lean.

She lay back on the bed. 'I wish I could retire,' she murmured, and then laughed. 'It sounds as if I'm a bloody business.' Well, she supposed she was really. Business was supply and demand, and she was supplying all right!

She reached out, picked up a framed picture of her mother and gazed at it fondly. 'Oh, why did you have to go and die on me, Mum?' The picture showed a young woman in a neat dress with flowing hair and a beautiful smile. She slowly replaced the picture. If her mother hadn't passed away with pneumonia when Jessie was sixteen, who knows what sort of a life she would now be leading, she thought sadly. Her father had tried to cope, but one day he'd signed on with one of the shipping companies, promising to send money home to her – and that was the last she'd heard of him. She felt her anger grow. It was because of her father she'd been forced on to the streets to survive. 'Bastard!' she cried. 'I hope you die a horrible death, wherever you are.'

She reluctantly rose from the bed and dressed. She slipped into a white blouse with a high lace neck she'd purchased from a second-hand shop, and a long black woollen skirt. Her coat had definitely seen better days, but she couldn't help that. Anyway, she always slipped it off her shoulders so any potential punters could take a look at the goods on display. She put on her shoes, but there was a hole in the sole of one of them so she lined it with a bit of old newspaper.

She thought she'd go to the Horse and Groom tonight. It was the toughest pub in town, but if there was to be any business at all, there would be the place she'd find it. Besides, the locals and the landlord, Jimmy James, knew her. And she felt safe if there was ever any trouble, and there often was. Not that she couldn't defend herself. She was well known for having a good right hook.

The public bar of the Horse and Groom was already busy by the time Jessie arrived. She was greeted by a few of the local men she knew as she made her way to the bar.

'Half a bitter,' she said to the barmaid, and looked around for any likely business, as she waited.

At a corner table was a group of three men. Her stomach turned over as she saw them: Jack la Salles sitting there with two of his henchmen. Jack was a small shrivelled little man with beady eyes. She took her drink to another table and watched them. Jack was looking at all the females with a lascivious expression. Jessie knew he wouldn't be interested in her – she was much too old. It was a known fact that Jack liked young girls; well, there were not many in the pub tonight. She watched him with distaste. She knew all about perverted sexual practices. But she wasn't into that with her punters; she always made that quite clear. Straight sex or a hand job, but no more than that. Some of the other prostitutes were prepared to go further, and that was fine – it was a personal choice after all – but they all had one thing in common: they despised Jack la Salles.

It was with some relief she saw the party get to their feet and depart. She sipped her beer and looked around. Well, she supposed she ought to start work. There were a few seamen in tonight and if she was lucky, she'd be able to make up for the lean pickings over Christmas.

Later that night, as she walked back to her room with her last punter, she passed what used to be the old builders' merchant's, and noticed a light reflected from the back of the house. She had seen some work being done there and wondered who had bought the property. No doubt she would hear soon enough. Nothing was kept quiet for long in the docklands. It was as if it had its own wire service. Eventually everyone knew everything.

It was the second week of January 1919, and the workmen were finishing off the final bits and pieces at Harwood House. Flora had found a place that sold her the iron beds she wanted for the dormitory. She had bought six to start with. She had hesitated about the purchase before getting permission to open, but she decided to be positive about things, and if the authorities came round, she wanted to let them see that she was ready. But she would wait before she bought the linen and blankets.

Father Duggan had called the previous day to ask if he could bring Richard Goodwin to see her the following evening after his surgery closed, and she was only too happy to agree. It was imperative to get his approval, she felt. She just hoped that she would like him; otherwise it could make things very difficult.

As soon as she saw the local doctor, Flora took to him. Richard looked somewhat like her idea of a professor, with his hair worn a little long in the neck, almost as if he'd not had time to visit the barber. He wore horn-rimmed glasses and looked very serious, until he smiled, and then it was as if the years slipped away, and Flora realised he wasn't as old as she had first thought.

'Miss Ferguson,' he said as he shook her hand, 'I'm happy to make your acquaintance. The good father here speaks very highly of you.'

'He's too kind. Please, sit down and I'll make us a cup of tea.' As she did so, she told the doctor what her hopes and dreams were; how she desperately wanted to be able to help the children walking the streets.

He gave one of his rare smiles. 'My goodness, it's a privilege to talk to someone who actually wants to do something about the problem. The situation is of great concern to both Patrick and me.'

After they had drunk their tea, Flora showed them both over the house.

Patrick remarked on the progress made. 'You are almost ready to open now, aren't you?'

'Yes, another few weeks should do it. But I don't know just how to go about it. What do you suggest?'

The priest turned to the GP. 'Do we have your support, Richard?'

'Indeed you do. I am happy to offer my services free should any child need medical attention.'

Flora looked at him with surprise. 'You are very generous, but you know absolutely nothing about me.'

'Father Duggan told me of your own medical background, which of course would be an advantage, and I admit I did have my reservations – until I met you. I can see by your enthusiasm this isn't just a whim on your part.'

Flora looked around. 'A whim? Whatever do you mean?'

'There is no polite way of putting this, Miss Ferguson, but there are women from a privileged background who sometimes take it into their head to "help the poor", but they soon tire of it.'

She was incensed. 'How could you think that of me?'

He smiled apologetically. 'Having met you, I can now see that isn't the case, but I had to be sure before I decided to give you my support. You do understand, I hope.' There was an anxious expression in his soft blue eyes as he awaited her reaction.

'Yes, I do understand, and thank you for your kind offer.'

'May I ask you one thing, though?'

'Of course.'

'How are you going to finance all this?'

Flora began to feel defensive. 'I have enough money of my own to keep it going for a year, if I'm really careful; in the meantime I will get financing to cover us in the future.'

He gazed intently at her. 'And how do you intend to do that?'

She looked stubborn. 'Frankly, Dr Goodwin, I have no idea, but I can assure you, I will get it!'

He chuckled softly. 'Patrick said you were determined. I can now see what he meant.'

'Do you still want to help us?' she challenged.

There was a twinkle of amusement in his eyes as he answered, 'My dear Miss Ferguson, I wouldn't miss it for anything.' He rose to his feet. 'I must make tracks. My wife expected me home an hour ago.'

As she showed him out of the front door, Flora thought he seemed an interesting man. One moment he looked so serious and severe, but another moment he looked quite different. It was amazing what changes a smile could bring, she thought.

She returned to the sitting room and Father Duggan. 'Well, I suppose that went well, didn't it? To be honest I'm not quite sure.'

He smiled benignly at her. 'Richard is in. I knew he would be, but you can understand the questions. He had to be sure you were serious in your intention.' Before she could answer he continued, 'Now what you must do is write to the chairman of the council, Mr Chivers, and ask for an appointment to see him. Just say it is to put something before him that you feel would be of benefit to the town and some of its inhabitants.' He sat back in the chair. 'I will have a word with him after church on Sunday.'

'Put pressure on him, you mean,' she said artfully.

'I wouldn't quite put it like that, Flora.' A slow grin spread across his features. 'But, yes, that's exactly what I intend to do.'

She burst out laughing. 'What would the Pope have to say about your methods?'

He wasn't upset by her remark at all. 'The Pope is a businessman as well. He would understand the necessity of this home, for the sake of the children. He would approve, I'm sure.'

'The end justifies the means,' she said, still highly amused.

'In this case, yes!'

'You'll be telling me next that the Lord moves in mysterious ways.'

'I don't need to. You already know that.'

As she escorted him to the front door, she asked, 'How are you getting along at the presbytery? Is your housekeeper back yet?'

'Not for another few weeks, but the ladies of the parish have sorted out a rota, so I'm well taken care of. I'll be seeing you soon, Flora. Good night.'

'Good night, Father Duggan, and thanks.'

As she settled down for the night, Flora wondered if,

even with the help of the Father and Dr Goodwin, she would be able to persuade the authorities to grant her permission. If they said no, what on earth would she do? She climbed into bed, angry with herself for her negative thoughts. She must believe in herself. If she didn't, how on earth could she expect the members of the council to do so? She turned over and went to sleep, after she had mentally written the letter to the chairman. Tomorrow she would put her thoughts on paper and post it. Then she would just have to wait.

Flora was beset by confused dreams. She was standing at the gates of Harwood House, which were barred. Outside were hundreds of children, crying to be let in, but there stood a stranger, flanked by policemen. The man was waving a piece of paper and calling loudly, 'The council will not allow these premises to open. You must all go away!'

Chapter Nine

Alderman George Chivers sat behind his desk in his office at the town hall, puffing on a large cigar, flipping through his mail. He placed the letters in different piles to be dealt with later by his secretary. He frowned as he started to read through one and glanced down at the signature. Miss Flora Ferguson – never heard of her. But here she was, this woman, asking to make an appointment to see him as she had a proposition to put before him that would benefit a certain section of the community. He was about to cast it aside when he saw the name of Father Duggan mentioned. He placed the letter in a drawer in his desk. He would see the father this Sunday at Mass and would have a word with him about this young woman. Maybe he could shed some light on the matter.

He sat back in his chair and looked around at the comfortable office with its plush leather chairs. It was befitting a man of his position, he felt. Yes, he had done well for himself. He had a thriving jewellery business in Above Bar, he was high up in the local masonic lodge, he had a wife who was capable of being the hostess he required for formal occasions, and who had given birth to his two children – and he also had a young energetic mistress, who certainly met his more basic needs. His wife did her duty, when required, in the marital bed, but with Daisy he could really indulge himself. Daisy had absolutely no inhibitions whatsoever, and he felt himself harden as he thought of the games they played together.

He was a good man, he thought. He knew that having a mistress was breaking his marriage vows, but he felt that as his philandering was hurting no one, what was the harm? After all, he did go to confession, so he was making amends in one way. He frowned as he thought of Father Duggan telling him to give up these sins of the flesh. It was all very well for him – he had vowed to lead a celibate life – but he, George Chivers, had not!

The following Sunday after the service, the Alderman waited for Father Duggan to finish shaking hands with his parishioners and approached him. 'Father! A word.'

Patrick turned to him. 'What can I do for you?'

'I had a letter from a certain Miss Ferguson, in which she mentioned your name. Now what's this all about?'

The priest walked him slowly down the path to the gate as they talked. 'Miss Ferguson wants to open a home for children. She has seen how many of them are deprived of care and wander the streets begging, and she wants to make this contribution to society.'

'And what's in it for her?'

Patrick looked at him wryly. 'Absolutely nothing. You know, George, there are people in this world who have a Christian heart and who ask for no reward. All she wants from you and the council is permission to open her home.'

Chivers glared at him. 'At what cost to the council?'

'Miss Ferguson is prepared to meet the cost herself. She has bought the old builders' merchant's along the docks, and had it painted and decorated inside in preparation.'

'What qualifications does this *sainted* woman have for such a task?'

'Excellent ones! She was a VAD for two years and served in France. Her nursing experience will be invaluable – *and*, Dr Goodwin has promised his services free if this all goes ahead,' Patrick said, adding strength to his cause.

George Chivers raised an eyebrow. 'Do I detect a *tour de force* here, Patrick? Are the troops gathering for a battle, perhaps?'

With a slow smile the priest said, 'Of course not, but Richard and I have long been concerned about these children, as you well know. The council have always said that something should be done about the situation, but have argued that the finances were not available. Now they are.'

'And you want my support!'

'Indeed I do. You and I have nice warm homes, food on our table, comfort – *from all different sources*.'

The alderman gave him a hard stare.

'But these poor children of the Lord have nothing. Would you deny them again, when this time there is no excuse? Richard and I would be only too willing to appear in front of the council to give our reasoning for supporting this venture.'

'I see. Well, I will get my secretary to make an appointment for me to meet this woman.'

Father Duggan smiled. 'Thank you, George. I'm sure you won't regret it.'

'I do hope not,' he said as he walked away.

And so the following week Flora made her way to the office of George Chivers, at his invitation, well prepared to put her case before him.

Once in the office, she sat down in the chair facing him across his desk as requested, and took an immediate dislike to the man, but she smiled as she said, 'It was very good of you to see me, Alderman.'

Chivers eyed her with interest. He didn't know quite what he expected this Miss Ferguson to look like – probably old and staid – so it was a great surprise to him to find himself gazing at such a good-looking young woman. She was dressed sedately in a smart suit, hat and gloves, but it was the gleam in her eye as well as her full bosom that attracted him.

'Good morning,' he said. 'Now tell me just exactly what you have in mind.'

Flora laid out her plans and expectations before him, explaining how appalled she had been to see so many children on the streets, obviously undernourished and neglected.

There was just a hint of censure in her voice, which put Chivers on the defensive. 'Of course, we do know about this problem, Miss Ferguson, and it does trouble the council that we are not in a position, financially, to deal with it, apart from the soup kitchen and the children's homes we have. But they can only take so many, you see. And, of course, the ending of the war has made a difference. So many wounded men returning home, and no employment for them, their families are suffering too. It all adds to our problems.'

Flora's eyes flashed with anger. 'You don't have to tell me about such men, Alderman. I nursed them when I was in France. I am horrified to see these poor devils, standing on street corners, selling matches, trying to earn a pittance. Some "land fit for heroes" this is! Lloyd George should be ashamed! I think it's disgusting, but at least I could do something for the children – if you let me.' It was as if she had thrown down a gauntlet, such was the note of challenge in her voice.

George admired the courage of this young woman. My, but she was feisty. How he wished his wife were like this. Had she been so, there would be no need for him to seek succour elsewhere. 'Perhaps I ought to come along and take a look at your establishment before I put it to the council. After all, I need to have all the facts at my fingertips.'

And that is all you'll have at your fingertips, thought Flora, recognising the predatory look in his eyes. 'Certainly, Alderman. If you can give me a time, then I will make sure I am on the premises.'

And I'll make damn sure that Father Duggan is there too, she decided. She didn't like this man but she didn't want to upset him, not until the necessary permission to open the house was signed and sealed. And so an appointment was made for Thursday, two days hence, at three o'clock in the afternoon.

Patrick was more than surprised to find Flora on his doorstep when he answered the front door to the presbytery. 'Flora! What a pleasant surprise. Please, come inside.'

She followed the priest into a comfortable sitting room. There was a large open fireplace, with logs burning, sending out a welcoming warmth as she sat on an old but comfortable settee. 'I've just had a meeting with the chairman of the council,' she told him.

'How did you get on?'

'Alderman Chivers is calling at Harwood House on Thursday at three o'clock. Could you possibly be there at that time?'

He consulted his diary. 'Yes, Flora. I am free then.' Noting the anxious expression she wore, he asked, 'Is everything all right?'

As always, she was very frank. 'Everything is fine, but I think the councillor is a dirty old man and I don't want to see him on my own!'

Patrick chuckled. 'What on earth makes you think that?'

'I have been dealing with men for the last two years and I recognise the look of lust when I see it.'

The priest rocked with laughter. 'Oh, Flora, you are quite a case.'

'I'm right about him, though, aren't I?'

Struggling to keep a straight face, Patrick said, 'You can't honestly expect me to comment about one of the town's most illustrious citizens, a member of my congregation – and a good Catholic.'

'No, I suppose not . . . but I bet it is interesting in the confessional when he's there!' she murmured.

'Flora! Please. Have a little respect for my calling.'

But she could see the merriment reflected in his expression.

'I do apologise,' she said, 'but I have seen the people on my mother's various committees, *and* the good churchgoers among them. As for their Christian beliefs, many of the women go to church to catch up on the latest gossip, and to see if they can outdo the other women in their new hats!'

'Ah, but that's the Church of England!'

She grinned at him. 'Actually it isn't. It's the Church of Scotland.'

He leaned forward. 'You know, I'm beginning to be really concerned about you.'

'Why?' she asked with surprise.

'You have a very cynical view on life.'

'You know, Father Duggan, you could be right.'

'Please call me Patrick. If we are going to be working together, we may as well be friends.'

'Very well, Patrick.' She rose from the settee. 'I'll be on my way. I need to see that all is in place for the alderman's visit.'

He took her to the door and opened it. 'I'll come a little early on Thursday afternoon and make sure I'm there before George.'

'He's that bad, is he?' she asked with a grin.

'*Goodbye*, Flora,' was his only response, but he could hear her laughter as she walked down the street.

It was Patrick who opened the door of Harwood House to the alderman. The priest tried to hide his amusement at the look of surprise on the face of the visitor.

'Father!'

'George. Come in. Miss Ferguson is in the kitchen, waiting for you.'

Chivers entered the kitchen and smelled the coffee percolating on the stove. He was very surprised at how clean and well equipped the kitchen was, and his surprise grew as he was escorted around the premises and saw the now completed rooms. He was struck by the cheerfulness of the place and felt that any child would love to sleep here, as there were now murals of animals decorating the walls of the playroom.

He turned to Flora and said, 'My word! I had no idea. You really have done a lot to this place.'

'Does that mean that you like it?'

'Of course I do.'

She showed him the dining room, which now had a long table and bench seats in it. 'This is where the children will eat,' she said. She took him to the comfortable sitting room and suggested he might like to ask her and Father Duggan any questions over a cup of coffee.

When Flora went to the kitchen to pour it, Patrick turned to the alderman and said, 'You must admit, George, she has done a fine job here.'

'Of course she has, but there are a few questions I want to ask.' And when Flora returned with the coffee, he said, 'What are you going to do about staff, Miss Ferguson? You obviously can't manage to run this on your own.'

'No, of course not,' she conceded. 'I want a permanent cook and I will require staff to help me to take care of the children and keep the place clean, but there is no point employing anyone until I know if I will get the necessary permission.' She looked expectantly at him.

He cleared his throat and said, 'I, of course, can't give you any indication of that until I put it before the council.'

Father Duggan spoke sharply. 'Now don't be evasive, George. I know that whatever you suggest will be acceptable to the others.' He gazed pointedly at him. 'After all, we know how persuasive you can be when you really want something.' He saw Chivers' neck redden and added, 'I can't believe you have any reservations about this place being suitable, or Miss Ferguson. Richard and I haven't.'

'Of course not,' the councillor blustered, 'but as you well know, I have to go through the proper channels.'

'Certainly you do. But I also know I can rely on you to do the right thing.'

George Chivers rose to his feet rather hurriedly. 'I must be off, Miss Ferguson. You'll be hearing from us in due course.' He shook her by the hand and allowed Father Duggan to escort him to the door. As he was about to leave he turned to Patrick and said, 'You are really using your position to pressure me, Father, and I think you are taking an unfair advantage!'

'I have no idea what you mean!' retorted the priest as he showed him out.

When he returned, Flora looked anxiously at him. 'Well?'

'I don't think you have a thing to worry about,' Patrick said.

'How can you be so sure?'

He shrugged. 'Nothing is ever certain, Flora. However, in this instance, if I was a betting man . . . In any case, the council meets next week, so you won't have long to wait.'

'I must say, you were very forceful. It was almost as if you were demanding he give the go-ahead.'

'I am not in a position to demand anything from anyone. After all, I am only the Catholic priest.'

She studied him for a moment. 'And that gives you a certain power.'

'What nonsense! Any more coffee in the pot, and I don't suppose you have been baking again, have you?'

Flora knew he was deliberately changing the subject, so she smiled at him and said, 'As a matter of fact I have. With your sweet tooth, Patrick, you'll end up like a barrel when you are an old man.'

'The way I have to rush around, never! I need such things to keep up my strength, to give me the energy to do my job. Now would you deny me that?'

She gazed at him and with a faraway look she said softly, 'All you Irishmen are the same. You have an answer for everything.'

'Of course,' said Patrick, suddenly remembering. 'Your young man was Irish, was he not?'

She nodded. 'From Dublin. He had the same persuasive

way with him.' She looked away and, as if to herself, she said softly, 'He could charm the birds from the trees.' She turned back to Patrick and said, 'Let's hope our charm worked on Alderman Chivers!'

A week later, Flora received a letter from Chivers' secretary asking if it would be possible for the members of the council to come and view the building on a certain day. Flora didn't hesitate, and wrote to confirm the arrangement.

This time when her visitors arrived, both Patrick and Richard were there. Flora set out some tea and home-made scones for the men to enjoy when they had been taken on a tour of the building. Flora left the doctor and priest to do the talking. After all, she was an unknown quantity to the men, until one of them mentioned that his son had been at the Battle of the Somme.

Flora sat beside him and they talked. The councillor was concerned that although his son was physically unharmed, he had become withdrawn. Flora tried to explain a little of what it was like to be in the front lines, without upsetting the man with any details. Then she said, 'If your son would like to come and see me, I'd be happy to talk to him. You see, the men who were at the front find it difficult to talk to their families, but to someone who has seen the war first-hand and understands, it sometimes helps.'

He was very grateful. 'He is our only son, you see, and his mother is beside herself with worry.'

'Of course she is. Ask your son to call round at any time. Just pop in. I don't have a telephone installed yet, but I'm usually here in the mornings.'

The man looked around the room. 'You have done a lot of work, Miss Ferguson, and you will have my vote. This sort of place is sorely needed in the town.'

'Thank you very much,' she said, and rose from her seat as she saw Alderman Chivers getting ready to leave.

'Thank you, Miss Ferguson,' he said in an officious tone. 'I'll let you know the council's decision in a couple of days' time.'

She smiled sweetly at him and thanked him, then showed everyone out. She returned to the kitchen and sat down. 'I am exhausted!' she exclaimed.

Richard laughed. 'It was a bit of an ordeal for you, being scrutinised like that. But the worst is over. Now it's a matter of waiting.'

Flora grinned broadly. 'Anyway, I have the promise of one vote.'

Patrick said, 'I saw you, charming the boots off Councillor Beckett.'

'We were having a serious discussion about his son, that's all,' she said as she poured them all some more tea. 'He was at the Somme.'

'And is still suffering,' said Richard quietly.

'Well, is it any wonder?' Flora retorted. 'Those poor devils went through hell out there. No one comes home unchanged.'

'Not even you, I imagine,' he said.

She looked up and saw the eyes of the softest blue staring back at her as he had removed his glasses to clean them. They reminded her so much of Flynn that for a moment she was thrown.

'Not even me,' she answered. 'I learned about life, about death, about suffering – and about bravery that was beyond belief.' Her voice faltered slightly. 'I learned how to love a man with every fibre of my being . . . and I learned how deep the pain can be when he died.' She sipped her tea and blinked hard, trying to keep at bay the tears that threatened. 'People say that as time passes, it gets better. It doesn't . . . it is just different.'

'Your loss is our gain, sadly,' the doctor remarked. 'Had your fiancé survived, you certainly wouldn't be here, would you?'

'No. I would be in Ireland training horses. But life is very strange. Just when all seems fine, it comes along and knocks the legs from under you.' She looked at Richard. 'And how has life treated you?'

'Rather better,' he said. 'I'm doing the job I love, I am married to a beautiful young woman, I am a fortunate man.' He paused. 'The only thing I miss is being able to ride. I used to do so when I was younger, and many is the time I would like to ride out into the country, away from everything.'

Flora was surprised. He looked such a scholarly man; she could picture him surrounded by books, but galloping across a field didn't seem to fit the picture she had of him, albeit formed on such a short acquaintance. 'Really?'

He laughed at her disbelief. 'Oh, yes, Miss Ferguson. I used to go to point-to-point meetings, and once or twice I actually participated.'

'Good heavens!' She looked across at Patrick. 'He doesn't look the type!'

Richard's eyebrows lifted. 'Whyever not?'

She suddenly realised what she'd said and she became momentarily embarrassed. 'I'm sorry, I shouldn't have said that.'

Richard looked bemused. 'I begin to wonder just what sort of picture you have of me, Miss Ferguson.'

'Flora, please. And I don't know you well enough to have any kind of picture of you.'

He chuckled softly as he got up from the table. 'I don't

believe that for one moment. I don't think you can help assessing everyone when you meet them. Forgive me, but I have a surgery to prepare for. Let me know what happens, Patrick.' He smiled at Flora. 'I'll keep my fingers crossed for you. I'll see myself out.'

'Nice chap is Richard,' Patrick said. 'Solid as a rock and a very fine doctor.'

'What is Mrs Goodwin like?' Flora asked, her curiosity aroused.

Patrick hesitated. 'Young. Much younger than he is.'

'Do I hear a note of disapproval in your voice?'

'No, not at all. But he is very dedicated to his work and I sometimes wonder if she understands the pressure his practice can bring.' He rose to his feet. 'I must be away now. Let me know when you hear from the council.'

'Keep your fingers crossed,' Flora said.

'I'll do even better. I'll pray for you and the home.' He opened the door. 'You might do the same, Flora.'

'I already do that, Patrick. Every night.'

As she cleared away the dirty crockery she couldn't help wondering about Mrs Goodwin. Patrick said she was young and Richard referred to her as beautiful. Richard sounded happy, but she couldn't dismiss the remark that Patrick had made about her. There had been something in his voice that led her to believe that the priest didn't entirely approve of the young Mrs Goodwin.

Just a few streets away, Jack la Salles, sitting at the bar in his brothel, had just heard there might be a children's home opening soon and he wondered what the ages of these youngsters might be. Would they all be little ones or might there be some teenage girls there? He would watch the place with interest.

Chapter Ten

In the hope that the council would grant her permission to open Harwood House, Flora had placed two advertisements in the *Southern Daily Echo*. One for a female cook and another for an assistant, stating the applicant had to like children. She wasn't necessarily looking for anyone with training – she could do that herself – but a love of children was essential. She wanted to get the staff organised so that if she could open her house she would be ready to go. By the time the applicants applied for the post, she should have heard from the council.

Her careful planning proved successful, as the following morning she received a letter stating that she now had official approval to open as a home for children. She danced around the kitchen with delight, waving the letter in her hand.

It was entirely coincidental that Father Duggan should appear at the open kitchen door at this precise moment. He stood watching her, unobserved, whilst Flora twirled around until she was facing him.

'Oh, my God!' she blurted out. 'Patrick! You gave me such a fright for a minute.' She waved the paper at him. 'We've got it!' she exclaimed. 'I am now official.' Then she paused and, with a look of consternation said, 'But how will I get the children? I can't go and drag them in off the street, can I?'

'Indeed you can't. You'll have the law after you! As a matter of fact I may have two children who have need of you. Their mother has to go into hospital next week and her husband must continue to work to keep the wolf from the door. Besides, he is so worried about his wife, I doubt if he could cope, poor man.'

'Sit down, Patrick, do. What is wrong with the poor woman?'

'Consumption,' he said sadly. 'To be honest with you, Flora, I don't think she is going to get better.'

'How old are the children?' she asked.

'Little Matilda, or Mattie as she's known, is nearly four, and Jake, her brother, is six.'

'Are they aware of how ill their mother is?'

Patrick shook his head. 'No. Mattie is too young, but Jake is very grown up for one so small. He's had to take care of his sister for a long time really, because his mother has been ill for the past two years. He's very protective of little Mattie, so he is. It's very touching to see, but also very sad.'

'I could make up one of the small rooms next to mine for them,' said Flora, giving the situation some thought. 'The two of them alone in an enormous dormitory would be frightening. I must go and buy the bed linen and blankets, now that I can go ahead.'

'Well, don't go mad and buy a lot,' advised the priest. 'After all, it will take some time for it to be known that you are available. I will inform the police that you are here. They'll be grateful. What about staff?'

Flora looked very pleased with herself. 'I have to interview some applicants tomorrow afternoon. I took a chance and advertised in the *Echo* a week ago. But if there are only two children, I can manage alone until I find the right people for the job.'

Patrick leaned across the table and patted her head. 'Well done, Flora. I'm pleased it all worked out for you.'

'I don't know that it would have without your intervention. I'm grateful for that.'

'There is no need to be, not at all. The reason I came round is to tell you I am having dinner tonight with Richard and his wife. He asked me to bring you along too. He apologised for the short notice, but he has been so busy and tonight he is unexpectedly free. Another doctor is on call.'

'How kind. I would love to come.'

'Good. I'll pick you up at seven o'clock. We can walk from here. He lives over the surgery in Bernard Street.' He rose from his chair. 'I'll see you later then. We can all celebrate this great news together.'

When she was alone, Flora went to her bedroom and rifled through her clothes, wondering just what to wear, bearing in mind that Mrs Goodwin was supposed to be a beautiful woman. She didn't want to appear a dowdy Scot, just dragged out of the heather. She had packed one or two nice gowns when she was at home, just in case she would have need of them, and these she now inspected, holding them up against her in front of the long mirror, twisting this way and that, grateful that she still retained the slim figure she had acquired whilst working in France on short rations.

She eventually chose a calf-length gown, one made of the finest wool, in a wonderful shade of emerald green. The high round neck was decorated with black jet beads, as were the cuffs to the long sleeves. It was simple, expensive and elegant, and intensified the colour of her green eyes. Apart from her engagement ring she wore only a pair of jet pendant earrings to match the trim of her dress. Her long brown hair, which in strong light had the sheen of the fruits of the horse chestnut tree, she twisted up on the top of her head and used her tortoiseshell combs to hold it. What she didn't realise as she met her reflection in the mirror was just how beautiful she looked.

This was not wasted on young Father Duggan when he arrived to escort her. For a moment she took his breath away. Until now he had mostly seen her working in the kitchen, busy baking, wearing an apron and looking after the workmen, or on his doorstep wearing an overcoat. Here was a different Flora Ferguson, elegant and sophisticated.

'You look lovely,' he said as he helped her into her overcoat. 'Fortunately, although it's a cold night out, it's dry. A nice brisk walk will keep us warm. Come along.'

Richard Goodwin's house was one of a terrace of imposing Edwardian buildings, which in earlier times had housed the wealthy. Even now it had an air of elegance. There was a shiny brass plate outside the surgery door with the doctor's name engraved on it, but it was to the main front door sheltered by an overhead porch that Patrick led Flora. She mounted the half-dozen steps and glanced down at the door leading into the basement, which had probably been used as the servants' entrance in the past.

Patrick pressed the bell, housed in a circular brass base, and waited.

Richard himself opened the door and ushered them inside the long carpeted passageway, with rooms leading off on either side. He took Flora's coat and, as he hung it on the hallstand, said, 'I am so pleased that you could come at such short notice. And how charming you look, Flora. I'm used to seeing you wearing an apron. Come along into the drawing room and meet my wife.'

It was a large room with settees facing each other in front of the wood-burning fire, a long low coffee table placed between the furniture. Other comfortable chairs were situated around the room, and in one corner on a plant stand was a potted aspidistra. Silver candlesticks were standing either end of the tall mantelpiece; in between these were several small photographs in oval frames, and miniature porcelain figurines. Standing beside the fire was Lydia Goodwin.

Flora's first thought was this young woman was deliberately posed to make an impression; her second was that Mrs Goodwin certainly was beautiful, with her slim figure, and her long blonde hair caught at the back of her head in a Spanish comb. But she noticed also the spoiled pout of the mouth and instantly knew why Patrick had his doubts about the doctor's wife.

'Darling,' said Richard, leading Flora towards her, 'this is Miss Ferguson, the lady I told you about.'

Lydia smiled politely and held out her hand. 'How do you do? My husband hasn't stopped talking about you, Miss Ferguson.'

'Flora, please. What a lovely home you have.'

Patrick approached to kiss Lydia on the cheek. 'Thank God for a good fire. It's enough to freeze a man to death out there, so it is.'

Richard poured them each a martini. 'I do hope you like this, Flora. It's my specialty.'

'And a darned sight better than communion wine, I can tell you!' joked Patrick as he put his glass to his lips and took a sip. 'This is truly nectar from the gods!' He glanced at Flora. 'Well, go on then; tell him your news.'

'Today I heard from the council. I now have permission to open as a children's home.'

'Oh, Flora, that's wonderful! You have no idea just how long Patrick and I have badgered the council for such a place.' He grinned broadly at her. 'And you are just the woman to make a success of it. Congratulations!' He turned to his wife. 'Isn't that really good news, darling?'

'Yes, I'm sure it is,' she answered. 'These two have never got this far,' she told Flora. 'So well done.'

'Come along, everyone,' Richard said. 'I'm starving. Let's go and eat.'

The dining room was comfortable but smaller than the drawing room. The mahogany dining table with matching chairs would have seated six people comfortably. Against the wall stood a matching sideboard, but there was no room for any more furniture. A maid carried in a tureen of soup and served it, then left.

Lydia didn't add much to the conversation during the evening. The men were telling Flora more of the history of Southampton and how important shipping was to the town and how, the previous year, Spanish flu had caused so many deaths.

'There were over two thousand deaths in London alone,' Richard said. 'And no doubt many where you were in France, Flora.'

'Yes,' she said. 'There were times when it felt like the last straw.'

'Let's not have such a cheerless conversation,' interrupted Lydia, as Richard was about to answer Flora. 'It's hardly a happy subject to have at the dinner table. You'll be talking about the latest medicines next, darling. Flora wants to get away from all that, I'm sure.'

'My wife is not interested in current affairs,' Richard explained, 'but ask her which are the best shops and she will be able to give you all the details. Isn't that right, Lydia, my dear?'

She laughed. 'I leave the workings of the world to those who are able to understand them. After all, whatever opinions I have make not a jot of difference!' She turned to Flora. 'But Richard is correct. If you would like me to recommend any shops to you for anything in particular, then I would be happy to do so.'

'Thank you, I'll remember,' said Flora.

'Might I make a suggestion?' Patrick asked, glancing in Flora's direction.

'Certainly.'

'You may find the children that come to you will be poorly dressed; it might be an idea to keep a few spare garments. There is a second-hand clothing store which I know keeps a stock of various items that are of a certain quality.'

Thinking of the children she saw on the streets and the worn and shabby clothes they wore, Flora knew exactly what he meant. 'Thank you, that is a really sensible idea.'

'You'll probably have to delouse them too,' said Richard. 'Some of their clothes would have to be burned anyway.'

Flora noticed the expression of distaste on Lydia's features. She certainly wouldn't be the type to soil *her* hands with waifs and strays, she thought.

The rest of the meal passed off pleasantly enough, and they all sat and chatted over coffee in the drawing room before Patrick suggested that he and Flora take their leave.

As they walked home together, Flora, her curiosity aroused, questioned her companion. 'I did enjoy the meal.

Thank you for taking me.' She remembered the pretty furnishings, and the quality of Lydia's dress, cut in the latest fashion. 'It would appear that Richard is well situated?' she pressed tentatively.

'Don't let appearances fool you, Flora. The house was his parents'. His father was a doctor too, and Richard inherited the house and surgery. He is an extraordinary man, a gifted doctor. He has private patients who pay for his services, and that enables him to do his work with the underprivileged. His wife is indulged by a wealthy father. He is the ruin of her, in my opinion!'

'I see. But they seem happy enough together.'

'Yes, thankfully.'

They continued in silence until they reached their destination. 'Would you like coffee or a nightcap, Patrick?'

'No, thank you. I need to be up in the morning. I'll let you know about the Thomson children, Mattie and Jake.'

As Richard and Lydia Goodwin were getting undressed for bed, Lydia said, 'Flora Ferguson has a certain beauty, don't you think?'

'Yes, although I confess I didn't realise it until this evening. Tonight she looked quite different from her usual working self.' As they climbed into bed he put his arms around his wife. 'But she's not nearly as beautiful as you are, my darling. Come here . . .'

Chapter Eleven

The following morning, Flora prepared to receive her applicants. Three were for the position of cook and the other, as her assistant. The first two who wanted to cook for the home were not impressive. One had dirty nails and a stained blouse beneath her coat, and the other hadn't had any training in the kitchen at all, but thought that cooking for a bunch of kids would be easy! Flora began to despair.

When she saw the third person, she felt more hopeful. 'Mrs Bennett, please come into the kitchen.'

The woman looked around appreciatively and gazed at the cooker with interest. She was of medium height, slightly plump, with square competent-looking hands, Flora noted. She invited her to take a seat by the table where she also sat, a pad and pen at the ready.

'Tell me something about yourself,' Flora invited.

'I'm forty year old, a widder woman,' Mrs Bennett answered, yet she smiled brightly. 'My old man went down with the *Titanic*.'

'Oh, I am sorry to hear that.'

The smile faded slightly. 'Well, miss, it was seven years ago now. I still miss the old codger, of course, but you gets used to it in time – being alone, I mean.'

'How have you managed?'

'I've been cooking! That's 'ow I kept myself going and paid the rent. First I 'ad a couple of lodgers, couldn't bear the empty house. I know Sid was away a lot, but I always knew 'e was comin' 'ome. When I knew 'e wasn't any more, well, I couldn't stand it, so I 'ad me lodgers.'

'Did you enjoy that?' asked Flora.

'It was all right to begin with; then they started asking me to do their washing and ironing. I didn't mind at first – it was extra money – but in the end it was like being married to two men, without the sex!'

Flora chuckled at the woman's reasoning. 'So what did you do?'

'I gave them their marchin' orders and went as cook in the local workmen's café. I'm still there now, three years on.'

'Then why do you want to change?'

Mrs Bennett's expression softened. 'Well, it's like this, miss. I love kids, didn't 'ave any meself. I always reckoned Sid was firing blanks, to be honest, but I am a good cook, love it in fact, and I certainly would like to do it for kids who ain't had much. So 'ere I am!'

There was something so fundamentally honest about the woman that Flora felt she would be a comfort to have around.

Whilst she was thinking this, Madge Bennett said, 'Now I don't expect you to take me on without trying my cooking, so I'll be 'appy to give you a taste of it. I could cook you an evening meal if you like. 'Ow about tomorrow?'

Flora thought it a splendid idea. She'd invite Patrick and get his opinion. 'That would be fine. I might have a guest, though.'

'All the better. What would you like? 'Ow about a

steak-and-kidney pie? I'm a dab 'and at pastry.'

'I'm sure that would be fine. I'll get the shopping in the morning.'

'Get some eggs as well, miss. I'll make you a nice *crème brûlée* for pudding.' At the look of surprise on Flora's face Madge grinned at her. 'I can do posh stuff as well, you'll see!'

Flora wasn't so successful when she interviewed the applicant for the post as her assistant. The woman was in her early sixties and told her that she was looking for employment in her retirement. She didn't smile and there was a hard set to her mouth as she said, 'I've been bringing up other people's children all my life. I can give you references from my families.'

'You must like children then,' Flora remarked, but somehow as she said it, she doubted that the woman did.

'Children are just like dogs,' she said. 'All they need is discipline and training.'

'But what about love and affection?' asked Flora softly, searching for some sign of compassion.

The very idea was dismissed out of hand. 'Humph! Go soft on them and discipline flies out of the window.' She stared haughtily at Flora. 'I'll make sure you have no trouble from any children in *my* care. If the remuneration is right, I can start as soon as you want me.'

Enraged by the callousness of her attitude, Flora rose from her chair and glared at her. 'Thank you very much, but I'm afraid you wouldn't do at all.'

The other woman looked startled. 'What do you mean?'

Flora didn't even pay her the respect of using her name. 'I want a person with a big heart, who can *care* about the children who will be here under my roof – someone who can give them comfort when they need it, a cuddle – not someone whose only thought is discipline. No, I'm afraid you are not the person for Harwood House.'

The woman got to her feet. 'Well,' she said, her face and neck crimson with rage, 'I have never been so insulted in all my life! I can see I'm wasting my time here.' She swept out of the kitchen, marched down the corridor and slammed the front door behind her as she left.

Making herself a cup of tea, Flora sighed. It was not going to be easy to find someone who was as dedicated as she was to helping these little ones, but she was prepared to wait. It was essential that she chose wisely.

Later she made her way to the presbytery to invite Patrick to dinner. She met him at the front door, just as he was about to leave.

'Flora! What can I do for you?'

She told him about Madge Bennett and what she had suggested. He looked very pleased. 'Of course I'll come. My mother had the fingers of an angel when she made pastry, so I'm a real good judge.' He paused, then said, 'Are you busy right now?'

'No, why?'

He took her by the arm and they walked down the path to the gate. 'I'm just off to see the mother of the two children I told you about. Come with me. You'll meet the family – not the husband, though; he'll be at work still.'

When they arrived at the abode in French Street, Patrick knocked on the door, then to Flora's surprise opened it and walked inside. 'It's always on the latch,' he explained, 'to allow the neighbours to pop in and out.'

Inside the tidy room was a shiny black-leaded stove with a small fire burning. On an old settee lay a young woman who smiled at the priest. 'Ah, Father Patrick, how good of you to come and see me.' She looked at Flora. 'Hello,' she said.

'A good afternoon to you, Hetty, my dear. This is Miss Ferguson, the lady I was telling you about. I thought you two should meet.'

Flora saw by the pallid skin and deep black circles beneath the eyes that Hetty Thomson was indeed a sick woman. She knew the woman wasn't long for this world; she had seen the same look on too many faces of the soldiers she'd nursed.

'Hello, Mrs Thomson.'

On the floor beside her was a little girl playing with a torn rag doll. She held up the doll for Flora's approval. Sitting on the floor beside the child, Flora picked up the doll and began to play with it, making it dance, waving its arms. The child chortled with delight.

At that moment a young boy entered from the scullery. He stopped when he saw Flora and she saw him cast an anxious glance at his mother. Then he recognised the priest and relaxed.

'Hello, Jake.' Patrick grinned across at him. 'And how are you doing, my boy?'

'Fine, Father, thanks.'

'This lady is Miss Ferguson.'

'The lady what's opening the home?' There was a nervous tremor in his voice.

'That's right, love,' said Hetty. 'How about making us all a cup of tea?'

Whilst Patrick and Hetty were chatting, Flora continued to keep Mattie entertained, but she watched the small lad set about his task with such competence, it was obvious he had done this many times. There was a quiet efficiency about him as he warmed the teapot before putting in the tea leaves that made her heart ache for him. And she wanted so desperately to take over and let him be the child that he was, but she knew not to do so.

When he was ready, Jake set out the cups and saucers on the table, the small sugar basin, and the teapot, which he covered with a cosy to keep it warm whilst he went to the larder for a jug of milk. When he returned, he removed the cosy, stirred the contents of the pot and, looking at Flora, said, 'I'll just let it brew for a minute, only Mum don't like weak tea.'

With a smile Flora said, 'Neither do I, Jake. There's nothing worse, if you ask me.' This seemed to please him and he poured a little milk in a cup and gave it to his sister, saying to Flora, 'Would you watch her while I see to the tea?'

'Of course,' she said.

Over the boy's head, Patrick looked at her and winked.

When he was ready, Jake invited the two of them to sit at the table.

'Well, isn't this fine!' declared Patrick. 'I don't get as good service in my own home. Indeed no.' The child swelled with pride at the compliment, but he didn't smile, and Flora wondered when was the last time this child had played and laughed. Then she glanced across at the mother. With such a responsibility, how could he?

'I've been telling my Jake that he and Mattie might come to stay with you when I have to go to hospital,' ventured Hetty, somewhat hesitantly, obviously uncertain as to what reaction this would bring from the son she loved.

Seeing the consternation in his expression Flora said, 'How would you like to bring Mattie to Harwood House for tea? Then you could take a look around. You would be my first guests, so that would make you kind of special.'

Looking at his mother for permission and seeing her nod her approval, he said, 'Thank you, we'd like that.'

Patrick looked at Flora. 'Today is Friday, how about Sunday afternoon?' He nudged Jake and in a conspiratorial voice said, 'If it's Sunday then I could come too. Miss Ferguson makes wonderful cakes, you know.'

'That would be fine,' she agreed.

'I'll tell you what, Jake, lad. Why don't I collect you and your sister, after I take Sunday school and we can all go together?'

The boy agreed. He looked shyly at Flora. 'Do you make chocolate cake?'

'If that's what you like, of course. I'll do one specially and you can bring what's left home with you to share with your family. How's that?'

His eyes shone and at last, he smiled. 'Yes, *please*, miss.'

As they left the small house and walked along the street together, Patrick turned to Flora and asked, 'Well, what did you think of them?'

'The mother is very sick, and I think you're right about her health, but the children . . . the boy breaks my heart. He is such a little soldier, coping the way he does. I wanted to hold him and tell him everything is going to be fine.' She looked at the priest and with a voice filled with sadness she added, 'But it won't be, will it? What is to happen to them later?'

'In my business I've learned to worry about one day at a time, Flora. My first consideration is to place them where I know they'll be cared for, their situation understood, and thankfully you have solved that problem.' He sighed. 'After that, we'll see.'

'At least if they come to me Jake won't have to carry

such a burden. He'll be the one taken care of, for a change.'

At the next corner they went their separate ways. Flora to do the food shopping for tomorrow's dinner and Patrick to return to the presbytery.

As he sat in his study he thought of this extraordinary woman who had entered his life such a short time ago. Flora Ferguson was so determined for one so young, yet owing to her wartime experiences, she was far more mature than other females of her age. The suffering she had seen, and had endured herself at the loss of her fiancé, only added to her compassion and understanding of others. He looked at the photograph of his family that adorned the wall of his study among the religious artefacts. Flora was also a disturbing young woman with her frank and open opinions. He smiled to himself when he remembered how she questioned the fairness of his mother putting him forward for a life in the priesthood. He of course, had questioned her decision to himself, but realised that he did have a genuine calling and was happy doing his job, but it would seem that Flora thought it a liberty taken unfairly. She was a strange girl.

He thought back to the previous evening when they had dined with the Goodwins, and the interesting conversation. Yes, this Scots lass was going to shake up a few people in the future, he mused. It was a pity the spoiled Lydia didn't possess a few of her attributes.

Whilst Father Duggan was mulling over his thoughts, the lady in question was preparing for an evening's entertainment, without the presence of her husband. Lydia sat at the dressing table in her bedroom, brushing her blonde silky tresses, twisting them up on the top of her head, then shaking them loose, splaying them over her bare shoulders.

She would wear her hair this way, she decided, but she would catch the sides in a pair of rather exquisite combs, studded with marcasite. Men liked long hair, and she was out to impress one particular gent this evening.

Earlier in the week, she had encountered a friend of hers in one of the stores, a daughter of one of the master builders in the town, a man with untold wealth. The family moved in the social circles she could easily have been a part of, if only Richard was interested in pursuing the social scene. His reticence to do so was a matter of great annoyance to her.

To her great delight she had been invited along to the family home to a private dinner. Richard too had been invited, but Lydia had made an excuse on his behalf, thinking he would probably decline the invitation, and she wanted a bit of excitement in her life. She said that she would be happy to accept, though. She lied to her husband, saying she was to dine with lady friends to celebrate a recent engagement.

It was the brother of the girl that had caught Lydia's eye. She hadn't met all the members of the family, and certainly not this young man, whom she imagined to be just a few years her senior. He was tall and handsome, with dark hair and smouldering eyes, which had seemed to pierce her innermost thoughts when they had been briefly introduced. But it was the way he had smiled that had excited her. It was a smile of invitation along with the hungry look in his eyes. Richard was the last person she wanted around when she was with young Douglas Slater.

Slipping into a deep plum-coloured silk dress, with slender straps that showed her bare shoulders, and a cut that flattered the gentle curve of her breasts and the roundness of her hips, she looked at her reflection in the mirror – and smiled with satisfaction.

★ ★ ★

Lydia was made welcome by the Slaters, who aired their disappointment at the absence of her husband, saying that they understood his presence at a medical meeting (her excuse) was more important.

She flirted playfully with the older men friends of the host and smiled sweetly at the wives, and deliberately ignored Douglas Slater, but was secretly delighted when she realised she'd been seated next to him at the dinner table.

Douglas Slater was no mean hand in the game of seduction and recognised, in Lydia, a willing participant. He also realised that during the pre-dinner drinks she had been playing her own game in ignoring him, yet he was aware that she knew exactly where he was every moment, as he moved among the guests. This amused him. Well, he was not above playing the game, but by his own rules.

He turned to her after they were seated and said affably, 'I am so sorry that Richard is unable to join us this evening. He is such an intelligent man; I always have such interesting conversations with him.'

There was such a guilty air about Lydia as she said, 'He was disappointed too,' that Douglas began to wonder if the good doctor even knew anything about the invitation.

'Never mind,' he said. 'I'll give him a call and take him out to lunch instead. I'll tell him it's to make up for this evening, and for him being so dedicated to his profession.'

He knew his instincts were correct as Lydia hastily said, 'I shouldn't bother at the moment, Douglas. Richard is so busy just now, but I'll tell him of the invitation and ask him to telephone you when he's free. Shall I?'

'If you say so. Now, how do you spend your time, Mrs Goodwin, when your husband is out and about saving lives?'

There was a certain arrogance in his voice that irritated her. She gazed at him as she daintily ate her grilled halibut and said, 'Now really, you men are never interested in such things. Tell me about yourself. I'm sure you don't go around saving lives, as you put it, so what *do* you do?'

'I am not so different from your husband as you might think. I try and make life more interesting and enjoyable for my female friends. That could be life-saving!'

She was sure he was baiting her. 'Are there very many of them?'

He gave a half-smile and said quietly, 'There is always room for one more.'

Further conversation was interrupted as other diners claimed their attention.

At the end of the evening, Lydia asked if someone could be sent for a taxi for her. Douglas walked over and said, 'That won't be necessary. I will drive Mrs Goodwin home.'

She gazed at him steadily and said, 'I wouldn't want to put you to any trouble.'

'Of course you would,' he said quietly, and helped her into her coat, his hands lingering on her shoulders.

They drove in silence down The Avenue, until he turned the car into a side road near the Common and parked.

'What do you think you're doing?' Lydia demanded. 'Why have you stopped here?'

He pulled her to him, slid his hand inside her coat and caressed her breast. 'So that I can do just what you have wanted me to since first you walked into my parents' house this evening.' His lips crushed hers, and he gripped her in his strong arms as she tried to struggle, until she began to relax and return his kisses with a growing hunger.

He released her bosom and pushed up the hem of her

dress, stroking the bare flesh above the tops of her stockings, then the inside of her thighs.

As he slipped his fingers between her legs, she moaned, 'My God! That is so good.'

As his fingers delved and explored, he said, 'My dear Mrs Goodwin, how long is it since you last had sex with your husband? You are so ripe for the picking!'

She suddenly pushed him away. 'How dare you?'

He laughed at her and said, 'Come now, my dear lady, let's not continue with the game. You want me and I want you.' He stroked the silken material of her dress covering her womanhood. 'Where and when shall we next meet? I promise you won't be disappointed.'

'You arrogant bastard!' She raised her hand to hit him, but he clutched hold of her wrist as he kissed her savagely at first, but then more gently, teasing her with his tongue, his hands caressing her until she ceased to fight him off; until she clung to him, returning his kisses with a fervour. And then, without pretence she looked at him and said, 'Soon, very soon, please.'

He chuckled softly. 'Darling, it will be my pleasure – and yours, I promise. I'll telephone you soon. What is the best time? I don't want your husband answering, do I?'

'About noon,' she said, 'when he is on his rounds.'

He started the car engine and drove her home, stopping a short way from the house at her request.

As she alighted from the vehicle, he leaned forward and said, 'I'll be in touch.' Then he drove away.

Chapter Twelve

Lydia let herself into the house, knowing that the maid would have been dismissed after serving Richard his evening meal. She closed the door quietly behind her and crept up the stairs to her bedroom. It was almost one o'clock in the morning and she didn't want to disturb her husband, but to her surprise the bed was empty. She switched on the light and saw the bedclothes were ruffled and assumed he had been called out to a sick patient, which suited her very well.

She slipped out of her clothes and left them on the floor, then standing in front of the long mirror, she studied her lithe body, running her hands over her pert breasts, down over the rise of her stomach, and then brushed the fair mat of curly hair, remembering how Douglas's fingers had invaded the intimate parts of her body. She writhed slowly as the memory stirred the unsatisfied passion within her.

She pulled her nightdress over her head and climbed into bed. She could hardly wait until she could lie with him and be made love to. It wasn't as if Richard was a poor lover – he was very accomplished – but there were times when he was too tired to make love to her; too tired to meet her needs. But Douglas Slater wasn't!

It wasn't that she didn't love Richard, but they led a

reasonably quiet life owing to his commitments to so many medical organisations, and she longed for a busy social life. She was bored! Doug Slater promised her the excitement she craved.

Richard returned home in the early hours of the morning, tired and drawn. He went into the kitchen and made himself a cup of tea. Tonight he had lost a patient, and despite his years of practice, such things still upset him. This one was particularly poignant, as he had delivered the young girl when he'd first opened his practice. She had become pregnant and rather than tell her parents of her predicament, had foolishly visited a backstreet abortionist. Later, alone in her room, she had started to haemorrhage, but it was some time before her mother found her in her blood-soaked bed. By then it had been too late.

He took his tea into his surgery and wrote up his notes. Taking off his jacket and trousers, he hung them over a chair and from a cupboard removed a couple of blankets and a pillow. He would sleep on the couch tonight, then he wouldn't disturb Lydia. As he settled down he hoped she had enjoyed her evening. He felt a stab of guilt, as he knew he had neglected her lately. He would take her out to dinner, just the two of them, and try to make her understand why he had been so busy of late. He sighed wearily, closed his eyes – and fell asleep immediately.

Lydia was still slumbering when Richard looked in their bedroom the following morning, so he sat at the breakfast table alone. After he had finished his surgery and enquired as to the whereabouts of his wife, the maid told him that Mrs Goodwin had gone shopping.

After making a few house calls, Richard drew up in front of Harwood House, anxious to catch up on the latest developments. As he stepped from his car, a young woman nearby tripped on a loose slab in the pavement and fell heavily, crying out with pain. He ran over to her.

'It's all right, I'm a doctor,' he said as he surveyed her ankle, which had already begun to swell. He took his overcoat off and placed it about the woman's shoulders. 'Just wait here,' he said. 'Don't move.'

Jessie Maxwell, her face twisted with pain snapped, 'How the hell can I?'

Richard rang the doorbell and waited, praying that Flora was at home. To his relief she answered the door at once. 'Richard!'

'Quickly, come and give me a hand,' he said without explanation.

Seeing the anxious look on his face, Flora hurried after him. They helped Jessie to her feet. 'Don't put any pressure on that foot,' Richard said sharply. He swept her up in his arms and, turning to Flora, said, 'Take my case out of the car, will you?'

Flora ushered them into the kitchen, where it was warm, and Richard carefully lowered Jessie into a chair. 'You have badly twisted your ankle,' he explained, having examined her injury. 'But you are very lucky. It's only a sprain; it isn't broken.'

'It bloody well feels like it!' she said with a grimace.

Between them, Flora and Richard held cold compresses over the sprained part to try to stop the swelling, and eventually Flora bandaged her foot.

'Where do you live?' she asked the young woman.

'Just down the road from here.'

'Do you have family at home?'

Jessie thought this was very amusing, despite her discomfort. Imagine being a whore and taking punters home to your family! She shook her head. 'No, I live alone.'

'Well,' said Flora in a matter-of-fact tone, 'you certainly can't manage alone with an ankle like that.' She looked at Richard. 'She'd better stay here until she's able to walk a bit.'

'Why would you do that, offer to look after me?' asked Jessie. 'You don't know me from Adam!'

With a smile, Flora said, 'I don't have to know you to be able to help you, do I?'

Jessie was completely nonplussed by such kindness and was at a loss for words.

Turning to Richard, Flora said, 'I have a room on the ground floor with a single bed in it for emergencies. She can stay there.' Of her new guest she asked, 'At least you can tell me your name.'

'Jessie. Jessie Maxwell.'

'Is there anyone we should contact, Jessie, to let them know where you are?'

There was a note of sadness in her voice as she replied quietly, 'No, miss. Me mother is dead and me dad . . . well, I haven't seen him in years.'

'Right,' said Flora. 'How about a cup of tea? It's a good thing for shock.'

Jessie felt shocked all right – not from her fall, but by the kindness of this stranger who seemed to have taken control.

Richard smiled at her. 'There you are then, Miss Maxwell. You will certainly be in safe hands with Miss Ferguson, and I'll pop by in the morning to see how you are faring.' He looked at Flora. 'I could really do with a cup of that tea you're making. I was up with a patient until the early hours.'

126

'I thought you looked a bit tired,' she said.

'P'raps you ought to come and stay here too, doctor,' grinned Jessie.

He laughed heartily and said, 'Believe me, that sounds almost too good an idea to turn down.'

Whilst Flora was making the tea, she told Richard about the two children who might be coming to her and the sad reason behind it. He listened intently.

'Unfortunately, consumption is still rife and it has no age barrier. Poor woman.'

'Poor children,' said Flora.

'Yes indeed. Look,' he said, lowering his voice, 'it's very good of you to take this young woman in, but she does have a point, you know. You don't know her or anything about her.'

'That's not strictly true,' Flora said, 'I have seen her around and I know where she works.'

'You do?'

'Yes,' said Flora quietly as she poured the tea. 'She's a prostitute.' She carried a cup of tea over to her patient. 'Here you are, Jessie. Drink this. When did you last eat?' she asked.

'Can't rightly remember. I had a sandwich last night, I think.'

'Very well, when the good doctor leaves I'll cook you something. How about bacon and eggs?'

Jessie's mouth watered at the thought. 'That would be lovely, but I don't want to put you to no trouble.'

Richard was astonished. Flora, knowing this woman was of the streets, felt no compunction at taking her in. He was filled with admiration and concern for her. 'Are you sure about this?' he asked.

'What harm can the poor girl do? I have nothing worth stealing and she can't run away, can she?'

He had never met anyone quite like Flora, with her modern outlook. It was probably due to the fact that she had seen so much harshness in the world when she was in France. But he admired her for her free spirit. Placing the cup and saucer down on the table, he said, 'Thanks. I'll look in tomorrow.'

Left with her guest, Flora fetched a leather pouffe and placed it beneath Jessie's injured foot. 'Best to keep this up as much as you can,' she said.

'Just who are you, Miss Ferguson, and what are you doing here?'

Getting the bacon and eggs from the larder, Flora said, 'I'm a nurse and I'm going to open this place as a children's home.'

Hearing the educated voice Jessie said, 'But posh kids don't need a home; they've already got one.'

'No, Jessie, not posh kids, as you say, but those poor little mites wandering the streets, begging, pinching food to keep from starving. This house is for them.'

'Bloody hell! Why would you, a lady, want to do that? It doesn't make any sense.'

'It makes a lot of sense to me. And I may be from a privileged upbringing, but why should that make any difference?'

''Cause folks like you don't do that sort of thing!'

Turning the bacon in the pan on the stove, Flora said quietly, 'I was a nurse during the war, stationed in France; I saw a lot of suffering there, Jessie: brave men badly injured, others dying, all for their country. We did what we could for them. Then when I came home and stayed in Southampton it didn't seem right to see little children starving on the streets and I felt that maybe I could help their suffering too.'

Jessie looked at her in awe. 'I've never met anyone quite like you, miss.'

'Call me Flora,' she said, highly amused by her unexpected patient. 'I'm not sure I've met anyone quite like you either,' she added with a broad grin, 'so we are both in the same boat.'

'No, Miss Flora, I doubt we would ever be in the *same* boat, but I am glad you was around today, and the good doctor. Blimey, when he lifted me up in his arms I thought me luck had changed!'

Flora started laughing. It was nice to have someone in the house. It seemed so empty, waiting for her first children, and she would walk aimlessly from room to room, wondering if there would ever be a day when the beds would be filled. She suddenly remembered that this evening Mrs Bennett was coming to cook a meal for her and Patrick. Well, now there would be one extra. She wondered what Patrick would make of Jessie!

Flora helped her to settle in the small sitting room, after giving her a change of clothes from her wardrobe, and helping her to wash herself, then taking Jessie's clothes, soiled by her fall, away to the outhouse to be seen to later.

Mrs Bennett hadn't been at all bothered by there being one extra for dinner.

When Patrick arrived, Flora showed him in, saying, 'I have someone staying with me.'

'Really?'

'Yes, a poor girl fell outside earlier today. It was fortunate that Richard happened to be here at the time. She's sprained her ankle. Come and meet her.'

As they entered the room, Patrick said, 'Hello, Jessie. Is it you that's been in the wars then?'

Flora saw the anxious expression in Jessie's eyes. 'Hello, Father. Well, I suppose the bloody game's up now.'

'Whatever do you mean?' Flora asked.

'Father Patrick knows me, and how I earn my living. You won't want me here when *you* know.'

'Why? Because you earn your living by prostitution?'

Jessie's mouth opened in surprise, but she couldn't utter a word.

'I already know that, my dear. I've seen you at the top of the Ditches, near the Horse and Groom, with your . . . punters. That's the word, isn't it?'

Jessie looked from one to the other, still speechless.

Patrick started to laugh. 'Oh my! Never in all my life did I think I would live to see the day when you, Jessie Maxwell, hadn't a word to say!'

She looked at Flora and asked, 'And you don't mind what I am?'

With a shrug Flora said, 'It's an honest living, isn't it? We all have to survive. Who am I to judge you?'

Looking at Patrick Jessie said, 'This woman is too bloody good to be true, ain't she, Father?'

He was grinning broadly. 'She's different, sure enough, I'll grant you that, my girl.'

At that moment, Mrs Bennett knocked on the door and announced that dinner was ready. Between them, Patrick and Flora helped Jessie into the dining room. As they sat down Patrick said, 'My, I'm looking forward to this.'

'Me too,' the two others said in unison, and laughed.

The pastry on the steak-and-kidney pie was so light it melted in their mouths and the *crème brûlée* was delicious. 'If you don't hire this woman, I will!' declared Patrick. 'My own mother couldn't make better. What do you think, Jessie?'

She leaned back and patted her stomach. 'I haven't had a meal like that in years,' she said. 'Not since me mother died, God rest her soul.'

Flora passed on the compliments to Madge Bennett and asked her if she would take up the position as cook, starting the following week. The woman was delighted to accept.

After the priest left, Jessie sat and told Flora about her parents and how she had to turn to prostitution to survive. 'If that sod of a father hadn't left, I could have been anything I wanted.'

'It must be a difficult way to earn a living.'

'I hate it when men run their hands over me, treating me like a piece of meat. I hate them – and I hate what I've become.' Tears filled her eyes and she blinked them angrily away. 'What I don't understand, miss, is why a lovely woman like you ain't married.'

'I was engaged to a pilot,' said Flora, 'but he was killed in the war. His name was Flynn O'Connor, and I was very much in love with him.'

'Life's a bugger, ain't it?'

'Yes, life's a bugger!' agreed Flora. 'Come on now, we'd better get you to bed or the doctor will be cross with me tomorrow when he comes to see you.'

Jessie allowed Flora to help her undress and thanked her for the use of one of her nightdresses. As Flora tucked the young woman in and made her comfortable, Jessie caught hold of her hand. 'Thanks for taking me in. You are the only person who has done something for me since me mum died.'

Touched by her sentiments, Flora said, 'I'm only too pleased I was here. You sleep well now. I'll see you in the morning.'

As she climbed into her own bed, she went over the day's events. She had seen Richard at work, Mrs Bennett had been hired and she had company for a few days. How strange life was. Poor Jessie, whose circumstances had dictated her way of life, Patrick's mother who had decided his, and the death of Flynn that had led her here – was it all a master plan plotted by some higher being, or was it purely circumstantial? And would she ever know the answer?

Chapter Thirteen

It was Sunday morning, and Flora was busy in the kitchen preparing for the Thomson children's visit. She beat the butter and sugar together, ready to make the chocolate cake she had promised young Jake. Flora had looked in at Jessie earlier and she was still fast asleep. The red hair was spread over the pillow, surrounding her head like a flaming halo. As she walked softly away, Flora thought how sad it was that the girl was earning her living in such a dangerous manner.

As she added the eggs, flour and cocoa powder, and folded in the ingredients, she worried that Jake wouldn't want to stay at Harwood House. Mattie was too young to understand what was going on, but Jake wasn't. She desperately wanted to look after him, give him the opportunity to be a six-year-old, without the responsibility he was having to endure at the moment. She wondered what the father was like. Would he be difficult? She hoped not.

Flora heard Jessie stirring, poured a cup of tea from the pot and took it into her. 'Did you sleep well?' she asked.

'Like a baby, Miss Flora. Ta.' She took the tea from her.

'I'll come back in ten minutes and help you to dress and wash, then you can come into the kitchen and we'll have breakfast.'

'I'm not that hungry after last night's meal,' said Jessie.

'Well, some good Scots porridge oats will soon put you back on your feet.' She added with a grin, 'It'll grow hairs on your chest!'

'That won't be good for business, will it!' joked Jessie as Flora left the room.

Later the two of them sat at the kitchen table, chatting. Flora told Jessie about the Thomson children and their problem.

'Poor little things. At least when my mother died I was sixteen, but they are just babies.' She shook her head and said sadly, 'Life seems so unfair, doesn't it? It makes you wonder if there really is a God!'

'Don't you let Father Duggan hear you say that!'

'Now there is a good-looking young man going to waste.'

'Jessie!'

She was not in the least bit contrite. 'It's true. He'd make a lovely husband for some lucky girl. I just think it's a shame the Catholic Church won't let their clergy marry.'

'Christ wasn't a married man.'

'Well, he didn't hang around long enough, did he, Miss Flora? He popped his clogs on the cross. A little more time spent with Mary Magdalene and who knows?'

'You are incorrigible,' chided Flora, but she had to laugh. 'You seem to know a lot about the Bible,' she said.

'Ah, well, I used to go to Sunday school. I loved all the stories, them parables. We used to get pretty pictures to stick in a book, I remember. I still have them somewhere.' Studying Flora she asked, 'After all the awful things you must have seen in the war, didn't you ever wonder about God?'

'No, I didn't. I found there was a lot of comfort in prayer.'

'Even when your feller was killed?'

'I'm not sure I thought about anything much. I just worked and worked, until all I wanted to do was sleep. When we've finished the breakfast,' said Flora, anxious to change the subject, 'you can help me prepare the vegetables for tonight's meal and after that I'll make some sandwiches and scones for tea. I'm not sure just how much the Thomson children have to eat when they're at home.'

They sat side by side, peeling the potatoes and carrots. Jessie said, 'If my mates could see me here now doing this, they wouldn't believe it.'

'What are they like, the other girls?' asked Flora out of curiosity.

Shrugging, Jessie said, 'All right, most of them. My mate Daisy's on to a good thing, though, lucky cow.'

'Oh, why's that?'

'She's an old man's darling. She's the mistress of Alderman Chivers.'

'George Chivers? From the council?' asked a surprised Flora.

'Yes, that's him. He spoils Daisy something rotten. He's always buying her things, giving her money.'

'But how on earth does he manage to keep that quiet? He's a married man.'

'Well, you see, Miss Flora, he's set her up in a nice little house in St Mary's.' Jessie chortled softly. 'But what he don't know is that she takes other men there too.'

'Other punters, you mean?'

'Listen to you talking about punters! A lady like you! What a scream. Yes, she makes a bomb out of him, but she isn't beyond earning a bit on the side, like.'

Thinking about the pompous man who had called on her, Flora remarked, 'He wouldn't like it if he found out.'

'Bloody right he wouldn't, but she's careful to do it when he's working or out on a do at night with his missus.'

Flora wondered if Patrick knew about George Chivers' philandering, and if he did, whether he'd used this knowledge to put pressure on the man when it came to his decision about Harwood House. She had an inkling that this did have something to do with the council's support! Wheels within wheels! as her father would say.

At four o'clock that afternoon, Patrick duly arrived with the Thomson children. Mattie came running in, quite unconcerned when Flora opened the door, but Jake kept close to the priest as they walked into the kitchen. Flora watched the boy look about him, then she saw his eyes light up as he espied the chocolate cake in the middle of the table.

He looked at Flora and said, 'You made one then.'

'Of course. Didn't I promise that I would?'

'Yes,' he said slowly, 'but people don't always keep their promises.'

Flora wondered just who had let this small boy down in the past. She also realised he would need eventually to be told the truth about his mother's illness, and this made her sad for him.

Everyone sat around the kitchen table on the bench seats, borrowed from the dining room. The kitchen was warm and cosy, and Flora felt that Jake would relax here.

Jessie chatted away to both children, made a fuss of little Mattie and spoke to Jake as an equal, and Flora thought what a natural she was with them. Patrick helped to pour the tea and they all tucked into the cress and egg sandwiches, the scones and, at last, the chocolate cake.

Jake took a bite, chewed on it and said to Flora, 'This is

lovely. My mum would like it, I know.'

'Well, Jake, don't you worry. There'll be plenty left for you to take home and you can give her some then.'

With that, he seemed content. Flora left Jessie entertaining the children and cleared the table with Patrick's help.

'That was a fine tea,' he said, 'and an excellent idea on your part to bring them here today. It will make their transition a bit easier for the boy.'

'How's Hetty?' Flora asked.

With a shake of his head, Patrick lowered his voice. 'Not well at all. The doctor wants to put her in hospital, but she's waiting until Jake tells her if he wants to come here and stay. If he isn't happy . . . then I don't know. She needs hospital attention desperately, Flora.'

'I see.' She walked over to the table and said to Jake, 'Why don't you bring Mattie upstairs and I could show you the room you would share if you decide you would like to stay for a while?'

Taking his sister by the hand he ascended the stairs behind Flora. She showed the children her bedroom, and then, opening the door next to it, she said, 'This would be where you would both sleep.'

The room was painted in a cheery yellow with green curtains; the twin beds were covered in green floral eiderdowns and on each pillow sat a teddy bear. Mattie ran over, picked one up and cuddled it, but Jake looked uncertain.

Flora sat on the other bed, picked up the bear and held it. 'When I was a small child and I felt unhappy about something, I used to go to my room, curl up on the bed and cuddle my bear,' she said softly. 'Somehow, afterwards, I used to feel so much better.' She stroked the short fur on the bear's body. 'I suppose because he felt so soft and cosy. Why don't you and Mattie play up here for a while? Come down when you are ready.' She handed him the toy and walked down the stairs.

Patrick looked at her anxiously. 'Well?'

She shrugged. 'We'll have to wait and see.'

Some little time later, Jake came into the kitchen with his sister, who was still clutching the bear.

Patrick said, 'It's time to go, Jake.'

'Thanks for the tea, miss.'

Flora handed him a cake box and said, 'Here. Don't forget the chocolate cake for your mother, and I'm sure your father would enjoy some too when he gets home.'

Mattie went to walk out of the kitchen clutching the bear, but Jake gently removed it from her hold saying, 'No, that's for when we come and stay here.'

Flora looked over the boy's head at Patrick and smiled.

The children moved in the following afternoon, escorted by Patrick, who carried a small suitcase containing their things.

'Hello,' said Flora. 'I am so pleased you could come. Have you had anything to eat?'

'I had a sandwich,' Mattie informed her. 'But I'm hungry.' She beamed at Jessie, who was seated in a chair by the fireside.

'Let's get your things put away upstairs and then I'll boil a couple of eggs for you, with some toast. How will that do?'

'Lovely! Can I go and get my teddy?' Mattie asked.

'Yes, come along the two of you.'

There was very little in the case: a thin pair of pyjamas each, clean vests and underpants, and two clean jumpers that looked as if they'd been shrunk in the wash. As Flora looked at the poor selection, she realised the wisdom of

Patrick's advice about purchasing clothes from the second-hand shop. She had popped in quickly the following day and bought some things in readiness, just in case the children did come to stay, but thought it prudent to let them wear their own clothes for a couple of days until they settled.

Patrick stayed to have a cup of tea whilst the children ate their boiled eggs. 'Now you're not to worry about your mother, Jake,' he said. 'She is in good hands in the hospital. They'll take good care of her.'

'Of course they will,' said Jessie. 'Those nurses are very good at their job.'

He just nodded slowly.

'I'll say a special prayer for her,' added the young priest. He rose from his chair. 'I must be off now.'

Flora saw the look of panic in Jake's eyes and said, 'How about I read you both a story? I've some books in the bookcase next door. There's a nice fire there and we can all curl up together.'

'Can I come too?' Jessie asked. 'I love a good story.'

'You go ahead,' said Patrick. 'I'll let myself out.'

And so they all settled in the other room, Jessie on the settee, foot on a stool, and Mattie on her knee, Jake sat beside her and opposite, Flora, who proceeded to tell them the story of 'Rumpelstiltskin'.

It was some time later that Flora took the children upstairs to wash. 'I'll take Mattie into the bathroom whilst you get undressed,' she told Jake, thinking to give him some privacy. 'Then you can have a wash whilst I help your sister to get undressed.'

As she eventually tucked them both in, she said, 'I'll leave the hall light on and your door open a little. Then if you wake in the night, you'll know where you are. I'm in the next room and I'll keep my door open too in case you want me. And you know where the toilet is.' She looked at Jake. 'All right?'

'Yes, miss. Thanks.'

'Sleep well then. I'll call you in the morning when I'm ready to get the breakfast, but if you wake up before then and hear me downstairs, come down to the kitchen.'

'Are they settled?' asked Jessie when Flora returned.

'I suppose so. Little Mattie's eyes were closing, but I don't know about Jake. With everything being strange he may take some time to settle.' But when she went up to check on them a little later, Jake was fast asleep, clutching his teddy.

'You know,' said Jessie as the two of them sat drinking a cup of cocoa before going to bed, 'you're a great softy. You really care about that kid, don't you?'

'Of course. How could anyone not do so?'

Jessie pulled a face. 'Listen to me, Miss Flora; you've got a lot to learn about people. Motherly love isn't always in abundance around here, I can tell you.'

'You'd be a good mother, Jessie.'

She stared into the dying flames of the fire, then said quietly, 'Fat chance I've got, in my line of business, meeting a man and settling down.' She turned to look at Flora with a deeply sad expression. 'It would be nice, though.' She drained the contents of her cup. 'Best be off to bed. You know, when the doctor sends me home I'm really going to miss you.'

'I'll miss you too. But you will come and see me often, I hope; have a cup of tea and a chat. See the children if they are still with me.'

'You don't want the likes of me coming here.'

'Why ever not?'

'You really mean that, don't you?'

'Of course. I'm surprised you have to ask.'

'You are a very unusual woman, you know that, don't you?' said Jessie, grinning broadly. 'And I'm really glad I came a cropper outside, otherwise I would never have met you.'

'Maybe it was fate that brought you here.' Flora stopped abruptly. Flynn had believed in fate and she used to question it, but maybe there was something in it after all. But if it was true, for what purpose had Jessie been brought into her life?

Chapter Fourteen

Flora gave the children their breakfast the next morning and left Jessie to take care of Mattie whilst she walked Jake to school, despite the fact that he told her he could manage on his own.

'I just want to make sure you know the way,' she said.

'You don't have to worry about me, Miss Flora, 'cause I have to do the shopping for Mum, so I know all these roads and shops.'

At that hour of the morning, the dock area was buzzing. Stevedores were already inside, working, and trains chuntered in through the gates, carrying coke and coal, to be loaded on to cargo ships. Seamen were scurrying about, some leaving a ship that had just berthed and others getting ready to join theirs. Street traders were setting up the odd stalls and the paperboys were yelling the latest headlines. The shrill cry of the train whistles rent the air. It was a cacophony of sound, the aria of the busy port.

Flora and Jake threaded their way through all this. 'You'll be all right to come home on your own then?' she asked as they arrived at the school gates.

'Yes, honest.'

'All right. But watch the traffic around the dock gates. I'll see you later, and don't worry about Mattie, she'll be fine. Come straight home, won't you?'

Jake nodded and ran into the playground.

When Flora returned to Harwood House it was to find Richard in the kitchen on his knees looking at Jessie's ankle. Jessie looked at her and winked.

'There, Miss Flora, would you believe it, I've got a handsome man at me feet!'

'I'm surprised to see you here at this hour,' said Flora. 'Don't you have a morning surgery?'

'Not until later. I have been making a few calls and Jessie is the last one. I could enjoy a cup of tea if there is one going,' he said, smiling.

As Flora poured the water from the simmering kettle into a teapot, he added, 'Your patient is well enough to go home now. The swelling has gone down, but she needs to take it easy, not do too much too soon and rest the ankle now and then. Another week and she should be as good as new.'

Jessie looked disappointed.

'That ought to please you,' said Flora.

With a grimace Jessie said, 'I know, but I have so enjoyed being looked after.'

'Of course, you could always come here and work for me.' Flora looked at Jessie. 'You are so good with the children, you would be a great help.'

Jessie's face was red with embarrassment. 'I couldn't possibly do that, Miss Flora. My place ain't here, oh no. That wouldn't do at all.'

'But why ever not?'

'I know where I belong, Miss Flora, and it ain't here working in a decent place. Let's leave it at that!' To cover her confusion she turned to the doctor and said, 'She's a bloody good nurse, you know, that Miss Flora.'

'I am sure she is, Jessie. This little one looks content enough,' he said, nodding in the direction of a deep armchair, where Mattie was sitting playing with her teddy bear. 'How's the boy?'

'All right, I think,' Flora assured him. 'He's at school now and insists he's capable of going by himself.'

'Most of the children round here have to be, I'm afraid. But at least they grow up to be independent.'

'By the way,' said Flora, 'the men came and installed a phone line a couple of days ago.' She scribbled the number on a piece of paper. 'Here,' she said, and handed it to him. 'How's your wife?'

'Lydia's fine, thank you. I'm planning to take her out to dinner this evening as a surprise. I have been so busy lately, she feels a bit neglected.'

Remembering the pouting, spiteful mouth of the young Mrs Goodwin, Flora thought she would make great demands on a husband, which was the last thing a doctor needed, certainly one as dedicated as Richard was supposed to be.

In fact, Lydia was feeling far from neglected as that morning the maid had brought up her breakfast tray, and an envelope that had arrived that morning in the mail. Ripping it open, she took out a card and read, 'Tonight at seven thirty. Holy Rood Church.' It was unsigned, but she knew it came from Douglas Slater. Who else could it be?

She lay in bed and stretched like a cat anticipating the pleasures before her. Where would they go? Surely they just wouldn't park the car somewhere, but she knew that whatever he planned, she would go along with it, just to feel his mouth on hers, his hands on her body. She would wear her prettiest underwear to entice him. Then she laughed. He wouldn't need encouragement at all, but even so . . .

When Richard came home late that afternoon, Lydia had just stepped from the bath and was standing in their bedroom with only a bath towel around her. He walked towards her and took her into his arms.

'Mm,' he said, nuzzling her neck, 'it seems that I have come home at just the right time.' He went to remove the towel, but she slipped from his grasp.

'Not now, darling,' she said, 'I am going out and need to get ready.'

'But I've booked us a table for dinner!'

She looked scathingly at him. 'Well, don't you think you should have asked me first?'

'It was to be a surprise! I've neglected you lately through no fault of mine, and I wanted to make up for it.' He held out his hand. 'Let me take you to bed.'

She turned on him, eyes blazing. 'How very like a man. When I want you to make love to me, you are too tired and turn away, but when you feel like sex, then I should be ready and willing. Well, my dear Richard, life isn't like that. This time *I* don't want to.'

'I see,' he said slowly. 'And where are you going, and with whom?'

'Oh, for God's sake! Don't come the heavy husband; it doesn't suit you at all. I'm going out with some lady friends. Their husbands are busy too, so we thought we would treat ourselves.'

'Lydia, be reasonable. You know I have a lot of commitments because of my profession.'

She glared at him. 'Strange, isn't it? I thought you were committed to me as your wife.'

'Now you're just being difficult.'

'No. You are the one who is. You forget, Richard, I am young, full of life. I don't want to rust away and gather dust, as you seem to be content to do. I want to live!'

Richard's anger was growing. 'You knew what life married to a doctor would be like. I made that very clear to you when I asked you to marry me.'

'Not clear enough, obviously. Now will you please leave me alone to get ready?'

'With pleasure!' He went out and slammed the bedroom door.

Richard sat fuming in his empty surgery. Was there no pleasing this woman? He did admit to being too busy, but the welfare of the poor was a particular concern of his. He was on several committees that dealt with such things. He would do anything he could to ease the suffering of people who were without the means to pay for medical treatment. And if it were absolutely necessary, and somebody was ill, this would come before his spoiled and overindulged wife. He dialled the number of the restaurant and cancelled the table, then stomped out of the house and climbed into his car.

The children were safely tucked up in bed and asleep, and Flora was sitting with Jessie, reading the daily papers, when there was a knock on the door. To Flora's surprise she found Richard on the doorstep.

'Forgive the intrusion,' he said, 'but Lydia had made other arrangements for this evening and I didn't relish being alone, so I thought I'd come round to see you and Jessie.'

'Come in,' Flora said. 'We were just reading the papers before getting some supper. You are more than welcome to join us.' They entered the small sitting room and Richard was greeted warmly by Jessie.

'Please forgive me. I should have called first, but it seems the only way I can run my life at the moment is to do things on the spur of the moment.'

'If you wanted a different way of life, you should have chosen a different profession,' Flora remarked with a smile.

He looked appalled at the suggestion. 'I couldn't envisage doing anything else but medicine.'

'Except riding point-to-point,' she said, remembering an earlier conversation.

He laughed, and Flora once again saw the change it made in him. His cares seemed to fade when he laughed, the years drop away, and he looked young and carefree.

'You remembered!' With a broad grin he said, 'You didn't think I was the type, I recall, and I wondered exactly how you saw me, Flora.'

She studied him thoroughly and eventually said, 'To be honest, I'm not quite sure.'

He looked amused. 'That's not like you at all.'

'How can you say that? You don't even know me.'

'You are not so hard to read.' He gave her a penetrating look. 'I would say you are a passionate creature. You believe strongly about everything you do.' He cocked his head on one side as he looked at her. 'I would say also that you have a very stubborn streak in you and once you have made up your mind about something, you are intractable.'

She chuckled softly. 'You've been talking to my father!' She rose from her seat. 'We are only having poached eggs on toast – will that be all right for you, Richard?'

'Perfectly splendid, and thank you.'

She left Richard talking to Jessie and went into the kitchen to prepare the supper. When it was ready she called them in. 'We always eat here in the evening,' she explained. 'It's warmer and we like it.'

As he sat at the table, Richard said, 'And so do I. They say the kitchen is the heart of a house.'

'You don't see very much of yours,' Flora remarked.

He grinned at her. 'That's true now, but when I was a boy I used to plague my mother and the cook we had. You should have tasted my pastry, or rather the bits left by the cook, which I rolled out again and again until they were like rock!'

Jessie started to laugh. 'I can't imagine you doing that at all!'

'I assure you, Jessie, it didn't last. After that it was listening to everyone's heartbeat with my father's stethoscope.'

They ate and chatted, and then Jessie excused herself and went to bed. Flora and Richard took their cups of coffee into the sitting room and settled down.

'Tell me about your time in France,' he said. 'Unless you would rather not talk about it?'

But Flora found it easy to talk to Richard about her experiences and his understanding about the difficulties of the medical staff was comforting to her.

'I can't imagine how you all coped,' he said. 'I feel quite guilty, staying at home, but I was persuaded by the powers that be to stay here and help them organise hospital beds for the wounded here, and in the surrounding areas, and to assist in getting the necessary medical supplies to send to France.'

'And quite right too.'

'And how about your fiancé? Are you coping with the loss?'

She suddenly looked sombre. 'Ah, Flynn. He was a

wonderful man. I knew the longer he flew the more chance he had of being shot down . . . yet somehow he was so full of life I began to believe he was invincible.' She shook her head sadly. 'But he wasn't. I still find it hard to accept that he is no longer with us and keep expecting him to suddenly appear out of the blue, and when the reality hits me, it is sometimes more than I can bear, even now.'

'One eventually learns to live with grief. I remember from when my parents died. But it takes time. But you, Flora, had no need to put yourself through all this, going to war, to the Western Front. Why did you?'

'Because I felt so damned useless! I wanted to make some kind of contribution, and I have never regretted it for a moment!' She saw him smile and asked, 'What's so funny?'

'I told you you were passionate about things. You should have seen the fire in your eyes just then . . . It was quite wonderful,' he said. 'That's how I feel about medicine.'

The evening passed quickly and she discovered that the usually serious doctor had a very sharp sense of humour. They shared similar tastes, and neither could suffer fools easily.

'Incompetence really makes me angry,' Richard declared. 'And bureaucracy. The council, for instance: full of over-stuffed dignitaries who have no real conception of the town's needs.'

'That sounds like fighting talk,' Flora remarked.

'Sorry, I do get carried away sometimes, but the council and I have crossed swords on many occasions.'

'Have you ever come out a winner?'

He gave a boyish grin. 'As a matter of fact, I have!'

'Good for you!'

He gazed at the beautiful girl before him and found

himself wishing that Lydia were more like her: supporting him, showing an interest in his work – how much easier life would be. But lately he seemed to be endlessly fighting his wife as well as the council.

Eventually Richard took his leave. 'Thank you so much for a delightful evening, Flora. You take care now.' And with a cheery wave of his hand, he left.

As she made her way to bed, Flora saw that Jessie's light was still on. She tapped on the door and opened it. 'Are you all right?'

'Yes, I'm fine. I thought I'd leave the two of you alone. Pity he's a married man, Miss Flora. You make a nice couple.'

'Jessie! The very idea! You go to sleep and no more of this nonsense.'

As she undressed, Flora thought of her words. Richard was indeed a nice man, but even if he was single, how could she even think of another man after her darling Flynn, who still lived in her heart. But hard as she tried, from her one meeting with Lydia Flora couldn't see her being in the least bit interested in her husband's work or sharing his deep concern for his patients, and she thought what a great pity it was, if this was so.

The last thing that Lydia Goodwin was thinking about at that moment was her husband – or his work.

Chapter Fifteen

Lydia Goodwin was lying naked on a bed, with Douglas Slater raining kisses on every part of her body, to her great delight.

'We're two of a kind, you know,' he murmured as he traced a finger between her breasts.

'We are?' she whispered, her voice soft and deep with desire. 'How?'

'We know what we want and go after it, and we don't give a toss about anyone else.'

She ran her fingers through his hair and asked, 'Is that wrong?'

'My dear girl, it's bloody marvellous. I have no conscience about bedding you, even though you're married, and you couldn't care less about your husband. What a wonderful combination.' He buried his face in the soft mat of her womanhood, and she squirmed with pleasure.

Douglas had driven to this small but exclusive hotel on the outskirts of Southampton. They had wined and dined on a grand scale and, slightly drunk from the wine and champagne, made their way to the room he had booked. There they had quickly removed their clothing, anxious to taste the forbidden fruits of desire.

As Douglas spread her legs and explored the most

intimate parts of her, Lydia moaned softly. 'Oh, my God. Douglas, Douglas, don't stop.'

'I wouldn't dream of it, darling,' he murmured as he moved over her and thrust himself inside her. She raised her hips and squirmed beneath him, urging him on, teasing him with her own intimate caresses until they both reached the zenith of their passion and lay side by side, hot and breathless, devoid of energy.

Lydia wiped the beads of perspiration from her brow with the back of her hand and let out a deep sigh of contentment. She rolled over on her side and caressed the broad chest of her lover. 'You certainly know how to please a woman,' she said softly. 'That was wonderful.'

He leaned forward and kissed her. 'Of course it was,' he said. Then with a slow smile he added. 'Life-saving, wouldn't you agree?'

She ran her finger over his full sensuous mouth and said, 'Absolutely.'

Douglas swung his legs over the side of the bed, and filled their glasses with more champagne, which they had taken with them from the dining room. 'Here, darling Lydia, I think you have earned this.'

'Have I, really?'

'Oh, yes. You are a wanton woman, in bed and out. I think we'll suit each other very well.'

It was very late when they eventually left the hotel after once again enjoying each other, but Lydia didn't care. Her body was still living the sensations of the sex she had enjoyed and she wanted to cling to this secret pleasure for as long as possible.

Douglas parked his small Morris Oxford two-seater a hundred yards down the road from the surgery. He took

Lydia into his arms and kissed her hungrily. 'I'll be in touch again soon,' he said. He watched until she was safely inside the house, before driving away.

Richard was fast asleep when Lydia opened their bedroom door, and she crept around with great stealth. The last thing she wanted was to disturb him. Slipping beneath the sheets, she listened to the soft breathing of her husband and then she lay on her back, reliving every sexual moment of her lascivious adventure.

At Harwood House the following morning, Jessie was preparing to take her leave. Mrs Bennett, who had taken up her position as cook that day, had presented Flora and Jessie with a full breakfast and made some porridge and toast for the children.

'I'll wash and return your clothes to you, Miss Flora,' Jessie said quietly.

Flora put her arm round her shoulders and hugged her. 'Don't be silly. You keep them. They look better on you than me anyway.'

'You know that's not true,' argued her guest, 'but anyway, thanks. What are you going to do today?'

'I have a woman to interview for the post of my assistant, but I don't hold out any great hope after the last lot. Still, fingers crossed. Are you sure you won't change your mind and work here?'

Jessie would love to have accepted but she felt totally unworthy of such a position. After working on the streets, in her mind it wasn't fitting to leave the paid-for sexual caresses of men for the innocent cuddles of a child. She felt soiled and unclean.

'No, honest, thanks, but I am flattered that you asked.'

Flora smiled across at Jessie, of whom she had grown

very fond in the few days she had known her. 'You take care now and don't forget, the children and I want to see you soon.'

With a smile of delight Jessie said, 'You try and keep me away.' She felt able to call on the children, whom she'd grown fond of, but thought that was as far as things should go.

Flora placed a hand on her arm. 'Be careful, won't you?'

Jessie felt a lump rise in her throat, knowing that this woman was really concerned about her. 'I will, I promise.' With that she threw her arms around Flora's neck and hugged her. 'Thanks for everything.' She turned quickly and walked out of the kitchen door, closing it behind her.

'I'll miss her,' Flora said to the cook. 'Now at the moment there are only the two children and me to cater for, Madge, but I hope before too much longer, there'll be more.'

Almost before she had finished speaking the telephone rang. It was the police.

'Miss Ferguson, early this morning we discovered four children sleeping rough near the Floating Bridge. At the moment we don't know who they are or where they came from, but they are very tired, very dirty and very frightened. Can you take them?'

'Of course. What ages are they?'

'They range from about four to seven.'

Flora felt a thrill of excitement rush through her veins. 'Of course, bring them along,' she said. She went tearing back into the kitchen to pass on the news to Madge.

'What a pity your young friend 'as gone. You could do with 'er 'elp now,' said Madge. 'Never mind, I'll give you an 'and.'

Twenty minutes later, everything seemed to be happening

at once. A police sergeant arrived with the children, three of whom were crying loudly, Patrick walked into the kitchen, and a young woman called Rose came for an interview.

Flora hustled the children, two boys and two girls, into the kitchen, thinking that some food would stem their tears, and settled them down at the table.

Turning to Rose, she said, 'I'm sorry but, as you see, I just can't deal with you now. We'll have to make another appointment.'

Rose Turnbull, twenty-seven, tall and muscular, removed her coat and said, 'It seems to me, Miss Ferguson, that what you need right now is another pair of hands, and I'm not going anywhere else in a hurry.'

She was a godsend. There was a no-nonsense approach about her, yet it was tinged with kindness. She and Flora fed the little ones with Patrick giving a helping hand, then the two women took the children up to the bathroom where they stripped them of their clothing, which was filthy and flea-ridden, and burned it. They scrubbed and washed the children's hair with a special liniment to get rid of the head lice, and bathed them before putting on some decent clothes, which were in Flora's store from the second-hand shop. She thanked God that she had had the forethought to spread the sizes as she sorted through them. Then they settled the children in the small sitting room with Mattie and a basket of toys and picture books whilst they sat in the kitchen and had a cup of tea and a minute to recover.

'Well, Rose, what can I say? I would never have managed without you.'

She grinned broadly at Flora and said, 'You could say I've got the job!'

Flora burst into peals of laughter. 'Oh, my. I'm sorry, I should have said, but in all the excitement I forgot. Indeed you have got the job and I'm happy to have you. Do you want to live in or out?'

'I've come up from Lymington so I need a place to stay.'

'Right then, there is a small bedroom upstairs near the dormitory. Let's have our tea and I'll show you around and you can tell me all about yourself.'

Patrick came and sat next to them, having been in the other room to talk to the children. 'It seems that they all live in Netley,' he said.

'Are they related?' asked Flora.

He shrugged. 'I don't know, that's all they would tell me, but there has to be some sort of story behind this. By the look of them when they arrived here, they have been on their own for a while, wouldn't you say?'

'Well, certainly more than a couple of days, I would have thought,' Flora said. 'Never mind, when they're ready they'll tell us. Meantime, at least they are out of danger. I would like Richard to take a look at them. I'll call his surgery later.'

'Good idea,' said the priest. 'I must be off, but, Flora, I'm so pleased to see your home being used so soon for the purpose for which it was intended.'

'How is Hetty?' she asked.

'Not well. Unfortunately the children won't be allowed to see her. She's in the isolation hospital. But the father asked if he could call and see his children.'

'Of course he can, at any time, tell him.'

'I will. Now I really must go.'

Flora went into the sitting room with Rose and they sat and played with the children, trying to find out some further information without pressuring them, but nothing more was forthcoming.

Rose remarked, 'It seems they are frightened of something, but what, I don't know.'

'I'm going to ask the doctor to take a look, just to make sure,' said Flora, and went into the hall to call Richard.

He came before his evening surgery. When Flora explained the situation he went into the sitting room and started talking to the children. He gained their confidence by letting them listen to each other's heartbeat through his stethoscope before using it on them himself and examining them.

After, as he stood in the kitchen, he said, 'They seem fine. Their temperatures were up a little but not too much, but if they've been sleeping outside that is to be expected. I would say they are malnourished, but there are no outward signs of bruising, which is a relief, and of course they are bound to be nervous after what they have been through.' His eyes narrowed and his brow furrowed. 'What I want to know is why were they alone, so far from home?'

'Wouldn't we all!' exclaimed Flora. 'Oh, by the way, this is my new assistant, Rose. She arrived in the middle of all the mayhem today, just in the nick of time.'

He smiled across at the young woman. 'How do you do, Rose?'

'Hello, Doctor. I'm fine thanks.' She turned to Flora. 'I'll just go back to the children.'

'She looks very capable,' remarked Richard.

'Indeed she is. She has a nice way with children, firm but kind. She'll fit in here very well.'

'And Jessie? Has she gone home?'

'Yes, this morning. I shall really miss her.'

He smiled benignly at Flora. 'Have you always picked up

waifs and strays, or is this a new habit?'

'Well, let's say that before it was usually animal life, now I've moved on to humans.' She raised an eyebrow and asked, 'Do you want saving, Richard?'

She expected him to laugh at her joke, but he picked up his bag and said softly, 'If ever I do, I will come here immediately.' And he walked out of the room, leaving Flora absolutely speechless.

The children settled, in a quiet sort of way. They played with Mattie, building bricks, drawing pictures with wax crayons, and eventually helped Cook to make small cakes, which they really enjoyed. She mixed up different coloured icing, put this into paper pipes and let them squeeze the contents over the cakes. It was certainly haphazard, but great fun.

Sitting watching Madge Bennett, Flora said, 'It's a great shame you didn't have children of your own. You would have been a terrific mother.'

The cook beamed at her. 'Never mind, Miss Flora. I'll borrow these and any others that come to stay.'

When Jake returned from school, he was very surprised to see the new faces. Flora took him to one side and explained their circumstances. 'So you see, Jake, they probably feel a bit strange.'

He nodded. 'Yes they probably do, but I expect they'll be all right after a day or two.'

'Will you try and make them feel at home?'

'Of course I will. We can play cards. I'll show them how to play snap, or five stones.'

As Flora watched him dealing the cards, she realised how good he was at looking after others, but then, he'd already had a good training, looking after his mother.

★ ★ ★

Jessie felt absolutely lost, alone in her bedsitter after the company and comfort of Flora's house. At six o'clock she couldn't stand the solitude any longer and, putting on her coat, she made for the Horse and Groom. Limping just slightly as her ankle was still a bit sore, she walked up the Ditches, looking in the shop windows as she tried to kill time.

She sat in the bar over half a pint of bitter and waited for the other prostitutes to gather for their nightly natter, before they started work.

'Hey, Jessie, love. Where the hell have you been?' asked one. 'We ain't seen hide nor hair of you for bloody days.'

'I fell over, didn't I? Tripped over a paving stone and twisted me ankle. I was laid up, couldn't walk.'

'Blimey! How did you manage?'

She tossed her hair back and said, 'I stayed at Harwood House.'

'Where the bloody hell is that?'

'You know, the old builders' place beyond the dock gates. It's now a home for children.'

They all roared with laughter. 'You're a bit bloody old for that, gel!'

Jessie glared at them. 'Now you lot listen here! Miss Flora what runs the place is a real nice lady and she took me in and looked after me, until I could get about.'

'Go on,' said one of her mates. 'If you fell down a bleeding sewer you'd come up smelling of fuckin' roses!'

Jessie grinned at her. 'Well, I certainly did this time. Honest, girls, she was lovely to me, not a bit stuck up.'

'So how's your ankle now?'

'Almost better. That smashing Dr Goodwin looked after me.'

'Oooh!' they all chorused. 'She had the bleedin' doctor, an' all.'

Jessie sat back in her chair and preened. 'Richard's his name. He carried me in his arms into the house.' She winked at them. 'Bloody lovely, it was!'

They all continued to exchange news until the bar began to fill and they separated and set about finding business for the night.

As Jessie took one of her punters home, they passed by Harwood House, and she was filled with sadness, knowing that had she made a different decision, she could still have been there in the warmth and comfort. Those few days had been some of the happiest in her life, and now she was back on the streets where she belonged. And she hated it!

Chapter Sixteen

The following evening, Patrick arrived at Harwood House with Jake and Mattie's father. He was a sad-looking creature, clutching his flat cap in his hand. He was obviously suffering beneath the weight of his wife's illness and the inevitable future without her.

Flora took him into the sitting room where the children were playing. Jake looked up and ran to his father, flinging his arms around him. The man stroked his head and muttered a few words, then he picked up Mattie in his arms and held her close. His love for his children was evident. Flora suggested they take their father up to their bedroom, thinking it would give them some privacy, away from everyone.

She and Patrick went into the kitchen and shared a pot of tea.

'Sure, and the man's beside himself,' he said. 'The doctors have given Hetty but a few weeks to live. He's a simple hard-working man, unable to cope.'

'Will the children be able to see her?' Flora asked.

'Under the circumstances, I'm sure they will. I think it's necessary for them to be able to say goodbye. We'll have to tell Jake when the time comes. Mattie is too young to understand the full implications.'

'As far as the children are concerned,' said Flora, 'they can stay here indefinitely. Will you let the father know this? It might help to ease his burden.'

'I will. You're a good woman, Flora Ferguson.' Patrick held up his cup to her and said, 'I salute you.'

She pushed aside his compliment. 'That's what I came here to do. This is what Harwood House is all about.'

During the next few days, the mystery of the new arrivals at Harwood House remained. The oldest child was a girl, who did at least reveal their names. She was Bella, seven years old, and the others, Mathew, four, and twins, Robert and Sylvia, both three. But they remained as secretive as ever, led by Bella, who was very protective of them.

When the subject was raised about her attending school, she became very agitated. 'I can't go to school and leave the others alone,' she declared. 'They need me to take care of them!'

Flora took her into the dining room and sat her down. 'Now listen, Bella,' she said gently. 'I am here to protect you all. That's my job. That's what Harwood House is for. I wouldn't let any harm come to anyone in my charge, you must believe me.'

Bella eyed her suspiciously. 'That's what they all say.'

Flora became watchful. 'Who does?'

'People like you who are supposed to look after us kids,' she said angrily.

'Well, Bella, you have been with us for three days now, you see how we take care of all of our charges, is there anything that worries you? If so I want you to tell me.'

The child squirmed uncomfortably in her seat. 'No, Miss Flora, but how can I be sure that things won't change? They were kind at first.'

Flora felt her pulse quicken. 'Who are they?' She sat and waited, watching the child battle with her thoughts and feelings. She reached out and took Bella's small hand in hers and asked, 'Do you trust me, my dear?'

She was uncertain and said reluctantly, 'I think so.'

'Do you feel safe with me and Cook and Rose?'

Bella nodded slowly. 'Yes.' She looked pleadingly at Flora. 'You wouldn't hurt us, would you?'

Flora reached for her and, gathering the small bundle in her arms, she held her firmly. 'Oh, my poor child, of course I wouldn't.' All Bella's resistance fell apart as loud sobs racked her body.

Hearing the noise, Rose poked her head around the door, eyebrows raised in question. Flora whispered, 'Keep the others out of the way.' The woman nodded and left, shutting the door quietly.

Flora let Bella cry until she managed to control her anguish. She gave the girl a handkerchief to wipe her eyes and blow her nose, then poured a glass of water from the pitcher on the table, and handed it to her. 'Better?' Bella nodded. 'Then why don't you tell me the whole story?'

It was a heart-rending tale.

'My dad's in prison and my mum's on the game. So I was sent to this house where I was supposed to be looked after.' She sniffed loudly and wiped her nose. 'At first things wasn't that bad. We didn't get enough to eat, though, and the other children cried because they were hungry.'

'What happened then?' prompted Flora.

'They got fed up with this and tied us to our beds and left us, and when it got dark and we called out because we were frightened, they didn't come.'

'What happened if you wanted to go to the toilet?'

Bella's chin trembled. 'Nothing. So we had to go anyway.

Then when they found the mess, they made us clean it up, and wouldn't give us anything to eat. They said we were naughty children.'

Flora was appalled and her anger grew, but she didn't let Bella see how much her tale of woe affected her. 'How did you get out?' she asked.

'I was there for three weeks and I couldn't bear it any longer and the babies were crying all the time. The next time we had to clean up the mess, they had to untie us. A stranger came to the front door while we were doing it and the lady and man went into the front room with him. I know because I was looking through the banisters. I watched them. Then when she closed the door, I grabbed some coats, collected the others and crept downstairs and got the children out the back way, and we ran as fast as we could.'

'Oh Bella!' Flora put an arm around her. 'That was very brave of you. Where was this place?'

The child shrugged. 'I don't rightly know, but it's in Netley somewhere. The lady what took me there said so.'

Flora lifted Bella on to her knee. 'Thank you for trusting me and telling me all this. Those people were very wicked and you did the right thing, but I promise, nothing like that will ever happen to you here. You do believe me, don't you?'

The child nodded and clung to Flora as a new bout of tears overtook her.

When at last Bella was comforted and had settled enough to go back to play with the others, Flora told the story to Rose, who was horrified. 'These people should not be allowed to get away with this. Their treatment was criminal!'

'I agree with you. I had better consult with Father

Duggan and Dr Goodwin. They will know how best to deal with this.'

Later that evening, when all their charges were in bed and asleep, the two men came to the house, alerted to the revelations by calls from Flora.

'I want these people found!' declared Richard. 'No wonder the children were malnourished. These people were crafty enough not to mark the children – physically, anyway. They deserve to go to prison for this.'

'I quite agree,' said Patrick. 'We need to report this to the police. I'll go and see them tomorrow.' He looked at Flora. 'They will probably want to question the children.'

'Then I want to give them another day or two until they really feel secure here. Poor mites have been through a great deal.'

Patrick looked mystified. 'I thought I knew all the children's homes, but I've never heard of one in Netley, have you, Richard?'

The doctor shook his head. 'No. I've been puzzling about that too. Perhaps it's a new one. The police would know.'

But the desk sergeant at the Southampton police station hadn't heard of one either.

'We'll have to talk to this little girl,' he told the priest. 'Perhaps she can give us some kind of clue to follow.'

'Give her a couple of days; there's a good man. Miss Ferguson wants to let her get settled and know that at last she's in a safe place.' He rubbed his chin thoughtfully. 'She was a brave little soul. God knows how many days they were wandering around.'

So the kindly sergeant visited Bella a few days later.

Flora sat with them as he asked Bella questions, but she was unable to shed much light on the whereabouts of her abusers.

'Do you know their names?' he asked.

'No,' said Bella. 'They said we were to call them mum and dad, but I wasn't going to. I already have a mummy and a daddy.'

'And this stranger that came to the door, did you know him?'

'No,' she said, 'but I got a good look at him.'

'Do you think you would know him if you saw him again?'

'I think so.'

The officer patted her on the head as he stood up to leave. 'You are a very brave young lady,' he said. 'And you did the right thing taking care of the other little ones. Were they there when you arrived?'

'Yes. I don't know how long, though.'

'Never mind that. You've been a great help. Thank you, my dear.'

As Flora went to see the policeman out she said to Bella, 'Go into the kitchen and ask Cook to give you a cup of cocoa and a biscuit. I think you've earned it.' The child scurried off with a look of delight.

At the front door, the sergeant paused. 'We'll do our best to find this place,' he said. 'I've got kids of my own, and such a tale makes my blood boil.'

But as the days passed, the police had not been able to discover how the children came to be there or the culprits, but the enquiries continued and the file was kept open.

Shortly after this, Patrick and Flora had the unhappy task of taking Jake and Mattie to the hospital to see their mother. Before they went, Flora and Patrick spoke to the young boy.

Patrick took Jake's hand. 'You know how ill your mother has been, don't you?'

'Yes,' he said quietly.

'Well, son, the doctors are unable to make her better, I'm afraid.'

The boy looked stricken. 'Is she going to die?'

'She's just going from this world to another, Jake. She's going to be with God.'

'Will He look after her?'

'He'll take real good care of her, because she's a good woman.'

Jake looked at Flora. 'Does she know?'

'Yes, she does, darling, and she wants to say goodbye to you. She's a very courageous lady, Jake, and I want you to try and be brave when you see her.'

'I'll try,' he said.

When they arrived at the hospital, Hetty asked to see Flora alone first of all.

As she approached the bed, Flora was saddened at the deterioration in Hetty, but the woman smiled bravely and asked Flora to sit beside her. 'I know how well you've been taking care of my kids,' she said. 'My hubby told me. He also said they could stay with you when I'm gone. Is that right?'

Taking hold of her hand, Flora said, 'I will be happy to look after them. You have two fine children, Hetty. You should be very proud of them.'

With a wan smile she said, 'I am. Mattie is still a babby, but it's Jake I'm worried about. He's a good boy. He'll be lost without me, 'cause he looked after me for some time, you know.'

'I know. Didn't I see him when I came to call with Father Duggan? But don't you fret. I'll make sure he's all right; watch his schooling. Help him with his homework. He's very bright, Hetty. He'll do well.'

'He don't get that from me.' She started to cough.

'He gets his courage from his mother, I know that.'

'My hubby is a good man, Miss Flora, a hard worker; he just can't cope with anything else. But he loves his kids.'

'He'll be able to see them as often as he likes.' She squeezed Hetty's hand gently. 'You don't have to worry about the children. You have my word.'

'I'll go to me Maker a happy woman knowing that. I'd better see the children now. Don't let them stay too long, Miss Flora. I get very weary very quickly. And thank you.'

Patrick took the children in to see their mother and Flora waited outside. She was impressed by Hetty's stoic way of coping with death, and thought she was extraordinarily brave. But she knew what it was like to lose someone you love, and she was concerned for Jake, knowing he would need a lot of kindness and love to help him through his grief.

Patrick came out with them after a short while and asked Flora to take the children home. 'I'll be staying with Hetty,' he said.

Flora took them either side of her, by the hand. As they walked, little Mattie said, 'My mummy said she was going to stay with the angels.'

She felt Jake's grip tighten. 'Yes, darling, that's right.'

'Do they have chocolate cake up there? Because my mummy loves chocolate cake, just like the one you made.'

Flora felt a lump in her throat at the child's innocence. 'I'm sure they do,' was all she could say, lest she give way to the deep sadness welling up inside her. The rest of the journey was made in silence.

When they got home, Jake asked if he could go to his room. 'Yes, of course,' said Flora. 'Would you like me to come with you?'

He shook his head and rushed upstairs. Mattie went to play with the other children and Rose, who was attending them.

In the kitchen Madge asked, 'How did it go?'

Flora couldn't answer.

'That bad, eh? Sit down. I'll make you a nice strong cup of tea.'

At that moment, Jessie arrived at the back door. When she entered the kitchen she took one look at Flora and said, 'Christ! What's wrong?'

Madge told her where Flora had been.

'Dying, is she?'

When Flora nodded Jessie asked, 'Where is Jake?'

'In his room. I asked if he wanted me to go up with him but he said no.'

'When I stayed here, Jake and me were mates,' said Jessie. 'Do you mind if I go up to him?'

'No,' said Flora. 'You are probably just the person he needs right now.'

Jessie walked up the stairs towards the child's room and knocked on the door, then walked in. The boy was sitting on the edge of his bed, clutching his teddy, sobbing quietly. Jessie sat beside him and took him into her arms.

'There, there, my darling, you let it all out.' Eventually, when his sobs had subsided, Jessie said quietly, 'A good cry does you good, you know. I do it sometimes.'

Jake looked up at her with red-rimmed eyes. 'You do? But you're a grown-up.'

'What difference does that make? If I'm unhappy, I'm allowed to show it. I bet Miss Flora cried too when her young man was killed.'

'I didn't know about him.'

'Oh, yes. He was a pilot, you know, in the war fighting the enemy. He was shot down.' She wiped the damp hair away from Jake's forehead and said, 'Everyone loses someone they love at some time in their lives, Jake.'

'Did you?'

'Yeah, my mum. She had pneumonia. I was sixteen. I thought it was the end of the world.'

'But you still had your dad?'

Jessie pulled a face. 'Not for very long. He buggered off and left me on my own.'

Jake looked appalled. 'Didn't you have anyone to look after you?'

'No. I didn't have a place like this to live in, or a lady like Miss Flora to look after me, and you still have your dad, don't you?'

'Yes. He's not going to die as well, is he?'

'We all have to die one day, Jake, but your dad looks like he's going to be around a long time yet – until you grow up, anyway. I cried a lot when my mum died. You do when you love someone, Jake, but your mum is a good person. God will look after her, and she'll eventually be looking after you, watching over you, making sure you come to no harm.'

'Do you think she will?'

'Most definitely. Mothers do, you know.' She smiled at him. 'How about you coming downstairs with me? I'll give you a game of snap. What do you say? I bet I can beat you!'

He gave her a half-smile. 'All right then.'

The two of them walked downstairs together. As they passed Flora, Jessie winked at her.

A little while later, Rose and Flora peeked into the room and saw Jessie sitting on the floor surrounded by children, playing cards.

Rose said, 'She's certainly got a way with kids, hasn't she?'

'She certainly has,' said Flora. And she was sad to think of her leading a life on the streets when she was capable of so much more. If only she wasn't so adamant about not coming to work at Harwood House.

Late that night, Hetty passed peacefully away. At her bedside were her husband and her priest.

The funeral was a quiet affair. There were several neighbours who had loved Hetty and had helped to care for her, popping in and out of the house with bowls of gruel, and food for the children – not that any of them could afford much, but they gave what they could with a good heart.

Jake stood clutching Flora's hand tightly as the coffin was lowered into the ground. He looked so upset as they walked away that Flora said, 'Your mother isn't there you know, Jake. When you die your soul goes to heaven. Your body is only a shell for the soul to use whilst you live in this world. Now she will be free of pain.'

'I don't understand,' he said.

'I know it sounds complicated, but all you really need to know is that she is now living with God and the angels.'

'Is it a long journey to heaven?' he asked.

'I don't really know,' she said, 'but I wouldn't think so.'

As they walked towards the cemetery gates, Flora looked up at the cherry trees, their branches waving gently in the

March breeze, the blossom beginning to flower, the branches of others now covered with fresh leaves. She thought how strange it was to be in the cemetery, which housed the dead, surrounded by trees bursting with new life.

Back at Harwood House Cook had prepared a simple buffet for everyone in the dining room.

Jake's father came over to Flora to thank her. 'When Father Duggan told me you were going to do this for Hetty, I didn't know what to say. But thank you.'

'I did it for her *and* Jake,' she said. 'You know you are free to see the children whenever you like. And if you want them to stay overnight with you at the weekend, that will be fine.'

'I don't know what I'm going to do without my Hetty,' he said.

Flora placed her hand on his arm. 'I know, I know.' She beckoned Jessie over. 'This is Bob, Jake and Mattie's father,' she said. 'Jessie made great friends with your children when they first came here,' she explained, and left them together.

'I'm sorry about your missus,' said Jessie. 'Miss Flora said she was a very brave woman.'

'That she was,' he said, his voice full of emotion.

'Well, Bob, I know it's tough for you, but now *you* have to be brave for your kids – more especially Jake. He's a fine lad and he too will be lost without his mum. He really needs you, you know.'

The man stood straighter, pulled a handkerchief from his pocket, blew his nose loudly and said, 'Yes, you're right.'

'Come on,' said Jessie. 'A drop of sherry is what you need to put you on your feet, and then you should eat. Don't suppose you've eaten anything today, have you?'

He shook his head.

'Men! I don't know . . .' she teased. 'Come on, you need looking after!'

Chapter Seventeen

Jack la Salles, sat on a high stool at the bar of his dingy club in the heart of Southampton's docklands, sipping his glass of beer, grumbling and cursing the inclement weather outside. Two cargo ships that were meant to arrive that night were anchored out in the Solent, waiting for the storm to abate, before they were able to dock. It was low tide and the Solent could be treacherous at such times.

He looked around the large room with its tarnished decorations, and low lighting that hid some of the peeling paint and shabby furniture. There was a collection of tables and chairs, an odd sofa or two, as well as the tall stools around the bar. The place was called the Mariners' Club, but it was just a brothel, with common prostitutes who called themselves hostesses. The clientele were mainly seamen, lascars, and the usual riffraff that a seaport generally spawns.

'Another bloody quiet night!' Jack grumbled to the barman, who looked as run down as the rest of the place, with his thinning hair brushed over his bald pate, and his velvet waistcoat, which had seen better days. He eyed his boss over a pair of glasses that were stuck on the end of his nose.

'Never mind, guv. When the men eventually gets 'ere,

they'll be panting for a woman.'

Jack looked around at the motley assembly of girls, draped over the sofas and chairs, chatting together – apart from one or two who did have clients – and thought to himself hell would freeze over before *he* panted over any of them. No, Jack liked fresh meat. Young and tender, untouched by hand if at all possible. But it was some time since his last encounter.

The girl had been sixteen, brought down for him from London. Half drugged to keep her quiet. He felt a stirring in his loins at the memory. What a young beauty she had been, with her almond eyes and straight black hair. She had been taken from the streets of Chinatown one dark night, when she had been returning home alone. In the quiet of the bar, lost in his thoughts, he relived the experience.

How smooth her skin was, he thought as he stripped the girl's limp form and ran his hands over her body. What a pity she wasn't conscious and able to enjoy what he was doing to her. Jack satisfied all his perversions on her whilst her senses were dulled with laudanum, and she was unable to resist his advances, but as the night turned to day, he tired of her drugged acquiescence, and started to reduce the dose. He wanted a woman who could respond to his sexual requirements. It was a big mistake.

After the girl had slept off the effects of the drug and was finally more or less in control of her senses, she sat up on the bed, and was suddenly confronted with the naked figure of this wizened little man, with his hunched shoulders and wrinkled skin. She went berserk. She screamed loudly, kicked and struggled, as Jack caught hold of her. She scratched his face with her nails, breaking the skin and drawing blood, then she kneed him in the groin, leaving him writhing in agony.

Grabbing her clothes from a nearby chair, she slipped her cheongsam over her head and made for the door. She was so near to making her escape, but at that moment one of Jack's bouncers entered the room after hearing the commotion, and caught the girl by surprise.

Jack, from his foetal position on the floor, snapped out his orders in a voice strangled with pain and anger. 'Get rid of the bitch!'

Her body was found, washed up by the tide, several days later.

He had been in severe trouble with the men who procured the girl, and when the news of the body hit the papers, Jack had a visitation.

One of the gang caught him by his coat lapels, lifted him off his feet and pushed him against the bar wall. 'You stupid little bastard! What the bloody hell were you thinking of, dumping her in the drink like that?'

Jack, scared out of his wits, screeched at the man, 'The little bitch fought like a tiger. She scratched me. Look! I've still got the marks.' He pointed to the two scars down the side of his face.

'You'll have a fucking scar across here if I have my way.' The man drew his finger across Jack's throat. He let go suddenly and his victim dropped to the floor. 'What you don't seem to understand, you useless piece of shit, is if the Triads get to hear of this, we are finished.'

'The Triads?' Jack's voice trembled. The Triads were a vicious, villainous group of Chinese criminals, spreading fear among the oriental community in the capital. 'What's this got to do with the Triads, for God's sake?'

The other man looked abashed as he said, 'Well, we didn't know it at the time, but the girl was a daughter of one of them.'

'What? Oh my God!' He struggled to his feet and stomped around the bar. 'You bungling incompetent idiots!' It was Jack who was now furious. 'You stupid buggers have put us all in danger! Well, you had better keep away from here, and if I was you I'd leave the Smoke for a bit too.'

And since then, Jack had kept a low profile. But he was getting restless. He wanted a woman.

Unlike Jack la Salles, Lydia Goodwin was far from restless. She was feeling very content with her sexual adventures. Douglas Slater filled her needs with great expertise. Their affair was progressing nicely, she thought as she lay in his arms.

He stretched languidly and asked, 'How the hell do you manage to meet me so regularly without making the good doctor suspicious?'

She gave a throaty laugh. 'I told him that several of us ladies gather once a week to discuss fashion and design.'

'You what?' asked Douglas with an expression of amusement. 'And he buys that, does he?'

'Of course. He knows how much I like new clothes and I tell him that we often go to London to a museum or fashion parade.'

'And I thought the man was intelligent!'

'He just wants me to be happy. And, let's face it, Douglas, at least it gives us a chance to get away from Southampton.' She looked around the hotel bedroom. Douglas always did her proud, taking her to good hotels in London, wining and dining her in style. He rolled towards her and pulled her close, running his fingers over her naked form. 'God, you are worth every penny that I spend on you, my little harlot. Your appetite for sex is insatiable. Just as I like my women to be.'

★ ★ ★

Now, because she was content, when she was at home with Richard they no longer quarrelled as they had in the past, and their relationship flourished once again.

In her own bed with Richard, she smiled in the dark, as he reached for her. 'Come here,' he urged, a husky edge to his voice.

She wound her arms around him and bent her body to his. She nuzzled his ear lobe and whispered, 'What do you want, darling?'

His hand brushed her breast. 'I want you.' His lips closed over hers and she kissed him passionately, then eased herself away a little. 'Are you sure you are not too tired?' she teased. And chuckled with delight as he pulled her on top of him. How she loved this game. Being desired by two men: who could ask for more?

March passed into April then May, and Harwood House was ticking over nicely. Flora now had several children sleeping in her dormitory. Some were there for short stays whilst a parent was in hospital, or until they were passed on to other relatives in other towns, or were put up for adoption, but she had a small nucleus of long-term children.

Bella was now happily settled, and went to school every day with Jake. They had become firm friends, each helping the other overcome problems. The younger children were cared for and played with by Flora and Rose, who were also teaching the little ones the alphabet and helping them build bricks, preparing them gently for the time when they too would be old enough for school. And Madge was in her element, cooking nourishing food for all, surrounded by children.

Although Flora was busy and fulfilled, her legacy was not stretching as far as she had anticipated and she knew that she would have to think seriously of getting some financial backing in the very near future, if her dream was to continue. She voiced her concerns to Patrick when he called round one afternoon.

He frowned as he listened. 'Perhaps we could get some of the big businesses in the town interested,' he suggested. 'It would be of little use to approach the council. Richard and I have been on their backs for such a place for years, always without success. They just don't want to know.'

She looked at him with anxious eyes. 'I *must* keep this place going,' she said. 'I *can't* let it sink without trace. We're giving a vital service here.'

Patrick couldn't bear to hear the anguish in her voice and put his arm around her shoulders. 'Don't fret, Flora, my dear. We'll manage somehow. We just have to find a way. I'll ask around.'

She said wryly, 'Don't tell me these businesspeople are part of your congregation, like the alderman.'

He laughed loudly. 'Sadly not. Now come on, Flora, it's not like you to be so dispirited.'

'My mother did warn me against my plan,' she said ruefully. 'I can hear her now: "I hope I don't have to tell you 'I told you so'." It would break my heart if she was proved right.'

It didn't help either that when just after Patrick took his leave of her, the telephone rang and she heard her father's voice on the other end of the line. 'How are things going, Flora my dear?'

'Dad! How lovely to hear from you. No, everything here is going well, thanks.' How could she tell him otherwise? It would be to admit she could face failure in her endeavours.

Having chatted to him for a while, she felt the need to get away from the house to think. She told Rose to hold the fort; she was going for a walk.

She walked along Canute Road, cut through the Ditches, making her way towards the park, when she saw Jessie, standing talking to another young girl.

'Hello, Jessie,' Flora said, coming up behind her.

She turned and smiled warmly. 'Miss Flora. How are you, my love? This here is Daisy, my friend. I mentioned her when I was staying with you, remember?'

And Flora did. So this flouncy young miss was the alderman's little doxy, was she? 'Hello,' she said.

'How do you do?' said Daisy. 'Jessie here is always singing your praises, miss,' she said and grinned cheekily. 'If I'm ever ill, will you take me in too?'

'Gerroff!' said Jessie, and turning to Flora asked, 'Where you going then?'

'Just taking a walk. I need to think over a few things and I thought a stroll in the park might fit the bill.'

'Don't you go talking to any strange men then,' teased Jessie.

As she walked Flora gazed at the neat flowerbeds being cleared of their spring bedding plants by the council gardeners, and hungered for the rugged countryside of her native Scotland. What she would love to be doing at this moment was riding Jasper at full speed through the heather – feeling the wind in her hair. But what she longed for more than anything was Flynn. If only he was here to hold and comfort her; tell her what to do. She felt very much alone and longed to be able to share her troubles with the man she had loved so much. A photograph of him was by her bed, and she would talk to it, but she yearned to be able to feel the strength of his arms about her, his soft Irish voice reassuring her. The emptiness she felt was indescribable.

As Flora was walking, immersed in her thoughts, Patrick was making his way back to the presbytery, filled with concern about the continuation of Harwood House. He was also worried about Flora; she had looked so woeful today. He admired her indomitable spirit, but it had not been visible that morning.

He let himself into the church and kneeled at the altar. As he asked for God's help for his young friend he thought of the tenderness she had shown as she dealt with a child who had fallen. She was a very special woman and she was a great asset to the community. He hoped that all would be well for her and Harwood House.

Chapter Eighteen

Flora's worries only increased when she returned from her walk and found Councillor Beckett waiting for her with the son he had mentioned when they had first met. She shook the young man by the hand, when he was introduced and offered both of them a cup of coffee, but the councillor declined.

'I'm off to a meeting,' he explained. He turned to his son and said, 'This place is desperately needed. If only the council could help financially, but we have overspent our budget.' He pulled a face and, turning to Flora, said, 'That's what this meeting is about. I'll leave Peter with you, if that's all right?'

'Of course it is.' She showed the man out and returned to the sitting room and her unexpected guest, thinking that here was another door closed to her. The council certainly couldn't help her keep Harwood House going.

The young man looked uncomfortable and said, 'I feel I'm intruding when you are so busy.'

'Not at all,' said Flora as she poured the coffee. 'Your father told me that you had served on the Western Front, during the war.' She handed him his cup. 'That wasn't a load of laughs, was it?'

'No,' he said sharply. 'I lost most of my battalion at the

Battle of the Somme.' He sipped his coffee. 'It was the complete waste of lives that I find so very hard to forgive and forget.'

'And no doubt you are filled with guilt that they are dead and you are still alive.' He looked at her in amazement. 'How did you know that?'

'So many survivors feel just the same, believe me, and find their good fortune the hardest thing to deal with. But you *are* alive, you have a life to lead. Your friends wouldn't want you to waste it feeling guilty, I'm sure.'

'I'm sure they wouldn't,' he agreed. 'But it is hard to cope with.'

They spent the next hour swapping experiences, and as Flora told him about her time spent in the field hospital and he realised just how much she had shared in the horrors of the same war, Peter was able really to talk about his time in the army: the responsibility he felt for his men; his feeling of failure that so many perished on the field of battle; as he saw it, the useless loss of lives of so many young and brave men.

Later, as he rose to leave and shook Flora by the hand, he smiled warmly at her. 'This is the first opportunity I have had to be able to get all that off my chest,' he said, 'and I can't thank you enough.'

'You're more than welcome,' she said. 'I was in the same position myself, but I poured all my bottled-up worries out to Father Duggan. It helped, I found.'

'I'm sure you're right,' he said. 'Good luck with Harwood House; you're doing a marvellous job here. I wish you every success.'

As she showed him to the door, Flora's thoughts, swung back to her immediate worries. Harwood House needed an injection of money pretty soon to keep it running, and she wondered if Patrick would be able to discover any benefactors among the business world.

Whilst Flora was worrying about her problems, Jessie had worries of her own. A new prostitute was working around the Southampton docklands, and Jessie was mightily perturbed, because the girl looked so young and some of the other women were giving her a hard time. She'd had to break up a catfight the night before as one of them took off on the girl and the discussion became physical.

'You keep off my bleedin' patch,' the prostitute screamed at the newcomer. 'I've been working here for years, so who do you think you are to come pushing in without so much as a by your leave?' With that the woman leaped at the girl, yanking her hair.

Jessie came between them and separated them, telling the older woman to 'Piss off and leave the poor kid alone!' She bustled the distressed girl into the nearest bar and, sitting her down in a corner, went and bought them both a half of beer.

As she settled next to the girl, who was sniffing loudly, Jessie said, 'Now listen, dearie, you can't just come on to a street and work without fixing it with the other girls first. It just ain't done.'

'I've as much right to earn a living as them!'

'I ain't saying you haven't, but you don't take another person's patch. 'You'll get yourself hurt. Anyway, what you doing down here? I ain't seen you around these parts before the other night.'

It was a sad story that Jessie had heard many times before. The girl had fallen for a man who spoiled her rotten for a while, and then he'd pushed her out on the streets to whore for him, after breaking her in sexually himself. 'I really loved him,' said the girl, 'and I thought he loved me. He said we'd get married, but he was just a bloody pimp with several girls working for him.' She wiped her nose on the back of her hand. 'He kept all the money I earned and gave me just enough to buy my fags, so one night I nicked some of the cash when he was asleep, and I lit out of there as fast as I could and got a train to Southampton. I thought being a seaport, there would be better pickings.' She looked around nervously. 'I can't go back to the Smoke. He'll kill me.'

She was a pretty young thing, thought Jessie, with her fair hair and long eyelashes. 'How old are you, darling?' she asked.

'Old enough,' the girl answered defiantly.

Jessie gave her a penetrating look. 'I don't think so. I would say you was . . . sixteen, seventeen at the most.'

'You won't tell no one, will you?'

Jessie shook her head. 'Bloody hell, girl, you're asking for trouble. You're bleedin' jail bait!'

Her eyes filled with tears as she looked at Jessie. 'What else can I do? My dad kicked me out of the house because of this man.'

'What's your name, darling?'

'Mavis.'

'Well, Mavis, have you got a place to stay?'

'Yes, I've got a room in Threefield Lane.'

'You go home for the night and I'll have a word with the others. I'll meet you here tomorrow evening about seven. All right?'

Mavis nodded.

Feeling sorry for the youngster, Jessie gathered together the other girls and eventually, after much arguing, they agreed between them on a small patch the girl could work.

'But if she so much as steps over her line,' said one, 'I'll bloody have her. OK?'

And so young Mavis joined the band of street women, who in time gave her advice and in fact began to mother her. As one said to Jessie over a drink in the Horse and Groom, 'Christ, if I had her looks and skin, I wouldn't be working the streets, I'd be set up in a nice flat in London.'

Jessie looked at her disdainfully. 'That's all very well for you to dream – she couldn't do that. Where would she get the money?'

'True,' said the other. 'We'd all like that, though, wouldn't we?'

'Not me!' snapped Jessie. 'All I want is to get out of this bloody game, but what chance have I got? None at all! Oh, bugger it, I'm going to have another drink.' She sat in silence, stewing over the fact that she had bypassed the chance of getting off the streets by turning down the job at Harwood House, and for the first time, she really regretted doing so. She shut her mind to her regrets and thought about Mavis. Now this was a sad state of affairs, a kid like that on the streets before she was really a woman, facing the degradation of prostitution at such a young age.

She shared her concerns with Flora when she called in at Harwood House the next morning. Flora was appalled when she heard how young the girl was. 'Can't she get a job in a shop or something?'

Jessie shook her head. 'There aren't that many jobs about for the likes of her, Miss Flora. The posh stores are choosy, like. You have to be able to speak proper and all that. As for the others who ain't so fussy, there's no vacancies. Besides,' she grinned broadly, 'she is doing all right. She has plenty of punters; a good-looker like her can't fail. We all keep an eye on her, see she doesn't go off with any of the weird bastards.'

'I really worry about you, Jessie,' said Flora. 'You are in such a dangerous occupation.'

Jessie rocked with laughter. 'Occupation! Bloody hell, I've never heard whoring called that before! I'll have to tell Father Duggan that one! How is he, by the way? I haven't seen him about lately when I pop in.'

'No, I haven't seen him either,' said Flora. 'I've been so busy – we had some more children in this week, you see – and I hadn't realised he hasn't been around.'

Father Duggan had been busy visiting the offices of some of the town's most important businessmen in an effort to convince them to sponsor Harwood House, but without much success. One or two of them had given him a cheque for a token amount, to ease their consciences and to get rid of him. He knew that asking for money made wealthy people feel guilty – but not guilty enough, he thought angrily, knowing that what he had been able to collect was like a drop in the ocean, and he prepared to visit Flora with many misgivings.

When, the following afternoon, he arrived at the back door of the home, everyone greeted him warmly. Madge rushed to make him a cup of tea and cut him a slice of the fruitcake she had made.

'I've been trying to raise some funds for you,' he said to Flora, 'but the pickings are sadly very poor, I'm afraid.' He produced some cheques from his pocket and handed them to her.

But she looked pleased. 'This will help to buy some

clothes for the children. Thank you so much.' She looked at the anxious expression on the priest's face and sat beside him. 'Don't you worry. I'll find some money. I haven't even begun to fight the people of this town yet.'

'Well, my goodness, this is a little different from the last time I saw you,' he remarked with surprise.

'I know,' she said. 'I was angry with myself for being such a ninny. You don't get anywhere by feeling sorry for yourself. I have decided that I need to toughen up. I'm not sure quite what I'm going to do, but no one is going to stop me giving these children a safe place. Come into the playroom and you'll see what I mean.'

There must have been a dozen children playing there. Some were colouring books and drawing pictures, others were building with bricks, and a few were looking at picture books. One or two were tumbling around, just playing, as children do.

'Good heavens!' he exclaimed. 'Where did this lot come from?'

'All over the place. It seems that what facilities the council have are bursting at the seams, and I've had a steady trickle coming in over the past two weeks.'

'Can you and Rose manage on your own?'

'It is hard to cope sometimes, but Madge often stays behind when she's finished in the kitchen. I don't ask her to, but she loves children and sometimes I have to bully her to get her to go home!'

As he watched the happy animation of her expression as she talked about her charges, Patrick was again filled with admiration and respect for this young woman, and for one moment he wondered what would have happened if they had met earlier in life, before he entered the Church, but he quickly tried to shut out such thoughts.

'Councillor Beckett brought his son round the other day,' said Flora.

'How was he? I heard he was having a hard time putting the effects of the war behind him.'

'We had a long chat and he told me all about his experiences, much as I did to you, Patrick. Let's hope it helped him.'

'Life is never easy,' he said. 'We all have some kind of burden to carry at some time or other.'

'Even you, Patrick?' she teased.

'Especially me,' he said, feeling he had failed her in his attempt to collect funds for the home.

'You sound as if you need cheering up,' she said. 'How about coming round to dinner this Friday? I'll invite Richard and his wife, and maybe Peter Beckett. What do you say?'

Without a moment's hesitation, Patrick agreed. 'Thank you, Flora. I would really enjoy that.'

'Good. Rose and I could do with a break too. I'll get in touch with Richard later.'

But when Richard arrived on the Friday evening, he was alone. 'I'm sorry, Flora, but Lydia isn't feeling well. She has a bad headache, so she's staying in bed. She sent her apologies.'

'That's fine. I do hope she feels better soon. How about making us one of your specials? The drink is on the side.' She went into the kitchen to tell Madge they were one short.

Peter Beckett was an interesting dinner companion. Before the war he had trained as an architect and had travelled extensively, studying styles of architecture in different countries. He regaled the dinner guests with interesting and amusing tales, and Flora was pleased to see the animation in his expression, and the seeming lack of stress compared with what she had seen when first they'd met.

Rose too proved to be a good conversationalist, and Flora realised that the two of them had been so busy they had not had time for long conversations about anything much other than the care of the children who were staying with them. She watched Rose and Peter talking together, and was pleased they seemed to be getting on so well. She was also relieved to see Patrick back to his old self, joshing with Richard as they ate their Dover sole.

It was towards the end of the meal, when they were drinking coffee, that Flora excused herself to go upstairs to check on the children. Jake and Mattie were fast asleep in their room, and as Flora picked up Mattie's teddy, which had fallen on the floor, she heard the sound of a child crying softly in the dormitory next door.

When she walked in, she saw by the low nightlight she kept on that one of the little ones was tossing in her bed. When she reached out and touched the child, she could feel the feverish forehead. She checked the others. Most were asleep but one or two were unusually warm. She called for Richard to come upstairs and look at them.

After he examined them, he said, 'I think you are in for a bout of measles, Flora. Several children in the district have gone down with it, and I would say that is probably the cause. We'll know by tomorrow.'

'I'll call Rose. We'll bathe them with tepid cloths and try and get their temperatures down. At least they will feel more comfortable.'

Patrick and Peter excused themselves on hearing the news. 'You'll have enough to do, looking after your charges,' said Patrick. 'I'll call round tomorrow.'

It was a long night. Rose and Flora changed out of their glad rags and worked hard as, one by one, most of the children developed high temperatures. Richard stayed to help. By dawn, when the children seemed to settle, he and the women were exhausted.

Flora made them all cups of tea and then sent Rose to bed to get a few hours' sleep. 'When you wake up, I'll get my head down for a bit,' she said. 'We are going to have a few disturbed nights, I would say, so we'll work in shifts. Get some sleep and we'll sort it all out later.'

When eventually Richard crawled into his own bed, he was careful not to disturb his wife, who was sleeping soundly. But he would have been livid had he known that earlier, she had been sharing his bed with her lover, as he dined at Harwood House, her headache being just an excuse to miss the dinner party and invite Douglas Slater over in Richard's absence.

'Don't you find this exciting, making love to me in my husband's bed?' she asked Douglas as she sat astride him, brushing her full breasts across his mouth.

He chuckled. 'You are a woman without any principles or morals, you know.'

She threw back her head and laughed. 'And are you any better? You were here quickly enough when I telephoned.'

'But I'm not the one here who is married, darling. If Richard ever finds out what a feckless bitch he's married, he'll kick you out.'

'Don't be ridiculous. Richard adores me. He wouldn't do a thing like that.'

Douglas raised an eyebrow. 'I wouldn't be too sure of

that if I were you. Unlike his wife, our good doctor is a man of principles, but you wouldn't understand that, would you?'

'Stop preaching and wasting time. Make love to me, that's what you came for,' she demanded, as she leaned forward and kissed him.

Chapter Nineteen

The next few weeks were frantic at Harwood House. One by one, the children went down with the measles. Flora and Rose were run off their feet looking after their fretful and unwell charges. They kept the rooms well ventilated, bathed the children to bring down their temperatures and washed them with a special fluid solution to soothe their rashes.

Madge moved into Rose's room, sleeping on a camp bed, helping out where she could when she wasn't working in the kitchen, trying to make tasty meals for children who had no appetite. She made delicious beef tea in the hope she could tempt the children to take some nourishment.

Jessie knocked on the door and offered to come in through the day to help with the laundry as the beds needed frequent changes.

Flora, with a frustrated expression, said, 'For goodness' sake, Jessie, when are you going to put your pride behind you? I need you desperately. For heaven's sake, come and work for me!'

Put like that, how could she refuse? And, frankly, she didn't want to. 'Right, you're on,' she said, and started to collect the dirty sheets.

Richard was also caught up with this sickness with his

own patients, as it seemed to have almost reached epidemic proportions in the town. When this became apparent, Lydia had immediately dispatched him to sleep in the spare bedroom.

'I don't want you coming home and infecting me with measles from your slum children!' she snapped. And from then on, she made sure they ate at different times so she was as far away from him as she could be. It was important to Lydia to keep her clear complexion and she didn't relish the idea of catching measles and maybe spoiling it. Besides, she didn't want to fall sick and have her love life spoiled with the exciting Douglas Slater.

Richard didn't care. He was so busy and desperately tired that he was grateful to be free to get on and do his job without any hindrance. He was also in daily attendance at the house, keeping a watchful eye on his little patients there. Most of them were following the expected path of the illness, with runny colds and rashes that covered their bodies, but one or two were really poorly, and little Mattie especially was giving them cause for concern. She was now suffering with a nasty cough as well as a cold.

Her father called round regularly to see how she was, and Flora tried to stop him from worrying, saying it was just one of those illnesses that children get. She knew how concerned he was, but Jessie was on hand to console him. She tried to be positive in her attitude when she talked to him, but in all truth she was as anxious as he was. These two children were special to her and she fretted quietly over little Mattie and was concerned for the father.

Patrick, who called as often as he could, was there one day at the same time as the poor man and sat talking to him. Bob Thomson looked harrowed. 'I couldn't bear it,

Father, if I was to lose Mattie as well as her mother. It would destroy me.'

Taking the man's hands in his, Patrick said, 'Listen to me, my son. We are all in God's care. All we can do is wait, and pray. Shall we say a prayer together now and ask God's help to make little Mattie better?'

'Do you think it would help, Father Duggan?'

'A prayer to our Lord is never wasted,' he said. The two of them closed their eyes and Patrick, still holding on to Bob, quietly began to pray. 'Dear Lord, our God, please hear our prayer. We ask you to watch over little Mattie, who is sick with the measles. The child has a pure heart and is dearly loved by us all. Please guide the good doctor and Miss Flora to do the right thing to help to make her better soon. We don't want to lose another member of this family. For Jesus Christ's sake we ask this. Amen.'

'Amen,' echoed Mattie's father. He looked at the priest. 'Now I suppose all we can do is wait?'

'You know she is in the best of care here. They will let you know if all is not well. Go and get some sleep. You look terrible, and this won't help your children. You need to be strong for them now.'

Flora saw Patrick soon afterwards and asked, 'Has Bob gone?'

'Yes. I sent him home to get some rest.'

'I'm worried about him,' she said.

'Flora, you have enough to do, let *me* worry about him.'

She smiled softly at him. 'You are a good man, Patrick Duggan. I think you worry about us all.'

'That I do.' He smiled back at her. 'It comes with the territory, didn't you know?'

'I suppose you are going to tell me we are all your children?'

'No, Flora. You are all *God's* children.'

He watched her walk away as Rose called her. He admired her spirit and powerful conviction, yet at the same time he knew that deep inside she was vulnerable too. Her experiences in France had taken their toll on her emotionally, as they had on everyone who had been involved with the horror that was war . . . and the loss of the man she loved had also affected her deeply. He saw a person who needed the Lord's protection and he would say a prayer for her.

Over the next twenty-four hours, Mattie's condition didn't improve, and when Richard called in the morning, Flora said anxiously, 'I can't keep her temperature down.'

He placed his stethoscope on the child's chest, listened and frowned. 'Her chest has a nasty rattle. I'll prescribe something that will help her to bring up the phlegm.' He looked at Flora and said, 'I don't want her to get bronchitis if I can help it. When she's hot, keep bathing her with tepid cloths, keep the covering on her as light as possible. Only increase it if she cools down, but don't put anything on her of any weight.'

'Is she going to be all right, Richard?'

'I hope so, Flora. I really hope so. I'll come back this evening.'

The hours through the night seemed like an eternity to them both. Mattie's breathing was worse. With Jessie's help, they boiled kettles to fill the air around her with steam to try to alleviate the congestion in her lungs. They also propped her up even higher with pillows, which seemed to help a little.

Whilst Jessie was speaking softly to the child in the hope

that she could hear her, Flora left to get a bowl of tepid water and several cloths. 'You take one arm and I'll take the other,' she said to Richard when she returned.

'This child is on fire,' Richard said as he lay a cloth over the skinny limp limb, then let the air dry the damp skin as he did the same with one of her little legs. He glanced up at Flora on the other side of the bed, doing the same.

'I know,' she said, but neither of them dared to put into words their deepest fears. Instead they spoke about other things whilst they cared for the child, watching for an improvement in her condition, sending Jessie away to get some rest.

They discussed their love of horses and as Flora told Richard of her home in Scotland, her family, and the stables that housed her beloved animals, he looked at her with admiration. 'You're from a privileged background, from what you've told me, so what on earth are you doing here?'

'I had to do something with my life after Flynn died, and the war came to an end,' she told him. She looked down at her hands and the cloth she was holding, as if trying to gather the words to explain how she felt. When she eventually met his gaze, Richard could see the rawness of the pains she kept hidden deep inside. 'I felt that a great part of me died with Flynn. Then after the suffering I saw when I was in France, I realised what an empty life I led and I couldn't go back to it. It would have been so superficial and meaningless. Almost obscene, I felt. Then when I saw how these poor children were fighting to survive, I knew I had to put a stop to it in some way.'

He stretched across the bed and took her hand in his. 'You really are an extraordinary woman, Flora.'

She gazed into the blue eyes of the man she respected so

much, and saw the kindness mirrored in his eyes, but then a bout of coughing from their young patient sent her scurrying for another kettle.

During the following hours, they worked frantically, trying to cool Mattie's temperature, continuously bathing her, boiling kettles until they were both exhausted. Jessie woke and joined them once again, helping in any way she could. It was not until the early hours of the morning, when the dawn began to break, that Mattie eventually showed a slight improvement and her temperature started to drop slowly.

After listening to the child's chest, Richard smiled wearily at Flora and Jessie and said, 'I really think she's going to make it.'

Flora felt the tears fill her eyes. Although she was a professional, this little girl and her brother had a special place in her heart, and she had been without proper sleep for days. The relief was almost too much. She looked at Jessie and they both burst into tears and clung to each other.

Richard walked round the bed and put his arms round both women. 'There, there,' he said, 'everything's going to be fine. You're very tired, Flora. What you need is a good night's sleep. And so do I.'

She looked up at him with tear-brimmed eyes and nodded. 'I know. But I really thought we were going to lose Mattie.' Her voice caught in her throat. 'Thank you so much, Richard. I don't know what I would have done without you.'

'You go to bed, Flora,' urged Jessie. 'I'll sit with Mattie.'

'Listen to the girl,' said Richard. 'I'm going to get some sleep too.'

Flora walked him to the front door. 'I'll be back after

surgery later this afternoon to check on Mattie, but if you need me, give me a call,' he said softly. Then he added, 'You really do need some sleep, Flora, or *you'll* end up being my patient.' With a quick smile, he was gone.

She walked back to the kitchen, her emotions in turmoil. She was filled with relief that Mattie was on the mend, and completely thrown by the fact that she suddenly felt a great affection for the doctor. She chided herself, thinking it was the drama of the moment. With such a traumatic time, her feelings were totally confused.

When he returned later that day, Richard just squeezed Flora's hand and asked, 'How is the patient?'

'She seems a little better. She took some beef tea from Jessie, which Madge made, and drank some water. Her temperature is a fraction lower, but she is so weak.'

They made their way to the child's bedroom. Mattie, pale and wan, smiled at Richard. He sat on the side of the bed and took her small wrist in his, timing her pulse. 'Well, young lady, you have been a poorly thing, but you are now getting better. I want you to try and eat a little something now and then so we can build you up into a strong girl again. Will you do that for me?'

She nodded. 'I'll try.'

He listened to her chest, took her temperature and glanced across the bed at Flora. 'It's still down a little.' He looked at the child. 'Poor Jake has been missing you, you know.'

'Has he? I miss him too.'

'Never mind, when you're better you'll be able to play with him again . . . and the other children.'

They left the child to sleep and made their way downstairs to Flora's office.

203

Richard closed the door and asked, 'Did you get some rest?'

'Yes. Rose took over just after you left. I've only been up a while.'

'Good. Have you seen Mattie's father, only I know he was deeply worried?'

'Jessie is with him now in the kitchen. He took the morning off work.'

In the kitchen Bob sat with Jessie, who made him a cup of tea with some toast. 'She's going to be fine,' she assured him. 'She's asleep now but before you go, I'll take you up to see her.'

He smiled shyly at her. 'Cook tells me that you were up half the night with her.'

Brushing his remark aside she said, 'Well, it's my job, ain't it?'

'I don't believe it was just that. I know you love my kids, and I want to thank you. How about coming out for a drink one night?'

Jessie looked astonished. 'You don't have to do that!'

'I know, but I want to. You have been good to my children and kind to me.' He looked at her appealingly. 'Please say you'll come. It's my way of saying thanks.'

'All right,' she said. 'That would be nice. Come on upstairs and take a peep at Mattie, but we mustn't disturb her if she's asleep.'

They stood on the threshold of the room. Mattie was curled up clutching her teddy bear, sleeping peacefully. 'There you are,' said Jessie. 'She's weak, of course, but we'll soon build her up, you wait and see.'

After Richard left, Flora made her way to the kitchen,

poured a cup of tea from the pot that Madge always seemed to have on the go, and sat down wearily.

Madge glanced at her as she made some pastry. 'The doctor gone, has he?'

Flora nodded. 'Yes. He has his other patients to attend to.'

'Nice bloke. Pity he's already married,' she remarked.

'Why do you say that?'

She rolled out the pastry with great concentration, not glancing in Flora's direction at all. 'You just seem so right together, that's all.'

Flora looked at her, but Madge carried on with her work and made no further comment.

Taking her cup and saucer, Flora went into the playroom and watched Rose with the children who were well enough to be up and about. 'Everything all right?' she asked.

Rose looked up. 'Yes. Are you? You look very down.'

With a wan smile, Flora said, 'Just tired, that's all.'

'Why don't you go for a walk and get some fresh air for a while?' Rose suggested.

But Flora didn't want to be alone with her thoughts. 'No, I'm fine. There are things I must do upstairs. Some of the beds need clean linen. I'll go and sort them out.'

Watching her employer walk away, Rose frowned. Something was on Flora's mind and it wasn't the children.

Later that evening, Patrick, hearing the bell, opened the front door of the presbytery to find Richard waiting.

'Good heavens! Come along in. You look shattered.'

'It's been a long day,' said Richard as he followed the priest into his study.

Patrick poured them each a Scotch and glanced at the doctor. 'Here,' he said. 'This is my prescription for what ails you, and it seems to me that something does.' He asked quickly, 'Nothing has happened to Mattie, has it?'

Richard shook his head. 'No, I think she's over the worst, thank heavens.' He took a sip from his glass. 'It was touch and go, though.' He looked up at his friend. 'I just feel such a sense of relief. Flora was magnificent. She is an extraordinary lady, isn't she?'

'Indeed she is. Go home, Richard. You need your bed and a good night's sleep.' He paused. 'There isn't anything else bothering you, is there?'

'No, no, nothing at all. I'm just weary.' He finished his drink and bade the priest good night, then climbed into his car. But as he drove he wondered. There was something nagging at him. It was the look of helplessness he had seen in the green eyes of Flora Ferguson as she had nursed young Mattie. He had wanted to take her in his arms and comfort her. He shook his head vigorously. Whatever was the matter with him?

Chapter Twenty

Jessie was frantic! Young Mavis hadn't been seen for two days. Jessie hadn't missed her at first, having been so busy helping out at Harwood House. When she actually did realise she hadn't seen the girl around and about and questioned the others, they came to the conclusion between them that she hadn't been on her patch for about forty-eight hours.

'Perhaps she's ill,' suggested one, but when Jessie called round at her room in Threefield Lane later in the day, the woman there said she hadn't been home for two nights. 'She'd better be here to pay her rent on Friday, or I'll let her room to some other tom,' she snapped.

Jessie looked at her in disgust. 'Are her clothes still here?' she asked.

'Oh yes, I checked. I'm used to those who do a moon-light flit, so I made sure.'

Jessie was so worried that she didn't spend time giving the woman a piece of her mind but went trawling around the local pubs that evening, looking for the young girl, but no one had seen her.

Back in the Horse and Groom later the same night, she berated the other prostitutes for not taking care of Mavis, much to the annoyance of one or two.

'Take care of her?' said one. 'It's all very well for you, now you've got a proper job, but she's doing more bloody business than all of us put together. She can afford to take care of herself!'

'Just because you're jealous of her, you bleedin' old hag, doesn't mean you don't keep an eye out for her, like we all do for one another.' Jessie drank up her beer, rose from her seat and marched out of the bar, to go in search once again for her protégée.

A few hours later, she returned to the Horse and Groom just before closing time.

Jimmy James, the landlord, served her. 'What's up, Jessie love? You look down in the mouth and no mistake.'

'It's young Mavis,' she explained. 'She's gone missing. I can't find hide nor hair of her anywhere.'

He thought for a moment. 'She was in here a couple of nights ago talking to a sailor, but I didn't see her leave. I was talking to Jack la Salles at the time.'

Jessie felt her blood run cold. 'He was here the same night?'

'Yes, I just said so, you daft bitch.' He turned away to serve another customer.

Jessie felt sick to her stomach. Mavis was just the age that Jack liked, but Jessie had warned her about him several times. She was beside herself with worry. How could she find out if Jack had taken her? She pondered this as she drank her beer, until the landlord called time.

On leaving the pub, Jessie made her way towards the Mariners' Club and hung around outside for a while, then she went round the back, being very careful not to be seen.

A tall rickety fence shielded the building from the public and, try as she might, Jessie was unable to see over it. She could see the curtained windows of the upstairs rooms and although there were lights on, there didn't appear to be any movement. She tried the gate, but it was locked.

She had little sleep that night. She tossed and turned in her bed, trying not to think of what Mavis might be going through, if indeed she was in the hands of the perverted brothel-keeper. But she felt sure Mavis wouldn't go away without saying something. She certainly wouldn't risk going back to London because of her old pimp. No, Jessie was convinced that she was in trouble, and that meant Jack la Salles.

Jessie kept a close watch on the back entrance to the Mariners' Club when she was off duty during the following two days. She had found an old beer crate that was just the height to enable her to peer over the top of the fence, if she stood on tiptoe on it.

She observed the barman putting out the rubbish to be collected. There was a lot of coming and going of staff during the day, but not much during the evening, and she realised they only locked the back gate around dusk. She knew she had to get in somehow and try to find Mavis, if indeed she was there.

On the third night, she couldn't contain herself any longer. Slipping in through the gates, she opened the back door slowly, only to close it quickly and press herself against the wall, her heart pounding. She had seen Jack walking along the corridor.

She waited for what seemed an eternity, then tried again. Peering around the door, she saw the place was quiet. She slipped inside, closing the door carefully behind her, then crept along the narrow corridor. She could hear laughter and the sound of voices coming from the bar area, and went swiftly to the stairs, running up them as silently as she could.

There was a long narrow corridor upstairs with several doors leading off and she wondered which to try first. She listened outside one, and heard the voice of a man and the sound of female laughter, and moved on. She did this to three of them, discovering them to be occupied, but the fourth one had a key in the lock and she could not hear a sound from within. Her heart was beating so hard, Jessie felt that everyone would hear it. With trembling fingers she turned the key and opened the door.

Inside was dark, but with the aid of the low lights in the corridor, she could just make out a shape on the bed. Creeping over to it, she whispered, 'Mavis, is that you?'

The shape sat bolt upright, startling Jessie so much she let out a muffled scream.

'Who's there?' asked a nervous timid voice.

Jessie's heart leaped for joy. 'Mavis! It's me, Jessie.' She took the key, then closed the door, locking it from the inside, and moved towards her. 'Can you get out of bed?' she asked.

'Yes, but I'm only in my underwear. He's taken my clothes away. Please get me out of here,' Mavis pleaded. 'I'll kill myself if I have to stay another night!'

'How on earth did you get here?'

'Two of Jack's men grabbed me off the street. They put a blanket over me and carried me to the club. Please help me,' she implored.

Jessie put her coat on the half-dressed form of her friend. 'Now, as quiet as you can, follow me.' She caught Mavis by the hand and made her way over to the door, but froze as she heard footsteps and the sound of Jack la Salles' voice outside. The two girls clung together, paralysed with fright, hardly daring to breathe. Jack tried the door but on finding it locked, cursed loudly. 'Who's taken the fucking key?' he demanded. There were muffled voices answering. He tried the door again and then they heard the footsteps move away.

Jessie waited, then turned the key and, with her heart in her mouth, opened the door slowly. The corridor was empty. Grabbing hold of Mavis again, she hurried her towards the stairs. Halfway down, they both crouched out of sight, trembling, as someone walked through to the gents' toilet.

As Jessie heard the door close, she said, 'Right, now come on, let's run for it.'

They tore down the rest of the stairs, along the corridor as fast as their legs would carry them and out of the back door, but the gate was locked!

'Oh shit!' exclaimed Jessie. With a feeling of desperation, she dragged a beer crate over to the gate and, urging her friend to climb on it, she pushed her over the fence, following swiftly behind, clambering awkwardly, falling, as she landed on the other side.

She got quickly to her feet and closed her mind to the discomfort of her scratched leg. She ran, hauling Mavis along behind her by the edge of her coat, until she stopped outside Harwood House. She stumbled to the back door and rapped loudly on it with her knuckles, calling urgently, 'Flora! Flora! Let me in!'

Hearing the commotion and recognising Jessie's voice, Flora hurried to open the door. She stepped back. 'Come in,' she said.

Once inside, Jessie turned and looked at Mavis, and was shocked. The girl was sporting a black eye and swollen lips. Beneath her eyes were dark, almost black, circles. She enveloped Mavis within her arms and held her, saying, 'You're safe now, love. You're quite safe here.' Over Mavis's shoulder she could see Flora gazing at them anxiously. 'Can we make her a cup of tea?' Jessie asked.

Flora ushered them into the empty kitchen, and made a pot at once. She looked at Mavis and, seeing the bruises, looked then at Jessie. 'Perhaps you had better tell me what this is all about.'

Whilst Flora poured the tea, Jessie quickly explained what had transpired. 'I brought her straight here. I hope you don't mind?'

'Of course not.' Turning to Mavis, Flora said, 'When you have drunk that tea, you had better let me have a look at you. It seems to me you might be in need of medical attention.'

Mavis looked fearfully at Jessie, but her friend smiled and said, 'This is my friend, Miss Flora, what you've heard me talk about. She took care of me when I hurt my ankle and I work here now. You can trust her – I would, with my life. Honest.'

A short while later, Flora took Mavis into the small surgery on the ground floor and examined her. She was covered in bruises. There were lacerations to her skin, but Flora didn't ask for an explanation until Mavis allowed her to lay her out on the couch and examine her internally.

'You were raped, Mavis, weren't you?'

The girl's eyes were filled with tears. 'That man is worse than a beast!' she cried. 'I wanted to die.'

'If you report this to the police, Mavis, you could have him put away.'

The girl looked horrified. 'I can't go into court and tell strangers what he did to me. It was disgusting. I can't ever tell anyone!'

Flora was full of sympathy. 'I understand. If that is how you feel, then I won't report it, but you must let my doctor look at you. I need to know if you are injured internally.' At the worried expression on Mavis's face, Flora explained, 'Dr Goodwin is a fine doctor and very understanding, I promise.'

After Jessie was called on to assure her friend, Flora phoned Richard at his house and quickly explained the problem.

'I'll come at once,' he said.

Whilst Flora held her hand, Mavis allowed Richard to give her a thorough examination. He was very gentle, and spoke softly to Mavis as he did his work, and Flora once again saw what an excellent doctor he was. When he had finished, he covered Mavis with a blanket, washed his hands at the washbasin in the corner and then sat beside his patient on the examination couch.

'I cannot begin to imagine what you have been through,' he began, 'but I can tell you that the injuries you have sustained are not serious. Your bruises will fade, you have been torn a little inside, but that too will heal. You will be sore and uncomfortable for a while.' He smiled at her. 'But I can give you something to alleviate the pain. What you need now is time, to help you recover.' He looked questioningly at Flora and raised his eyebrows.

She knew what he was asking. 'You can stay here, Mavis. We'll take care of you.' Seeing the tears welling in the youngster's eyes she said, 'I'll go and get Jessie to sit with you whilst I prepare a room. All right?'

The girl nodded. 'Thanks, miss,' she whispered.

Once Jessie was with her friend, Flora and Richard went into her office.

He looked outraged. 'Whoever did this should be locked away in a mental home. She has been raped in a most brutal manner.'

'It was Jack la Salles, by all accounts,' Flora told him, 'but the girl won't go to the police, and can you blame her?'

He shook his head wearily. 'That man should have been put away years ago, but the police never seem to have enough evidence to convict him.' He looked at Flora and asked, 'I don't suppose she would change her mind?'

'I shouldn't think so.'

'If this man finds out that you are sheltering her, you could be in danger, you do realise that?'

'In what way?'

'Think about it from his point of view. You are harbouring a young girl who could put him behind bars! He's not to know she won't report him.'

With an angry shrug, Flora dismissed the warning. 'Well, I'm certainly not going to turn her away!'

Richard gave a rueful smile. 'I didn't think you would, but do take extra precautions. Make sure everything is locked up and secure at night. I don't imagine he would be stupid enough to try anything during daylight hours, but be careful.' He caught hold of her shoulders and stared into her eyes. 'I don't want anything to happen to you when I'm not around.'

After Richard had departed, Flora and Rose made up a small room with twin beds, which they kept for emergencies. She quickly told her assistant what had transpired and warned her also of the dangers they might face by taking Mavis in.

'Of course we must take her!' said Rose. 'We can't leave her alone at a time like this. Who knows what her mental state might be after such a dreadful experience!'

Flora looked at her and said, 'Thank you for that. But we will have to be vigilant.'

'And we will be, but the most important thing is to get the girl better.' She frowned. 'It is just as well that Jessie is here full time, because we are going to be pushed to cope.'

Jessie came to the kitchen to get a drink for Mavis. She looked at Flora and said, 'Poor Mavis. What a bloody state to be in at her age.' She slowly stirred the cocoa in the cup and said, 'You don't really know just how much it means to me to be working here with you all. It means that I don't have to have another man touch me unless I want him to. It means, Miss Flora, that I can feel like a woman and not some cheap tart.'

'Oh, Jessie, don't say that. You had to do what you did to survive.'

'I know, and I hated every moment.' She smiled, but there was sadness in her eyes as she looked at Flora. 'You have given me a fresh start and I'll never forget it – or you taking Mavis in like you did me. I would do anything for you, you know that, don't you?'

Her sincerity made Flora embarrassed. 'All you need to do for me is be your usual self with the children and help us take care of Mavis. Come on, we can move her into the room you'll be sharing . . .'

Back at the Mariners' Club, Jack la Salles was going berserk. He was cursing and swearing at his staff, accusing each of them in turn of letting his captive free. When at last he half believed they had no part of it, he screamed angrily at them all. 'I want that little bitch found. She could put me behind bars.' He looked around menacingly. 'And I don't care if she's dead or alive!'

His head man said quietly to him, 'Take care, Jack. We don't want trouble like we had last time with the Chinese bint.'

Jack just glared at him and repeated, 'Dead or alive.'

Chapter Twenty-One

Jessie had settled nicely in to her new position, which took a lot of pressure off Rose and Flora, and Mavis was slowly getting better physically, but her mental state worried Flora. The girl had dreadful nightmares and occasionally her screams woke and frightened some of the children.

When Richard called to see his patient Flora spoke to him privately of her concerns.

'Well, it's not surprising really. We have no idea just what that young girl went through. It could scar her for life.' He scratched his chin thoughtfully. 'If you could get her to talk about it, it might help.'

'I'm not sure that she'll ever be able to do that,' Flora said, thinking how impossible it would be to put the perverted actions of Jack la Salles into words when you had been the victim.

Richard reached out and placed a hand on her shoulder, stroking her cheek, as he did so. 'I hate to see you look so worried. You already have enough on your plate with the children, without this added problem.' With a note of anxiety in his voice, he asked, 'Have you been troubled at all by any of Jack's men?'

Flora was startled by the question. 'No. Have you heard anything?'

'No, but you really need to be careful. If la Salles sees Jessie working here, he may put two and two together.'

'Oh! I hadn't thought of that. But I can't expect Jessie to hide away for the rest of her life, can I?'

'Of course not, but I've been thinking, the very fact that she isn't around her usual haunts might cause suspicion. Now if she were to be seen at one or two of the pubs she normally frequents, it might put Jack off the scent. Of course, Jessie wouldn't have to take on any clients,' he added hurriedly.

Flora gazed affectionately at him. 'Oh, Richard, what would I do without you?'

He smiled at her and said, 'You would manage just as well. I had better get back to the surgery. I'll look in again soon.'

When Flora entered the kitchen she was surprised to see Patrick sitting at the kitchen table chatting to Madge, with a cup of tea beside him and a slice of half-eaten sponge cake on a plate. He looked up. 'Hello, Flora. How are you? Madge sneaked me in the back door.'

'You know you never have to sneak in here. You are always welcome.' She then told him about Mavis and the bad condition she was in.

'Can I help in any way?'

Shaking her head Flora said, 'No, I really don't think so. The male sex isn't her most favourite thing at this moment, even a man of the cloth.'

'Well, and that's no surprise, is it?'

'No, sadly not.'

The priest finished his cake and rose to his feet. 'Well, Flora, my dear, if I can be of any help, just let me know.'

She made her way to the playroom where Jessie and Rose were keeping the children occupied. 'Jessie, can I have a word?'

Flora told her of Richard's idea about her behaving as normal to allay the suspicions of the brothel-keeper. The girl listened intently. 'You know, Miss Flora, the doc is a smart man, and he's right. I'll pop off to the Horse and Groom tonight. Then if Jack or any of his men are around, they will think everything is hunky-dory.'

Later that evening, Jessie pushed open the door of the public bar of her local and walked in, to be greeted like a long-lost friend by her mates.

'Where the hell have you been?' asked one.

She had given the matter a lot of thought and although she trusted her fellow prostitutes, she had decided to take no chances and was not about to confide in them. 'I've had a bleedin' touch of the flu,' she said, 'and I've been laid up.'

'Did you stay at that place again?' queried another. 'You know, like when you hurt your ankle.'

Shaking her head, she said, 'No, of course not. I didn't want any of the kids there to catch it, so I stayed home.'

'And what about Mavis? Did you find her? We ain't seen nothing of her.'

'I searched high and low,' she said, 'but I couldn't find a trace of her. I reckon she's gone back to London.' At that moment she saw Jack la Salles enter the bar with a couple of his henchmen. He stared across at Jessie and said something to his men as he sat at a nearby table watching her.

Jessie felt her stomach tighten beneath his scrutiny. She finished her drink and told her friends, 'I'm still feeling a bit rough, so I'm off home and an early night.'

Jack la Salles muttered to one of his men, 'Keep an eye on that bitch. She was very chummy with that little whore who ran away. Maybe she knows where she is. Don't touch her – well, not until we find the girl, and if she's got something to do with her then she will pay for giving me so much trouble.'

But Jessie was prepared for this, and once outside the bar she took to her heels and shot up a side street, making a long detour and ensuring the man wasn't following her before she arrived back at Harwood House.

Jack's man returned to the Horse and Groom sometime later.

'Well?' asked his boss.

The man shook his head and, not wanting his boss to know he'd lost her and face his wrath, he said, 'She's holed up for the night with a punter. She ain't going nowhere else.'

Jack grumbled beneath his breath. 'Just keep an eye on her,' he snapped, and got up and left. His man went and ordered a beer, thankful that he hadn't been found out.

Lydia Goodwin was in despair. Doug Slater was getting bored with her – she knew the signs. No longer did they journey to London for their nights of passion. Now it was a second-class hotel on the outskirts of Southampton, and not nearly as frequently as before. Before, he would spend hours flattering her, buying her presents, and in bed the foreplay used to be wonderful and unhurried. Now . . . now, if she was honest, she felt he treated her little better than a prostitute!

When she pouted and complained to him, he would ignore her or tell her briskly to grow up. But now she had a serious problem – she was pregnant. She knew the child was Doug's because ever since the measles epidemic in the town, she had banished Richard to the spare room and they hadn't had sex for several weeks. Tonight she was going to break the news to her lover and she wondered just what his reaction would be.

She began to run through the different ways he might respond to her news. Would he be overjoyed? She was not at all sure. Would he be angry? For no reason in particular, this seemed the most likely to Lydia. Although Doug had been an attentive lover, until recently, he had made it abundantly clear he was free to come and go as he pleased. She gave a wry smile. What a poor choice of words that was!

That evening she dressed with particular care, wearing her most alluring underwear beneath her gown. She would have to handle the situation with care.

To her great relief, Doug was in a good mood when she climbed into the passenger seat of his car, at their usual meeting place, away from the house. He greeted her with more affection than of late, pulling her towards him and kissing her lovingly before putting the car into gear and driving away.

'You look wonderful, darling,' he said as he placed his hand on her knee and stroked her leg.

She smiled at him and caressed the back of his neck. 'I've missed you,' she said softly.

'Of course you have,' he replied with his usual arrogance. 'Tonight you can show me how much.'

They dined at a small hotel outside Southampton, in Otterbourne, a sleepy little village. The hotel was tucked away behind several small cottages and Lydia wondered how Doug knew of its existence. Had he brought other women here? He probably had – but how recently? Before their affair, or during it? She really didn't want to know the answer.

Once they were in their room, his display of affection continued, and her fears began to fade as he whispered words of love to her between kissing and caressing her body. She had been imagining his loss of interest, she told herself, as his lovemaking and demands became more passionate. All her doubts were dispelled as she let her body answer to his manipulative fingers, and she allowed the feelings of desire to sweep her away.

When eventually they lay exhausted and replete in each other's arms, she let out a deep sigh of satisfaction. 'Oh, that was so good,' she murmured, and stretched languidly.

'Mmm . . .' was his only reply as he reached for a cigarette.

'You do love me, Douglas, don't you?' she asked.

'Of course I do,' he said quickly and without feeling – as he always did.

'No, *really* love me,' she insisted.

He lay on his side, looking at her as he puffed on his cigarette. He chuckled to himself. 'What is it with women that they all demand to know if you love them?'

'Because it's important!' she snapped, irritated by his attitude.

He put his cigarette in the ashtray, and then, turning towards her he ran his finger between the cleft of her breasts, and down the soft rise of her stomach. 'I love you madly,' he said, as his hand slipped between her thighs.

'I'm so happy to hear you say that,' she said, 'because I'm pregnant with your child.'

His fingers stopped their gentle movement and he sat upright, staring at her. 'You what?'

'I'm carrying your baby.'

The expression in his eyes was cold and his voice had an icy edge to it. 'How can you be sure it's mine? It could easily be your husband's.'

She traced the shape of his lips. 'No, darling. Richard and I haven't slept together for almost two months. The baby is definitely yours.'

He swung his feet over the edge of the bed and stood up. Casting a glance in her direction he said, 'Well, that's that then!'

She sat up, pulling the sheet up to cover her naked form. 'What do you mean, "that's that"?'

He started to dress and said, 'It's been fun, darling, but now it's over! It's time to move on.'

'Move on!' She was furious at his air of dismissal. 'What the bloody hell do you mean, "Move on"?'

He tucked the tail of his shirt into his trousers and did up his flies. 'Precisely what I said. You must go back to the faithful Richard, and I'll find a replacement for you.'

'And your child?' she demanded.

He shrugged and laughed cruelly. 'You must make Richard believe the child is his.' He tossed her clothes at her. 'Get dressed!'

Lydia flung the sheet aside and leaped out of bed. 'You callous bastard!'

His laughter echoed. 'You always knew that, Lydia, my dear. It was part of the attraction, admit it.'

The fact that he spoke the truth enraged her even more and she raised her hand to slap the smile from his face, but he was too quick for her and grabbed her wrist, twisting her arm, making her cry out with pain as she fell to her knees.

He looked down at her with contempt. 'Don't tell me that you envisaged a future for us together. What you wanted from me was wonderful illicit sex – and that's what you got!' He released his hold and she rubbed her wrists. 'I have never ever led you to believe that there was anything more between us – have I?'

She didn't reply. How could she argue? He was right.

They dressed in silence, then made their way downstairs and out to the car. Doug always paid for their room in advance.

As they entered the outskirts of Southampton and drove down The Avenue, he said, 'There's no point in sulking, Lydia. We both had fun and enjoyed each other, but now it's over. It had to end sooner or later.'

She couldn't answer. She was fighting back tears of frustration, of fear, and she was damned if she was going to let Doug Slater see just how much she cared.

When eventually he brought the car to a standstill, his tone was gentler, and he put a hand on her arm as she went to open the door. 'Listen, darling, you are a terrific woman. I have really enjoyed our time together, but I'm not the marrying type – you know that.' He stroked her arm and said, 'You need to seduce your husband, and you can; you're good at it. He will be delighted at the resumption of his conjugal rights and he'll be thrilled, eventually, to think he's going to be a father.'

'Unlike you!' She spat the words at him, but he just laughed.

'Unlike me.' He kissed the tip of her nose. 'Goodbye, Lydia. It's been fun.' He leaned across her and opened the car door. 'Take care.'

And she knew this was his final dismissal.

The worst of the mini-epidemic was over and most of the children in the home had recovered. Mattie took a while longer to rebuild her strength, but she was progressing satisfactorily. Jake was very solicitous over his sister, spending time with her, telling her about his day at school and generally cheering her up. Their father was greatly relieved at Mattie's recovery and still called regularly to see his children.

Once or twice he took Jessie to a local pub where they sat over a couple of beers and chatted about the children.

One evening Bob looked at her and said, 'I'm surprised you ain't married, Jessie – a nice-looking woman like you. Especially as you're so good with kids. Mine adore you.'

'And I love them too,' she said.

Jessie didn't know what else to say. She really loved these two children and was getting fond of their father, but she couldn't let him go on with a false impression of the sort of woman she was. Staring straight into his eyes she said, 'In my old game, marriage was the last thing on a man's mind,' and she held her breath.

He patted her hand. 'I know you used to be a tom, my girl. But thanks for being honest about it.'

'You knew?'

He grinned broadly. 'Of course I did. Good God, Jessie, I've lived in Southampton all me life – don't you think I've seen you working in the Ditches?'

'Bloody hell! And it don't make no difference?'

'No, it don't,' Bob said softly. 'It's what's inside a person that's important, girl. There's many people who live blameless lives, and right bastards into the bargain they are too, but you, Jessie, you have a good heart. That's much more important.'

Back at Harwood House in the kitchen, Madge was airing her views about Bob. 'What that man needs,' she declared in her down-to-earth way, 'is to find a good woman to make a proper 'ome for those kids.' She looked at the shocked expression on Rose's face. 'What?' Madge asked.

'It's only been a short time since his wife died!'

'I know that! I don't mean in the next few weeks, you daft 'a'p'orth, but some time in the future.' She glanced at Rose. 'I reckon our Jessie would fit the bill nicely.'

Rose agreed with her. 'Well, she already treats Jake and Mattie as if they were her own.'

Madge cast a sly glance in her direction. ''Ow's it going with that young man of yours?'

Rose blushed. She had been meeting Peter Beckett occasionally. 'He's not my young man!'

Madge grinned broadly. 'But 'e'd like to be. Don't you go losing 'im, my girl. Good men are 'ard to come by, and that one is all right.'

Although she was embarrassed, Rose smiled slowly. 'You think so, do you?'

'Yes, love, and I'm a good judge of character. I wish that nice Dr Richard wasn't married. He and Miss Flora would make a nice couple.'

Rising to her feet, Rose said, 'You stop your meddling, Madge.'

The cook grinned at her. 'It's the only fun I 'ave these days.'

'Then you find yourself a man and leave Flora and me alone!'

With a hearty laugh, Madge said, 'I've 'ad my day, my girl. I 'aven't got time for any more truck with the male sex!'

When Richard sat down to dinner that night, he was very surprised when Lydia, dressed most beautifully, joined him. He looked at her and her finery and asked, 'Are you going somewhere special?'

She smiled sweetly at him and said, 'No, not at all. Now the measles scare has all cleared up, I thought it was time I

226

saw something of my husband.'

Richard was immediately suspicious. 'And why would that be, Lydia my dear? You have taken great pains over the last two months to ignore me completely.'

'Now you are being unkind, darling,' she wheedled. 'After all, you can't blame me for taking precautions against the measles, can you?'

'But it wasn't just that was it, Lydia?' he said, remembering a furious row they'd had just after he'd moved into the spare room. 'You told me I was too old and staid for you . . . and boring, if I recall correctly.'

She remembered every word and she had meant it at the time, but now she desperately needed to repair fences with her husband. 'I'm really sorry,' she said. 'I was in a foul mood. I didn't mean what I said and I apologise.'

'And now what do you expect?' he asked.

'Now we can revert to normal.' She stared at him provocatively. 'I've missed you. An empty bed is very lonely.'

'You haven't seemed to mind until now. After all, two months is a very long time.' He cut into his pork chop. 'Frankly, I've got used to sleeping alone, and if I get a call during the night, it doesn't disturb you. And considering how you used to complain—'

She interrupted him. 'Richard! I can't believe what I'm hearing. It's a husband's duty to share his wife's bed.'

This angered him and he snapped at her, '*You* didn't think so when you insisted I sleep in the spare room. Duty wasn't mentioned then, as far as I recall!' He added, 'And if you remember, when you told me I was far too old for you and I was boring, you ranted on like a spoiled child, adding for good measure that you were sorry you married me in the first place. Now you expect me to forget all that!'

Lydia was getting more and more agitated. If she couldn't persuade Richard to share her bed, how could she seduce him and make him believe he was to be a father? Time was of the essence. She rose from her chair and walked over to him. Standing behind him, she nuzzled his neck. 'Don't be angry with me, darling.'

He moved away, saying, 'Please, Lydia, I've had a very long day and I'm hungry.'

She returned to her seat, but just played with her food. She had suddenly lost her appetite. She cursed Doug Slater beneath her breath and looked across the table at Richard. How distinguished a man he looked. If only he had more time to spend with her all this foolishness could have been avoided. She would have to bide her time, but she couldn't wait too long. She would work on Richard a little more every day. There would be a moment when his defences would be down, and then he would be hers.

For his part, Richard was still smarting from Lydia's cruel words because he knew that she was unhappy and their marriage had deteriorated. Why had been a puzzle until she'd blurted out her feelings. His hurt had been deep. Was he a bore, he had asked himself. Yet he had done his utmost to please his wife, and he was still angry enough to ignore her apology and keep her at bay.

Chapter Twenty-Two

Flora was sitting in her office poring over the books. She was meticulous in keeping her accounts up to date and it was very clear, as she read the figures, that she was in deep trouble. Her funds were now really low. She did have a small overdraft facility at the bank, but that wouldn't keep her going for long, and how would she pay it back? She had been aware of the problem, but the measles epidemic had prevented her from tackling the situation earlier, and now things were dire. What on earth could she do? She had a full house at the moment. Jake and Mattie were well settled, and Bella, Mathew, Sylvia and Robert seemed happy and secure, although the mystery as to their previous dwelling remained unsolved. Apart from those children, she now had others. No, she couldn't let all this disintegrate. It was far too important.

There was a tap on her door and Madge came in with a cup of tea and some toast on a tray. 'Now then, Miss Flora, you missed breakfast this morning and that won't do, so you jolly well eat this.' She looked at her employer and said, 'Whatever is the matter, love? You look as white as a sheet.'

There was something so comforting and motherly about Madge Bennett that Flora poured out her troubles. 'I'm running out of money to keep Harwood House open, and I *don't* know what to do about it.'

Madge drew up a chair and said, 'Well, we can't let that 'appen, can we? We need to put our 'eads together. Now 'ow on earth can we raise some money?'

'I don't know. I'm sitting here racking my brains for an idea.'

'The trouble, Miss Flora, is that people are not aware of the good work that is done 'ere. If they knew about it then I'm sure they would be only too 'appy to 'elp.'

'Father Patrick went around various businesses trying to raise funds, but they were not interested – but, of course, as you say, they don't really know what we do,' agreed Flora.

'Mm.' Madge was deep in thought. Suddenly she looked up and with a smile she said, 'I 'ave an idea.'

'What?'

With a knowing look she said, 'I know all about big businesses. They all need publicity. If it were known to one and all that they were subsidising this place, it would do their reputations the world of good. But the public need to be able to *see* what you do. You need to 'ave an open 'ouse.'

Intrigued, Flora asked, 'What do you mean?'

'You need to open the 'ouse for a few hours one afternoon and invite the press to see the work that you are doing. Invite the mayor at the same time, to make it official, and then send invitations to all the 'eads of the large businesses in the town, and the members of the council. Let them know the press will be 'ere. They won't want to miss 'aving their pictures in the paper. It's all about publicity. Then put pressure on them – all of them – in front of the reporters.'

Flora looked at her cook in astonishment. 'Wherever did

you learn about such things?'

'Before I married, I worked in an advertising agency and I picked up a few pointers.'

'What did you do there? Were you a secretary?'

Madge doubled up with laughter. 'Lord, no, my love. I was the cleaner, but I kept my ears and eyes open.' She winked. 'You would be surprised at what interesting things you can find in a wastepaper basket, and the gossip that flies around an office. I could tell you a thing or two, and no mistake!'

'Oh, Madge, you really are wonderful! I love the idea. I'll talk to Father Patrick and Dr Richard and see what they have to say, but I'm sure they'll see the sense of it.' She smiled. 'Thank you so much for your suggestion. To be honest, I was beside myself with worry.'

The cook rose from her seat. 'Don't you fret, my dear,' she said as she walked to the door. 'This place will be closed over my dead body!'

Flora called a meeting with her colleagues for the following evening, when the children would all be in bed. Jessie, Madge and Rose sat round the table in the dining room, with Richard and Patrick.

'I'm really sorry to have to call such a meeting,' apologised Flora, 'especially as I was so adamant that I would be able to get the funds to enable us to continue to run the home. There I have failed.'

'Don't be so hard on yourself, my dear,' interrupted Father Patrick. 'You have had too much to cope with recently, and I too feel I've failed, trying to interest the businessmen of the town without much success.'

'Well, Madge has come up with an excellent scheme and I think we should all listen to her. Madge . . .'

The cook laid out her idea very succinctly to everyone, and it was met with enthusiastic agreement by all.

'Surely once they see the children and the security they now have, and the care,' said Rose, 'they will be only too willing to help.'

Richard gave a slightly sardonic smile. 'Madge is right: as long as the companies get lots of publicity, they might be drawn. There is never something for nothing in business.'

'That's a rather embittered outlook, isn't it?' remarked Flora.

'Not at all, my dear. I have had to deal with these people; I know.'

'Well, I feel we should make a big splash,' said Flora. 'We'll put up bunting and flags. The more folk who know about us, the more pressure we can put on the men with money. Besides, ordinary souls are always generous, even if only in small ways.'

'If we do it in the afternoon,' suggested Madge, 'the children can bake cakes and we can serve tea.'

'It would be as well to keep all private rooms locked,' advised Patrick. 'If you are having people wandering around, you will need a certain amount of security.'

'What about Mavis?' asked Jessie quietly. 'We must keep her out of sight.'

'She can stay in my office, which I'll lock. No one can look inside, as there are no windows. She'll be safe there.' She looked at Jessie. 'Do you think that man will come here?'

'I wouldn't put it past him.'

'Then we must keep her well hidden.'

'Should I join her, do you think?'

Flora thought for a moment. 'You can't keep swanning

in and out of the Horse and Groom for ever to try and fool him. I think the time has come when we face up to reality. He's bound to find out you work here one day, after all. We have just gained a little time.'

Jessie beamed at her. 'I think it makes sense.'

They decided on a date two weeks hence, to allow Flora to advertise the event and interest as many people as possible. Now the meeting was ended, Madge invited them all to join her in the kitchen. 'I've made a few sandwiches and sausage rolls,' she said.

Flora grinned across at Rose. 'Any excuse,' she said, knowing Madge's penchant for entertaining, especially Father Patrick, who was a decided favourite with her.

As the others rose to follow the cook, Richard caught Flora by the arm and said, 'Stay a minute, please.'

When they were alone she asked, 'What is it?'

'I just wanted a moment with you to say it worries me that you are in financial difficulties and I am unable to help you.'

She smiled at him and said, 'But I am not your responsibility, Richard.'

'Then tell me why I feel so responsible for you?'

'I don't know, I really don't know, but it is nice of you to do so.'

And so it was, two weeks later, on a Saturday afternoon in the late summer, that Harwood House was flying bunting from every possible structure. The gentle breeze kept the flags moving. Bouncing lines of fluttering colour gave the place a joyous feel, and passers-by stopped to read the posters outside and see just what was going on. Those who read the local paper were aware that the mayor was to preside at this fund-raising day.

Flora said, 'We may as well do the best we can and damn the expense. After all, this is our last stand.'

'Who the hell do you think you are, Flora? General Custer? If I see any Indians around here, I'm off!' joked Jessie.

The one person who didn't share in the excitement was Mavis. She was terrified that Jack la Salles might come looking for her. Everyone tried to reassure her that she would be safe behind the locked door of the office, and that an eye would be kept open if indeed the man did come on the premises. And so with much trepidation she was led to safety.

The mayor was due to arrive at two o'clock. Harwood House had been cleaned from top to toe, Flora and the members of her staff were adorned in their spotless uniforms, giving as professional a look as was possible, and in the playroom, children were being read to by Jessie, some were sitting, colouring books, and others were in the kitchen helping Madge with the baking. The air was filled with pungent, inviting aromas, tempting the visitors to purchase a cup of freshly brewed tea and home-made cakes. Already members of the public were filtering through the gates, to be greeted warmly by Flora, who invited them to look round.

Richard and Patrick were on hand to do their bit, and Flora smiled to herself as she heard them telling folk of the important work being done by her and her staff. She listened to one or two comments.

'I had no idea this place existed,' said one woman, watching the children in the kitchen. Her expression softened as she saw them icing the small cakes. 'Poor little souls,' she said. 'Imagine not having a home with parents to look after them.' She opened her purse and withdrew a five-pound note. Looking around, she saw Flora and, walking over to her, said, 'Will you take this and put it towards something for the children?'

'Thank you so much,' said Flora. 'This is very kind of you.'

'I hope you manage to raise the funds you need,' the visitor said. 'I'll tell my friends about you.'

Flora's eyes shone brightly at such news. 'If you could do that, madam, I will be eternally grateful, and so will the children.'

Alderman George Chivers arrived with several members of the council. He puffed and bluffed his way around the building, talking to various visitors. Flora was incensed as she listened to his conversation. He made it appear that the council were responsible for Harwood House. 'I'm not having that!' muttered Flora as she strode over to the small group, listening to his postulations.

'Good afternoon, Mr Chivers. How nice of you to come.' She turned to the others. 'Unfortunately the council were unable to help with the funding of this house,' she said clearly, 'so I am pleased to see members of the council here today. Perhaps when they see how important a job we are doing, they may be able to help us in the near future.'

Chivers gave her a thunderous look. One of the reporters, who had been standing by, writing all this down, sidled up to Flora. 'Good for you, miss. I can't stand that pompous ass. I'll give you a good write-up in the *Echo*, because I think you are doing a fine job.'

Flora thanked him, and walked on. At that moment the mayoral car arrived. Flora saw Chivers making a beeline for the door, but she got there first and, catching hold of his arm, she held him back as she walked past him. 'Thank you, Alderman, but today it is *my* place to greet the mayor.'

The press were in evidence with their cameras, taking pictures of Flora greeting the mayor and lady mayoress on the steps. One of the smallest children presented the mayoress with a small bouquet and curtsied prettily.

Flora took them on a tour of the building, explaining the layout of the house, the children that were there permanently and the others who were just on a limited stay.

'What would happen to the children who are here all the time if this place was to close?' asked the mayoress.

'I have no idea,' admitted Flora. 'I suppose they will be found places elsewhere, but I know for a fact that there is a dire shortage.'

The lady just shook her head, but said no more.

The mayoral party took their tea in the kitchen with the children, which delighted the press. It was a great photo opportunity, and Flora made sure that only the children and none of the councillors were in the pictures with the dignitaries. Eventually, as the official party were about to take their leave, on the steps of Harwood House the mayor made an impassioned plea for the gentlemen of the business world to sponsor this wonderful project, and then he invited Flora to speak.

She stood erect and proud, speaking clearly. 'Ladies and gentlemen, and most of all, children, as a nurse on the battlefields of France during the war, I saw the terrible suffering of men who were heroes, and when I left that behind at the end of the war I thought never to observe the like again. Yet here,' she indicated the children, some of whom were standing next to her, clinging to her skirt, 'are victims of a different kind of suffering: cruelty beyond belief, neglect and, in many cases, the result of poverty and the inhumane treatment of one human being by another.

This is yet another battlefield.

'These children need care, love, medical attention, food and clothes. All, of course, require the funds to keep things going. The children need books to stimulate their minds; school uniforms, because we are very mindful of their education. We want them to grow up to be young people who can hold their heads up high and feel proud of themselves, despite having such a traumatic and tragic start in life. For this reason alone I urge you to help me to continue to fund Harwood House. Thank you.'

There was a spontaneous burst of applause at the simple but heart-rending appeal.

The reporter from the *Southern Daily Echo*, circulated among the local businessmen. 'Gentlemen, you are men of intelligence and influence – are you going to help fund this fine project?'

'Of course,' answered several, anxious to please the press.

'Splendid!' said the reporter. 'I'll be able to print that in tomorrow's edition with the names of your companies.' He stared at them. 'I'll call on you in a few weeks' time and do a follow-up article. After all, this would be excellent publicity for you.' He tipped his hat. 'Thanks, gents.' He walked away, chuckling to himself, knowing he had guaranteed Harwood House funding from several organisations.

Members of the public remained for quite some time, fascinated by the children. Some even stayed to play with them. Jessie, keeping an open eye on the proceedings with Rose, suddenly looked up to see Jack la Salles watching her. She froze for a moment and then met his gaze, daring him to say something.

He walked over to her and said, 'What are you doing here? Why aren't you skulking around the alleyways where you belong?'

She glared at him. 'I've changed my profession,' she said. 'Not that it's any of your business.'

The gaze that held hers was cold and threatening. 'And where is that little whore who was your mate? Is she skulking around here too?'

'I haven't seen her in weeks. She's gone back to the Smoke, for all I know. Why are you interested?'

He didn't answer but leaned closer and said, 'If I thought you had anything to do with her disappearance, you would be in real trouble. You remember that!' He turned on his heel and left the building.

Jessie placed her hand on her heart, which was beating so fast it almost hurt. She only hoped that he believed her, but at least he now knew she was working at Harwood House. She no longer had to pretend to be on the game.

Flora, urged by the reporter who gave her the names of the businessmen who had said they would help, went up to them one by one, thanked them for their generous offers and blatantly asked when she could expect something concrete from them. Taken aback by her forthright manner each one told her she would be hearing from them shortly.

When at last all the visitors had left, everyone gathered in the kitchen, drank a welcome cup of tea, and ate a sandwich. They all agreed that it had indeed been a profitable afternoon. When Flora told them how Alderman Chivers had behaved, they were all furious, but they laughed when they were told how she had thwarted his games.

Father Patrick looked at her with undisguised affection. 'Oh my, Flora, you are indeed a force to be reckoned with once you are roused!'

'I had an ally in the *Echo* reporter,' she said. 'He was a great help.'

'Ah, well,' said Patrick, 'he was an orphan, so he understands.'

'Well, that explains it then.'

'Jack la Salles was here,' said Jessie quietly.

'Was he any trouble?' asked Richard.

She looked perturbed as she said, 'I really don't know. I'm not sure he believed me when I said I didn't know where Mavis was.'

'Oh my goodness,' said Rose, 'Poor girl, she's still in the office.' She rushed to go and free her. When she opened the door, she found Mavis huddled in a corner on the floor. The girl was trembling from head to foot.

'I heard him!' she cried. 'He tried to open the door. He called my name. He knows I'm here!'

Alarmed at the state of the girl, Rose hurried to get Richard, who came at once. He gave Mavis a sedative to calm her, letting Jessie take her to her room and put her to bed.

Turning to Flora, he said, 'If that girl doesn't get away from Southampton and that man, she'll have a complete breakdown.'

Thinking quickly, she asked, 'Is Scotland far enough? I'll send her up to my home. She can stay there, and when she's recovered enough she can work in the house if she wants to. It will give her something to occupy her mind, and the air will do her good. La Salles won't find her there. What do you think?'

'I think it's inspired.'

'I'll ring my father tomorrow and arrange it,' she said.

Mavis's fears were completely justified because when la Salles returned to the Mariners' Club he said to one of his men, 'I'm sure that bitch Jessie at Harwood House knows something. I have a gut feeling that that little trollop is hiding my girl somewhere there.'

'Didn't you have a good look round for her?'

'Of course I bloody did. There were some private rooms locked, but one downstairs, which looked as if it was probably an office, was also locked, but I'm sure as I tried the handle I heard someone move inside. I called her name but then it was quiet. I just know she's there.'

'What are we going to do about it?' asked the man.

Jack was quietly thoughtful for a while and then he smiled slowly. 'Perhaps we ought to try and smoke her out!'

Chapter Twenty-Three

George Chivers returned home in high dudgeon, furious that that chit of a girl had usurped his authority today. Here had been a wonderful opportunity to put himself forward, especially with the members of the press present, but she had thwarted his every move. He was also annoyed that she had done such a good job with Harwood House, earning today many plaudits for doing so, and getting the backing, which had always been denied him, from the top men in the business world. Had the council funded the home in any way, today would have been a day he could have sat back and been congratulated for his foresight. Instead, he'd been sidelined, and he didn't like it – and what was more, she wasn't going to get away with it!

He leaned back in his chair and lit a cigar. He had recognised one of the town's most notorious prostitutes today, who appeared to be working with the children. Now he was sure that no businessman would want to be a part of a sponsorship where a woman of low repute was being employed. That wouldn't do anything for their own moral standing with the public, and he was just the man to inform them if they weren't aware. But first he would make that Scottish upstart squirm. Would he dictate a letter to her, telling her of his intentions? No. No, he would take the pleasure of visiting her and telling her to her face! That would give him the greater satisfaction. Yes, that's what he would do, but he would wait a day or two; let her get carried away with the idea that all was well in her little world, and then he would wipe that smile off her face.

As Richard opened the front door of his house, his emotions were very mixed. Today had been such a success and if everything came to fruition, Flora's financial worries were over, which brought him a feeling of great relief, but also the realisation that he was falling in love with her. A ludicrous situation. He was a married man, for God's sake. But there was something between them – a spark, a certain chemistry – and he thought that she too might be aware of it.

Lydia emerged from the drawing room. 'Darling! There you are. How did the afternoon go? Was it a success?'

Richard looked at his wife with some surprise. This was the first time that he could remember her ever taking an interest in anything that he did, and she did seem genuinely interested.

'Yes, it went well. Flora now has the sponsorship she needs from several companies in the town.'

'I am pleased.' Lydia put her arms around his neck and said softly, 'You look tired, darling. Let me go and run you a bath. That will make you feel better.'

He did feel drained mentally, and a bath was just what he needed to help him relax. 'Yes, that would be nice,' he conceded, and followed her upstairs.

As he lowered himself into the softly scented hot water, he lay back, resting his head on the back of the bath, and tried to let his mind go blank, to shut out all thoughts of Flora. He felt the tautness of his body gradually relax and closed his eyes. Twenty minutes later, he got out of the tub, put a towel around his waist and, picking up another, started to dry his back as, without thinking, he walked into the bedroom he used to share with Lydia before he moved into the spare room. She was laid upon the bed, scantily clad in a very feminine ivory slip. His gaze rested upon her bare breasts nestling beneath the delicate coffee-coloured lace bodice and he caught a glimpse of her smooth thighs. A sexual longing surged through him. God, it had been a long time since he had desired his wife, he realised. It was time to put his foolish notions about Flora out of his mind and try to repair his ailing marriage. Lydia held out her arms to him, and after a moment's hesitation, he released the towels and walked towards the bed.

Two days later, Flora answered a knock on the front door and was greatly surprised to find Alderman Chivers standing there. Without waiting for an invitation, he pushed past her.

'Shall we go into your office?' he demanded.

With a sense of foreboding. Flora took him there. He sat in a chair as she moved behind her desk and took a seat. 'What can I do for you, Alderman?' she asked.

All the spite that had been brooding inside the man was unleashed on the unsuspecting woman. 'I suppose you are patting yourself on the back now, after your fund-raising day!'

There was such a note of accusation in his voice that Flora was immediately on her mettle. 'What seems to be the problem, Mr Chivers?' she asked. 'From the tone of your voice, you are not here on an errand of mercy.'

'Indeed not! I am here to stop you making complete

fools of our captains of industry. The men who have offered to support you.'

Her eyes narrowed as she tried desperately to guess this man's intentions. 'I'm sorry, but I don't follow you.'

'These men have put their reputations on the line to put money into Harwood House. How do you think they would feel if they knew you were hiring a prostitute as a member of your staff? What sort of teaching will she be giving these innocent children? Children that you have placed in her care. She will only corrupt their minds, and I for one will not stand by and let you do this!'

He was, of course, referring to Jessie. It all suddenly fell into place and Flora saw through him immediately. She glared at him across the desk. 'Ah, now I see. You didn't like having to take a back seat the other day, did you? No, that's not your style, Alderman, is it? So now, out of spite, you are prepared to put the future of my children and many others who might come here in the future at risk, just to satisfy your wounded ego!'

His face flushed red and he blustered, 'How dare you speak to me like that?'

But by now Flora's wrath was unstoppable. 'And how dare you come here and behave in such a petty manner? You, who have everything – and these poor souls who have nothing. Your behaviour is obscene! Don't continue down this path, Alderman, because you will live to regret it, I promise you!'

'Are you threatening me, Miss Ferguson?'

'Damn right I am!' She tried to calm down. 'After all, Alderman, you have a penchant for ladies of the night yourself, don't you?'

She thought he was going to explode.

'You what?'

'No, not me, *you*, sir. A young lady called Daisy, I believe, is a very close friend of yours.'

There was such an expression of hatred on his face that Flora sat back in her chair in an effort to distance herself further from her adversary, but she was not to be deterred. 'I will not let you endanger the future of Harwood House. These children need a home and you won't stop them from having one. I'll fight you every step of the way.'

But the councillor was a mean old buzzard. He recovered and gave a sly smile. 'If you were to try and prove my relationship with this young lady, I would have you up for slander. You see, Daisy would deny any such liaison. She wants to keep a roof over her head. She likes the things I can give her. She would never let a chit of a girl like you deprive her of them. My advice to you, Miss Ferguson, is to keep your own counsel about this matter, because I'll wipe the floor with you!'

He rose from his seat. 'In two weeks' time I am attending a business federation luncheon with these men and I intend to put the facts before them.' He leaned across the desk. 'I am going to close you down!' He turned on his heel and left the room, slamming the door behind him.

Flora was devastated. George Chivers had called her bluff and she knew he would outwit her if she pursued her threat to expose his debauchery. She looked down at the list she had been making of things that were required at the home: more blankets, clothes, shoes, and things she would be able to buy when the new funding arrived. She made her way to the door, opened it and called loudly, 'Jessie!'

There was no reply and as she walked towards the playroom young Bella tried to stop her. 'Miss Flora, I've got something important to tell you.'

'Not now, Bella.'

'But it's about that man. The one who just left. I've seen him before.'

Pausing, Flora said, 'Yes, he was here on the open day.'

'I didn't see him then, miss, but he's the man who came to see the people who looked after us at Netley. He was the man they took into the front room when me and the others ran away.'

'Who? Alderman Chivers?'

Bella shrugged. 'I don't know his name but it was him.'

Flora looked astounded. 'Are you sure? This is *really* important.'

'Yes, I'm certain. I remember thinking what an ugly fat old man he was. When I heard his voice I recognised it.'

'We'll have to tell the police about this, you know, darling.'

The child nodded. 'I don't mind that, 'cause I know you'll take care of me.'

Kneeling down, Flora embraced Bella. 'Of course I will, and you haven't done anything wrong. In fact, the police will be pleased with you because this will help them to discover what's going on and where this place is. After all, we don't want these people to look after any other children the way they looked after you and the little ones, do we?'

'No! They were horrid, not like you and Rose.'

Kissing Bella on the cheek, Flora said, 'You run along now and play. I'll let you know what the police say, but *you* don't have a thing to worry about, honestly.'

'You won't let anyone take us away, will you?'

Seeing the look of desperation on the little girl's face, Flora said, 'Absolutely not! I promise. Cross my heart and hope to die!' She crossed her heart with a finger, then held up her hand as if to swear on oath, imitating a favourite chant of the children's.

Bella gave a smile of relief and left to play with the others.

Flora rushed to the kitchen, calling for Jessie and Rose to follow her there, where she told them and Madge what had happened since the visitation of the alderman.

On hearing that he wanted to close them down all their voices were raised in anger at once, and Flora had to calm them. 'But that's not all!' She then proceeded to tell them Bella's strange disclosure.

'Well, I never!' exclaimed Madge. ''E's up to no good then, being mixed up with the likes of them sort of people!'

'Maybe,' said Flora, 'but we don't know that, and won't until the police are informed and start to investigate. By then he will have destroyed our chances with our sponsors.'

Jessie was desolate. 'This is all my fault!' she cried. 'If you hadn't taken me on here, that bastard wouldn't have no reason to ruin everything!'

Putting an arm around her shoulders, Flora tried to pacify her. 'Now don't be silly. You have a natural gift for handling children. I know of many so-called respectable people who are cruel and unkind and don't understand children at all. I can remember such a woman coming to me for a job. I turned her down. No, Jessie. I wouldn't have things any different. The welfare of the children comes first.'

With a sniff, Jessie said, 'Maybe, and it's kind of you to say so, but what will all those businessmen say when old Chivers goes and tells them about me?'

Flora rubbed her forehead and closed her eyes, trying to think. 'I really don't know. We have to do something to stop him. Maybe the police will turn up something about him before his meeting. We'll just have to hope so. I'll telephone the desk sergeant now.'

Madge was stomping angrily around the kitchen, muttering beneath her breath, 'Just when everything was going to be all right . . .'

Flora returned to the kitchen after making her call and said, 'The sergeant was very interested in what I had to tell him, and he'll be sending someone round in the morning to question Bella. We'll just have to see what transpires.'

The following morning, a constable came to Harwood House and listened carefully to what Bella told him. He looked at Flora and said, 'Maybe the alderman can cast some light on these people. We need to know who and where they are to further our case of neglect against your children. I'll be in touch.'

Now Flora was in a dilemma. She thought of approaching the chairman of the business federation and putting forward her case to him personally. But if Chivers was bluffing, and didn't mention Jessie, she may jeopardise her position herself. She had no choice but to wait. If he carried out his threats, then she would appeal to the chairman. It was taking a gamble, waiting to see what transpired, but she felt she had no choice. With a sigh she realised she had one more problem to solve – that of Mavis. She picked up the telephone receiver and put a call through to Glasgow.

It was so comforting to hear the familiar voice of her father, but she couldn't let him know of her troubles. She couldn't even tell him the truth behind the condition of Mavis. If her father thought Flora herself might be in any danger from the brothel-keeper, he would demand she return to Scotland, and she wasn't going to give up everything for anyone. One way or another Harwood House would continue.

Unwillingly, she concocted a tale about Mavis being one of her workers, who needed a complete change of scene to help her to recover from an illness. She must have been convincing because her father didn't hesitate.

'Of course, my dear. Send her to London on a train and I'll meet her at the station. We'll take care of her.'

Knowing that Mavis wasn't in a fit state to travel alone, Flora decided to send Jessie with her as far as London. 'I'll send a companion with her, Dad. She has fiery red hair; you can't miss her. I'll find out the trains and then I'll let you know the day and time. And thanks.'

'I told you if there was anything you needed, didn't I? Is everything all right, Flora?'

'Yes, why do you ask?'

'I don't know – something in your voice, I suppose.'

She forced a laugh. 'Just tired, that's all. Love to Mother.'

When she returned to the kitchen, both Rose and Madge were waiting for her. Rose said, 'We've been talking, Madge and me. We don't mind working without any wages until you get back on your feet.'

Flora was choked with emotion. 'That's really good of you, but I can't expect you to do that.'

Madge in her usual outright manner said, 'It 'asn't got nothing to do with you, love. Me and Rose 'as decided. We'll all scrape by. Me – I can make a meal out of nothing. We'll manage for a bit longer, you see if we don't.'

Two days later, Jessie and Mavis were dispatched in a taxi to the station with full instructions to follow to meet Mr Ferguson.

'Don't you dare tell him what's going on here,' she told the two women. 'I don't want him to know anything. If he asks, everything is fine. All right?'

Jessie looked at her and said, 'If that's the way you want it.'

'It is. Now have a safe journey.'

There was nothing to do now but wait to see if the police came up with anything against George Chivers, or even Jack la Salles, that would help their cause.

Chapter Twenty-Four

Jessie returned from delivering Mavis safely into the hands of Flora's father. 'What a lovely man,' she enthused. 'He insisted in taking us into the buffet and giving us sandwiches and coffee before we parted.'

'How was Mavis?' asked Flora.

'A bit nervous, of course, but your dad soon put her at her ease. She went off all right.'

'You didn't say too much, did you?' Flora knew how Jessie liked a good natter.

She looked quite peeved. 'Fancy asking me that. I'm no grass!'

Flora had to smile. 'No, of course you aren't. Sorry.'

'That's all right. No news from the police about the alderman, I suppose?'

'Not yet. It's a bit soon. I'll give them a few days then I'll walk down to the station and see for myself.'

With so much on her mind, Flora couldn't sleep and at two o'clock the following morning, after tossing and turning in her bed for what seemed an eternity, she decided to go down to the kitchen and make a hot drink. Knowing her way around the house so well and with a low light always on in the upstairs hallway, she made her way downstairs. It wasn't until she reached the kitchen that she turned on the light. Suddenly, she heard a clatter outside. Picking up a heavy torch, which was by the door, she turned the key in the lock and opened it. The smell of petrol filled the air and she heard the sound of running footsteps. She flashed the light of the torch across the yard and saw the outline of a man running through the now open gates.

'What the . . .?' she uttered. Walking towards the gates she saw by the beam from the torch that the chain and padlock were on the ground. With closer inspection she could tell that the chain was broken in half. Picking it and the padlock up, she closed the gates and returned to the kitchen, where under the strong lights she saw that the chain had been cut.

Going back to the door, she flashed the torch around on the ground outside where, to her horror, she saw an upturned can of petrol, its contents seeping across the yard. Putting down the torch, she quickly put the can upright, filled a bucket with water and swilled the ground outside. She did this several times, sweeping the petrol away with a stiff yard brush.

'What the bloody hell is going on?'

Flora gave a scream and jumped with fright. Jessie was standing in the kitchen doorway. 'Flora! What on earth are you doing?'

It was only then that she stopped and looked down at her feet. Her slippers were soaked through. She took them off, leaving them outside, went in, and, picking up the broken chain from the draining board, she held it out towards Jessie.

Jessie looked at the chain with the padlock still attached, and then up at Flora, with a startled expression. 'Is that petrol I can smell?'

Flora nodded and pointed to the can outside near the door.

'Jack la Salles!' they both said in unison.

Flora's eyes blazed with anger. 'That bastard was prepared to set fire to this place. Christ, he could have burned all the children. What sort of a monster *is* he?'

'You don't want to know,' said Jessie. 'A body of a young Chinese girl was washed up in the docks some while ago. There was a rumour that it was la Salles' work.'

'I'm calling the police!' said Flora.

Half an hour later, a police car pulled up outside and a sergeant and constable entered the building. When Flora told them what had transpired, they looked around the back yard. The sergeant picked up the now empty can with a stick and said, 'We'll take this away to have it fingerprinted. Now, who do you think would do such a thing?'

Both Jessie and Flora answered, 'Jack la Salles!'

The policeman looked surprised. 'Why on earth would he be involved with you, miss?'

Flora hesitated for a moment, then said, 'He thinks I have a young lady staying here.'

Looking somewhat puzzled the sergeant asked sharply, 'Just what exactly has been going on, Miss Ferguson?'

She realised that she could no longer keep the truth hidden. After all, the safety of the children was now in question. She told them how Mavis had been rescued from the Mariners' Club and brought to Harwood House to be cared for.

'You didn't report this?'

Flora shook her head. 'The young lady was badly injured and traumatised. She refused to talk to the police. I did ask her to,' she added.

The officer cursed. 'That la Salles has been sailing close to the wind for far too long. With her help we could have put him away. After all, kidnapping is a very serious offence – apart from anything else he did.'

'I told her this, but she was terrified for her life.'

'Is she here now?'

'No, she isn't and don't ask where she is. I will tell you that she is being looked after, hundreds of miles from here, but that's all I'm prepared to say. Besides, it is the present I'm concerned about. Had this man set fire to this place we could all have been burned alive. What are you going to do about it?'

'What can I do, miss? You have no proof that it was la Salles. Did you see who the person was who ran away?'

'No, only that it was a man.'

He shrugged his shoulders. 'Then what can we do except look at the petrol can for fingerprints.'

Flora was incensed. 'What do you want? Do you need to see the charred remains of all the children here before you do anything? Is that it?'

'Now calm down, miss.'

'Calm down? What do you expect of me, officer? My staff and I are the only ones here responsible for my charges. Can't you at least keep a watch on the place?'

He looked somewhat nonplussed. 'I can ask the officers on the beat to keep an extra eye open.'

'And that's all?'

'Well, miss, I'm afraid so, until we have some kind of proof.'

'In which case, you may as well leave,' she snapped. 'You are wasting my time and yours. I just hope that nothing serious happens to the children. It would be on *your* conscience if it did!'

'I'll have a word back at the station, Miss Ferguson, see if there is anything more we can do. I know this is a serious situation, but my hands are tied.'

'Thank you,' replied Flora coldly. 'I'll show you out.'

When they had gone, Flora fumed. 'The police are useless!'

'Well, they did have a point,' said Jessie. 'There *is* no proof. But don't you fret. I know a few villains. I'll have a word in the right place. They'll put the frighteners on la Salles, don't you worry. I can do it now that Mavis is safe.'

'I don't want you getting intro trouble, Jessie. We have enough to cope with!'

'I'll be fine, honest. But you had better get another chain in the morning.'

'A lot of bloody good the last one did!'

Jessie grinned at her. 'Just listen to your language! A lady like you. Tut tut!'

Flora started to laugh. 'My mother would disown me. Oh dear, Jessie, but this is enough to make anyone swear.'

'I know, love. Come on, get back to bed. There's nothing more we can do now.'

Flora wasn't the only one who was furious. Jack la Salles was incandescent with rage when he learned that his plans had gone awry. Hearing that the police had been called, he knew he would have to keep a low profile for a while, despite not knowing where that little whore was. Until she was found and dealt with, he wasn't safe.

'We'll give it a week and then you'll have to try and break in one night; search the place. I won't rest until I know for sure if she's there or not. But I'll give them something to think about meantime.'

He waited until the early hours of the morning, and then he rang the number of Harwood House.

Flora woke with a start. She was a light sleeper and, hearing the sound of the telephone ringing, especially at that hour, caused her to rush down the stairs. Who on earth could be calling, and so late, she wondered. With a beating heart, she lifted the receiver from its cradle.

A low menacing voice said, 'You had a lucky escape, Miss Goody Two-Shoes. If you are sheltering that little whore Mavis you should be very worried, because I'll get her!'

Although scared, Flora was absolutely livid. This was the man who could have killed all her children! Burned them to death! Anger overcame her fear. 'Now you listen to me, you sick little man. I don't have the girl here and, I warn you, if you try anything else, I'll make sure the police get you. Understand?'

He laughed at her. 'Brave words, my dear lady. We'll see if you are telling the truth, make no mistake. For your sake, I hope you are!' And the line went dead.

As she replaced the receiver she realised that her hands were trembling. She knew these were not idle threats. She sat on the bottom of the stairs wondering what to do. She heard a door open, and looked up to see Jessie coming down the stairs.

'What's up? I thought I heard the phone, then I thought I'd been dreaming.' She saw the anxious look on Flora's face and asked, 'What's going on?'

'Jack la Salles rang,' said Flora, and then proceeded to tell her what he had said.

Jessie's expression was set as she listened. 'Right,' she said. 'It's time to sort that little sod out.'

'Whatever do you mean?'

Jessie put her arm round Flora and said firmly, 'Never you mind. Come on now, back to bed afore you catches your death.'

As she stood up, Flora said, 'I don't want the others to know about this phone call. It will only cause them concern and we all have enough on our plates as it is.'

Madge and Rose were shaken when in the morning, over breakfast, Flora told them of the happenings of the previous night. 'You went outside without waking me?' demanded Rose. 'Are you mad? You might have been attacked.'

'I never gave it a thought.'

'What a wicked bugger!' snapped the cook when Flora explained whom she and Jessie thought the perpetrator was, but omitted to tell them about the telephone call. 'Mind you, seeing the state of that poor girl, I'm not surprised 'e's worried. God knows what that poor child went through. If it was up to me, I'd cut his balls off!'

The very idea of Madge doing such a thing broke the tension, and both Rose and Flora started laughing until the tears rolled down their cheeks.

'I believe you would too,' Rose managed to splutter as she gasped for breath.

'The trouble with most men is they keep their bloody brains in their trouser pocket,' stormed Madge. 'All they think about is sex, sex, sex! Why can't they think like a woman?'

'Now you're asking for the impossible,' said Flora, wiping her eyes. 'Oh, my. I really needed that. A laugh is as good as a tonic any day. However, we must be vigilant. If Alderman Chivers ever heard about this, it would only give him more ammunition.'

'Do you think we'll get another visitation from that rotten little pimp?' asked Madge, looking suddenly perturbed.

'Hopefully not,' said Flora, not wanting to alarm the others. 'After all, I interrupted the arsonist, and no doubt Jack will have heard that the police were called. If the policeman on the beat is on the lookout, as the sergeant said, la Salles may have been put off.'

'I do hope so.'

There was a tap on the back door and it opened to reveal Patrick, who hurried in. 'I just heard about last night,' he said. 'I met the constable on the beat just as I came in. Are all of you all right?'

They assured him that they were, but when Flora told the priest they had another problem now with Chivers threatening to have them closed down, Patrick was furious.

'I'll pay him a visit,' he said. 'I'll soon put a stop to this.'

'I think that would be unwise,' said Flora, and then explained to him about Bella recognising the councillor. 'The police are investigating him, Patrick. I don't think you should interfere at this point.'

'But what could he have to do with this lot in Netley?' he said with a puzzled expression.

'You take his confession,' remarked Flora tartly.

He cast a glance in her direction and quietly said, 'I do, and what is told to me in the confessional is private. But I have no knowledge of this situation whatsoever. You didn't tell me any of this, Flora.'

Letting out a sigh she said, 'What was the point? There was nothing you could do about it and almost as soon as he left, I informed the police of Bella's revelations. No one can do anything at the moment. We'll just have to wait and see what happens.'

'And if nothing does and he goes to this luncheon and stops your sponsors, what then?'

'Then I shall go to the chairman of the business federation and appeal to him personally. What else can I do?'

'Yes, I see your predicament. My dear Flora, this is so unfair. You don't deserve such treatment.'

'When was life ever fair?' she asked angrily, 'and please don't tell me you'll pray for me because right now, it is of little comfort!' And she hurried out of the room.

'She didn't mean that, Father,' said Madge. 'Last night was an unnerving experience for her.'

'I know, my dear, I know. I'd better get back to work. I'll look in again.'

But as he walked down the road, Patrick worried about Flora. She had achieved so much since her arrival in Southampton and it would be criminal if it were all to be taken away because of a man with such a mean spirit as Alderman Chivers. He pressed his lips together in a determined line, wondering just how he could help, other than with prayer. There must be something he could do . . .

That evening, Jessie left Harwood House and made her way through the dark mean streets of the docklands of Southampton. This was no place for a woman to wander around alone, but it held no fear for Jessie, who had spent so many years working the area. There was nothing she could do to help Flora with the problem of the councillor, but she could help sort out Jack la Salles.

She headed for a billiard hall tucked away up a narrow alleyway, and knocked on the side door. The darkness was only disturbed by the sound of rats scuttling about in the gutters. Moments later the door was opened but a few inches, and a man with a face that only a mother could love peered out. 'Whatcha want?' he growled.

'I've come to see Frank McAvoy. Tell him it's Jessie.'

The door was shut in her face, but she waited until it opened again and the big man nodded and let her in. She walked up the narrow staircase, lit only from the low light in the hallway downstairs, and entered a room when she reached the top.

There wasn't much in the way of furniture in the room – a couple of shabby, torn armchairs either side of an unlit fireside – but there were four men sitting round a table, playing cards. One of them looked up.

'Hello, girl. What brings you here?'

'I need a favour, Frank,' she said.

'Do you now?' A soft smile played at the corners of his mouth. 'That's not usually your style, Jessie. You are normally far too independent – as I recall.'

She grinned at him. 'You remember then?'

'How could I ever forget?'

Jessie was flattered. Years before, when she was first on the game, Frank McAvoy had been a regular punter of hers. Their sexual relationship grew into something more serious and he wanted her to give up her life on the streets and be his girl, but she had declined. By then Frank was becoming established in the criminal world and she had wanted no part of his life and refused him, but they had remained friends.

'It's Jack la Salles,' she said.

The others looked up, and Frank let out a mouthful of expletives. 'That foul piece of human shit! What's he been up to now?'

Jessie proceeded to tell him the sad tale of Mavis, ending with the abortive attempt to burn down Harwood House. 'All those kids, Frank, think about it. I don't want this woman who runs it worried by him again.'

'Yeah, I've heard about her; doing a good job by all accounts.' He smiled at Jessie. 'Leave it with me, darlin'. I'll sort it out.'

'Thanks, Frank. I owe you one.'

'No, Jessie. It's on the house – for old times' sake.'

She blew him a kiss and left the room, walked down the stairs and out into the darkened alleyway, well pleased with her visit. She knew Frank so well. If he said he'd sort something out, it was as good as done. She badly wanted Harwood House to continue the good work, and *she* desperately needed to feel an important and useful part of the community. This was the only chance she would get to live her life as a decent human being, with some self-esteem, not just as a piece of flesh used by men for their sexual gratification. No, she needed Harwood House just as much as every young child who had found love and safety within its walls.

Chapter Twenty-Five

It was almost a week after the attempted arson at Harwood House that Richard heard about it. There had been no reason for him to visit the children's home in a professional capacity, and he had stayed away and tried to repair his relationship with Lydia, after returning to the marriage bed. But this particular day, he was having lunch with one of the senior officers of the Southampton police force, who, knowing of Richard's association with the place, mentioned it.

He was shocked. 'What do you mean, someone tried to burn it down?'

The officer then told him the details and mentioned the young lady who had been implicated, although he didn't know her name.

'Yes, I treated her.'

'You what?'

'I treated her. She was in a sorry state.'

'And you didn't report this?'

Richard looked at the angry man sitting opposite him. 'It's no good you losing your rag,' he said. 'The girl refused to see the police and without her, you didn't have a case, and my patient's wishes had to be respected.'

'But look what might have happened, because of that.'

'Everything you say is true, but what choice did I have?'

His companion continued to complain until Richard was forced to say, 'I am like a priest; you know that. Whatever my patient says to me is confidential. Without her permission I can do absolutely nothing. I trust everyone there is fine after their ordeal? How is Miss Ferguson?'

'Angry! She sent my sergeant on his way with a flea in his ear.'

With a broad grin Richard said, 'That sounds like Flora.'

After the luncheon was over, Richard drove straight to Harwood House. As Flora opened the door to him he stepped inside and asked, 'Are you all right? I only heard today what happened.'

At the anguished look in his eyes, Flora felt her colour rise in her cheeks. This man really cared, and although she felt the intensity of his concern was more than was proper for a married man, she was glad of it.

'We're all fine,' she assured him.

He took her hand in his and said, 'Oh, Flora, if this man had succeeded, the consequences are unthinkable.' He gazed intently into her eyes.

She gently released his hold. 'That's not the way to think at all, Richard. Just think how fortunate we were that he was discovered in time. But it's kind of you to be so solicitous. Would you like a cup of tea?'

He shook his head. 'No, I've just finished lunch. I wanted to see that you were all right, that's all.' He walked to the door. 'The children all right? No one needs me?'

She smiled softly. He really was a dear man. 'No, honestly.'

Somewhat reluctantly, he made his way to his vehicle, struggling to keep his feelings and concerns in a proper perspective.

* * *

Whilst the doctor was wrestling with his problem, Frank McAvoy was solving another. That evening, he and his men called in at the Mariners' Club and sat at the bar. The barman, with great trepidation, walked towards them. If McAvoy was here it was for no good reason. The man's reputation in the underworld of the docks was fearsome enough to make those around him who were not a part of his organisation extremely nervous.

'Large Scotch,' the villain demanded, 'and none of that crap you keep in the optics for your clients. Give me the real stuff. The one you keep under the counter!'

'Yes, sir.'

Frank took a sip and asked, 'Where is that little runt?'

'If you mean Mr la Salles, he's in the office, sir. Shall I go and tell him you're here?'

'You bloody well stay where you are.' He downed the drink and, nodding to one of his men, he walked out of the bar into the corridor that led to the office, and kicked the door open.

'Now, you little shit,' he said to Jack, who cowered in his chair when he recognised his visitor.

'What do you want?' he asked in a voice that had risen to a screech with fright.

Frank slowly took a cigarette out of a packet in his pocket and sneered at him. Then, to his own man, he said disparagingly, 'Just look at him now. This quivering wreck is a twisted piece of so-called humanity. He beats and rapes young girls, he sends his man to set fire to a children's home. I don't suppose he has had one good thought in his head from the day he was born. What do you think we should do about him?'

His companion grinned. 'If he likes fire so much, guv,

perhaps we should roast him.'

La Salles let out a squeak of terror.

Taking out a cigarette lighter, the villain flicked it open and lit it, glaring at Jack as he did so, watching with pleasure as his victim shook from head to foot. 'No. The smell of him burning would pollute the air.' McAvoy looked down at the brothel-keeper and said, 'I am only going to tell you once, you little squirt, that if I hear even a *whisper* of a rumour that you are going to interfere with anyone or anything to do with that children's home, I'll burn you alive, just like those poor little tykes would have been burned if you had had your way. Do I make myself clear?'

Jack nodded.

'I can't hear you!' snapped McAvoy. 'Speak up!'

'Yes, yes!' came the loud reply.

Catching hold of the edge of the desk in the office, the visitor tipped it over, sending pens and papers flying, then walked out. When he reached the bar he said to the barman, 'Give me that bottle under the counter. Your boss will pay.' Snatching it, he walked out of the club.

Once he realised that the town's biggest villain had left his premises, Jack quickly regained his courage and stormed out to the bar. 'I'll pay that bastard back!' he screamed. 'Who does he think he is, coming in here and threatening me like that? Well, I certainly won't let this pass, I can tell you!'

But the barman and Jack's cohorts took little notice. It was a brave man who went up against McAvoy and none of them believed that their boss had the balls to do it. But Jack was a perverted creature, mentally as well as physically, and you could never be too sure just what he would do. It made for a very unsettling atmosphere in the underworld.

★ ★ ★

Lydia Goodwin lay back in her bath and smiled content-edly. Everything was going according to plan. She had tricked Richard back into her bed and soon it would be time to break the news of her pregnancy. She quickly dismissed the fact that when the child was born he might be suspicious that the baby was full term and not prema-ture. By then their relationship would once again be on solid ground and she foolishly felt she could persuade him that he was the father. She would of course be under the care of another doctor during the coming months, which would help her cover her deceit.

She climbed out of the bath and towelled herself dry. Standing in front of a long mirror, she studied her body from every angle. She was very careful how much she ate, as she didn't want to put on too much weight and give the game away. She ran her hand over the slight swelling of her stomach – and longed for Douglas Slater.

Despite his cruel dismissal of her, she still yearned for him – to feel his hands caress her, tease her, excite her; satisfy her, as only he could. Richard was a competent lover, but the thrill of the illicit was no longer there, and therefore the excitement was missing.

She felt, however, she had achieved a great deal. Her husband spent more time at home these days. He still sat on several committees, but his involvement with the new children's home seemed to have petered out, for which she was more than a little relieved. She thought that Flora, that Scotswoman, was far too attractive, and she was also very aware that Flora and Richard had so much in common. Lydia had not forgotten the night that Flora and Patrick had dined with them. Richard couldn't keep his eyes off the woman, and she had wondered from time to time since, if there was anything between them. Not that she really cared then, as she was so enamoured of her lover, but now she couldn't let anything or anyone come between her and her husband. Oh no. She needed a father for her baby.

Richard was the last person on Flora's mind at the moment. Tomorrow was the business federation luncheon, and everyone at Harwood House was on tenterhooks. The children, as if sensing the tension in the air, were playing up, and the staff all had their hands full.

Flora had paid a visit to the local police station that morning to see if there was anything forthcoming about the enquiries into the alderman.

'We have nothing for you at the moment,' Detective Inspector Blake, leading the investigation, told her, after he had taken her through to an interview room where they could talk in private.

'Haven't you asked him what he was doing there?' she demanded.

'It's not as simple as that,' he explained. 'We are quietly looking into his financial affairs to see if there is any evidence there first. We don't want to alert him at this stage, because if he has anything to hide he could cover his tracks.'

Flora could see the sense behind this, but she was frustrated beyond measure. 'He has threatened me with closure,' she said. 'I was hoping you would be my saviour.'

Inspector Blake looked at her sympathetically. 'I am really sorry, Miss Ferguson, but we may only have one bite of this cherry, so we must be thorough. We owe it to those poor children.'

She rose from her chair 'Thank you for your time,' she said.

'Please don't worry, miss. We'll get to the bottom of this mystery eventually. You have my word.'

And with that she had to be content. But it wasn't going to save her if Chivers carried out his threat on the morrow. She realised that having Jessie, with her colourful past, now working for her was going to be a very difficult situation if Chivers did tell the federation, but she hoped that if he had been discredited, it might balance the scales in her favour.

And George Chivers had no intention of losing the opportunity. He was strutting about his office at this precise moment, practising just what he was going to say to the assembled businessmen. He was going to enjoy every moment.

The following day, George presented himself at the luncheon, bought several drinks at the bar, and was effusive in his praise of the men he held in conversation. He sipped his drink and thought: there is no hurry.

The meal was good and the conversation interesting and controversial, as always. George waited until the port was passed around the table before saying loudly, 'Gentlemen, I have something of the utmost importance to tell you.' A hush descended on the gathering as they all waited with anticipation.

Chapter Twenty-Six

It was three days after the business federation luncheon that Flora had any indication of what had taken place. Three gut-wrenching days in which she found it hard to concentrate on her work. She didn't have long to wait. The morning post brought forth just the kind of news she had been dreading. She opened one envelope after another. They contained similar letters, all saying the same thing. Her eyes blurred with tears of frustration as she read one of them.

It has come to our notice that you have in your employ a woman of questionable character. As we have to protect the good name of our business and all who are associated with it, it means, unfortunately, that this precludes our being able to support you financially in the running of Harwood House, and therefore we have to withdraw our offer.

Flora banged her fist on her desk in temper. How could George Chivers bring himself to do this to the children? Well, she wouldn't let it rest there.

Putting on her coat, she marched into the playroom and said to Rose, 'I have to go out.'

Seeing the expression on Flora's face, Rose asked, 'The chairman of the business federation?'

'Exactly! The letters are on my desk if you want to see them. The alderman has done as he threatened, so I'm off to plead our case.'

Rose put her arms round her employer and gave her a big hug, saying quietly, 'Good luck.'

'I'm going to need more than that,' Flora muttered angrily as she walked along the corridor towards the front door.

She entered the office of the federation and demanded to speak to the chairman. His secretary informed her that his morning was fully booked, but she would be happy to make an appointment for her.

Flora froze her with a look. 'Tell him Miss Flora Ferguson is here,' she said as she walked over to a chair and sat down, glaring defiantly at the woman behind her desk. 'I'll wait here until he sees me,' she declared.

Observing the determined set of Flora's mouth, the secretary rose from her seat, tapped on the office door and entered, reappearing a few minutes later. 'The chairman can spare you five minutes after his present appointment,' she said frostily.

Flora waited for what seemed an age, her anger growing by the minute. She fought hard to control her indignation, knowing that what she had to say was vital to the children in her care, and this would be her only chance to appeal to the better nature of the business world.

When eventually she was ushered into the inner sanctum, she was calm, although the brightness of her eyes betrayed her anger. She removed a glove and held out her hand towards the chairman. 'Good morning, it was nice of you to see me at such short notice, but as you are aware, the reason I'm here is of the utmost importance – to me and the children in my care, anyway.'

The man was not unsympathetic. He had no liking for the alderman, but he was also a businessman. 'I'm listening,' he said.

'You saw for yourself on our fund-raising day the conditions in which the children live and, indeed, if my memory serves me well, you were full of praise for Harwood House.'

'Indeed I was.'

'I am truly blessed with my staff, and the assistant in question was on duty that day. She was in the children's playroom – a lady with red hair.' She could tell from the man's expression that he remembered Jessie.

'It is quite true that before she came to me, she earned her living as a whore.'

James Newman looked startled at Flora's outspoken approach.

'Why mince words?' she said. 'But this young woman has a very special way with children. First, and this is critical, she loves and understands them, but secondly, she has a natural gift in handling them. The children learn from her, they are loved by her, but above all, they trust and love her in return, and that, sir, as you are shrewd enough to know, has to be earned, as children can spot a fake a mile away.'

He smiled. 'This is true.'

'It is obvious that the bad reputation of this young lady is the one that Alderman Chivers has put before you, but the girl was earning an honest living on the streets and that is not something that everyone in business can say!'

'I have to protest at that remark, Miss Ferguson.'

'Protest all you like; you know I speak the truth. But I ask you, would it be better for the children to have someone work for me to whom it was just a job and who didn't care about them at all, but whose credentials were impeccable?'

'That's a leading question.'

'It would make things more comfortable for the consciences of you gentlemen of industry, but it wouldn't be the best for my children, and it is they who are important here, not some overblown councillor who has had his nose put out of joint!'

There was a twinkle in the eyes of the chairman, but he said, 'Most of what you say is true, Miss Ferguson, and I have to tell you, the discussion about you and your home was very heated, but in the end it came down to the appearance of morality.' He shrugged his shoulders and said, 'This may sound superficial to you, but we have our reputation and our stockholders to consider. We must be seen as beyond reproach. I'm so very sorry.'

'And that is your final word?'

'That is my final word.'

Flora pulled on her glove, slowly and deliberately, giving herself time to cover her disappointment. She rose to her feet. 'I will not detain you a moment longer, Mr Newman,' she said, and walked towards the door. With her hand on the doorknob, she turned back and said, 'Of course, those who were arguing for us could always help us anonymously but then there would be no kudos for the companies, would there?' And with that, she left the office.

Walking back towards the docks, Flora racked her brains to try to think how she could raise some money. What did she have that she could sell that was worth anything? There was enough left of her legacy to keep the home open for about two months, if they were very careful, but after that . . .

When she arrived home, she went straight to her office and placed a call to her father. When he came on the line, they exchanged pleasantries and family news, then Flora said, 'Dad, will you do me a favour?'

'Yes, of course, dear. What is it?'

'Will you sell my horses for me?'

There was an exclamation of surprise from Mr Ferguson. 'Whatever for?'

Trying to keep her voice as natural as possible, she said, 'Well, goodness knows when I'm going to get home again. I think they should go to a stable where they will be ridden regularly, where someone will spend time with them.'

'Flora, my dear, are you sure this is what you want?'

'Yes, Dad, and as soon as possible, please. You can put the money from the sale into my bank account here. I'll give you the number. Do you have a pen handy?'

At the end of her conversation, she put the phone down with a feeling of relief. It broke her heart to have to do this, but she needed the money to buy her time to come up with another idea.

In his office in Glasgow, Alistair Ferguson put down the receiver and frowned with concern. What on earth had made Flora take the decision to sell her horses, which she adored? What was wrong way down there in Southampton? She always assured him that things were fine whenever he enquired, but obviously this wasn't so if she was desperate enough to make this sacrifice.

Flora gathered all the staff together in the kitchen and told them of her meeting. Jessie, of course, was desolate. 'I'll leave!' she said.

'You will not!' Flora insisted. 'George Chivers would only have dug up something else to ruin our chances. He is a spiteful, mean, egotistical misfit!'

With a broad grin Jessie said, 'I don't quite understand what some of that means, but I like the sound of it. But what happens now?'

'We have enough cash to keep us going for another two months, and I'm hoping for a little more to add to that, and then we'll have to keep our fingers crossed that the police come up with something that will discredit the alderman. Then I can go to the business federation and say, "You say you must be seen to be beyond moral reproach, yet you have this sort of person on your committee. Is this fair?" At the moment, that's all I can come up with.'

The following Sunday, after the church service, Father Patrick approached George Chivers, who had not been to confession lately, and said, 'I am greatly disappointed in you, George.'

But the councillor was not to be shamed. 'I would have thought you would have agreed with me about that whore working with children. It's immoral.'

'How can you say such a thing – a good Catholic like you? Don't you recall the teachings of the Bible? Have you forgotten how Christ forgave Mary Magdalene? Do you put yourself above our Lord?'

Chivers' face turned red with embarrassment and indignation. He turned on his heel and hurried away. Patrick pursed his lips. Damn! It looked as if he had made things worse.

Jessie, on the other hand, was grimly determined to get back at Chivers. She left Harwood House and stopped at the nearest public telephone. She put her pennies in the box and dialled the number of the *Southern Daily Echo*. She asked to speak to the reporter who had covered the open day, and when he came on the line, she chatted to him and arranged to meet him that evening at the Horse and Groom.

The reporter, when he arrived, bought them a couple of beers and they sat at a table. It was early in the evening and the pub was quiet. Ron Forbes looked around the bar and said, 'The last time I was in here was a year ago, to cover a story about a stabbing.'

'I remember that,' said Jessie. 'I was in the bar when it happened, but I soon scarpered before the Old Bill arrived.'

'So . . . Jessie, isn't it?'

She nodded. 'Yeah.'

'You said you had a story for me.'

'Yes, I do, but before I tell you anything, there are a few assurances I want from you. Understand?'

'Fire away.'

Jimmy James, the landlord, looked over at the table where Jessie sat, wondering just what she had to say to a reporter of the local rag. Whatever it was, the man seemed delighted and surprised. He was making plenty of notes, anyway. He must remember to read the paper every evening to find out what it was all about.

At the doctor's house in Bernard Street, Lydia Goodwin sat at the dining table, dressed in her most alluring finery, and smiled across at Richard. 'A good day, darling?'

'Reasonably quiet inasmuch as nothing untoward happened. The Barton baby seems to have recovered from the croup, thank heavens. And you?'

'I went along to see Dr Bailey this morning.'

Richard looked surprised. 'Whatever for?'

'Darling, I have some wonderful news. I'm pregnant!'

He almost choked on a mouthful of coffee. 'You what?'

'I'm pregnant, just over two months. It must have happened the first time when you came back to our room.' Nervously she asked, 'You are happy about it, aren't you, Richard?'

He quickly covered his surprise and rose from his chair. Hurrying round to Lydia, he put his arms about her. 'That's absolutely wonderful. Wonderful! Especially after we have tried for so long without success.'

Yes, well, she thought, that's because she had used a douche every time after having sex. She hadn't wanted to lose her figure with childbirth, but she hadn't told her husband this.

He looked at her affectionately and kissed her gently. Returning to his chair, he smiled at her. 'Now we must take good care of you. When is it due?'

'Next June,' she said. 'A summer baby.'

'Excellent. April and May are not too hot, so you won't be too uncomfortable during the final weeks.'

She gazed at him, and with an inviting smile she said, 'I asked the maid to put a bottle of champagne on ice. I thought we could take it upstairs after dinner and have our own little celebration.' She ran her fingers up and down the stem of her wine glass and dared her husband to refuse.

As they walked upstairs together she thought how very easy it was to manipulate men – most of the time, anyway. She had managed it with Doug up until she became pregnant, and now Richard would delight in telling his friends he was to be a father. He hadn't questioned it, and why would he? The difficult time would be when the child was born.

Dr Bailey wasn't fooled. After his examination he told

her she was nearly four months gone. She was quite blatant with the doctor. 'For all intents and purposes, I am only two months along. Please remember this, if my husband should ask.'

His eyes narrowed. 'You don't think your husband will be fooled, do you? Especially when the child is born? Good God, woman, he's a doctor!'

'That is not your concern, Dr Bailey, it is mine. All I require from you is to keep me well during my pregnancy and my confinement.'

'Very well, Mrs Goodwin. I just hope you know what you're doing!'

And she knew he was right. At the birth, she would have her work cut out, but she could be really convincing when she wanted to be, and she was a good actress.

That night Richard lay awake, stunned by Lydia's revelations. He wasn't sure why – after all, they had been living a full married life – and yet he *had* been surprised. He was pleased, of course he was, but deep inside he still had these feelings for Flora and sometimes his conflicting emotions would tear him part. Now, of course, he was totally committed. He and Lydia were bringing a child into the world, and maybe it was the best thing that could have happened. He would now have a reason to put his past feelings away for ever.

A sentiment that was shared by Patrick when his friend told him the good news. 'Wonderful!' said the priest, who had watched Richard and Flora working together, recognising their compatibility, and sensing there was a certain chemistry between them. He was concerned that with so much in common, their relationship could develop into something more. 'I'm so very happy for you both.' He placed his hand on Richard's shoulder and said, 'There, your life has worked out after all. Now you have the baby and its future to think of. There's nothing like a new life to focus the mind! I'm delighted for the pair of you.'

But when Richard had left to do his rounds, Patrick wondered just how Flora would feel on hearing the news.

Chapter Twenty-Seven

At the Southampton police station, two detectives were poring over George Chivers' bank statements, obtained under warrant.

'There is a large monthly payment here from Forest Holdings. What the devil is Forest Holdings?' asked Detective Inspector Blake.

'It's a property company,' replied his colleague. 'I have been through the town's companies' records. Among the directors is one George Chivers, the other is his wife.' He grinned across the table. 'You'll never guess which property in the dock area belongs to them.'

'Well?' said the detective inspector. 'Which one?'

'The Mariners' Club!'

Blake was astonished. 'La Salles' place?'

'The very same. There's a house in Bevios Street, *and* there is a property in Netley also.'

'Now we're getting somewhere,' Blake said with great satisfaction. He rose from his chair. 'Come along,' he said. 'Let's go and take a look.'

'Should we get a search warrant, guv?'

Blake thought for a moment, then said, 'No. Let's go and see if they are interested in taking a couple of children into care. My brother's, for instance, the one whose wife has just died.'

The other man grinned broadly. 'Yes, I like that idea,' he said.

The two policemen arrived at the house in Netley and stood across the road, looking at the building. Outside, the front garden was neat and the curtains at the window were clean.

Blake said, 'It looks very presentable, doesn't it? You would never know what was going on inside. Come on.'

They crossed the road and knocked on the front door. Blake said, 'I'll do the talking.'

It was the woman of the house who opened the door. 'Good morning,' she said, looking at them somewhat suspiciously. 'If you're selling anything, we don't want it.'

'Good morning, madam,' said Blake. 'We aren't selling anything, I can assure you. We're here because I'm hoping you can help me.'

A watchful expression crossed her countenance. 'In what way?'

Blake looked crestfallen. 'You see my brother's wife has just died and he has two children aged two and four. Poor man just can't cope, I'm afraid, and a friend of mine on the council recommended that I come and talk to you.' He waited expectantly.

Her expression changed and she smiled. 'I see. You had better come in. Follow me.'

She took them into the same front room as described by Bella. 'Please sit down.' She waited until they settled and, perched on a high chair herself, she said, 'We do take children on a private basis, from people who have been recommended. Unfortunately the few children's homes that are provided by the council are mostly full all the time, so we try and help out these poor unfortunate children who belong to those who can pay.'

Blake felt his anger rising as he looked into the features of this woman with her chubby face and florid complexion. But he noticed the mean line of her mouth as he said, 'I don't know how long they would need to be in your care. It's just until he can make other arrangements. He has to work, you see, and the difficulty is finding someone to look after the two little ones.'

'I fully understand.'

'Perhaps we could look over your place.' This didn't please the woman at all, but he persisted. 'After all, I need to see where they would eat and sleep so I can pass on the information to my brother; reassure him that this is a good place for his children to be; maybe look at the other children. I suppose you do have others?'

'We have four at the moment.' Then somewhat reluctantly she said, 'Come with me.'

The woman took them upstairs to a room that contained two beds, and where the four children were sitting on the floor with a few sheets of paper and pencils.

'They don't have any toys,' Blake said.

'Indeed they do,' she snapped, 'but my husband has taken them away to give them a wash. You know how dirty they can get when they are in constant use.'

One of the children came over to them and stood looking at them out of curiosity. Her towelling nappy was obviously wet and it smelled. Blake saw the flash of anger in the woman's eyes but she quickly picked up the child and said, 'I'll just have to go and change her.'

The two men could hear the woman scolding the child who, when they returned, was crying loudly. 'She's teething,' they were told.

They were quickly taken back downstairs to the front

room. 'When do you want to bring the two children?' she asked.

'I'll have a word with my brother and I'll let you know. How much do you charge?' Blake asked.

'Twelve and six each child per week,' she said. 'That includes all meals as well as a bed and care.'

He rose from his seat and said, 'Thank you, Mrs . . .?'

'Johnson. Agnes Johnson. My husband, Norman, helps me, but he's down at the shops right now, buying some sweeties for the children.'

I doubt that very much, thought Blake. 'Thank you for your time,' he said. 'You'll be seeing me again very soon.' Once outside he turned to his colleague and said, 'Did you see the state of the floor in the room where the children were? It was badly stained, and by the smell, it is probably urine and worse. Now I believe every word that little Bella told the officers who spoke to her. And there were only two beds in that room. I wonder if all four have to share, sleeping head to toe perhaps. It wouldn't surprise me. Chivers should be horsewhipped, along with that couple.'

'But he hasn't broken the law, guv. He owns the property. But he could deny all knowledge of what goes on there.'

'True,' said Blake, 'but if we had those two in on charges of cruelty, they would sing like a couple of canaries and implicate him.'

'Do you think so?'

'I'd bet money on it!' said Blake angrily. 'Come on, let's get back to the station.'

Unaware that the police were slowly closing in on Alderman Chivers, Flora was still battling with figures, working out a tight budget to keep the home open as long as possible. In the morning post there had been a couple of cheques: one personal one for fifty pounds from the chairman of the business federation, and another from one of the directors of a company who had promised to help, but had withdrawn their offer. In all she had accumulated seventy-five pounds. She smiled softly, thankful that there was still some spirit of human kindness around. This and whatever money she received from her father from the sale of her horses would keep her going for a while if she were very careful. But oh, what a battle, she thought as she sat at her desk.

At that moment there was a knock on the open door and Father Patrick walked in. 'How are things going, Flora?' he asked.

She told him about the money she had received.

'Well, and isn't that grand!' he said. 'You must never lose your faith in people.'

'Things could be worse,' she admitted. 'My father is selling my two horses and that will be a big help. After all, I'm not at home to ride them, am I?'

Knowing her love for these animals, he knew this was a sacrifice on her part. 'Any news about Chivers?'

She shook her head. 'Not as far as I know. Still, the children all seem to be fit at the moment, thank God! I haven't had to call Richard in lately so we have a lot to be grateful for.'

It was then that Patrick told her the latest news. 'You wouldn't have heard then. Lydia is pregnant.'

The smile on Flora's lips froze for just a second and then she said, 'That's wonderful news. I'm really happy – for both of them.'

But Patrick could see behind the smile, and was sorry he'd mentioned it. He rose from his seat and said, 'I've bought some books for the children. I'll just take them into the playroom and give them to Rose.'

Once there, he took Rose to one side and said, 'Keep an eye on Flora. She has so much on her mind at the moment.'

'I will,' said Rose. 'Nothing seems to go right for her just now. But don't worry, Father, we all look after each other here.'

He patted her arm. 'I know you do. That's why I mentioned it.'

Alone in her office, Flora stood looking out of the window, watching the trains trundle through the dock gates. She saw the policeman on duty salute the mayor, who passed by in his car, his flag flying on the bonnet. And she watched a barrow boy push his cart, now empty, back to wherever he kept his stock.

Her heart was heavy. She supposed she should be pleased that Richard was to become a father. Despite all her efforts to control her feelings, she at last admitted to herself that she was in love with the doctor and this she couldn't deny. At the same time she was racked with guilt that she could love another after her wonderful Flynn. And to feel this way about one who was married was even worse.

Meanwhile, at his house outside Glasgow, Alistair Ferguson was in earnest conversation with Mavis. They were walking around the garden together. 'How are you feeling now?' he asked. 'Cook tells me that you are much better and that you would like to stay here and work in the house. Is that correct?'

Mavis looked so different from the poor pale creature she had been when she first arrived. Her cheeks had a healthy bloom and her nerves, which had seemed to be at breaking point not that long ago, had settled down with her removal from the docklands. 'Yes, sir, I really would.' She looked around her. 'It is so beautiful here. So peaceful, I never knew there were such beautiful places as Scotland and the country – this house and garden. It's like living in a different world, a world that is peaceful and safe. I would very much like to stay and work for you. I don't ever want to go back to Southampton.' She looked at him with uncertainty.

'Well, my dear, if that is what you want, I know Cook could do with another pair of hands, and Mrs Ferguson is willing to take you on.'

She beamed at him. 'Oh, thank you, sir. You won't never regret it, I promise.'

'I'm sure I won't, but I do want you to do me a favour, Mavis.'

'Yes, sir, what can I do for you?'

He stopped by a garden bench and indicated to her to take a seat. When they were comfortable he turned to her and said, 'I want you to tell me the truth about Flora and Harwood House.'

She looked suddenly wary and said, 'I don't know what you mean.'

'I think you do. Flora assures me that all is well there, but I have a feeling that that is far from the truth. Flora is my daughter and I'm worried about her.'

Mavis looked uncomfortable as he stared at her. 'But I promised,' she said.

'Please, Mavis. Unless I know what's going on, I won't know what to do to help.'

She shuffled her feet whilst she made her decision and then she looked at Alistair and said, 'Well, it's like this . . .'

She bravely told him about Jessie saving her from the clutches of Jack la Salles, about the measles epidemic and about the open house. 'You see, Miss Flora needs money to keep the home open, but one of the men on the council is making trouble for her and all the businessmen who were going to put money in have pulled out. I know because I had a letter from Jessie.'

'I see,' said Alistair slowly. That would explain why Flora wanted to sell her horses. 'Thank you for being honest with me, and I'm so sorry that you had such a dreadful experience with that awful man.'

'You do realise, Mr Ferguson, that I was on the game when all this happened? If you don't want me to work for you now, you know, I'll understand.'

He smiled benignly at her. 'You have been very honest with me, Mavis. You need not have told me this, and I can assure you that it makes no difference at all, but if I were you, I would keep that bit of information between us. All right?'

'Yes, sir. You are a gent, Mr Ferguson, and I won't forget that.'

He rose from the bench and said, 'You go and tell Cook you can start work whenever she likes.' He watched as Mavis hurried away and shook his head, thinking how life dealt some very difficult hands to some poor souls, but his brow furrowed as he considered the plight of his daughter. This needed some considerable thought before he made any decisions. Flora had been through so much: her time in France; the loss of the man she loved; and it sounded to him as if she was still on a field of battle, albeit of a different kind.

Jessie had taken herself off to one of the silent movie

houses. She had suggested to Flora that she might like to come as well and have a laugh, as ever since Father Patrick had called that morning, Flora had seemed down in the dumps, but she had declined. Now the film was over, Jessie thought she'd like to catch up with the gossip from her old friends and so she walked along to the Horse and Groom.

Here the women whose life on the streets she had shared greeted her warmly. 'So how does it feel to be an honest working woman?' one asked.

'Excuse me,' retorted Jessie, 'whoring is an honest job!'

'Quite right,' agreed another.

'Seen any more of that lovely doctor lately?'

Jessie shook her head. 'No, not since all the kids recovered from the measles. But I overheard today that his wife is pregnant, so he's a virile bloke, anyway,' Jessie said with a grin.

'Is he sure it's his? Only I heard Mrs Goodwin was having it off with that Doug Slater. You know, that horny little bastard whose father has pots of money – the builder.'

Jessie was intrigued. 'Tell me all about it,' she urged.

It seemed that it was common knowledge among the upper set of the town that Lydia Goodwin had been having an affair and that Doug Slater had dumped her.

'Someone I know works as a maid at their house,' said one of her mates, 'and she sometimes used to take messages from "Lady Lydia", who thinks she's better than most. I don't suppose the lovely doctor knows.'

'No, I'm sure he doesn't,' murmured Jessie, thinking it was a pity that he didn't. Looking around the bar she asked, 'Has Jack la Salles been in lately?'

'No, he don't come in here often these days, not now that Frank McAvoy seems to have made this his local.'

'Frank? In here? This was never his stamping ground.'

'I know,' said one of the women, 'and another strange thing: there have been a couple of Chinese blokes hanging around too.'

'Chinese?' asked Jessie. 'What the devil do they want around here?' But no one seemed to know.

As she walked back to Harwood House, Jessie pondered over the supposed affair of the doctor's wife. What if it were true? That really would be a turn-up for the books. She wouldn't mention it to Flora, but she would tell the others.

Chapter Twenty-Eight

The following morning over breakfast, Jessie passed on the gossip about Lydia to Rose and Madge. The cook looked down her nose and said, 'I never did like the sound of that woman. You 'aven't told Flora, 'ave you?'

'No, of course not,' said Jessie. 'What good would it do?'

'None at all,' said Rose. 'It makes me so angry. Flora and the doctor are so right for each other, and if this is true, it doesn't seem fair.'

Whilst all this speculation was going on, Flora was in the playroom with the children, helping them to paint pictures. She watched them all, wearing old shirts to cover and protect their clothes. Mattie, now at last putting some flesh on her bones, was concentrating hard on her picture, her tongue protruding from the corner of her mouth.

'What are you painting?' asked Flora.

'A picture of my mummy. She's in hospital, and that man there,' she pointed to a large blob on legs, 'is Dr Richard. He made me better. Perhaps he can make my mummy better.'

The innocence of the remark pained Flora. It was obvious that the small child didn't realise that her mother was dead, and Flora thought there was nothing to be gained by trying to explain once more. When she was older and was able to understand would be the time.

Moving on, Flora asked Mathew what his picture was about. 'A train in the docks,' he said proudly. 'I wants to ride on a train.'

'And one day you will,' she told him. She looked at Sylvia's splashes of colour, but didn't ask what it was, as the child was so involved with adding even more shades of paint. Her twin, Robert, was laid out on the floor, pushing a wooden horse and cart around. As she watched the twins and Mathew, Flora wondered if they would ever discover their parentage. Until the mystery of the house in Netley was solved, no one would ever know. Her other charges, who were playing on the floor with building bricks, all had their backgrounds securely on record.

She thought about Richard's child and wondered if it would be a boy or a girl – but whatever the sex, the baby would be secure, with a home and family, whereas these poor mites had only her and Harwood House. She prayed that she would be able to solve her financial problems somehow, even if she had to get a job to bring in some money, leaving Rose in charge during the day, because if she had to close she couldn't bear to think of the consequences.

Rose and Jessie arrived with the children's milk and biscuits, and Flora left them to manage, whilst she went into the kitchen and discussed the food shopping with Madge.

'We just need some vegetables from the market. I bought a scrag end of meat from the butcher yesterday, so I can make a good stew for tomorrow,' she said, 'and today we've got fish pie.'

Flora marvelled at the ability of Madge to make a feast

out of so little. The budget had been severely cut, but the cheery cook still turned out really tasty meals.

'I'll walk down to Kingsland Square then. Have you made out a list?'

Madge had done so. Taking a basket, Flora set off.

She hadn't gone very far when she saw Richard's car parked outside one of the houses. Her steps faltered for a moment and then she began to hurry, hoping she wouldn't meet him. But fate was cruel, and just as she was passing the house, the doctor emerged.

'Flora!'

She had to stop; she had no choice. 'Richard. How are you?' Her heart missed a beat as she saw in his eyes the look of affection that she recognised so well. 'Congratulations,' she said quickly. 'Patrick told me about the baby.'

'Thank you,' he said.

'You must both be thrilled.'

'Yes, of course,' he said. There was something in her voice, an expression in the eyes as he looked at her. He stepped forward. 'Flora . . .'

'I must be off,' she said quickly, 'or Madge will think I'm lost. Give my best wishes to your wife.' And without waiting for a reply, she hurried away.

The unexpected sight of the man she now loved was playing havoc with Flora's emotions as she made her way to the market. Oh, why did Flynn have to die? If he was still alive, they would be in Ireland now, and she would never have met Richard – or Jack la Salles – or the wretched George Chivers! Why was life so beset with problems? She wanted to scream out loud and give vent to her frustrations.

Richard watched her, wanting to run after her, take her

in his arms, comfort her, but he knew she wouldn't welcome it. He felt guilty at seeing the strained look on her face. He realised that this wasn't all down to him, but he also knew their meeting hadn't helped. With a feeling of despondency he threw his bag into the car and cranked the starting handle until the engine purred into submission.

If she didn't have the other worries, Flora told herself, she could have coped with Richard's situation. After all, wasn't she a fighter? A survivor? Then why the hell didn't she feel like one? It was all because of that bloody man Chivers.

Anger always gave Flora strength, and she started racking her brains as to how she could make the business federation change its mind in her favour. There had to be a way. The decision hadn't been unanimous – the very fact that she had received two cheques proved that. She just had to have a strong plan of action – something that would sway the others.

Oblivious and unconcerned about the mayhem he was causing, George Chivers put the key into the door of the small house in Bevios Street that evening and stepped into the front room. Daisy was waiting for him, wearing a broad smile and very little else. His eyes feasted on the swell of her breasts plumped up by the black corset, her tapering waist, and legs encased in black stockings kept up by red lacy garters.

'Hello, George, darlin'. I've been waiting for this moment all day long.' She held out her arms to him. 'Come here,' she said in a husky voice.

He was almost salivating with desire as he went towards her and picked her up. She wound her slender legs around his waist and kissed him, her tongue slipping into his mouth.

His hands were round her plump bottom, kneading the soft flesh as he returned her kisses. Daisy never ever wore drawers when she was with him, the very thought of which drove him wild. He put her down and divested himself of his clothes with unseemly haste, but she just watched him and chuckled.

She lay on the rug in front of the fire and stroked her breasts, spreading her legs, showing George exactly what was on offer. 'Come on, George. I know you can't wait to fuck me!'

The language of the gutter always turned him on and he threw his trousers over a chair, removed his underpants, and stroked his erection. 'Are you ready for this then, my little cherub?'

'Yes, yes, hurry up, I can hardly wait,' she lied.

Whilst George was thrusting himself into her body, Daisy looked up at the ceiling with boredom. For God's sake, hurry up, you stupid old bastard. My back is killing me and I'm desperate for a cup of tea, she thought.

Once he had spilled his seed and was content, Daisy stroked his chest, ran her fingers over his paunch and slipped her hand around his now flaccid manhood. 'You are wonderful, darlin'. There ain't a man in Southampton who can fuck like you.'

He pulled her closer and kissed her, his mouth moist with spent passion.

Whilst George Chivers was being serviced by Daisy, outside, across the road, waiting in a shop doorway, was Ron Forbes, the reporter from the *Southern Daily Echo*. He looked at his watch by the light from a match and smiled to himself. That Jessie had put him on to a good story all right, and he had enough on the alderman to make a great headline: 'Alderman Found in Love Nest.' A mate of his who worked at one of the banks had told him on the quiet that the police had taken away copies of Chivers' bank statements. Ron had quickly got in touch with a copper he knew, who had tipped him the wink that a story about the councillor might break soon and he would give him the nod when he knew any more. And so Ron Forbes was biding his time, collecting information in readiness for what he hoped would be a great scoop.

He already had the full facts of the businessmen pulling out from their agreement over the sponsorship of Harwood House because of this old bastard, and he was just waiting to tighten the rope around the man's neck and kick the chair away from beneath him.

When Richard arrived home that evening it was to find Lydia in a filthy temper. Whatever he said or did was wrong.

'What *is* the matter with you?' he demanded eventually, when she had bitten his head off for the umpteenth time.

'I'm sick of this baby! I'm losing my figure, I don't feel well, and my clothes won't fit!'

'What do you mean, you don't feel well?' Richard asked, immediately concerned. 'Perhaps you had better come into the surgery and let me examine you.'

'Oh, for goodness' sake, will you stop fussing!'

'Fussing? I'm not fussing. You say you are not well, and you are pregnant with our child – of course I'm anxious about you.'

The last thing Lydia wanted was her husband to examine her. He would be likely to discover that she had lied about the baby's expected arrival. 'I'm all right,' she insisted. 'I'm just a bit tired, that's all. Let's have dinner. I'll probably feel better after I've eaten.'

As they sat quietly, Lydia glanced across at Richard, but he was busy filleting his fish. What had really upset her was her unexpected meeting in town that day with Doug Slater. She had been walking up the High Street when he came out of the Star Hotel. He greeted her warmly.

'Lydia! How wonderful you're looking. They always say a pregnant woman blooms, and you look quite radiant.' He gave a lascivious grin and said, 'I have a great urge to take you to bed and ravish you. I have a spare couple of hours – what do you say?'

'You want my body, but you don't want your baby!'

'Darling, don't be a bore; there's a good girl. What we had between us was purely carnal, you know that. It wasn't your mind I was interested in.'

'You absolute bastard!' She spat the words at him, but he just laughed.

'I have never denied that. How's Richard? No doubt proud to be a father-in-waiting. Give him my best regards.'

And before she could reply, he walked away.

The meeting had upset Lydia on many levels. She was angry that Doug had no interest in his unborn child, furious that he could so easily expect her to fall into his arms, and livid with herself, because she had wanted to. He still managed to get beneath her skin and she still desired him. It was only her anger and her pride this morning that had saved her from making a fool of herself – again. What she really longed for was Doug Slater to come banging on her front door, confronting Richard, saying, 'The child Lydia is carrying is mine, not yours, and I am taking her away with me.' But this was never going to happen and that stirred her anger even more, and Richard had borne the brunt of it.

She looked speculatively at him and wondered just what he would say if he knew the truth. Would he throw her out of the house, or would he stand by her and bring the child up as his own? But these were mind games she was playing and all they did was unsettle her.

'Are you feeling better?' Richard asked as the maid cleared away the dirty plates.

She forced a smile and said, 'Yes, I am, thank you.' But already she was asking herself, could she bear to have Richard continue to believe he was the father of this child? She wanted to shout it to the world that it was Doug Slater who was the real father. How could she live with this lie? Spend years watching Richard bring up what he thought was his, maybe meet Doug as the child grew? Keep this secret? She wasn't at all sure if she could – or if she wanted to.

She rose from her chair. 'I have a slight headache,' she told her husband. 'I'll just lie on top of my bed.'

Once he was alone, Richard poured himself a glass of port and dismissed the maid. All he could think of was Flora. Ever since they had bumped into each other, she had haunted his thoughts and he had had difficulty that day concentrating on anything else.

He felt an absolute cad. Here was his wife, mildly stressed about having his child, and he was thinking of another woman. But not *just* another woman – Flora Ferguson could never be that. He wanted to help her in any way he could. Patrick had told him she was still in financial difficulties, which he sadly couldn't solve, and he saw today what an effect this concern was having on her. But he was at a loss to know what to do, so it was best that he kept his distance, unless his calls at the house were of a professional nature. He pushed the glass away, got up from the table, put on his coat, and went for a walk along the waterfront to try to clear his head of these disturbing thoughts.

Chapter Twenty-Nine

Jack la Salles returned to the Mariners' Club one evening after spending a couple of days with a friend who ran a nightclub in Portsmouth. He had felt the need of a break and had enjoyed the change, especially when his friend, who was aware of his particular penchant, supplied a young girl for his private entertainment.

He was checking with his top man that all had been well during his absence when he suddenly noticed that one of his regular prostitutes was wearing a cheongsam. He strode over to her and demanded to know where she got it.

'I've got a new punter,' she explained. 'He took a shine to me and when he came back the second time, he gave me this. He's Chinese,' she said, 'a really nice man.'

Jack felt his blood run cold. 'Where's he from?' he asked.

'Hong Kong.'

'Not London?'

'I don't think so. He said he'd docked here a few nights ago, after catching a ship from Amsterdam. As far as I know he's been here ever since.'

But Jack was nervous. He questioned everyone in the club about the man. The barman told him, 'He seems all right, boss – quiet little fellow. No trouble.'

But Jack was filled with trepidation. After the débâcle

over the Chinese girl, any oriental made him uneasy, and when the man returned that night Jack watched him very carefully.

Lee Chin seemed harmless enough. He bought his chosen woman a few drinks and then they left the bar for a room upstairs. An hour later, he emerged, smiled at Jack and left the club.

But when Lee Chin stepped into the street, he was no longer smiling. He walked purposefully along the road, turned up a small alleyway and knocked on the door of a shabby-looking house. A fellow countryman of his opened the door, and Lee stepped inside, exchanging a few words in his native tongue.

The following day Detective Inspector Blake, accompanied by two uniformed constables, knocked on the door of the house in Netley. In his hand was a search warrant. When the door was opened by Mrs Johnson, he pushed his way past her and said, 'I have here a warrant to search your house. Is your husband about?'

At that moment Mr Johnson, a large portly man wearing a pair of trousers and a sweat-stained vest, emerged from what turned out to be the kitchen. 'What the bloody hell is going on?' he demanded.

Blake instructed one of the constables to keep the couple in the kitchen, and raced up the stairs, two at a time. He made for the bedroom where on his previous visit he had seen the children had been housed. He opened the door. The strong smell of urine caught the back of his throat. He looked around. 'Christ!' he exclaimed.

The children were tied to the legs of the bed on lengths of twine that allowed them limited movement. Their nappies were soiled and the floor where they sat was covered in excrement. He closed his eyes in disgust.

He went back to the kitchen and instructed the constable to take the Johnsons down to the station in the Black Maria, waiting outside. As the two began to complain he said, 'I am arresting you on a charge of child cruelty,' and he read them their rights. He opened the front door and beckoned to the occupants of a car, parked behind the Black Maria. Two women in nurses' uniforms stepped out.

'Upstairs, back bedroom,' he snapped. 'Clean the poor little perishers up before we take them away. Put them in the bath, if there is any hot water, and look around for clean clothes and nappies. There must be some somewhere.' He stepped outside and lit a cigarette, his jaw pulsating from the anger he was fighting to control.

Some time later, the two women emerged with the children, who were crying and looking confused.

'We'll take them to the station,' Blake said, 'give them some milk and a sandwich when we get there, because God knows when they were last fed. I'm going to interview Mr and Mrs Johnson.'

In an interview room, Blake and one of his colleagues sat opposite the wife. Blake took out a cigarette and lit it, then he looked contemptuously across the table. 'You should be horsewhipped and at this moment I wish it was me that was doing it!'

The woman started to make excuses.

'Shut up!'

The sudden shout from Blake silenced her. 'If I have my way you two are going to be sent down for a very long time. I saw those poor kids today, and,' he said firmly as Mrs Johnson tried to interrupt, 'we also have the four children who managed to escape your clutches a few months ago, safe and in care. Bella remembers you clearly.' He waited to let his words sink in.

'Now tell me, Mrs Johnson, as you seem to be the one with the most lip, where do you get these children and exactly what does Alderman Chivers have to do with anything?'

The look of surprise on her face made him smile. 'You didn't think you could get away with this for ever, surely? Now I advise you to tell me everything, or you'll only make things worse for yourself, and they are already pretty dire.'

He emerged from the interview room an hour later, leaving his colleague to take a statement from the prisoner, then he questioned the husband. After, he formally charged them. When this had been done, and the Johnsons locked up in separate cells, the two detectives left the station and drove to the office of Alderman Chivers.

'The alderman's secretary was very surprised when the two detectives entered the outer office and showed her their official badges, but she was severely shaken when they took her into the councillor's office and told her and her boss that they were to be taken to the station for questioning.

Chivers began to protest strongly but Blake was taking no nonsense from him and calmly said, 'You walk out of here with dignity, or in handcuffs. The choice is yours!'

As the small party walked down the steps of the council's office, Ron Forbes was waiting at the bottom with a photographer. He smiled broadly as Chivers put his hand up to cover his face. Forbes winked at the detective, and waited for the cameraman to put his equipment away, then they both hurried off to the offices of the local paper.

★ ★ ★

It was Rose who came rushing into the kitchen of Harwood House with the evening edition of the *Southern Daily Echo*. She put it down on the table and in a breathless voice said, 'Look at the headlines!'

'Alderman and Secretary Arrested,' it said. Rose ran out of the kitchen and returned, pulling Flora after her. 'Look! Look!' she said.

Flora picked up the paper. There was Chivers, hand up, trying to blot out the camera. Beside him a very fraught-looking woman. The article just said that Alderman George Chivers and his secretary had been taken to the local police station that morning and were being held for questioning.

'I was out with Peter and I couldn't believe my eyes when I saw the headlines. What do you think it means?' Rose asked.

Flora's eyes glittered as she said, 'I would think that at last the police have come up with a few answers. I wonder just what the business federation think of their member now. This would seem a very good time to go and find out, don't you think?'

But the others tried to curb her enthusiasm. 'Why don't you wait a couple of days?' suggested Rose. 'There is bound to be more information then. They may let him go, but if, on the other hand, he is charged with something, you can at least appeal to their consciences. They won't want to appear hypocrites, even if they knew nothing of the alderman's activities.'

And Flora had to agree that this was good advice, but she was like a scalded cat, waiting for developments, and when Patrick dropped in the following morning she asked if he knew anything about the alderman.

'Only as much as you, my dear Flora. I was shocked

when I read the paper. I can't imagine what is going on.'

But Chivers knew. He refused to answer any questions until his solicitor was present. And then all he would say was, 'No comment,' which infuriated Blake.

'Either charge my client or let him go,' insisted the solicitor.

'I don't think so yet,' said Blake. 'Take Alderman Chivers back to his cell,' he instructed the officer standing by the door of the interview room. 'Perhaps the gentleman would like a little time to reflect on his lack of co-operation.'

'You can't do that!' exclaimed the solicitor.

'Indeed I can. I don't have to let him go just yet.'

Chivers looked at his solicitor for confirmation, but the man just shrugged his shoulders in helplessness, and George had no choice but to be led to the cells.

'That old bastard isn't going to give anything away,' stormed Blake. 'But that's fine. He can stew in his cell for a while and I'll charge him later. I've more than enough evidence to hold him.'

Meanwhile, Ron Forbes was interviewing Daisy at the house in Bevios Street. 'So this is where you used to meet the alderman, is it?'

Daisy grinned broadly. 'Yeah, that's right. He used to come here as often as he could. Randy old bugger, he was,' she confided.

Ron smiled and continued to write on his reporter's pad. 'This place his, is it?'

'Yeah. He bought it so we'd have somewhere to meet. He couldn't risk going to a hotel, you see.'

'No, I suppose not. Did he pay you well?'

'Oh, he gave me a weekly allowance. He was quite generous. Now the stupid bugger's got himself in trouble, *I'm* out of pocket! I got used to that steady income. It isn't fair!'

'What did you spend the money on?'

'I used to buy saucy underwear with some of it – he liked that,' she told him. 'Are you really going to put my picture in the paper?' she asked excitedly.

'Yes, darling, I'm going to make you famous.'

She gave a squeal of delight. 'I've always wanted to be famous. What shall I wear?'

Ron couldn't believe his luck. 'How about one of those saucy outfits the alderman liked so much?'

Daisy rushed upstairs to change, as the photographer set up his camera.

When she came down wearing the black corset, he let out a whistle of approval. 'That's sensational,' he said. 'Stand over there, by the fireplace. When your punters see this picture,' he said, 'you'll be able to charge more!'

'Yes, I suppose so. Well, I'll need to since I won't be seeing no more of George!'

When he left the house, Ron slipped her a pound note. 'Thanks, darling. You did very well.'

'Thank you,' she said archly. 'You wouldn't like a little bit before you go? I've got the time. I'll give you special rates.'

He chucked her under the chin. 'I'll hate myself in the morning, but I've got to get back to the office. You take care now. What are you going to do about living in this place?'

'Well, I'm damned if I'm moving! George bought this place for me, and here's where I'm staying!'

'Quite right! After all, why should you be inconvenienced? If I was you, I wouldn't move out until I had to.'

Forbes walked down the street chuckling. 'Can't you just picture it?' he said to his photographer. 'When Mrs Chivers discovers her old man owns this house, she'll be down here like lightning to kick his whore out.'

'You are a wicked bugger!'

'Not at all,' laughed the reporter. 'Just think what a good story *that* would make!'

'You're all heart,' quipped the photographer as they both walked away laughing.

The headlines in the paper the following day were even more lurid. Above a picture of Daisy in her underwear it said: 'Alderman's Love Nest Discovered'.

Flora read the article and started to chuckle. So Chivers had got his comeuppance after all, and that gave her a great deal of satisfaction. She picked up the telephone, dialled the number of the office of the chairman of the business federation, and asked for an appointment.

'I'm sorry, madam, but the chairman is fully booked today.'

'And what about tomorrow?'

'Tomorrow, the morning is full and then he's going to a federation lunch and won't be returning to the office.'

'I see. Can you tell me where the luncheon is being held?'

'At the Dolphin Hotel,' she was told.

'Thank you,' said Flora, and replaced the receiver. She was really desperate. If she could only persuade these businessmen to change their minds, then Harwood House had a chance. With the revelations about the alderman, maybe one or two may have weakened in their resolve.

At the business federation lunch the following day, the conversation was all about George Chivers. He was not a popular man and the remarks were ribald as more wine was consumed and the tongues became loosened.

'Mind you,' said one man, 'after seeing that picture of old George's doxy, I'm not surprised! She looked a right little goer. There would be no inhibitions there, I'll be bound!' There was laughter all round.

'Well, I have met his wife,' said another. 'A pillar of the Church and a good Catholic to boot, but rather staid, I would have said. Not much fun in the bedroom.'

'Gentlemen! Please, a little decorum,' begged the chairman.

'And to think he was so bloody self-righteous about the woman who worked at Harwood House. Hypocritical old sod. And there he was having it off himself with a prostitute. Really!'

At that moment the door to the private room opened and Flora walked in.

'Good afternoon, gentlemen,' she said to the stunned diners.

The chairman stood up. Flora noticed the twinkle in his eye as he looked at her and said, 'Miss Ferguson, this is a surprise. To what do we owe this visitation?'

Flora stood erect and proud. Gazing at each man in turn she said, 'I am drawn here today out of sheer desperation to make a final plea for your financial help for Harwood House.' She moved slowly round the table as she spoke. 'I now have in my care, twelve children. Children whom for the first time in their sad lives have clean clothes, food in their bellies and the loving care of my staff. Staff who are so anxious to keep the home open they are at the moment working without pay.'

There was a murmur among some of the men. 'This is the strength of their dedication. We also have the backing of Father Patrick Duggan, a respected member of the community and the free services, should we need them, of Doctor Richard Goodwin.'

From her large handbag, Flora produced a sheaf of papers and handed one to each of the men. 'You will see, gentlemen, I have prepared a list of figures showing the running costs of the home, and the amount we need monthly to keep going. You will agree I'm sure that there is not one shilling there that is unnecessary. We run a tight ship.'

She gave them a moment to digest the information before them, then added, 'Many of you have a family, and thank God, they are well cared for. All I ask is for you to spare a thought for the children in *my* care, who have nothing. At the moment I can give them security and the knowledge that someone is there to look after them and love them.' She sighed deeply. 'If I have to close, there is little guarantee they will ever have this again. Their future is in your hands. I plead with you to be generous in your consideration and forgive me for interrupting your meeting.' She walked with great dignity to the door, and left.

Chapter Thirty

During the walk back to Harwood House, Flora felt exhausted. Although her adrenaline had been flowing during the confrontation at the Dolphin Hotel, the episode had drained her mentally and physically, and she felt all in. This was her final shot at the businessmen and she knew if she failed to move them, she was still in deep trouble. She hadn't yet received any money from the sale of her horses, but she knew her father would be selective about the buyers, knowing just how much the animals meant to her, so she was still hanging on by the skin of her teeth. It was a great and pleasant surprise, therefore, when she opened the kitchen door and saw her father sitting drinking tea, and talking to Madge.

'Dad!' she said, and hurried to greet him with a kiss.

'Hello, Mr Ferguson,' chirped Jessie, who had been to the shops for Cook. 'How are you?'

He shook her warmly by the hand. 'Just fine, my dear, and you?'

'Hunky-dory!' she replied.

Flora asked Jessie and Rose to take the children through to the dining room and give them a drink. 'Bring your cup and come with me, Dad,' she said. 'I'll show you round when we've caught up on the news.'

Once settled in her office, Alistair gazed at his daughter and noticed the strained look about her. 'I have brought you some money,' he said.

Despite what this would mean she felt her face drop as she realised the sale of the horses must have gone through. 'Thanks.'

'I believe you are in dire need of it.'

She looked at him in surprise.

'I wormed it out of Mavis, who was very reluctant to renege on a promise, so don't be cross with her.'

'How is she?'

'Mavis is fine. She's fully recovered from her ordeal. Oh yes, I know about that too,' he added as Flora's eyes opened wide at his comment. He leaned forward. 'Why on earth didn't you tell me about these difficulties?'

'How could I? Mother thought I would fail, and I couldn't give her the chance to say "I told you so".'

'You two are the most stubborn people I have ever met!' he said angrily. 'And what is the situation now?'

Flora told him the whole story. He chuckled when she got to the part she had just played at the luncheon. 'Oh Flora, you should have been born a man! And what was the outcome?'

She shrugged. 'I'll have to wait and see . . . Who bought the horses?'

'You have no need to worry about them; they are in a good home.'

'How long are you staying?' she asked. 'Only I haven't any spare room here, I'm afraid.'

'That's all right. I've booked in at the Star Hotel. I have a couple of days free, and I thought I would like to spend some time with you.'

The sight of her beloved father sitting in the same room

as her was almost too much for Flora, after all her troubles, and she fought back the tears as she said, 'That's absolutely wonderful. Come on, let me show you around.'

Alistair Ferguson was very impressed when he saw what she had done to the building, how well the rooms were decorated and how many beds in the dormitory were full, apart from the small rooms, occupied by the staff and herself.

'You have done so well, my dear,' he said, his voice full of pride. By now they were standing in the dining room where the children were eating. He looked at all the little ones and said sadly. 'What a terrible indictment of our society that all these little souls should need protection.'

She shook her head. 'You have no idea, Dad.' Then she told him the sad tale of Bella and the other young ones she had saved. 'We still don't know how they came to be there, although it seems that very soon it may all come to light.'

She took him back to her office and showed him the newspaper articles. He read them with disbelief. 'And *this* is the man who spoiled your chances with the business federation?'

'Yes. Amazing, isn't it?'

'There must be something we can do,' he said. 'Look, come and have dinner with me this evening at the hotel, and we'll talk. I have some calls I must make, so I'll leave you now. Would you like me to pick you up later?'

'No, Dad. I'll come round to the Star about seven thirty. By then the children will have settled for the night and I'll be free. Rose and Jessie will be here on duty. I'll meet you in the residents' lounge.'

She walked her father to the front door and opened it for him. He gave her a hug and kissed her forehead. 'You are looking tired, dear. A change of scene is just what you need.'

It was so good to feel her father's arms about her. She felt like a child again, being protected by this strong man who had always managed to chase away her fears when she had been the age of many of her wards. But she was no longer a child. She was a woman with great responsibilities, and she held the wellbeing of many in the palm of her hand.

'I almost forgot to give you this,' her father said, and put a hand into the inside pocket of his jacket. Then he handed her a cheque.

She looked at the amount. At least that was some consolation for the loss of her horses. 'Thanks, I'll see you later,' she said. Although the money meant that now she had a bit of breathing space, it gave her little pleasure, knowing how it had been raised.

Alistair Ferguson walked slowly back towards the Star Hotel. He was in no great hurry, as he needed time to think. Flora was in desperate need of help and he was racking his brains, trying to think of the best way to set about giving her some support. Although he loved all his children he had to admit that Flora was the one he really understood and the one whom he felt had always needed him the most. Not that this was a weakness on her part in any way – quite the opposite. She was as brave as a lion, fiercely independent, but oh, so headstrong. And stubborn! She would rather die than ask for help.

When he arrived back at the hotel, he went to the public telephone in the reception area and asked to place a person-to-person call to Mrs Janet Ferguson in Glasgow.

★ ★ ★

Not long after her father's departure, Flora had another visitor. Detective Inspector Blake called on her, and when he was settled in her office, he said, 'Well, at last I have some news for you, although I'm sure you have seen the local papers, so I don't suppose my being here comes as any great surprise?'

'I imagined that I would hear from you soon,' she admitted. 'Have you information about the children who are here with Bella?'

'I have, and a sorry tale it is. I'll start at the beginning. The house in Netley is owned by Alderman Chivers, and a couple called the Johnsons, who run it, are in his pay.'

'Pay? For what?'

'Looking after children, and we both know how well they did that! Apparently, the twins are orphans and none of their relatives wanted to look after them, so they paid to have them cared for.'

'What about Mathew?'

'He was found abandoned, and as all the homes were full at the time, Chivers had his secretary take him to Netley and he is claiming money to take care of him. And Bella – well, Bella was to be there but a few days before she was to be moved to one of the council homes.'

'But how could he get away with this?'

'The alderman had a set of books in his office where he had registered the house as a nursing home, and was filching money from the council budget to finance it. He persuaded his secretary to help him in his dealings – I'm not sure how, because she seems a nice enough woman, but of course we don't know what he promised her for doing so.'

Shaking her head, Flora remarked, 'How could anyone be so wicked?'

'We found four children there, Miss Ferguson, all under

the age of five; they were in a sorry state. They have been taken to the hospital for examination, but apart from being malnourished, they are fine. Do you have the room to take them in?'

'Where did they come from?'

'We're not quite sure, but we think they were wandering the streets. The police are looking into the matter. Goodness knows who was paying for their care!'

'Bring them along,' said Flora. 'We'll move the beds in the dormitory closer together and I'll find room. But I have to tell you, Inspector, I'm not sure just how much longer I'll be able to keep this place open.'

'I'm sorry to hear that. Why?'

She explained about the business federation and Chivers. 'I'm keeping my fingers crossed that the members may change their minds about their financial backing, but it is in the lap of the gods.'

He got to his feet, shook her hand and said, 'Well, good luck, Miss Ferguson. You're doing a fine job here. It would be a great pity to see it close. The other children will be here within the hour.'

Flora passed on the latest information to the others, who were appalled to hear of Chivers' involvement, and then she, Rose and Jessie went up to the dormitory to prepare for the new arrivals.

All this extra activity made Flora late for her appointment with her father, and at about eight o'clock, she hurried into the residents' lounge, apologising profusely.

'Sit down, Flora,' said Alistair. 'You look a little fraught. I'll order you a drink. What would you like?'

'I'll have a gin and tonic, please. I could really do with one.' And while she waited, she told him of the latest occurrence. They discussed the different facets of the case and then made their way to the dining room.

During the first course, Flora, wanting to put behind her the concerns of Harwood House, plied her father with questions about the family. All, it seemed, was well, north of the border. Her sisters were busy being wives and mothers, and Janet was as usual involved with her committees.

Alistair looked at Flora and said, 'I do wish you had a man behind you, dear, who could support you through these troubled times. You seem to be climbing such a high mountain – and doing it alone.'

She smiled at him and said, 'Well, Father Patrick and Dr Goodwin are there if I need them.'

'You know what I mean.'

'Goodness, Dad. You're beginning to sound like Mother, trying to get me married off!'

He laughed loudly at that. 'Heaven forbid!'

At that moment, Richard entered the dining room, alone. He spotted Flora, walked over to the table and asked how she was. She had no choice but to introduce him to her father, but seeing him so unexpectedly had thrown her completely.

'What are you doing here?' she asked.

'Lydia is spending a couple of days with her parents, and I felt the need to get out of the house.'

To her great discomfort, Flora listened as her father said, 'Why don't you join us? We have just ordered our main course, but you can catch up.'

'That's very kind of you, sir. I'd like to.'

The waiter hurried over at Alistair's signal, placed a chair beside Flora's, and quickly laid out the cutlery, handing Richard the menu.

Flora tried to behave as naturally as possible, but every

nerve in her body was tingling. Her heart was pounding and she dropped a knife through her nervousness. Both she and Richard stooped to pick it up at the same time, and clashed their heads together.

As she put a hand to her forehead, Richard quickly apologised, caught hold of her wrist, pulling her hand away, and said, 'Here, let me take a look.' He delicately felt her brow.

To feel his touch was almost too much. She brushed his hand away and said sharply, 'Don't fuss, I'm fine.'

He said quietly, 'You may have a bruise tomorrow, but yes, there's nothing more.' Then turning to Alistair he asked, 'Have you seen Harwood House, Mr Ferguson?'

'Yes, I was given the tour today. It's a great place.'

'Flora has done so well, don't you think? We all have a lot to be grateful for since she arrived in Southampton.' He turned to her and said, 'The papers have been having a field day with old Chivers. Have you had any news about the children from Netley?'

She passed on all that she had been told, and watched the anger grow in Richard's expression. 'Well, I hope they throw the book at all of them!' he retorted. 'It makes my blood boil when I hear things like this!'

Alistair said, 'You sound a lot like my daughter.'

With a slow smile Richard said, 'Yes, we have quite a lot in common, don't we, Flora?'

'Yes, we do – professionally. How's Lydia?' Before he could reply she turned to her father and said, 'Richard is to become a father soon.'

'That's splendid. Will this be your first?'

'Yes, indeed.'

Although she had brought up the subject, Flora now couldn't bear to hear it discussed and quickly moved the conversation along a different path. 'Richard used to ride point-to-point, Dad.' Knowing this was something dear to his heart, she sat back and let the men talk while she ate her roast beef. It was easier this way. Yet the close proximity of Richard and the sound of his voice played havoc with her emotions.

At the end of the meal, they all sat and drank coffee, then Flora said she simply had to go, she was so tired. 'I'll see you in the morning, Dad.'

'I'll walk you home,' he said.

'No need,' said Richard. 'My car is outside; I'll take her.'

Flora was by then too weary to protest. She kissed her father good night and he promised to come round to the house after breakfast. Shaking hands with Richard he said, 'Well, it's nice to know that Flora has someone to turn to when she needs them.'

Outside the hotel, Richard helped her into the car, then drove her back to Harwood House. Once they had arrived, he turned off the engine. 'Dear Flora, you look so weary,' he said softly.

It had been a long and quite traumatic day and the gentle tone of the doctor's voice was almost her undoing. She wanted him to hold her and comfort her as Flynn used to, but she knew that was not possible. 'I must go,' she said. 'Thank you for bringing me home.'

'Flora, wait!'

But she had opened the car door and alighted, ignoring his call, and walked to the front door, tears trickling down her cheeks. Tears for the poor children in her care, tears at the comforting sight of her dear father, tears of frustration because of the uncertainty of her future. And tears because Dr Richard Goodwin was a married man.

Chapter Thirty-One

The following morning, Flora received a telephone call from the chairman of the business federation. 'Miss Ferguson,' he began, 'I thought I would let you know that after your visit yesterday, the federation have decided to hold a meeting next week to discuss once again the financial backing of Harwood House.'

'Really? How wonderful.'

'Now don't get too excited,' he warned. 'We do have a few old sticklers for convention among us, but there is always hope.'

'That's extremely kind of you. I'll keep my fingers crossed. Would you please let me know . . . either way?'

'Of course I will. Goodbye for now, Miss Ferguson.'

Flora sat at her desk and closed her eyes with relief. At least they were going to discuss it; that was something. They hadn't dismissed her appeal out of hand.

Alistair Ferguson arrived at Harwood House early, which didn't surprise Flora, who was used to his early morning ritual. 'I walked around the town,' he said, 'and down to the waterfront. It was very bracing.' He kissed her cheek. 'How are things? What are the children doing?'

'Come and see for yourself,' she said, and led him into the dining room, where Rose, Madge and Jessie were doing the rounds of helping those children who couldn't feed themselves, and urging the others to eat up.

'My goodness, you ladies have your hands full. Can I help?' And before you could say knife, he was sitting beside Mattie, helping her with her porridge.

'I was very ill once, you know,' said Mattie cheerfully.

'Were you?'

'Yes, I had the measles, but Dr Richard made me better, and Miss Flora. They boiled kettles in my room – not in the kitchen!'

He looked across at Flora. She nodded. 'Yes, she was very poorly, and had bronchitis as well. The steam helped her to breathe.'

'Well, you look very well now,' Alistair said.

'I'm all better and I'm getting much fatter,' she proclaimed proudly.

As Alistair put another spoonful of the cereal in Mattie's mouth, he said to Flora with a broad grin, 'I used to do this for you, and your sisters when you were this age. Oh my, how it takes me back.'

And it was true. Although the Fergusons had a nanny, Alistair always used to come up to the nursery every morning and help the girls with their breakfast, to Nanny's annoyance, Flora recalled. Janet never did, thinking that that was what you paid a woman to do, but Alistair enjoyed his children, and there was the great difference, Flora realised, watching him. Her mother never seemed to get the pleasure from her brood like her husband did, and that was probably why they were never close. Not that Janet wasn't a good mother. She was efficient, but she wasn't affectionate.

After the breakfast was over, Flora took her father into her office and told him about her call from the chairman.

He looked pleased. 'Well, that's a step in the right direction,' he said. 'Let's hope the powers that be do change their minds.' He looked across the desk at Flora and said, 'I thought that Richard Goodwin was a nice young man. I really liked him. Nice solid type.'

As her father stared at her Flora thought, he knows!

'You're in love with him, my dear, aren't you?'

She nodded. 'Yes, I am. I've tried to be sensible, but I can't help myself. Not that anything can come of it. After all, Richard is married and soon to be a father.'

'And he is in love with you, that was fairly obvious from the way he looked at you. I do urge you to be careful. I feel I'm looking at a time bomb, waiting for the explosion!'

'Please stop your worrying. Richard and I have never ever admitted to our feelings for each other.'

'But you are both aware of the chemistry between you.'

'Oh yes.'

'Haven't you been through enough already? The war, Flynn, this place and all its worries – and now Richard. Whenever you are going to do things the easy way?'

'I don't know. I didn't choose the path that life threw at me. I just take one day at a time. I'm sorry if I disappoint you, Dad.'

'My dear child, nothing you could do would ever disappoint me – don't you know that? But I do worry about you. I always have.'

'Oh dear, have I always been such a problem?' she said with a grimace.

He smiled wryly. 'Most of your life! All I want is for you to be happy.'

'I am happy, at the moment. If only I could be sure of the future of Harwood House, I would be content.'

He raised a quizzical eyebrow. 'Really?'

'Well almost.' Not wanting to continue the conversation, she said, 'Come on, I could do with a walk. Let me show you the seedy side of Southampton!'

She walked her father up to the Ditches and they looked in all the shop windows. The Jewish tailor tried very hard to sell Alistair a handmade suit, which amused Flora immensely.

They walked up to the Horse and Groom. 'This is where the ladies of the night usually gather,' Flora told her father. 'This used to be Jessie's pitch.'

With a grin Alistair said, 'She's quite a girl, that Jessie, but she's great with those children, isn't she?'

'Yes, indeed.'

Then they walked to the Bargate, which was part of the old town's gateway, which still straddled the road, letting the trams through the great archway in the middle.

'I can see why you like it here,' he remarked. 'And I have to say it's much warmer than Glasgow. I have to leave in the morning, so what would you like to do this evening?'

'How about a trip to the Palace Theatre? They have a really good variety show.' And after reading the programme outside, that was what they decided to do.

Madge insisted on cooking a meal for Flora's father and, after sitting down to guinea fowl with a selection of vegetables and a light sponge pudding to follow, he and Flora set off. Flora had always promised herself a trip to the Palace, but until that evening had not been there. There were jugglers, tap dancers, and Marie Lloyd topped the bill and sang the songs that had made her so popular: 'My Old Man Said Follow the Van' and 'I'm One of the Ruins that Cromwell Knocked About a Bit'. It was a thoroughly enjoyable evening, and as they walked home, Flora knew she would miss her father, when on the morrow he returned to Scotland.

He went with her to Harwood House for a cup of coffee before returning to the hotel. 'Now promise me,' he insisted, 'that you'll let me know what happens about the finance.'

She promised that she would.

'And don't keep things from me, Flora.'

'No, Dad, I won't. I promise. Give my love to Mother and to Mavis. I'm glad she's settled down there with all of you.'

'She's a good worker, but she's happy and that's the main thing.' He caught her by the shoulders. 'Take care, my dear.'

She kissed his cheek. 'I will. Don't you worry, I can look after myself.'

'I know. That's what worries me,' he said with an affectionate smile. 'I'll be in touch.'

As she watched him walk down the road, she wished with all her heart that he could always be around. When she had the time to think, she did miss the highlands of Scotland, but most of all, she missed him.

Flora rang Father Duggan to tell him the good news about the latest meeting of the business federation, and he called around later in the day to see her. 'I've written to the chairman to tell him how much we need this place and you, and how much of an asset Jessie is, in the hope that my words may add a little weight.'

'Thank you so much,' Flora said.

'And how are you?'

'Fine. On tenterhooks, of course.' Then she told him of her father's visit.

325

'I would so liked to have met him.'

'Well, if he comes again, I'll see that you do. This visit was completely unexpected,' she explained. 'I came home and found him sitting in the kitchen with Madge. He did meet Richard, however.' And she explained how this came about.

'And how is the good doctor? I haven't seen him for a few days.'

'Fine.'

Father Patrick held her gaze. 'It's good that those two are about to start a family. A child cements a marriage, I always think.'

There was something in the tone of his voice that made Flora ask, 'Are you trying to tell me something, Patrick?'

'Like what?'

'I don't quite know, but it sounded as if you were about to scold me like a naughty child!'

She knew he was playing with words, and if her father could see that she was in love with Richard, was it possible that Patrick also recognised her feelings? 'Life is so easy for you, Father,' she said. 'Your rules are strict, carved in stone, laid down by the Pope. And you never deviate from them, but life isn't quite like that for the rest of us.'

He rose to his feet. 'I wish my life was as simple as you make it sound, my dear Flora. But you're a good woman; I don't see you breaking too many of life's rules. I must away. Let me know how you get on with the business federation.' And he took his leave.

George Chivers was paying the price for breaking the rules. He had been up before the magistrates, charged with fraud, and an accessory to child cruelty, and if the police could prove it, he would later be charged with living off immoral earnings, when it became known that he owned the Mariners' Club. He was held without bail.

Jack la Salles was extremely nervous when he read of the alderman's arrest. He had run the club without the prostitutes practising their trade for a while, certain the police would be ready to pounce when they discovered that Chivers owned the property. He paid George a handsome percentage of his earnings for him to turn a blind eye to the use of the place – not that Chivers had ever been there; he wasn't that stupid, but he enjoyed the money earned for him by the girls, which was paid regularly into a special bank account.

So for Jack, business was slack and this made him restless. He would walk up and down, cursing his luck. There was always a certain bar trade, of course, and the girls still entertained the men, but not for sex – for the moment. The Chinaman still called regularly. He would sit at the bar and talk to his girl and now, without Jack's knowledge, he used to meet her off the premises and take her to his flat, where he paid for her services.

She became so used to being with him that she relaxed and was only too willing to talk about her life at the club and of the things she had seen whilst working there. One night she was so drunk that her tongue ran away with her as she told him – with a little prompting – of the beautiful Chinese girl who had been brought in one night, in a drugged state, but who several days later had disappeared. In her alcoholic haze, she had forgotten about the body being washed up.

A few days later, Jack was surprised to see three other Chinese men arrive with Lee Chin.

'These are my friends, who arrived from Amsterdam this morning,' he explained.

They all bowed to Jack la Salles, who was completely embarrassed by this. He couldn't abide all these strange foreign habits. Muttering to himself, he left them drinking at the bar.

At the end of the night, as the regulars were leaving, Lee Chin approached Jack and said, 'My friends like to play cards and gamble. Could we stay behind? We would want plenty booze but no women.'

As business had been so bad, Jack was delighted. He knew that orientals loved to gamble, and if they wanted drinks, he could at least make some decent money.

He dismissed the barman when it got really late and stood behind the bar himself. They had already spent a great deal, and he watched the pile of money on the table change hands several times. But once the men gave the barman enough time to clear the building, the real reason for their visit became apparent as they pounced on Jack, and tied him to a chair.

'What are you doing, you bastards?' he screamed. He was shaking with fright and cursing his own lack of foresight. He had become careless and now he was to pay for it. He knew who they were as they wasted no time in telling him.

'You had a Chinese girl last year,' said one of the men. 'She was brought here against her will.'

'That's not true!'

The man caught hold of Jack's little finger and bent it. Jack cried out in pain as he felt it crack in two. 'She belonged to our family,' the stranger continued, ignoring his victim's pain. The Chinaman looked at him. 'Have you heard of the Triads?'

Jack's eyes widened in terror.

The man looked at Jack with disdain as a wet patch spread down his trousers. 'I see that you have. You need to be frightened, my little man. I hope you enjoy pain as much as I do. Strip him!' he ordered. Another man tied a gag around Jack to stifle his cries. He struggled, but to no avail. He looked around in desperation, but there was no one to save him. He started to sob like a child.

'You killed Mai Lee,' said his accuser.

Jack shook his head frantically.

'Then you had someone else do it!'

Jack gave a whimper. He knew he was a dead man.

The barman at the Mariners' Club had a key, so the following morning he wasn't too perturbed when his boss wasn't on the premises when he arrived. He picked up an overturned chair and cleared away the dirty glasses and washed them. Then he swept the floor. But as evening approached and Jack didn't show, he became increasingly worried, but then thought perhaps Jack had gone to another club and forgotten to tell him, which was not unknown, if not a very regular occurrence. But when Jack didn't show up by the following evening, the man called the police and reported him missing, explaining he had last seen his boss entertaining three Chinese gentlemen.

Detective Inspector Blake questioned the customers and the girls, including the one whose regular punter was Chinese, but who hadn't been seen these past two nights. They took her to the flat where she told him they used to meet, but it was empty, and his fellow countrymen seemed to have disappeared also. Jack was officially reported missing and the club closed down for the time being.

* * *

A few days later, a cargo ship sailed smoothly out of port, heading for the Atlantic Ocean. On board were a small group of Chinese gentlemen returning home to Hong Kong. They were in a good mood and had plenty of celebratory drinks on their journey to their own country after their business had been satisfactorily concluded.

Several days later a sack was found floating in the Hamble River. Inside was the mutilated corpse of Jack la Salles, his penis stuck down the back of his throat.

'This man has been severely tortured,' the coroner told DI Blake. 'Never seen anything like it. He must have gone through all kinds of hell before he died.'

Blake wasn't sympathetic. 'In his time he tortured a few young ladies, and I believe disposed of at least one.' As he left the building he thought, at least we don't have to waste valuable resources any longer looking for him.

Chapter Thirty-Two

A week later, Flora received a telephone call from James Newman, the chairman of the business federation. 'I have good and bad news, Miss Ferguson,' he said.

With her heart in her mouth Flora said, 'Well, you had better give me the bad news first.'

'Several of our businessmen, the old sticklers I told you about, are not prepared to alter their first decision, and are declining their help.'

She was so disappointed she couldn't speak.

'But,' he continued, 'three of us would very much like to be a part of Harwood House, but this means, of course, that the total amount of sponsorship will be far short of what you had been promised in the beginning.'

The feeling of relief overcame Flora for a second. Whatever help she could get would be a great bonus. 'Thank you so much. May I ask the names of the three generous directors?' When he told her she said, 'Of course, I will be writing to thank them, and you. I don't know quite what else I can say.'

'There is no need to say anything. I'm only sorry that my news isn't better.'

'Believe me, it is such a help to know that at least I do have a certain amount of money coming in.'

'What will you do to make up the shortfall?'

'At this moment, I don't know, Mr Newman, but I'll think of something.'

'I'm sure you will, Miss Ferguson. The first cheques will be in the post in a few days. From then on, they will be sent to you on a monthly basis. Is that acceptable?'

'Absolutely!' she said. 'And thank you.'

As she replaced the receiver, Flora didn't know whether to laugh or cry. The generosity of the three directors was a help, but not nearly enough to ensure the continued running of Harwood House, and so her problem had not been solved, only slightly alleviated, and she didn't know which way to turn. She picked up the telephone and placed a trunk call to her father.

'Flora my dear, how are you?' he asked when she was put through.

'I am not really sure,' she said, and told him her news. 'What am I to do?' she asked.

'You carry on, for the time being. You have the money from the sale of your horses, and the cheques that will arrive this week,' he said. 'Leave this with me, and I'll see what I can come up with.'

'Thanks, Dad. I am completely at a loss. There is no other way for me here, no organisation but the business-men who have the cash to help. I can hardly have a flag day, can I?'

'I don't want you to worry, Flora. You have enough to cope with as it is. I'll be in touch, dear.'

She sat back in her chair and thought, how can I stop worrying? But being the resilient person she was, she tried to work out another budget, incorporating her new funds. She had to be able to pay her staff something. She couldn't let them work for nothing any longer – it just wasn't fair – but she could see it was going to be a great struggle.

Another person in Southampton who was having a struggle, albeit of another kind, was the wife of George Chivers. Hilda Chivers had been mortified at the incarceration of her husband, and the damning articles in the local paper, but the pictures and article about her husband's mistress had been the final straw. She went to visit George at the local police station where he was waiting to appear before the bench. She sat in an interview room, seething with indignation, whilst the police sergeant went to collect her husband.

George Chivers entered the small room, filled with trepidation. He leaned forward to kiss his wife, who turned her head away.

'I suppose you're proud of yourself!' she began.

'Hilda—'

'Shut up!' She glared at him across the table and her anger poured forth. 'To think I've put up with your imperious ways for years,' she said. 'Been ordered about by you: "Do *this*, Hilda, do *that*, Hilda." And I did it because I thought you were a man of stature. Of importance. Well, *you* certainly thought you were!'

'Now look here—' he began.

'No, you look here!' The expression of disgust on her face shook the alderman. 'You filthy, dirty old man! All the time you were meeting that whore. Fornicating with her, and then coming home to me. I could have caught a disease! I bet you never even thought about that.'

He looked away, unable to face her.

'All the years we have been married, I've done my duty as a wife. I've kept a fine house, made sure your life was comfortable in every way, and this is how you repay me. I've spent hours on my knees asking for God's guidance.'

'If you had spent a little less time on your knees, and a little more time in the bedroom, maybe this wouldn't have happened!' he snapped, unable to take any more.

She gave a harsh laugh. 'You think you gave me any pleasure in bed, with your clumsy fumbling, your pushing and shoving. You didn't make love, you behaved like a pig at a trough!'

The policeman standing at the door listening to this tirade, suddenly had a fit of coughing to cover his amusement, but Hilda ignored him.

'And now I discover that you own the house where your whore is and another, which is some kind of club. Secrets, George. Lies, George. They always find you out.' Her expression darkened and her voice was filled with sadness. 'But what I can't forgive is you being involved with child cruelty. I've heard the rumours: that couple in Netley, and you the owner of the house where the little ones were treated so badly. How much lower can you sink?'

Chivers was beaten. 'Why have you come here, Hilda?'

'I want you to give me power of attorney.' She saw the startled look on his face and said, 'You are going to be put away for a long time, and whether you like it or not, you have a duty to me as your wife. I have to survive. I want to sell the house in Netley, and this club, whatever it is, and the one in St Mary's, and then I'll have the money to live on. That much you owe me!'

'Very well,' he said. 'Get my solicitor to draw up the papers and I'll sign them.'

She was coldly dismissive. 'I just want the means to look after myself. After all, I have been used to a certain

standard of living – why should I give that up – for you?'
She pushed her chair back and got to her feet. 'That's all I
have to say. The solicitor will be in touch.' She walked to
the door, and when the constable opened it, she left the
room without a backward glance.

Two weeks later, the bailiffs and the police evicted Daisy,
kicking and screaming, from the house in Bevios Street,
and Ron Forbes was there with the photographer to cover
the event as an estate agent put up a For Sale sign. The
house in Netley was already empty, the personal belongings of the Johnsons removed, and that house too, was put
on the market.

Detective Inspector Blake was highly amused. 'Well
done, Mrs Chivers,' he said as he read the paper. 'At least
she has something to make up for her public humiliation.'
And he wasn't surprised when the family home was put up
for sale, as Hilda decided to move away from Southampton
and the scandal, which would always have dogged her had
she remained.

It was now three weeks before Christmas, and despite the
shortage of money, Flora was adamant that the children
would have a fine time. They cut strips of coloured paper
and pasted them together to make paper chains. She
searched the town to find inexpensive toys. Madge, Jessie
and Rose had unravelled second-hand knitwear, washed
the yarn and re-knitted it into new jumpers. Flora sorted
through her wardrobe for clothes of suitable material to be
cut down and made into party dresses for the little girls,
and the children sat with paints and crayons making
Christmas cards.

Patrick arrived during this busy time and was greeted

warmly by all, who expressed their delight with the tall Christmas tree he dragged in. He also brought a scene of the Nativity, the figures made of plain clay, and small pots of paint for the children to colour the Holy Family and the stable animals. He sat telling the children the Christmas story. It was like old times to see him in their midst, and the air was filled with merriment as the children sat singing carols with him.

He looked at Flora and grinned broadly. 'You have three more weeks until Father Christmas calls,' he said with a wink. 'These children will never last, they are so excited.'

'Don't I know it!' said Flora, but she was enjoying it all, nevertheless. 'Do you remember last Christmas Day, Patrick?'

'Indeed I do. The two of us sat down to a fine meal on our own. This year will not be nearly as quiet.'

At that moment, Richard walked in with several small parcels and a couple of jars of sweets for the children. The two men shook hands warmly.

'How are you?' asked the priest.

'Fine, busy. There are one or two babies due over the holiday period. Every year it is the same, almost as if people time it especially.' He glanced over to Flora. 'You all right?' he asked. 'Only I thought I had better bring this stuff over before I get snowed under.' He put the parcels and jars on the side.

She thanked him. 'My word, a doctor giving sweets to the children – what about their teeth?' she teased.

'It's Christmas, Flora. Everyone is entitled to a few treats.'

'You're right,' she said, 'and thank you. Like you, I'm rushed off my feet but my children have already arrived.'

She separated two who were fighting. 'This excitement is almost too much for them. Things are a bit hectic, as you can see.'

'I'm sorry I can't stop,' Richard said, 'but Lydia and I have been invited out to a pre-Christmas party at the Slaters' house. I was all for refusing because of Lydia's condition, but she insisted we go, so I must return home and get changed. It's a black-tie do. I would sooner be here with you all,' he said, looking longingly at her.

Flora tried to act normally, aware of his gaze. 'Go and enjoy yourself,' she urged. 'It will do you good.'

He smiled and said, 'Well, I do like the family, and Doug Slater and I are friends. He's always good company. I'll see you sometime tomorrow if I can get away.'

Lydia Goodwin sat on the edge of her bed after forcing herself into a corset to try and hide her bump. Despite the fact she'd been careful not to eat anything fattening, she had quite a bulge. She had bought a midnight-blue evening dress, with folds that softly draped her stomach, helping to disguise the growing child within her. She was a beauty still, and the hairdresser earlier that day had dressed her hair on top, with ringlets cascading down one side. She couldn't wait for Doug Slater to see her.

'How do I look?' she asked Richard when she was ready.

'You look beautiful, Lydia. Are you ready?'

'Oh, yes,' she said. 'I'm ready for anything!'

There were already several guests gathered at the Slaters' house when the Goodwins arrived. A maid took their coats and another offered them champagne. Lydia looked around at the palatial room and said, 'Now this *is* the way to live.'

Richard, who was always appalled at his wife's covetousness, said, 'If you like this sort of life, and have the money to do it.'

'Well, that's one thing you'll never have to worry about,' she snapped, and went over to greet her hostess.

Richard sighed. He had a feeling this was going to be a long night.

'You all right, old chap?'

He turned and saw Doug Slater. 'How the devil are you?' asked Richard as he shook his hand. He knew young Doug was a rascal with the women but he liked his ready wit.

'Fine, Richard, fine.' He looked around the room at the guests. 'I'm wondering what talent my father has got together tonight,' he said. 'The old man likes to gather interesting and diverse people, then throw them all together and see what develops. Your wife looks especially ravishing tonight. Lucky man. Congratulations, by the way. When is your baby due?'

'In the summer, I've been told.'

'Lydia, of course, isn't your patient?'

'No, but she is under a good doctor.'

Doug smothered a grin, wondering if she *had* been under him, and excused himself to go over to speak to her. 'How are you, darling? You look very tempting tonight. I'm surprised to see you here at all,' he said with a laconic smile.

'Why wouldn't I be here? Are you afraid I might let slip that you are the father of my child?' Her eyes glittered dangerously as she looked at him.

He was unconcerned and drew deeply on the cigarette he was smoking. 'You wouldn't be that stupid,' he said. 'Now excuse me, I have to mingle.'

'Yes, you're good at that,' she remarked, and watched

him cross the room to another group.

The dinner gong went soon after the canapés had been passed round and another drink served, and Richard took Lydia into the dining room. They read the place cards and were soon seated. Lydia was furious to see that Doug was at the far end of the table next to an older, but good-looking woman, and she seethed as she watched him charming her with his conversation. She herself was seated next to an elderly gentleman who was down from London for the weekend – apparently an old school chum of Mr Slater, the host.

Lydia tried to be polite, if only to show Doug that she didn't care, but he caught her eye once or twice and smiled, and she knew she hadn't fooled him a bit. The corset was far too tight, and just before the dessert was served she felt suddenly faint. She got unsteadily to her feet. 'I'm so sorry,' she said as she began to sway. Then she realised that Richard was beside her, leading her from the dining room.

Everyone was very solicitous and she began to feel a fool. Richard insisted they leave. To his host he said, 'I'm really sorry to disturb your dinner, but I think I should take Lydia home.'

Mrs Slater was really concerned. 'You are not in any pain are you, my dear?'

Lydia wanted to scream at her and tell her to shut up, but she controlled herself and said, 'No, I'm fine. Perhaps I shouldn't have had that glass of wine after the champagne.' And before she knew it Richard had her outside the house and in the night air.

'How are you feeling now?' he asked.

'Just take me home,' she snapped, 'and stop fussing. I'm fine.'

* * *

Once she entered the house she insisted that Richard get her a glass of water and leave her alone to get undressed, knowing if he saw the corset he would be furious. She slipped her dress off, and quickly undid the hooks and eyes of the offending garment. The relief was intense, and for a moment she sat in a chair and put her head between her knees as the room began to swim.

When her husband knocked on the door to see if she was all right she said, 'Yes, I'm fine, you can see for yourself, come in.'

He sat on the bed and took her pulse. It was up. He felt her forehead; it was warm. 'Do you have any pain at all?' he asked.

'Richard, you're my husband, not my doctor!'

'And as such I need to know that you are all right. Tonight was probably not a good idea,' he said. 'Try and get a good night's sleep. I'll look in later. I've got some paperwork that I can do.' He tucked the bedclothes around her, put out the light and left the door slightly open.

As he made his way downstairs, he frowned. Lydia seemed all right. She was probably unwise to drink wine and champagne, but he would watch over her carefully from now to make sure. He also wondered if there were twins in her family as he had noticed she seemed much bigger than he would have expected. He would call her doctor and have a quiet professional word.

He was also concerned about Lydia's mental attitude towards the baby. She showed no maternal feelings towards it at all – quite the opposite. It was almost as if she hated the child. Perhaps when she had actually given birth and held the baby, she would feel differently. He desperately hoped so.

Chapter Thirty-Three

When Richard called Lydia's doctor the following day, the man assured him that his wife was well. He was unable to discuss his patient with Richard, of course – it wouldn't have been ethical – and when, at the end of their conversation, the doctor put the receiver down he thought, poor man. It was obvious that the wife was playing a devious game, and he had to smile when he had been asked to think in terms of twins! In time, of course, the young woman would really have to come up with a good story because her husband, being a doctor, was not going to be hoodwinked with tales of a premature birth. He would know this was a full-term delivery as soon as he saw the child, and Dr Bailey wondered what would happen then. Shame, because Dr Goodwin was a decent chap.

It was Christmas Eve and Harwood House was buzzing with activity. Days before, notes had been written to Father Christmas, and posted up the chimney, and the children were anxious and excited to see what they would find in their stockings the following morning. Carrots for the reindeer, and a small glass of sherry and mince pie for Father Christmas had been placed outside the front door.

Madge was busy in the kitchen making more mince pies and putting the final touches to the icing on the Christmas cake. Flora's mother had sent them a huge hamper from Scotland, full of good things to help them celebrate the festive season. There had been a whole cooked ham, pots of preserves, bottled fruit, shortcake, Christmas crackers for the children, boxes of sweets, mixed nuts, dates, Turkish delight and sugared almonds for the ladies. There were several scarves and woollen hats in various children's sizes, made by the members on some committee or other, and small gifts for the staff from Alistair. And for Flora, a small framed painting of her beloved Highlands to hang in her office. As they had unpacked this manna from heaven, she'd had to blink away the tears at her parents' thoughtfulness.

In between services on Christmas Eve, Patrick had called to give each child a small picture book with stories from the Bible, promising after Christmas to come along and read to them. He looked around at the decorations and the magnificence of the tree, bedecked with baubles bought in the market.

'But doesn't it all look so grand!' he remarked. To Flora he said, 'My dear girl, I know that things have not been easy for you, but when I look around and see the happy faces of these poor deprived children, I thank God for you and Harwood House. Here,' he added, 'this may be of help to you at times and I would like you to have it.' He handed her a small book of prayer.

'Thank you, Patrick. How very kind you are.' She handed him a small package. 'I thought I'd bring a little colour into your life!' she said, her eyes sparkling mischievously.

'May I open it now?' he asked.

'Of course.'

He tore at the wrapping like a child and burst out laughing at the contents. Two pairs of socks in a colourful, yet tasteful Argyle pattern.

'*You* bring colour into my life, Flora, but these will make the congregation sit up when I wear them instead of my usual black ones!' He kissed her cheek. 'Thank you, and God be with you.'

The children all woke early, so they gathered in the dining room where Flora had lit a nice log fire. It was a truly joyous occasion. Flora watched the faces of the children, which were filled with wonderment as they unwrapped their presents, knowing that many had never before experienced such a time.

Jake had become more confident since first he had joined them. He and Bella were firm friends, and he looked after his sister, Mattie, with the same caring manner he had showed his mother. He was thrilled to know that his father had been invited to join them for Christmas dinner.

Jessie too was happy about this, as she and Bob had been seeing each other quite frequently. He visited the children regularly, occasionally having them to stay overnight at the weekend, when, if she was off duty, she would accompany them when they made trips to the pier, or walked through the parks.

Bella proclaimed she was never going to leave Harwood House and the others chorused their agreement. 'We are going to stay for ever,' proclaimed one.

'And what happens when I am an old lady?' asked Flora.

'*We'll* look after *you*,' they said, and she was overcome by their innocence and love.

Lunch was a busy and lively affair, with crackers being pulled and food being eaten with great relish, and when it was over, the younger ones, now very tired, were laid on cushions or mattresses, to nap in the warmth of the sitting room where another fire burned, made safe with a large fireguard in front of it.

When the washing up had been cleared, the adults sat down, completely exhausted.

'What a lovely meal, Madge,' said Flora. 'I'm too full to move.' Rose and Jessie agreed.

'It's one of the best meals I've ever had,' said Bob. 'And the nicest Christmas for many a year.' He looked across at Jessie and smiled.

She blushed and touched the brooch Bob had given her, a small bow set with diamanté, which she had pinned to her jumper.

Rose was going around to Peter's house that evening, but Madge was content to stay put, and Flora and Jessie were on duty. But Bob had been asked to stay on for a light supper and to help to put his children to bed.

'With all the excitement today, they all ought to sleep like angels,' said Flora. 'We'll just top and tail them tonight. That's all they'll be fit for,' she said.

'That's about all I'm fit for,' said Jessie.

There was not such a happy atmosphere at the house of Lydia's parents. Lydia was fractious all day and her father, who usually satisfied her every whim, finally lost patience with her. 'For goodness' sake, will you stop your whinging? Good God, your mother never made this fuss when she was pregnant!'

Lydia sulked for the rest of the day, but at least it was more peaceful.

But Richard was worried about her. According to his father-in-law, there were no twins in the family, and he was getting concerned.

When at last they arrived home, she brushed him aside as he tried to help her. 'I want a stiff drink!' she said.

'Now, Lydia, you had two glasses of wine with your lunch. I don't think you should have any more. It isn't good for the baby.'

'That's all you think about, the damned baby! What about me?'

'Of course I worry about you too. You are my wife and you are carrying my child.'

Without anyone's knowledge, Lydia had been hitting the sherry bottle, and with the wine she had had she was slightly drunk. She was also in a filthy temper.

'Your bloody child! That's all I bloody well hear, and that's all I'm going to hear for the rest of my pregnancy. I can't bear it! Well, I have news for you, Richard. This baby isn't yours – and it's about time you knew it!'

His face went ashen. 'What are you saying? Of course it's mine.'

She stood before him, swaying a little, a malicious smile on her countenance. 'No it isn't. Doug Slater is the father of my baby – not you!'

Richard sat in the nearest chair and looked askance at his wife. Eventually he said, 'I think you had better explain that remark.'

Now there was no reason to pretend, Lydia was enjoying herself. 'I had an affair with Doug and he made me pregnant.' With a malevolent look she added, 'He was a wonderful lover!'

'How long did this go on for?' he demanded.

'Months!'

'And where did all this take place?' Richard's eyes flashed angrily.

She tossed her hair back and said, 'In hotels, here and in London.' And with venom in her voice she leaned forward and said, 'We even made love here.'

Richard was livid. 'Here – in *my* house?'

She laughed. 'In *our* bed!'

'What!'

'Yes. When you went to that Scotswoman's place for dinner with Patrick, and I told you I was unwell.'

'And I suppose you rang Slater!'

'Yes I did – and he came running!'

Richard glared at her. 'I have never raised a hand to a woman in my life, but at this moment I can fully understand how murder is committed.'

There was such a coldness about him that for a moment she was frightened.

'Then why, if this was going so well, Lydia, did you pretend the child was mine?'

The defiant expression slowly began to crumble as she had to confess, 'He didn't want me when I said I was pregnant, so I tempted you into my bed and told you it was yours.'

'And how far into your pregnancy are you, really?'

'Six and a half months.'

He shook his head, wondering how he could have been such a fool. It was all very hard to take in at this moment, but he was outraged by Lydia's duplicity. He looked up at her. 'You are a devious, calculating bitch!'

'Richard!' She had never heard him use such wild language, and even in her drunken state, she was shocked.

'And I do hope you don't think that I am going to sit back and bring up another man's child, knowing the true facts.'

'Then what are you going to do?' There was a note of panic in her voice now.

'You'll find out soon enough. Now get to bed. I can't bear to look at you a minute longer!'

He got quickly to his feet and walked into his surgery, slamming the door behind him.

Sitting at his desk, his hands to his head, Richard was furious with himself and thought, what kind of gullible fool am I? *Me* a doctor, thinking my wife is carrying twins because she was so big! Had she been a patient of his and not his wife, he would have realised immediately, but then he had no reason to doubt what she told him. He got to his feet and started to pace up and down. And he supposed all those trips out with her lady friends so interested in fashion were a pack of lies too. The more he thought about it all, the more difficult it was to believe. Doug Slater – whom he had always liked, who was always so friendly to him, so polite and amusing, and all the time – bedding his wife in his own home! Congratulating him at the pre-Christmas party on becoming a father . . . to his child! How treacherous could a person get? To think that *he* felt so guilty about being in love with Flora! He had struggled so hard with his feelings for her, trying to be noble, do the right thing, when all the time, Lydia was enjoying sex with another man! But what really stuck in his craw was the fact she tried to pass off another man's child as his. That was pure wickedness and totally unforgivable. Well, he wasn't going to just sit back and do nothing. Tomorrow he'd start to sort out this situation. Not today. He was so shocked and angry that if Doug Slater were within an arm's length, he'd kill the bastard!

The next morning, when the maid arrived, Richard said to

her, 'After serving the breakfast, I want you to help Mrs Goodwin to pack; she's going to stay with her parents. When she's ready to leave, send for a taxi to take her there.' He went up the stairs two at a time and threw the door of the bedroom open.

Lydia sat up in bed with a startled look. Her hair was dishevelled and she looked decidedly hung over. He went across the room to the bed, and pulled the covers back. 'Get up and get washed and dressed. Agnes will be up to help you pack.'

'Pack? What do you mean, pack? I'm not going anywhere.'

'Indeed you are. You are going to live with your parents. I don't want you and Slater's child in my house. If you want any breakfast come downstairs!' And he swept out of the room.

Richard sat eating his breakfast alone. Upstairs he could hear crashing and banging as Lydia packed her things with obvious bad humour. Well, for goodness' sake, what did the woman expect? How could they continue to live together in the circumstances?

Two hours later, Lydia came downstairs, arrogantly walked up to Richard and said, 'I suppose you are driving me to Mother's.'

'Then you suppose wrong. I am on call. Agnes was told to ring for a taxi when you were ready.' At that moment, there was a knock on the door. 'It appears that it has arrived,' he said, after glancing through the window. 'Off you go, Lydia,' he added coldly. 'I'll be in touch, and I'll get the rest of your things packed up and sent to you.'

'What do you mean?'

'I mean I'm sending you home to Daddy. He always spoiled you to death – well, let him do so now, or would

348

you prefer I send your clothes to the Slaters'?'

Lydia was speechless. She turned on her heel and walked out to the car, the driver behind her, carrying her cases. Richard closed the front door and summoned the maid into the surgery. He handed her a piece of paper.

'I have to go out,' he said. 'If I am needed, call me at this number. I'll be with Mr Slater.'

Chapter Thirty-Four

Guy Slater himself opened the door to Richard. He stepped back to let him enter and said, 'We had better go into my study.'

The room was panelled and a hymn to the tanning industry. There was a leather-topped desk, three brown leather chairs, a leather-backed blotter and a large leather briefcase. Guy walked around the desk and sat down, indicating to Richard to take a seat opposite him. 'I was surprised to get your call this morning,' he said. 'What's this all about? Cigar?' He pushed a box full of them towards Richard.

'No thanks, but I must say they are very appropriate.'

Guy frowned. 'I don't understand.'

'Very soon you'll be able to hand them round to your friends. You are about to become a grandfather.'

'I don't know what you're talking about. As far as I know my daughter isn't pregnant and they already have two children.'

'No, it's Doug who is soon to be a father. Lydia is carrying his child!'

'What!'

'Yes, it came as a shock to me too when she told me yesterday. They had an affair for months, it seems, then she got pregnant and your son dumped her . . . so she told me the baby was mine.'

Guy, the ever-shrewd businessman, asked, 'Are you sure you're not mistaken and the child really is yours?'

Richard shook his head. 'Lydia is six and a half months into her pregnancy. At the time of the child's conception, there was the measles epidemic. I didn't sleep with my wife for over two months.' He looked at Guy and said sadly, 'Why would I lie? Do you think this is easy for me?'

Slater rose from his seat and, walking over to a drinks cabinet, opened it, took out two goblets, and poured a measure of brandy into each. 'Here,' he said, 'we can both do with this.' He didn't doubt Richard's word. He was a man of integrity and it must have cost him dearly to be here telling him this. And after all, the man had been cuckolded – and Slater knew his own son. This was bound to happen one day, but Lydia was not some cheap totty – even if she behaved like one.

'What do you expect me to do?' he asked.

'I expect your son to take care of his child – *I'm* damned well not going to! I have already sent Lydia back to her family to live, and I intend to sue for divorce.'

'What about the scandal? Divorce could affect your career.'

'I'll take that chance,' Richard said coldly. 'After all, I'm not the one at fault.'

Guy rang the servants' bell and sent the maid to summon Douglas.

When Doug Slater breezed into his father's study, he was taken aback when he saw Richard there. He glanced from one to the other and, seeing the hostile expressions on both Richard and his father's faces, he knew the game was up.

That stupid bitch, he thought. Lydia has opened her mouth and told the truth.

His father said, 'I'm sure you will know why Richard is here?'

Bluffing to the end Doug said, 'No. Should I?'

Guy glared at him and said, 'Don't arse about, son. You're in enough trouble without looking even more of a fool. Lydia Goodwin is carrying your child!'

Doug looked at Richard and said, 'She told you then?'

Richard gripped the arms of the chair to control his anger. 'You cheeky young bastard! Not only have you been sleeping with my wife, you had the bloody gall to do it in *my* house, and in *my* bed!'

Doug Slater shouldn't have grinned. Richard shot out of his chair, grabbed him by the front of his jacket and punched him hard on the chin, sending him flying across the room.

Guy rushed around the desk to separate them, but Doug was out cold. Looking down at his son, he asked Richard, 'Is he all right?'

'I'm afraid he is! He's just unconscious, that's all,' he said, after giving him a brief examination.

'I need another drink,' said Guy, 'and so do you.'

The two men sat quietly drinking, ignoring the young man on the floor. 'I have never known what to do with this kid,' said Guy, despairingly. 'He had too much too soon and, frankly, he didn't deserve it.' He sipped from his glass. 'Well, I think it's about time he learned about responsibility. You're getting a divorce, you say?'

'Yes, I am.'

'Right, then he'll have to marry Lydia and give the child a name.' He looked at Richard. 'Do you think she'll give us any trouble?'

'About marrying into this family?' He laughed heartily. 'Oh dear me no. She'll be ecstatic!'

Doug slowly came to his senses, and rubbed his jaw, which was already swelling. He looked first at his father and then at Richard. 'What's going on?' he asked as he got to his feet.

'We have just been discussing your future, my boy.'

Doug's eyes narrowed and he wondered why Richard was sitting with such an expression of satisfaction. 'And?'

'When Richard's divorce comes through, you are going to make an honest woman of the mother of your child.'

'No I'm not!'

Guy was unperturbed. 'Fine. Then tomorrow you can pack your things. It's time you stepped out into the world without my financial protection. It will do you good; make a man of you!'

Doug paled. 'You wouldn't do that, Father.'

'Indeed I would.'

'So what am I supposed to do? What do you want from me?'

Richard sat back and listened. This was giving him a lot of pleasure.

'Your playboy days are over, Douglas.' Guy puffed on his cigar. 'After the festive holiday, you will start to learn the building trade . . . from the bottom. Out on the site.'

Doug looked horrified and said, 'I wouldn't know where to start.'

'I know,' said his father, 'that was a big mistake on my part. But now you will earn your money. Then when the baby is born, you can start learning to be a father too.' Guy gave a sardonic smile. 'You will learn for yourself how difficult that can be sometimes.'

He rose to his feet and held out his hand to Richard. 'I

think we understand the situation. Everything will be taken care of. I'll be in touch.'

Richard, not wanting to return to an empty home, drove to Harwood House and was surrounded by children on his arrival, all wanting to show him their Christmas presents. Flora rescued him when he said he had to use the telephone. He rang his house and told the maid where he was in case he was called out. He was standing by the telephone after he replaced the receiver, deep in thought, when Flora came along.

'Is everything all right?' she asked. But she was shocked when Richard looked up and she saw the expression of abject misery. 'Richard! Whatever is it? You had better come into the office,' she suggested. At least there they wouldn't be disturbed.

He sat in a chair and said, 'I am not the father of Lydia's baby!'

'What!'

'The father is Doug Slater, a young man I really liked and who I thought of as a friend.'

'Oh, Richard.' Flora was at a loss for words. 'How do you know this?'

'She told me. It would seem that my dear wife has been having an affair for some months.'

'I don't know what to say.'

Richard took out a cigarette from a case in his pocket and lit it. 'The strangest thing is, apart from being extremely angry at her duplicity, I'm not sure that I really care!'

'Of course you must care,' Flora retorted. 'You were looking forward to being a father!'

'Yes, that bit is true. As you know, I love children.' He

gave a hollow laugh. 'The most ironic thing about this whole situation is that while Lydia was throwing convention to the winds, I was trying to live by them.'

'I don't know what you mean.'

He gazed into her eyes and said softly, 'You must know that I'm in love with you, Flora.'

'Richard, please. You're upset . . .'

'Yes, I'm upset. I have been in love with you from the night you came to dinner with Patrick. It grew even deeper during the time we worked together through the measles epidemic. I tried to fight it – I couldn't, but I said nothing. Did nothing, thinking I had a wife, and then a family on the way. What a fool I was!'

'What are you going to do?'

'I have already sent Lydia packing to her parents and I told Guy Slater what his son had been up to. He was not a happy man . . . neither was young Lochinvar!' He gave a wry grin. 'Especially when he knew I was going to divorce Lydia, and his father insisted he made an honest woman of her afterwards.'

'But, Richard, a divorce! Think of the scandal.'

'What would be worse, Flora? My wife living with her parents and having the baby, then staying there, not living with me? What would my patients think then? Divorce is clean and final. I am not the guilty party here!'

Flora fought against the urge to go to comfort him. This was not the moment.

But Richard had other ideas. He leaned forward and took her hand in his. 'Tell me that I'm not wrong to love you; that you feel the same way.'

She couldn't lie. How could she? She too had shelved her feelings, trying to live by the rules. Now was the time for truth. 'Yes, you know I do.'

'If you had said no, I don't know what I would have done.' He rose from his seat and, walking round the desk, caught hold of her hand and gently pulled her to her feet. 'I have wanted to do this for so long,' he said as he lowered his mouth to hers and tenderly kissed her.

As he released her, Flora looked into his eyes and said, 'Oh, Richard, I never thought I would feel this way about another man after Flynn.'

'You don't feel guilty about that, I hope,' he said, hearing the note of uncertainty in her voice. 'Life is to be lived, my darling. Flynn wouldn't want you to live out the rest of your years in the past, would he?'

'No,' she said. 'He was a free spirit.'

'And so are you, Flora. Free, brave, wonderful, and I love you.'

They clung together in a warm embrace.

'It will take some time,' said Richard, 'until I am free. Will you wait for me, my darling?'

'I will,' she promised. 'Oh yes, I will.'

Just at that moment Richard was called to the telephone. On his return he said, 'One of the Christmas babies is about to arrive and it's a breech. I must go. I'll see you tomorrow.' With a quick peck on her cheek, he left.

Flora sat quietly thinking about this turn of events. At last she was able to show Richard how much he meant to her, but there would be many a long day until they would be able to tell others. In his position, he would have to be very discreet, especially with a divorce pending. Besides, there was still the big problem of keeping Harwood House running. She hadn't heard anything from her father and Flora knew there was little point in ringing him. If he had anything to tell her he would have been in touch. She would look in the *Southern Daily Echo* for a job. Rose could run the home and whatever money Flora could earn would help to keep things ticking over. And much as she hated to admit it, her mother had been proved right after all.

The following day Lydia, accompanied by her father, stormed into the house, full of indignation at having been sent packing, and her father also voiced his opinion at what he thought was shabby treatment of his spoiled daughter.

Richard listened silently as they both ranted and raged, then quietly but firmly said, 'I will be getting in touch with my solicitor tomorrow to start divorce proceedings. I will be citing Doug Slater as co-respondent.' He saw the fleeting glimpse of fear in Lydia's expression.

'It will be in all the papers!' she cried.

'I am afraid it might be.'

Seeing that Richard was not to be swayed, her father appealed to him. 'Why not let Lydia divorce you? You could take some woman to a hotel and be found by a detective. It's done all the time.'

'But not by me,' snapped Richard. 'As for the baby, you obviously haven't heard, but Doug Slater is going to make an honest woman of you. Your baby will eventually bear his name.'

Her expression changed immediately. 'Really?'

'I called on them yesterday and we discussed the situation.'

Lydia preened. 'So Doug wants to marry me,' she said, a satisfied smile spreading across her features.

'Well, actually he doesn't.'

The smile faded.

'But don't worry, my dear, his father insisted. He also

insisted that your lover now has to work for a living, so there will be little swanning around, staying in hotels. He won't have the time or the money for it!'

The disappointment on her face made him smile. 'But, Lydia, you have always admired the way they live; it seems your prayers are to be answered.'

As she thought about it, it was patently obvious to both Richard and her father that she was happy with the solution.

Richard studied her for a moment and thought how very superficial she was. He said, 'Of course, with Doug for a husband, you will never be sure if he is being faithful to you. There is an old saying, Lydia. Be careful what you wish for because you may get it.'

She was made to remember these words when eventually Guy Slater arranged for the two of them to meet at her parents' house. Lydia rushed up to Doug and flung her arms about him, only to be pushed roughly away.

'You stupid bitch! Now you've ruined both our lives! Well, you needn't think I'll be staying in at night because of the baby. You will have my name, and when I feel like it and there's nothing better on offer, we'll have sex. You were not a complete loss between the sheets, as I recall, but that's all you'll have! But if I find you with another man and making a fool of me like you did Richard, I'll send you packing, just as he did.'

She was not without spirit. 'So it's all right for you to have a good time, but not me, is that it?'

'Precisely. You always knew I was a bastard. You used to like it.' He pulled her to him and kissed her roughly. 'At least being married will save me from other women thinking they can get me to the altar. I'll be able to tell them I have a wife and child, this is just for fun!'

'You *are* a bastard!'

'Yes I am, and you'll just have to make the best of it.' And he walked out of the room.

She sat in a chair and started to cry.

Chapter Thirty-Five

It was the beginning of February, and Flora was weary as she trudged home to Harwood House from her job as a nurse at the South Hants Hospital. She had been working on the wards for three weeks now, but she realised her meagre wage wasn't going to solve her problem in the long run. Rose was coping admirably, running the home during Flora's working hours, but it meant they were one person short and the workload was heavy. But they were all coping – or hanging on by the skin of their teeth, more like, thought Flora, as she arrived at the kitchen door.

' 'Ello, love,' said Madge. 'Come in out of the cold and I'll make you a nice cup of tea.'

Flora sat down by the kitchen fire; removed her gloves and blew on her frozen hands to warm them. 'Everything all right?' she asked.

'Fine,' said Madge. 'Now you drink that and I'll get you something to eat.'

'A bit later, Madge, if you don't mind. There are things I must do first.' And she quickly drank her tea and left the room.

The cook sighed deeply. Flora looked all in but she knew she would do what she always did before settling down, and that was to visit the children, check on Rose and Jessie,

361

and see if everything was in order.

As usual it was all running smoothly. In one corner of the playroom, Rose was trying to teach some of the children the alphabet, and the younger ones were gathered around Jessie as she read to them. The fire was low in the grate as they were trying to eke out the coal supply. The children were wearing warm clothes, with socks and jumpers knitted from used wool, but Flora was always amazed how the young didn't seem to feel the cold.

Before they stopped for the midday meal, the children would be taken outside into the yard to run around. This served two purposes: to keep them warm, and to help allay their high spirits, which on rainy days could easily turn to arguments and squabbles. It was a neverending task to keep them occupied as well as keep the house clean and the laundry up to date. They had long dispensed with outside help for these tasks for the sake of economy.

'Have you seen this evening's *Echo*?' asked Jessie.

Flora shook her head and read the paper that was thrust into her hand. The headlines read, 'Alderman Sent Down for Seven Years'. The Johnsons had been given three years each and forbidden ever to care for children again. Well, at least that was a result, thought Flora – and it seemed that George Chivers was to pay dearly for his misdeeds. She cursed the man. Without his interference, the children would have been secure, but she knew that she was going to have to close Harwood House and put it on the market, without much chance of selling it in today's climate.

Only the docklands of Southampton were maintaining the town's economic health. For ordinary people, times were hard. Many other businesses were having to struggle, not having recovered totally from the effects of the war, and Flora realised she was lucky still to receive some money each month from the three firms who fortunately were in a position to help. But it wasn't enough to keep her going.

Richard called to see her as he always did before the evening surgery; it was the one thing at the moment that brightened her days. He entered her office and walked round the desk, pulled her into his arms and held her.

'Hello, darling. You look tired. Another heavy day?'

Tears welled in Flora's eyes. 'Oh, Richard, I came to Southampton with such high hopes – a dream really – and I've failed.'

'Darling Flora, you haven't failed. Think of the children that are here. Even if they will have stayed only a while, you have given them love and attention and a grounding which will help them as they move on.'

'But where will they go and how will I know that they will be really looked after as we would do?'

'You don't, and in all honesty, I don't think anyone will give them the same kind of attention, but they will remember it, that's the main thing.'

'Then there's Jessie. I will have let her down.'

'What nonsense! Jessie is now in a position to apply for a post looking after children; she's had the experience. Rose too. And a good cook can always find a place.'

'I haven't told you,' she smiled through her tears, 'Rose and Peter are getting engaged.'

'That's wonderful news!'

'Yes, it is. He's so much better now, and he has a job with the council, helping them to plan a new housing project.'

'It's you I'm worried about, my darling,' he said. 'What are you going to do until the time comes when we can get married?'

'To be honest, I don't know.'

'If only you could move in with me now,' he said.

Flora looked horrified. 'That would give Lydia grounds to divorce you for adultery, ruin your career and,' she smiled, 'it would make me a scarlet woman!'

He kissed her gently. 'You will always be my scarlet woman.'

'Tomorrow,' she said, 'I'll have to go to the authorities and warn them of the imminent closure of Harwood House so they can start to arrange places to house the children. How on earth am I going to tell them when the time comes, Richard?'

'It will be very hard, but I'll be on hand to help you. When are you planning to close?'

'The beginning of April. We can't possibly carry on after that.'

He held her close and stroked her hair. 'I am so sorry,' he said.

'So am I,' came the muffled reply as she hid her face in his chest to stay her tears of sadness and frustration. 'I must call my Father tonight and tell him.'

'I am really sorry, Flora my dear,' Alistair said when she told him the news, but he didn't offer any reason or excuse for not having got back to her when he had told her to leave things with him, and Flora, although disappointed, concluded that after all he hadn't been able to find a solution. And how could he? What did she expect from him, she wondered.

'I wish you could come home to Scotland for a break,' he said. 'It sounds to me as if you could do with one.'

'There is too much to do here,' she told him. 'Tomorrow I'll get in touch with the estate agents to put the building on the market.'

'Try not to be too sad, Flora,' he said.

After their conversation had ended, she thought it was strange to be told such a thing. Her father understood her better than anyone. He would know how devastating this closure would be for her! For the first time in her life, she felt he had let her down.

The estate agent walked around the building with his tape measure, making notes. 'The building is in good order, Miss Ferguson,' he said. 'But to be honest, I don't quite know how to market it with the changes you've made. I suppose it could be a guest house; it's not up to hotel standard and no longer is it a builders' merchant's.' But he closed his book and said, 'I'll get back to you when I've had a word with my boss.'

A week later, after all the children had been settled for the night, Flora gathered her small staff in her office and gave them the bad news. 'I am having to close Harwood House the first week in April. I'm telling you now to give you a chance to find other positions. I'm so sorry it hasn't worked out as I planned, but you have all been absolutely marvellous – and I don't know what to say.' The words stuck in her throat.

'That bloody Chivers!' snapped Jessie. 'He was the one that did for us. Bastard!'

'Well, duck,' said Madge, 'I'm 'eartbroken but it 'as been a privilege, Flora. I wouldn't 'ave missed it for the world.'

'Me neither,' said Rose. 'Are you sure there is nothing more we can do to keep it going?'

Shaking her head Flora said, 'If only there was. The building is going on the market tomorrow.'

'What will you do, Flora?' asked Rose.

'I'll keep working at the hospital until the place is sold. After that, I don't know.' She turned towards her two assistants. 'You can both stay here, of course, until you get jobs and places to live. It'll save me rattling around the empty building alone, after the children have gone.'

'When will you tell the children?' asked Rose.

'Not until the last possible moment. It will only unsettle them.' Flora sighed. 'Life is a bugger, isn't it?'

The For Sale sign went up outside the following day and as Flora left to go on duty at the hospital she gazed at it with a deep feeling of sadness. As she was standing there, a woman tapped her on the arm.

'Miss Ferguson, isn't it?'

Flora looked round. 'Yes, that's right.' The woman's face looked familiar, but she couldn't place her.

'I was the mayoress on your open day.'

Flora remembered her then. 'Of course, forgive me.'

'What's happening here?' the woman asked.

'I am having to close.' And then she explained all the circumstances.

'I can't tell you how sorry I am,' the stranger said. 'I was so impressed that day. When is the home closing?'

'The first week in April.'

'That is so sad.'

'You'll have to excuse me,' said Flora, 'but I have a job at the South Hants, and I'll be late for my duty.'

'I'm sorry to have met you under such unhappy circumstances,' the woman said, 'but I won't keep you any longer.' She smiled and walked away.

Later in the week, a man from the council visited Harwood House, and Flora gave a list of the children's names and their particulars to the authorities. 'I want them cared for properly!' she insisted. 'I will be keeping a close eye on them, I can promise you that and, believe me, I will cause you a lot of problems if I find they are not being looked after properly!'

The bemused man with whom she spoke assured her all would be well. 'I wouldn't like to upset you, Miss Ferguson,' he admitted.

'Good!' she said as she opened the door. To her surprise there was a woman standing there, a suitcase in her hand.

'Mother!'

Janet marched in past the man from the children's department of the council and put her case down. 'Hello, Flora.' She kissed her daughter on the cheek. 'Now what *is* going on here!' she demanded.

Flora showed her council visitor out and took her mother into the sitting room. 'What on earth are you doing here?' asked Flora.

'It seems to me,' said Janet, 'that you are in dire need of help. But first show me around this place.'

Flora immediately felt like a small child again and did as she was told. She took Janet upstairs and showed her the dormitory. 'Are all these beds taken?' asked her mother.

'Yes, they are.' Then she showed her the other rooms and then they made their way to the playroom where Flora introduced her to the others. To a surprised Rose and Jessie she said, 'This is my mother.'

Janet, as usual, was economical with her words, and just nodded and said briskly, 'Good morning.' She watched them work with the children, inspected the toys and the books and then said, 'And where do they eat?'

So Flora showed her the dining room with the long table and benches, and took her to meet Madge in the kitchen.

Madge wasn't thrown a bit. ' 'Ow about a nice cup of

tea, Mrs Ferguson? And strangely, only yesterday I made some shortbread. I'd appreciate your opinion.'

Janet raised her eyebrows and said, 'Right, thank you.' They all sat at the kitchen table. Janet tasted the shortbread and said, 'Excellent. You have a good cook, Flora.'

Flora by now had recovered from the shock of seeing her mother and asked again, 'What are you doing here?'

'I would have been here sooner except I was held up with the plans I was working on, but at last everything is settled.'

Flora looked puzzled. 'I don't understand.'

'Your father and I have been working on a scheme to save Harwood House and at last everything is in place.'

Flora felt the blood drain from her face. 'Whatever do you mean?'

'Alistair told me what a grand job you were doing here and about your financial troubles, and so we set up a committee to make Harwood House a charitable institution.'

'What?'

'As you know, Flora, I am involved with several committees that run various charitable outlets, and one of them is involved with child care. It has branches all over the United Kingdom.'

'I didn't know that!'

Janet smiled for the first time. 'Well, my dear Flora, you never have understood what I do, have you?'

'No, I suppose not.'

'We have taken Harwood House as one of our places to help provide the necessary homes for those children brought up in difficult circumstances. In short, Flora, we will finance you!'

Madge let out a scream of delight and went rushing out

to the others to spread the good news.

Flora was stunned. 'You mean we don't have to close? I don't have to sell?'

'That's right. Your father and I have worked hard together on this, but it is all signed and sealed.'

'But he didn't say anything.'

'How could he raise your hopes until it was all settled? We did have a phone call from our member in Southampton who had seen this place and knew it was up for sale. Her opinion counted for a great deal.'

'Who on earth was that?' asked Flora.

'She was the mayoress a year ago. I believe you met her again recently and told her you were closing.'

This time Flora had no trouble in placing the woman. 'Yes, I know who you mean.'

She was near to tears when she said, 'Oh, Mother, I don't know what to say.'

Janet softened as she said quietly, 'Flora, my dear, ever since you were a small child I have never been able to understand you, but now, here with this establishment, I could see what a fine thing you wanted to do. This I *could* understand, and fortunately I was able to help.'

For the first time in her life, Flora felt close to Janet. She walked over to her and hugged her, kissing her on the cheek. 'You will never know how much this means to me – never ever. Thank you.'

'And when am I going to meet this nice doctor your father has told me about?'

Flora looked at her in astonishment. 'You know he's married and getting a divorce?'

'Yes, your father told me. But, Flora, my dear, when did you ever do things the easy way?' And they both laughed.

★ ★ ★

Shortly afterwards, Flora rang the estate agent to tell him to take his board away, the house was off the market, and then she rang the authorities to tell them the home was to remain open. The man she had spoken to before said, 'I am delighted, Miss Ferguson, and, to be honest, greatly relieved. I was worried you would be on my back for months ahead.'

She had the grace to laugh. 'You were probably right to worry.'

'May I ask why you have changed your mind? What has happened?'

'We are now a registered charity.'

'Excellent news! Good luck, young lady. You have done a splendid job and long may it continue.'

Then Flora rang Richard, who was thrilled at the news.

'My mother wants to meet you, by the way,' Flora added.

'Oh dear, will she be gentle with me?' he laughed.

'I don't know. It will be interesting to find out.'

'Then I had better make my way over,' he said.

As soon as she introduced Richard to her mother, she knew everything would be fine. Richard was his usual self, and Janet was charmed. They all went out to dinner that night and, to Flora's surprise, he and her mother found lots of common interests to discuss.

'You must come up to Glasgow with my daughter,' invited Janet. 'I'm sure she could do with a break when all this is settled. I believe things haven't been easy for either of you.'

Flora was amazed.

Seeing her expression, Janet said, 'I don't know why you look so surprised. Do you think your father and I have always had an easy life?'

'I suppose I don't really know,' she admitted.

'Well, we have had our problems but we overcame them. Marriage with the right partner is a very happy state, and I do believe you and Richard are right for each other.'

'Despite all those awful men you introduced me to!' teased Flora.

Janet had to laugh. 'Well, I was only trying to get you settled.' She sipped her glass of wine. 'Tomorrow we have some papers to go over and which need your signature. Then I can get home to your father.'

'I must call him when I get back and thank him. Have you booked a room anywhere, Mother?'

'Alistair booked me into the Star Hotel where I believe he stayed. I am very tired now. I travelled overnight and it's been a long day.'

'We'll drop you off,' said Richard.

'Thank you. I expect you two have a lot to talk over,' she said with unusual diplomacy.

When they were alone at Harwood House in the sitting room, Flora and Richard sat curled up on the settee. 'I will never understand my mother!' said Flora.

Richard was highly amused. 'I thought she was the one who didn't understand you!'

'It seems she is an amazing woman and I have never given her credit for that.' She snuggled up to him and said, 'No wonder Dad didn't say anything. Oh my God! I've forgotten to ring him.' And she flew out of the door on feet that scarcely touched the floor.

Richard sat back and listened to Flora's animated conversation from a distance. He couldn't hear what she said, but from the tone of voice he could tell she was deliriously happy. Well, she certainly deserved to be, he thought, and he was thrilled for her.

When she entered the room, she was smiling and her eyes were shining. 'Darling Richard,' she said as she returned to his welcoming arms, 'I am so very happy. I thought my world was falling apart, and now I know Harwood House will always be here for any child who needs shelter and care – and I have you too.'

He kissed her tenderly. 'We'll have to wait a while before I can make you my wife but, you'll see, the time will pass quicker than we think, and we have the rest of our lives together.'

She cradled his face and kissed him. 'And what woman could ask for more?' she said.

As they sat snuggled up together, lost in their own thoughts, Flora remembered her days in the hospitals of France, and the horrors she had seen. She thought of her darling Flynn, who would forever hold a special place in her heart, and then she thought of the children who were already living at Harwood House and of the children who would now be able to find refuge there in the future, and she silently thanked God for bringing it all to fruition.

She gazed adoringly at the man beside her. Flynn would be happy for her, she felt. Richard and he were alike in many ways. Both had strong beliefs and integrity. Flynn would say that it had been fate that had played a hand in it all. She smiled contentedly and mused that maybe he was right at that. But whatever it was, she felt privileged to have known and loved two such fine men. To have been the lover of one and eventually in time, the wife of another. And that *would* be for ever.

Epilogue

The following year, Flora was married to the man she loved, in a civil ceremony near her home in Scotland. She wore a gown made of ivory silk, with the latest dropped waist and scalloped hem. Her groom looked very distinguished in a smart dark grey three-piece suit. Alistair was in full Scottish regalia with his kilt and sporran, and Janet was most elegant in a pale blue suit and matching hat. The reception was held at the Fergusons' grand house, and Flora proudly introduced her husband to his new sisters-in-law, their spouses and offspring. Surrounded by her family and friends, Flora was ecstatic. She was back in her beloved Scotland.

Flora and Richard were to spend their first night in her old home, before touring the rest of the country, but as the reception ended, Alistair said to her, 'Take Richard to the stables. You'll find your wedding present there.'

As they strolled across the garden, Flora said, 'Father still has a couple of horses stabled – perhaps when we come back before going south, you and I can ride out together.'

'Yes, I would really like that,' he said.

They turned into the stable block, still talking, when Flora stopped as she heard a whinny from the far end. She started to run.

'Flora! Whatever is it?' Richard asked as he ran after her. He found her with her arm around the neck of a very fine-looking horse, rubbing its nose, talking to it. Then she moved along to the next box and let out a cry of joy.

'Richard! These are my two horses, Jasper and Sheba. Dad didn't sell them after all. Oh, darling, isn't it a wonderful surprise?'

'It is indeed. I know how much they mean to you.'

'It's the end of a perfect day,' she said and, flinging her arms around Richard's neck, she kissed him.

Whilst the happy couple were on their honeymoon, back in Southampton, looking after Harwood House, were Flora's faithful staff. Rose had been promoted to matron, and Madge still presided over the kitchen, but now there were extra staff to lend a helping hand.

Jake and Mattie now lived at home with their father, who had married Jessie, and seemed very happy, but every Saturday morning they came to call, and stayed until after lunch, playing with the children that were there, reluctant to break away totally. Jessie still worked there part time, as she loved the place and the children so much.

Lydia eventually got her wish and married Doug Slater, then moved into the house she so admired, to stay with Doug's parents until he could afford to pay for a home of their own. She closed her eyes to her husband's philandering, content to be part of the social circle she had always coveted.

Once Flora and her husband returned to Southampton, and settled down, she was able to help him with his work for underprivileged children as well as oversee the running of Harwood House, which in time became the flagship for future homes for children in the district. And so, finally, Flora had achieved her aim of making a difference, but to far more people than she ever could have envisaged.

Now you can buy any of these other bestselling
Headline books from your bookshop or
direct from the publisher.